Voices of Deliverance

VOICES OF DELIVERANCE

INTERVIEWS WITH QUEBEC & ACADIAN WRITERS

by Donald Smith
translated by Larry Shouldice

Anansi

Toronto   Buffalo   London   Sydney

Originally published in French as *L'Ecrivain devant son oeuvre.* Copyright © 1983 Editions Québec/Amérique.

Cover design and layout: Laurel Angeloff.
Photographs courtesy of Editions Québec/Amérique, Montréal. Photo of Jean Barbeau: *Le Droit.* Photo of Jacques Ferron: Daniel Fontigny, Les Presses de l'Université du Québec. All other photographs by Adrien Thério.

The translator wishes to thank Denise Provençal, Donald Smith, Sheila Fischman, James Polk and Ann Wall for their co-operation.

Translated with assistance from the Canada Council. Published with assistance from the Canada Council and the Ontario Arts Council, and manufactured in Canada for

House of Anansi Press Limited
35 Britain Street
Toronto, Ontario M5A 1R7
Canada

Canadian Cataloguing in Publication Data

Main entry under title:
Voices of deliverance: interviews with Quebec and Acadian writers

Translation of: L'Ecrivain devant son oeuvre.
Includes index.
ISBN 0-88784-148-1

1. Authors, Canadian (French)—20th century—Interviews.*
2. Authorship. I. Smith, Donald, 1946—

PS8081.E2713 1986   C840'.9'0054   C86-093031-9
PQ3908.E2713 1986

86 87 88 89 90 91 92 93 5 4 3 2 1

I would like to thank Larry Shouldice for his excellent and inspiring work. Our numerous letters and conversations were both stimulating and revealing. A special thanks to James Polk for his sound advice and professional editing. I would like to thank as well my colleague Michel Gaulin for his suggestions concerning the original French manuscript.

Initial versions of the interviews here were published in the magazine *Lettres québécoises*, except for the interview with Adrien Thério, published in *Voix et images*. All the interviews in *Voices of Deliverance* have been extensively updated and reworked, and in some instances an additional interview with the writer was necessary. Both writer and translator have revised certain passages in the French edition for the convenience of the English reader.

To Adrien Thério, an inspiration to generations of writers, critics, and readers of Quebec literature.

Contents

Introduction

In 1976 when the magazine *Lettres québécoises* was founded, I
undertook a series of interviews with Quebec writers.[1] From
my work as an interviewer, I started to recover the wonder
and joy of my first experiences as a reader. Almost as if I'd
gone back into my childhood, I started learning again that
reading is a way of life, that one needs a certain openness
and receptiveness to enjoy literature. Anne Hébert says it
well in a beautiful passage from "Poésie, solitude rompue,"
her introduction to *Mystère de la parole*: "Poetry isn't explained;
it's experienced. The reader must remain open and attentive
like a young child who is learning his mother tongue." A
book should not be considered an object, a cold, dead collection of impossibly smooth pages. After all, it is permeated
with the life of an individual, an individual who has struggled
to communicate to others his or her realities, dreams and
inner world. Félix-Antoine Savard taught me to look at paper

through new eyes. The author of *Menaud, maître-draveur* wrote on unfinished paper that still showed traces of bark and knots. It had all the imperfections of life. Savard "wrote on trees," and for each individual, trees are — or can be — a source of incalculable wealth. For Savard, trees were living beings that inhabited the mountains of his mind. And in order to teach *Menaud* you have to enable students to grasp the meaning of the mountains; to get them interested and set them on the right track, you have to explain how ascending the mountain represents a kind of spiritual elevation, an act of courage, and how Menaud's madness can be understood only when the significance of the mountain and the trees has been understood.

Reading is thus an act of communication between one living being and another. Each writer I interviewed spoke of at least one object, one person or one element that, even in the course of a simple conversation, took on a "literary" meaning. This was the case with Jacques Ferron, who led me off to see the Juneberry tree which he used as the title of his book *L'amélanchier*; for his character Tinamer and for the whole of Quebec literature, this tree represents what the vegetation in Wonderland represents for Alice and for all world literature. In the case of Gilbert La Rocque, the symbol he lived with in his everyday life is that of the spiders he used to feed in his garden; thus what in his novels is an obvious image of decomposition is also something that is dangerously real. Marie-Claire Blais' characters like watching people in public places. For them, the world is a spectacle. And this sense of observation, which becomes the art of transformation, is one I myself witnessed in the bar where I met Ms Blais. There are a number of observations of this sort in *Voices of Deliverance*. My hope is that in their own small way they will help provide a glimpse into the marvellous world of symbols. For the writers in this book, literature is basically a curious, uncontrollable mixture of the real world turned inward and the dream world turned outward.

The most revealing question I asked the writers being interviewed is clearly the following: "What does the act of writing represent for you?" The answers will no doubt help reinforce the idea of literature as a way of life, an act of liberation. Here are a few typical answers, selected more or less at random: a descent into our internal images (Bessette); the mysterious power of memory, a return to childhood, the music within us (Savard); phantasies, dreams, internal cinema, a passion (Thério); a flash of lightning, experiences perceived in images and rhythms (Anne Hébert); a tale, a fable (Thériault); salvation, deliverance (Marie-Claire Blais); a marriage of poetry and reality (Antonine Maillet); surprises, tricks played by one's deepest self, a release of unconscious powers (La Rocque); an endeavour to mask, transform and transmute things, an act that allows a reinvention of the world, the best drug in the world (Godbout); the power to reconstruct the world (Barbeau).

The act of writing is a vital necessity for the writer. However, in a way it is also a vital necessity for everyone, because without "deliverance" through the word (as it is written, spoken or even read, since reading is a sort of writing or rewriting), life itself runs the risk of being dull, banal and overly predictable.

Voices of Deliverance deals with more than simply the act of writing. A complete survey of each writer's work is also presented, and questions are asked about his or her production in an overall sense. The essentials of the plot of most books are also provided, so that the reader can follow the conversation more easily.

While the themes of a particular work of the imagination have no doubt appeared elsewhere in the form of social ideas, writers still need to set their phantasms, their "poetry" (their "creation," in Greek) into the framework of reality — although they do this to varying degrees, depending on the genre they have chosen to work with — novel, tale, play or poem. Images and symbols in the pure sense have never reached a very wide audience, perhaps for the very reason that they inevitably come to life in real, chronological time.

The reality described by Quebec and Acadian writers has one point in common, one basic leitmotif: it shows a concern for the fate of the little people, whether they be from ethnic or linguistic minorities or are simply men and women who have been exploited. Does a continuing concern for the powerless arise from the fact that most writers in Quebec and

Acadia live in a country that doesn't correspond to their deep desire for a homeland, for a place where their identity can be fully assumed? Have these writers discovered that defending the people of their own land leads them naturally to defend other groups struggling with problems of identity? Although this seems quite probable to me, the ultimate answers will have to come from literary sociologists. One thing that is sure is that if the political and national problem is ever resolved in the minds of the writers, the thematic framework of their writing will change direction and quite naturally start dealing with other realities. Actually, this process has already begun. Since the Parti québécois came to power in 1976, several writers have moved off in other creative directions, leaving it up to the politicians to build the country that Quebec's creative artists have been claiming, articulating and celebrating. Contemporary writers have turned their attention to investigations of language, of "modernité," while the feminists are inventing a liberating mythology for the women of the future.

Quebec and Acadian writers tackle the problem of survival in different ways: with Savard, the notions of freedom and economic self-reliance take precedence; with Bessette, the focus is on the phantasms of individuals repressed by a theocratic society, or on the more universal primitive phantasms that lie deep within us all; Anne Hébert breaks with social prohibitions in order to deal with characters on the fringes of society — the sick, the obsessed, the possessed — because, as she says, "everyone is marginal in some way"; Yves Thériault rises to the defence of the aboriginal peoples and social outcasts; Marie-Claire Blais and Michel Tremblay recreate the worlds of lesbians and homosexuals, and explore the psychology of the poor and the alienated; Jacques Ferron and Antonine Maillet rewrite the history of their respective homelands; Gatien Lapointe articulates the land and, finally free of this obsession, explores the human body; and Pierre Morency's "torrents" reconcile the poet with the collective origins of childhood.

Reading every book by the fourteen novelists interviewed in this collection made me realize how rich and varied their styles are. Having grown up in societies in which the oral tradition plays a central role, Quebec and Acadian writers show a particular fondness for the tale; the light-hearted, concentrated style of the tale is apparent even in novels and plays, although the tone may range from the supernatural to the brutally realistic, from the epic, the mythological and the fantastic to the socially ironic. Such variation in styles is encouraging for the future since changes in style are a great deal more difficult to bring about than changes in theme.

Rooted in the North-American continent, influenced first by American and then by French writers, and immediately afterwards by the writers of Quebec and South America, the writers presented in this book have created a gigantic library. They speak with a multiplicity of accents and emotions. *Voices of Deliverance* is an attempt to confront these writers with their books, with themselves, with my impressions as a reader, with the judgements of other critics and with the imagination in general. The resulting confrontations and discoveries are often unexpected, such as Antonine Maillet's contention that the Québécois are essentially a people of masculine symbols, while the Acadians are a people of feminine symbols. And so there are agreements, disagreements and surprises. I thank these writers for their unforgettable excursions into the world of the imagination.

Donald Smith

Félix-Antoine Savard:
The Wonders of Nature[1]

> "A nation should strive
> for its own survival in the
> same way nature does."
> (Félix-Antoine Savard,
> in the film *Le pays de
> Menaud*, Quebec Film
> Institute)

As I was about to interview Félix-Antoine Savard, I could not help thinking to what extent his name is synonymous with the protagonist in *Menaud, Maitre Draveur* (translated as *Boss of the River* and *Master of the River*). I knew that Savard signed his letters "Menaud," and I had often been told that the writer identified so strongly with his character that even the way Savard spoke brought forth images of Menaud. Nevertheless, I decided to conduct the interview in my usual manner: I would arrive with a series of questions dealing with the man and his work, I would tape-record our conversation, and if necessary I would take notes. With Savard, however, taking notes proved to be impossible. Certainly, there was no lack of subject matter: he had a great deal to say, and he said it slowly, deliberately, thoughtfully. But I was so moved by the poetry of his language and the obvious warmth of the man that I didn't even dare to turn on the tape-recorder, for fear of making him uncomfortable or impeding the flow of his simple, friendly conversation.

I was lucky enough to spend an entire evening with Monsignor Savard in 1976, at a banquet given in his honour by the Association for Canadian and Quebec Literatures. The first part of this interview deals with my reactions to him on this occasion. I later mailed him a list of more specific questions, and he kindly replied to them in writing.

I was struck by the importance of three phenomena in the life of Félix-Antoine Savard: nature, fraternity and faith. "Respect" is perhaps not quite the right word to sum up his attitude towards nature, since his reaction is rather one of humility and admiration for the miracle of creation and the many messages it contains. To reach an understanding of what it means to be human, and more specifically, to be Québécois, Savard suggests that one must open one's eyes and ears to the natural world: water (whether in rivers, ponds, lakes or marshes), vegetation, animals and landscapes. "I am a *coureur de bois*," Savard used to say, and being a *coureur de bois* means moving through the land and learning from nature how important it is for human beings to live in harmony with one another. In Sophocles, Savard admired "the truths of light and shadow that produce harmony." In his own work, light symbolizes both sacredness and the nation, whereas darkness is perfidious and funereal. Savard explained to me that one must "go back to nature" and study religiously "the life of plants, as Saint Augustine did," in order to comprehend "the seminal reasons for order and balance." In the context of Savard's literary works, "order" and "balance" often refer to the Québécois and French Canadians.

When the Association for Canadian and Quebec Literatures presented him with a magnificent lithograph by Roland Giguère, Monsignor Savard exclaimed: "It's marvellous! All those fall colours, those trees thrusting upwards, growing towards the future. It's like a nation of people." For him, nature is inevitably associated with the collectivity, with the idea of belonging to a French race living on the American continent. The French must now recover their full share, but they must do so without creating tensions or making enemies, so that both the French and English can be masters of their own lands, their own industries and their own respective languages. In this way both Québécois and Canadians could finally live in freedom and harmony, just as things do in the natural world.

Later I accompanied Savard back to the home of his friend, the composer Roger Matton. Upon hearing the name Savard, the young man driving our taxi immediately recognized his favourite writer. "Not all teachers know how to analyse your books, Monsignor," he said, "but I think they're beautiful and I really admire them." Responding to the compliment — "It's the first time a taxi driver's ever been nice to me," he remarked — and as we drove past the Hilton and the concrete jungles that have increasingly isolated Quebec City from the essential realities of nature, Monsignor Savard proceeded to tell us the story of a caribou he once saw standing by the side of a lake. Feeling an immediate sense of identification with the animal — "What a magnificent beast, so noble and friendly and human!" — and wanting it to eat from his hand, Savard motioned to it and imitated its call. The animal leaped into the water, as if to run away, but suddenly it turned and moved back towards the man, eventually eating out of his hand. "I kept my distance, since it was a wild animal," he said, "but we looked at each other carefully and we understood one another."

As we drove through the Americanized streets of Quebec, Monsignor Savard also confided that his love for the natural wilderness had earned him the nickname "Caribou" when he was in college. In his writings, animals and birds show how necessary it is for each human being and for every race to be free. It might also be mentioned that Monsignor Savard, out of love, tenderness and respect, used to raise chickadees at his summer retreat in Saint-Joseph-de-la-Rive. As our G.M. taxi rolled on through the night, a kind of implicit understanding arose among André Vanasse (from the University of Quebec in Montreal), the taxi driver, and myself. We had hardly said anything, and yet the story of the caribou told by the "Caribou" himself made us realize how urgent it is to protect the natural environment.

I also couldn't help thinking of an embarrassing incongruity that had become apparent at the banquet earlier in the evening. We were in the Jacques Cartier Room — a name worthy of Savard, who has always stressed the French origins of the Quebec people. In this context it was rather shocking to hear, coming from the room right next to the "Jacques Cartier," the "tacky" American music of a totally conventional piano bar pushing its way insistently through to our table. I was unlucky enough to have to cross through this noisy nightclub in the company of Monsignor Savard, whose only comment was "What a place!" I thought of the log-drivers' dance in *Menaud, Maître-Draveur*:

> The blaze seemed to arouse the sluggish blood of their race. Under branches abloom with sparks, the moment Bourin had taken out his accordion and tapped his feet, there was a breaking loose, an explosion of release that was like revenge for these beings immobilized by cold and fatigue.
>
> As soon as one dancer grew weary, another rose in his place: face flaming, voice afire, eyes lost in a mysterious dream glimpsed through the pattern of blazing branches where the fire spirits limned for the pleasure of each one the faces he longed to see.
>
> It seemed to issue from the very depths of their being. It was a reminder that from sea to sea and even in all their dangers, their forefathers had been the blithest of men, faithful echoes of this resounding world of theirs, passionate lovers of this nature with its images of beauty ever renewed, to which all, on plain, river, or mountain, had offered a song of love and an anthem of liberty.
>
> No one spoke now of the drive. The dance went lightly, on tip-toe, as if on the brink of flight, and decked out in fire.
>
> (*Master of the River*, p.26, translated by Richard Howard)

I wondered how Savard felt about the rock music and the disco dancers. I also thought of the theme of the ancestors in

Savard's work and the way he answered when I'd asked him if he liked to sing. "Yes, sometimes," he said, "especially the songs I remember from my childhood."

The episode in the taxi, however, had restored my confidence. As the taxi driver so aptly put it, Monsignor Savard "always talks in parables." He was fascinated by "the narrows of death," the name of a treacherous passage on the Columbia River in British Columbia, which he used as the title for one of his plays. The future of the Quebec people, he felt, is as dangerous as it was for the *voyageurs* to cross through the "narrows of death."

The words "fraternity" and "fraternal" often cropped up in Monsignor Savard's conversations with people. "Quebec should welcome people of various national origins and should respect their distinctiveness, but French obviously has to be the foremost language." Savard's maternal grandmother, Mary-Ann Nathalie O'Neil, was Irish, although she came from Louisiana. "She taught me how to chase after an alligator, which is a fairly rare occurrence in Chicoutimi," joked Savard. In any case, her foreign blood was "reconciled" to the Quebec people, and Mrs. O'Neil became a true Québécois.

According to Savard, the possibility of achieving harmony between the Québécois and other groups can be learned from the rivers of our land, which all flow into one another "miraculously." Monsignor Savard further explained his point-of-view by using the image of an orchestra: "Each instrument has its own voice, but it's when they play in unison that you achieve harmony."

Félix-Antoine Savard did not believe in the political separation of Quebec. "They tried to get me involved in that," he explained, "but I've held back. I'm neither a political scientist nor a sociologist. Menaud's idea is that the land has been sold, but nevertheless Menaud is *in* the land." The house has been sold — the rivers, plains and mountains as well. The Québécois have become tenants. And this is the situation that Savard deplored. In his work, the only "political" ideology was that the national heritage had to be reappropriated. But even if Savard didn't like the idea of separation, particularly because of the francophone minorities living outside Quebec, it seems to me he would have more or less agreed with the concept of economic and cultural sovereignty. In that regard Félix-Antoine Savard admired the lucidity of Louis Hémon, the author of *Maria Chapdelaine*, although he didn't approve of his using the word "barbarian" to describe foreigners. "Young people are more and more aware that key industries and our national heritage shouldn't be in the hands of outsiders," he said. Menaud retreated into the mountain to "get away from the quarrels and find peace of mind. He takes refuge. He sees things from above. He keeps going higher. I'm doing the same thing myself." Menaud, a name that Savard heard for the first time in the Charlevoix region, is in fact a "combination of several people"; "Menaud tried to find help, but no one would listen. I could have written a sequel to *Menaud*, showing that French Canadians are foreigners in their own country."

After our discussion of Menaud, I spoke with Savard about the importance of faith, which for him had a very broad meaning. For Savard, Protestant and Catholic were trivial considerations compared to Christian brotherhood. T.S. Eliot, "a great Anglican friend," he added, smiling, incarnates the idea of "redeemed patience." Solzhenitsyn, he claimed, "has a human dimension," and believes in "spiritualism."

* * *

In the whole of Savard's work, there is one title which seems to me of particular significance: *Le bouscueil*. "*Le bouscueil* is a strange title," writes the poet in his preface to the collection. "It is a word from the Petite-Côte-Nord area of Quebec, used to refer to the spring break-up on the rivers.... It can also be applied to certain mental processes in which the mind, like an ice-jam in a river, suddenly finds its release in the spoken and written word." The same can be said of Savard's writings. His poetic prose flows freely and is highly charged with meaning, much like a spring "break-up" that provides release and surges towards springtime and freedom: freedom in nature, in work, in love and in faith. His writings illustrate the mysterious, liberating power of the word that has finally been communicated.

After his ordination in 1926, Monsignor Savard soon felt himself removed from people and nature. Only when he had moved to Charlevoix and freed himself from a religious life that was too austere and isolated did the priest finally discover his true vocation: working with the people in Saint-Agnès, La Malbaie and other localities. Having become a parish-priest and eventually a curate, the future writer met the working people of Charlevoix, savoured their rich way of speaking, and quickly became aware of the scandalous degree to which they were being exploited. It was a contact that he later described as "a wound from my youth," a wound that is still there. In this beautiful but exploited land of Charlevoix, there are still too many people who have not yet heard Menaud's message.

At the height of the Depression, Savard helped the underprivileged people to escape from their terrible poverty. He founded two parishes in the Abitibi region and he set up a paper factory in Saint-Joseph-de-la-Rive. The paper produced by this factory is left in its natural state. It is as beautiful as the birch-bark it resembles, and since Monsignor Savard used it for his letters, for me it remains yet another symbol of this upright, proud man, a "guiding light" for any who wish to follow his example.

In *L'abatis*, Monsignor Savard presents his recollections and poems from the years he spent in the Abitibi region. Here, he is in "the service of his own people." He admires the long, laborious work of the pioneer farmers, and as in *Menaud*, his observations of nature always result in a poetry that is universal in rhythm and images, and national in the relevance of the lessons it contains. Take, for instance, the wild geese, which "struggle blindly against everything, made strong by the burden they carry: the fragile eggs, the precious treasure of the future, the ultimate destiny of the race... oh, admirable creatures, so intrepid and faithful: I learn so much from you!"

Savard's second novel, *La minuit*, is a sort of reply to *Menaud*. A truly tragic novel, it denounces greed, materialism, ideological revolt and injustice, and at the same time teaches the evangelical morality of brotherliness. *Le barachois*, a collection of poems and reminiscences, emerged from the writer's contacts with the sea-faring people along the coast. Long before Antonine Maillet's *La Sagouine, Le barachois* sang the praises of the Acadian "fishermen": their fertile imaginations, their lives spent in constant harmony with a symbolic environment, and as in *Menaud*, their exploitation at the hands of the capitalists. *Martin et le pauvre* is yet another magnificent poetic prayer about poverty, charity and compassion; while it has clear affinities with popular speech, it also moves in the direction of chants and fables.

Fascinated by language in general and especially by the direct, natural way rural people tend to express themselves, Savard also wrote plays for the theatre. *La folle* is a lyric drama which extols the merits of charity; its style combines elements of Greek theatre with those of Christian theatre in the manner of Claudel. *La dalle-des-morts*, a historical drama set in 1830, is a "deeper study of the themes in *Menaud*"; it also alludes to Maria Chapdelaine, who stares through the kitchen window at the clearing, dreaming of freedom and escape. The main character, Gildore, faithful to the ways of the *voyageurs* and the *coureurs de bois*, leaves behind his fiancée, Délie, and eventually perishes in the "narrows of death." Monsignor Savard's characters are often haunted by the wide, open spaces still waiting to be claimed or reclaimed. This represents no small matter, for at stake is the question of whether the French Canadians will sit back and let their French identity wither away, or whether they will take up the challenge of ensuring a partially French North America and a predominantly French Quebec. The adventures of Gildore and Menaud lead to death and madness, but here the death and madness are Savard's way of reminding us that we must always listen to the voices of the land.

Félix-Antoine Savard was awarded a number of Quebec, Canadian and international literary prizes. A firm believer in the importance of popular traditions as the source of a nation's vitality, he founded, with Luc Lacourcière, the Archives of French-Canadian Folklore at Laval University, where he was also a distinguished professor. A former president of the Quebec Geographic Society and the *Société du parler français*, he helped codify the French language as it is spoken by his people: one cannot help but associate his name with such typical Quebec words as *draveurs, abatis, barachois, bouscueils, huards, outardes, bleuets,* and *quenouilles*. In his long and varied career, Savard has left the people of Quebec a rich heritage indeed.

In the course of the past few years I had the privilege of corresponding a number of times with Félix-Antoine Savard, and I learned a great deal from his letters. On November 12, 1977, in an envelope bearing a stamp with the picture of a magnificent caribou on it, I discovered he was very fond of Eliot. "For a number of years now, one of my close companions has been the great poet, T.S. Eliot. I turn to him often, and it does me good... If you come upon his poems (the English version presented and translated by Pierre Leyris, Editions du Seuil) or *T.S. Eliot* by Georges Cattaui (Editions universitaires), you'll see how much influence he's had on me." On September 16, 1976, a letter informed me that, to celebrate his eightieth birthday, Msgr. Savard was leaving "for several days on a long trip in the forest...to give my head a rest!" Even when ill and elderly, Menaud liked to stay close to nature. On January 20, 1977, Menaud wrote me again: "I listen to *inner music*. And memories keep coming back...coming back: yesterday it was the song of the hermit thrush, the virtuoso of our great coniferous forests that I used to listen to when I was young — a song that purified my soul!"

Later, after a year or two of silence, I once again felt a need to write to Menaud: "I often think of you, especially in November when I discuss your work with my students. The landscapes in the Ottawa region are starting to grow bleak, and suddenly, almost magically, I find myself in the land of Menaud. It's impossible for me to be bleak myself when I think of Menaud's mountain taking shape within me. Your writings bring hope — hope in fraternity, in the renewal of people and things, in a better future." On November 28, I was able to read to my students the following advice from Félix-Antoine Savard: "You're lucky to be in contact with young people. Give them the best of yourself, I mean what's finest in you. You must awaken their *appetite for beauty*. Open them up to *Nature*...If you manage to plant a single *beautiful* tree in those young peoples' hearts, you'll have done a very great deed." Félix-Antoine Savard knew, better than any professor lost in a jargon that reduces literature to graphs and diagrams, that to teach literature is above all to teach the pleasure of reading, to awaken the universal "inner music" that we all have within ourselves. On August 24, 1982, Menaud died, leaving behind him thousands of men and women who read and marvel at the exemplary landscapes his words have given us.

* * *

F.-A. S. — You've asked me a number of very serious questions, and you've done so in a way that is friendly and tactful. A few years ago a professor asked me to answer 52 of them; I've never seen the bootlicker again!

It's very difficult to explain the mysterious forces that motivate a writer. Memory is one of them. The Mother of the Muses never forgets a thing. Memories come back to me at the most unexpected moments, even from very far into the past, even my childhood and adolescence.

I was ten years old when my father first took me into the woods around where we lived. My amazement has lasted all this time. It was as though I'd become the *Little Prince* of a wonderful kingdom, the Saguenay region, and I've never entirely left it.

Like so many others, I studied fairly seriously: courses in Greek, Latin, French. And they marked me for life. They immunized me, so to speak, against a certain kind of vulgarity. In those days they taught the Classics as best they could. We even learned long passages by heart. I can still recite lines by Aeschylus or Virgil, and excerpts from Bossuet, La Fontaine, Pascal or Chateaubriand. Later I added to this intellectual storehouse, with Valéry, Claudel, Baudelaire, Verlaine, Rimbaud and that dear Abbé Brémond, who replied so well to the questions I had been asking myself about Poetry. I even became a good friend of T.S. Eliot.

These great writers are still sacred to me. To use the exact word that Tacitus wrote in his life of Agricola, they've entered into my *penetralia*, the recesses or sanctuaries of my soul. They've acted as a refuge for me, where I've taken shelter against all forms of barbarism, linguistic or otherwise.

D.S. — Do you consider these authors to be neglected these days?

F.-A. S. — Yes, unfortunately! Many of the people who pride themselves in being called educators should think about this distressing phenomenon. No longer studying the classics has deprived young people of an irreplaceable cultural heritage. And this is a very serious misfortune that threatens the future of our civilization.

I should add, however, that certain so-called private institutions are working to save traditional humanism. That's where the hope lies.

D.S. — You've been speaking about your studies, but in your books there are characters who are proudly referred to as illiterates. It seems that you're very fond of them and that they've taught you a lot.

F.-A. S. — I've been extraordinarily lucky and happy to be able to know and spend time with simple, natural people: *coureurs de bois*, woodsmen, settlers, and so on. They're wonderful: pure natives in the Greek sense of autochthonous — people who have grown out of the land and woods of my region in the same way as a tree would, or grain, or the *gourgane* beans of the Charlevoix area.

In *L'abatis* and *La dalle-des-morts* I celebrated the heroic lumberjacks and raftsmen of our epics. These people still live within me, and they pop up all over the place in my writings.

To digress for a moment, athletics are very much in fashion now, but we tend to forget that for three centuries of our history we had Olympics that had nothing to do with games...Our heroes braved death but they're not very well known now and sometimes even completely forgotten. It disgusts me to think of all that. History is so terribly ungrateful.

D.S. — In your work, certain words take on symbolic or even mythic dimensions...

F.-A. S. — It would take hours and hours to reply to that question. The world we try to express is *new every moment,* as Claudel put it.

    There are words in dictionaries, and they're immutable, scientific. Many of them have been established forever in their abstract meaning. They express the genius of a particular language. But poetic words change as living beings do, as the poet himself does. And you see the poor worker with words, stuck in his poem shop, trying to express, to stabilize what is constantly moving and changing; sometimes he's lost and almost hopeless in his forest of symbols. Great poets have gone on hunting expeditions for live vowels and consonants. But these days so many come back empty-handed and vent their anger by massacring words and ideas. They want to create things that are new but all they invent is disorder. Certain collections of poetry are frightful. They're enough to make you shake in your shoes.

D.S. — You seem pessimistic, at least as far as language is concerned...

F.-A. S. — I am a bit pessimistic, in spite of myself. But the deeds and misdeeds are there for all to see. In certain areas of our colleges and universities, the basic level of language is at its lowest. And it's the ideas themselves that are mortally affected. We forget that, except for religion, our language is our greatest treasure. "The French language is both the most perfect product and the most perfect record of our national heritage," as Claudel put it.

D.S. — Are there any cures for this degradation of language?

F.-A. S. — Of course! Young people can be educated to be aware of language, first by their parents and later at school — providing the school is worthy of its name.

    If I were a teacher, in primary school I'd have my pupils learn a dozen or so fables by La Fontaine. The language they're written in is perfect, and very close to nature. And not only do they always use exactly the right word but they also present syntactic constructions that are as varied as they are marvellous. *Le bonhomme*, for example, illustrates the workings both of geometry and precision, as Pascal spoke of it.

With writers who respect the truth, the most important word for their writings is *work*. And *patience*, I might add. It's a word which can't be put into practice without suffering. And patience refers not only to the heavens, as the poet says, but to patience that is obstinate, long-suffering, respectful of the most humble creatures.

D.S. — I'd like to hear you say more about the interaction between the poet and the world.

F.-A. S. — Man is always faced with the question God asked Adam when he invited him to name the creatures: *quid vocarat ea?*

Before his fall from grace, man's vision was pure and clear; it went right to the heart of things, and it was also poetic, since man was trying to create in God's image and likeness. Adam must have sung so many beautiful poems: we hear echoes of them in the sublime *Song of Songs*.

Pride clouded man's vision, but the need to name things and celebrate them has remained in the human soul. It's one of God's gifts to man. That explains why the respectful use of language is a sort of religion, a sort of sacrament of love, which we find even with so-called pagan peoples.

This reminds me of a sublime expression from Roger Bacon, a famous monk who was both a very learned man and a poet. I've become particularly fond of him in recent years, expecially his treatise dealing with methods of delaying the infirmities of old age and preserving one's faculties. I'll quote Bacon...Do you understand Latin? Excellent! *Mundus*, he said, *mens mea, conjugan connubio stabili.* What a commentary could be written about that: a wedding of the soul with the world of nature! What an inspiring combination for truth, beauty and goodness! It makes me think of the saints, including the ones we've forgotten: all those men and women whose sense of charity strengthened and purified man's vision and his language. I also like to think of the innumerable multitude of sinners who were finally able to wash their eyes clean in the fountainhead of grace. *Domine, fac ut videam!* Lord, make me to see! I'm very familiar with that blind man's prayer...

D.S. — Where do you get these ideas, which sound so strange these days?

F.-A. S. — ...but which are still fundamentally true, and a lot more common than you might think.

"Far from people and noise," as La Fontaine put it. I'd like to write extensively on that theme; it would bring back such memories...

I was raised in Chicoutimi and taught to respect language. For us, language — especially the written language — was honest and clean, and occasionally sprinkled with fine old words from the Quebec countryside. As early as the second year of my studies, I was introduced to etymology, and ever since then I've never stopped looking deeper and deeper into the origins of words. I still like to pick out words as if they were precious stones found in a piece of ore; I get a great deal of pleasure in polishing them, looking for their original brilliance in Latin, Greek or even Sanskrit. My mind has never been divorced from the language of my ancestors. I'll be faithful to it till I die.

D.S. — The name of God is found all through your work. God seems to be made manifest particularly in nature, in warmth and in the beauty of the land. The light of heredity and the light of divinity are practically one and the same. Could it be that you're more interested in God's appearance in nature than by His appearance through revelation?

F.-A. S. — "It is through Him that we have life, movement and being," said Saint Paul at the Areopagus. There is a sacred path that leads the soul to God, and it goes through fields and water and forest. I've spent a lot of time walking in the forests of my land — that is, in a natural world where I discovered what Saint Augustine called "the seminal reasons."

They can be found everywhere, even in the lowliest moss beneath your feet. They certainly haven't been created by man. I used to pray as I walked. I've never forgotten a wonderful thing said to me by an old hunter named Rousseau. I was telling him that it worried me to see him go off into the bush alone for weeks on end in the Saguenay area. He replied: "I'm not alone. The good Lord is with me...I speak to Him and He speaks to me." The great saints couldn't have said it better than this *coureur de bois*.

D.S. — For many people you'll always be the man who wrote *Menaud*.

F.-A. S. — But there was something that set if off, that triggered it. As you may well guess, it was *Maria Chapdelaine* — a masterpiece! I had stood up for it at college, because there were some people who, out of sheer vanity, felt they had to criticize it or people would take them for hicks. Imagine!

I have in front of me a picture of Louis Hémon's gravestone in the cemetery at Chapleau, Ontario, where he's buried. It still hurts me to think of the sad fate that befell him. There's a Fides edition of *Maria Chapdelaine* for which I wrote the preface, and I did so with love and admiration. His *voix du Québec (voices of Quebec)* were ringing in my heart.

As for *Menaud*, it's a book that I actually lived and that still goes on living within me. I've already said that it originally resulted from my being "wounded" as a young man. It would take too long to explain everything, and anyway, a writer should never explain his book; if he did, he'd do a very bad job of it.

I'll talk briefly about the raw facts that led me to write it. From the time I was quite young, I'd been aware that the natural resources upon which our liberty as a people depended were being taken away from us. Our nation still hasn't completely recovered from the trials of its history. Personally, I had worked on log drives, I knew how terrible conditions were for the men — my own people — working in the lumber camps, and I suffered because of it. Dostoevsky's famous title *The Insulted and the Injured* often ran through my mind, as it did with a lot of my compatriots.

It's hard — it's insufferable — to admit that you've been defeated forever after having discovered and mapped out the greater part of the North American continent. And that's what made me cry out in revolt. Others have written theses on the subject, and I'm aware of their value, but a fixed genre like that won't do for a young man thirsting after justice, a *coureur de bois*, as I then was.

With all these problems of honour and freedom, of a life worthy of our history and our civilization, what exactly was Menaud's *madness?* My own madness, to some extent. That's why, whenever I can, I take off for the High Country, the mountains of Charlevoix; there I'm above and beyond the miseries, dissensions, divisions and quarrels of my dear homeland.

[1] An earlier version of this interview was published in Félix-Antoine Savard's diary, *Carnet du soir intérieur*, vol.1, pp. 178-193.

Anne Hébert and the Roots of Imagination

Born in 1916 in Sainte-Catherine-de-Fossambault, Portneuf County, Anne Hébert has produced over some forty years a rich and fascinating body of work. In the impressionistic and surrealistic poems of her early career, she provides a most eloquent testimony to the deeply-rooted sense of alienation felt by most French-Canadian writers in the Forties and Fifties. Here the poet proceeds in a painterly fashion, creating striking images of disjointed, dismembered corpses. In the early Sixties, Anne Hébert played an important role in expanding the horizons of Quebec writers. Through her exploration of the senses and her sensual discovery of the world and the flesh, the way was opened for the liberated, passionate poets of the Sixties. Her exaltation of the natural world anticipates such works as Gatien Lapointe's *Ode au Saint-Laurent* and Paul Chamberland's *Terre Québec*, in which the poets are concerned with articulating the land, to name it and establish its cosmogonical foundations. Anne Hébert's first collections of poetry provide a link between Nelligan, whose images of snow, darkness and cold, along with a self-destructive personal mythology, give expression to turn-of-the-century alienation, and such poets as Brault, Chamberland, Miron and Lapointe, who were able to reach beyond their solitude.[1] It is in part thanks to Anne Hébert that protest and confrontation became the watchwords at those spectacular poetry readings and shows for the "Résistance," where singers and entertainers toured Quebec and eventually produced a successful movie entitled *La nuit de la poésie*.

As a novelist, Anne Hébert has created historical frescoes of epic dimensions such as *Kamouraska* and "*Un grand mariage*" in *Le Torrent*. *Les fous de Bassan* (1982) is a part of this "historical cycle" set somewhere between the real world and an imaginary one; in it, Reverend Jones and other anglophone characters, fictionalized versions of the Loyalists who settled in the Gaspé region in the 18th century, are left to their dynamic and delirious devices. In *Les enfants du sabbat* and *Héloïse*, Anne Hébert has plunged into a Manichean world in which the Satanic and the Christian rites of good and evil reflect the inherent ambivalences between love and hate, selfishness and charity, violence and tenderness. The author expresses this quest for human identity in terms of a concrete, fantastic universe marked, on the side of life, by springtime, fire, light, mountains, forests, wind, birds and water; and, on the side of death, by darkness, cold, blood, drought and bones.

Mme Hébert was good enough to invite me to her Paris apartment to talk about her work and her life. I was deeply moved by both the kindness and the warmth she showed me. Paris and Montreal had for a moment become one and the same place for me: the shrubs and flowers in the writer's balcony garden contrasted strangely in my mind with the painting hung over her sofa — a work by Jean-Paul Lemieux entitled "Kamouraska," which shows a terrifying, snow-covered field stained with blood.

* * *

D.S. — Were you deeply influenced by your childhood, growing up in Ste-Catherine and Quebec City? I have the impression that the landscapes in Portneuf have been a rich source of literary images for you and an inspiration for dreams and story-telling.

A.H. — Those years were very important to me, but then they are for everyone. I think that childhood, especially early childhood, is the greatest influence on one's life; since I was lucky enough to grow up in the country, I'll always feel very close to nature and the trees.

D.S. — And then you left the landscapes of Quebec behind. What is it that keeps you in Paris? You've been living in France since 1954, I believe.

A.H. — Not quite since 1954. I'd have to think back. First I spent three years here without returning; I had a scholarship that I was able to keep for three years. Then I went back to Canada. I spent two years in Montreal. After that, I spent every other year here. Until 1965 I would spend one year in Quebec and one year in Paris. Since 1965 I've mostly been in Paris, although I do go to Canada quite often.

D.S. — Did you decide to live mostly in France because you felt uncomfortable in Quebec, at a time when women writers who dared to speak of love and freedom were looked down upon by the Quebec establishment?

A.H. — No, I don't think so. There have always been women writers in Canada. There have always been some good writers who were women, and I didn't ever really feel any discrimination. I found that it was difficult to get published, but it wasn't because I'm a woman. At that time it was very difficult to get *Le torrent* published, for example, because it was considered too violent.

D.S. — Your father was a civil servant, a poet (author of the *Cycle de Don Juan*), and a literary critic. Did he have a decisive influence on your career as a writer? I know your father took great pride in being French Canadian, and that he often talked to you about his ancestors, who were deported Acadians, I believe.

A.H. − My father always took a great interest in whatever little thing I might be scribbling. That was really very encouraging. I was writing little plays of sorts. My father would read them and encourage me. It's so easy to stifle a child. He spoke the French language admirably well and he would correct my grammar and syntax. He was the one who taught me my grammar.

D.S. − You were very sick during your childhood. You even had to quit school. Could you speak a bit about your illness and the effect it had on you?

A.H. − I was never seriously ill. It was a custom in my mother's family, and in certain other families in Quebec City, that very young children didn't go to school. They had a private teacher. And so I had a private schoolmistress until I was eleven years old, not because I was sick but because it was the custom. This meant that when I did go to school, I was completely lost. With the other children, I was so shy it was crazy. I couldn't bring myself to recite the lessons because I was too shy. I'd rather get a zero than open my mouth. I was a scapegoat for the other children. Starting to go to school was an enormous shock for me but later, of course, things gradually fell into place.

D.S. − You grew up in a stimulating intellectual environment. Writers such as Jean Le Moyne, Robert Elie and of course your cousin Saint-Denys Garneau were all friends of yours.

A.H. − Yes, but they were teen-age friends. Saint-Denys Garneau was a little bit older than I was. When I was very small, Saint-Denys was already a tall young man and he didn't play with me very much. I used to play more with his brothers. But when I was 15 or 16, I became very friendly with him and his friends.

D.S. − I wonder to what extent Saint-Denys Garneau's poetry had an influence on you. After all, your cousin was, a bit like yourself in your earliest poems, a poet of dispossession, a writer who, as he says in one of his poems, "walked beside his joy" and who showed in his writings that the austere society of the time more or less killed him. But there is nevertheless one basic difference between your poetry and Saint-Denys Garneau's, and that is that you were able to go beyond loneliness and isolation.

A.H. — Yes, but it's very difficult to establish a parallel because Saint-Denys Garneau died very young. We don't know what he would have done. At some point he too might have opted for life. He was in total despair, but you never know what might have happened if he'd lived longer.

D.S. — You once said, in a film made by the NFB and the Quebec Film Institute, that writing is a driving force towards the absolute, a risk one takes without knowing how it will end. Could you explain more fully how you conceive of the act of writing?

A.H. — I think it's the same thing for music, painting or any art form. You try to reach a sort of absolute, a sort of perfection, but you know very well that you'll never attain it. The simple fact of doing everything you can to reach it, never sparing yourself and giving everything you have — that's the only way to work, with a kind of thrust of the whole being towards the fullest possible expression of one's gift.

D.S. — After having gone through all your writings, I've concluded that, for you, literature takes root in dreams and internal obsessions, in what you call the "troubled waters of the imagination." Everyday, external reality plays a secondary role in the way you write, does it not?

A.H. — I believe that the roots of the imagination are physical roots, real roots. In *Les enfants du sabbat*, for example, some very real things are being looked at. In Sainte-Catherine I knew a woman who called herself "la Goglue" and who actually did sell moonshine. All I did was push the whole thing towards the point of absurdity. However, in the beginning it is real before it becomes surreal.

D.S. — Perhaps we could talk about your poetry now. At the very beginning of your career, you published poems in several magazines, including *Gants du ciel*, which was edited by the literary critic Guy Sylvestre. In that magazine, Father Hilaire wrote an article called "From Francis of Assisi to Anne Hébert," in which he analyses the themes of crucifixion and resurrection. At that time, did you consider yourself a Catholic writer? I know, for instance, that you were strongly impressed by Claudel.

A.H. — Whenever I reread those poems, I'm astonished. I was very Catholic, like everyone else in the country at that time. I was profoundly religious — I was a believer. And so it was normal for me to speak about it. It was part of everyday reality.

D.S. — Your first poems do in fact show an explicitly Christian form of suffering, a kind of crucifixion one must undergo in order finally to break free of the sometimes masochistic images of pain. The Catholicism of your childhood seems to me to have been both a source of suffering and a source of poetic imagery.

A.H. — Yes, it was a source of richness as well, and I think that the Québécois today who have completely cut themselves off from religion have also cut themselves off from a great source of richness — the richness of the Bible — which is cutting themselves off from a source of culture that was their own. For me it was very constricting, but very rich at the same time.

D.S. — Your first collection of poetry, *Les songes en équilibre* (1942), expressed a sense of being absent from the world.[2] The poet is blind but she wants to give herself eyes so she can discover two "landscapes": her own body, and nature. You adopted the forms of modern poetry — a poetic prose through which you note your impressions. I find the title (literally "Balanced Dreams") particularly striking, and I suspect it could be applied to your entire literary output. Why did you choose a title that emphasizes dreams?

A.H. — Dreams are very evanescent, they're balanced on a tightrope, and they dissolve spontaneously. I had the sense that my poems were as fragile as dreams.

D.S. — Ten years or so after *Les songes en équilibre* was published, *Le tombeau des rois* presented a new grouping of inter-related themes: a discovery of the body and an awakening of the senses, despite the apparent obstacles symbolized by bones, ashes and night. Water comes to be associated with the symbols of death and a celebration of life is imminent, despite the lure of the tomb. It seems to me that the hands become the most important symbol in the collection. What was it about hands that so mystified you?[3]

A.H. — They're beautiful both as symbols and in reality. People's hands are very significant. They're almost as expressive as the face; you can discover things in a hand that you can't see in the face. For example, a person's character is never completely revealed in his face, but his hands may suddenly add some unexpected dimension.

D.S. — In *Le tombeau des rois*, one has the sense that the poet is blaming someone else for her own state of submission, sadness and repression. You wrote:

> There is certainly someone
> Who once killed me
> And then walked away
> On the tip of his toes
> Without breaking his perfect dance.
> (trans. F.R. Scott)

A.H. — Yes, if you're referring to the things that one might find restrictive and confining, there was certainly the Jansenism that existed in Quebec at that time, those families closed in upon themselves and quite cut off from the world.

D.S. — In *Mystère de la parole* (1960), the restrictive forces have been overcome and the poet exults in her ability to participate in the world. *Mystère de la parole* made an enormous contribution to the intellectual awakening of French

Canada. To Nelligan who cried out in despair, "My window is a garden of frost," you reply: "Joy set to crying out, a new mother smelling of game-birds/ among the reeds. Spring delivered was so fair that it took/ our hearts with one hand" (trans. Alan Brown). In the introduction to *Mystère de la parole*, you state that poetry breaks through solitude. What did you mean exactly?

A.H. — I wanted to say that for someone who is alone, who complains of being alone and not communicating with other people, the simple fact of writing shows that he wants to engage in communication. And when one writes, usually one gets a response; people speak to us about what we've written.[4]

D.S. — I believe, like you, that the poet is the one who is closest to the deep, hidden meanings of words. In *Mystère de la parole* you state that the poet "who has received the function of the word" must take in charge "his darkest brothers, all feasts engraved in secret" (trans. Alan Brown). Could you explain further what you see as the poet's function, at least in the context of *Mystère de la parole* and Quebec in the Fifties?

A.H. — I believe that the poets in Quebec really took charge of their inarticulate brothers and gave them expression by expressing themselves. This was very important in the liberation of Quebec.

D.S. — In your poems both the sonorities and the semantic structure are very carefully crafted. These structures involve equivalences, parallels and oppositions that spontaneously generate meaning as the poem unfolds. The reader has the pleasure of discovering a form that creates meaning. Did it require a great deal of work for you to construct this poetic architecture, this subtle arrangement of words?

A.H. — When I was writing poems — I'm now writing fewer and fewer of them — a large number came of their own accord. There was a large part that simply came to me. It's like lightning, something that flashes upon you brutally and violently, a sudden bolt of illumination. There are always a few small things left to arrange, but very few. The part that comes to us — is given to us — is even larger than the part that comes of our own volition. After the first draft, I almost never rework the whole thing, only specific words, words that don't manage to embody the image closely enough. I also tend to reduce the text, to condense it.

D.S. — HMH published a book of letters you exchanged with the English-Canadian poet Frank Scott, who translated *Le tombeau des rois*. What did this dialogue on the translation of your poems mean to you?

A.H. — With Frank Scott I peeled my poems to the core, to use a rather down-to-earth expression, as if they were foreign to me. That made me aware of all sorts of things I had done quite unconsciously. Since I had to provide him with explanations, and since he had to look for English equivalents, our discussions forced me to scrutinize the poem much more carefully than I had ever done before. It was a process that made me much more aware of what I had written.

D.S. — *Le torrent*, published in 1950, is your first prose work. The critical response at the time was not at all favourable to this book of fantastic short stories about children who were deaf, abandoned, punished by adults and victimized by a repressive Catholic morality.[5] To what extent did you want to demystify the values of your childhood and exorcize a repression that had become unbearable for you? I'm thinking here of the references to the educational system and of what you refer to as "a childhood tortured by the strict prohibition of any form of intimate knowledge."

A.H. — You musn't forget that even if I criticize the educational system, I myself had had a very unorthodox education and barely went to school at all in the real sense. I escaped all the repression that is present in *Le torrent*, but I observed it in other people. The story of the boy who was supposed to become a priest came from what I had noticed in young people whose mothers had reserved them for the priesthood.

D.S. — Dispossession is an essential theme in *Le torrent*. The teenager in the first story is thwarted in his attempts to possess the elements of the natural world. The evolution from dis-possession to possession is perhaps the most important theme in your work, at least until *Kamouraska* was published.

A.H. — I think that's quite true. Our religious education taught us to divest ourselves of everything, not to have any-thing of our own. It's a fine thing to give, but giving must be done spontaneously: you mustn't give because the educa-tional system forces you to. True giving is a free act, and the more self-possessed we are, the more we have to give. If you completely deny your own self, you have nothing left to give, and since you have nothing left to give, you don't exist.

D.S. — The narrator in the story "Le torrent" claims that "every man carries within him a crime that constantly seeps out of him and must be expiated." You seem to be quite concerned by man's destructive impulses.

A.H. — I'm more concerned with the original sin they taught us about at that time. Little children were taught that they had Original Sin within them and that they had to be baptized and confirmed — that they had to right the wrong that had been committed before them, long before their parents and grandparents. It's a very harsh thing to teach children, when they believe it. Personally, I took it very seriously. Guilt was cultivated in a way that was terrifying. They had a gift for making children feel guilty. We felt almost guilty just for being alive.

D.S. — A deaf boy, a crippled girl, a woman who's depressed by her work and unhappy in love, a nun who dreams of freedom and springtime — all these scenes from *Le torrent* might indicate that you have a tendency to see the world through the eyes of people who are sick or on the fringes of society.

A.H. — Everyone is marginal in some respect. If you look at people's lives, you see that they're much less ordinary than they might want to let on. People appear to stick very closely to some standard of normality; they talk like everyone else, they think like everyone else, but once you've scratched the surface, you see that on the inside people are all quite peculiar.

D.S. — Perhaps we could now talk about the tone in *Le torrent*. In that collection, as in all your writing, one senses the influence of mythology, the Bible and fairy tales.

A.H. — Yes, definitely. As a child I read a great many fairy tales, and I also read what at that time was called religious history.

D.S. — You know, Quebec critics have often claimed that there's no social commitment in your writing and that you're therefore outside the main current of Quebec literature. Now I don't agree with this at all. Even in *Le torrent* you have ironic descriptions of the "irreproachable bourgeois" and "nice patronizing ladies." You show a good deal of sympathy for the common people and people from the wrong side of town, for what you call the "castes in decline."

A.H. — I think you're right. Obviously I'm not in the business of writing tracts; if I was, I'd put the good guys on one side and the bad guys on the other. It's much more blurred than that, much more mixed-up, as it is in life. But the fact remains that in "Un grand mariage" (*Le torrent*), I never said that the bourgeois characters, Marie-Louise and Augustin, were particularly nice people.

D.S. — Let's now look at your first novel, *Les chambres de bois* (1958). This novel presents three of the most important themes in your work: a rejection of fear and insecurity; learning to experience joy and sensuality; and an appreciation of nature. At the time you wrote *Les chambres de bois*, you were also writing poetry. I suspect that for you, writing was then mostly an experience akin to dreaming.[6] This is no doubt why your first novel is much more poetic than realistic and why dreams come across as being more important than actions. For instance, you could have put more emphasis on actions in the story of Catherine, the young wife who falls victim to her husband's insensitivity.

A.H. — The writing is very close to poetry in *Les chambres de bois*. It could have been much more like prose.

D.S. — I wonder if you think Catherine's problems with her husband, who simply treats her as some kind of ornament, are shared by many other women? I might mention in passing that *Les chambres de bois* is often included in courses on feminist writing.

A.H. — I don't think Michel is cold or insensitive as a husband. Michel is neurotic and he's in love with his sister. He's a deeply selfish man who married Catherine in a moment of despair because his sister had gone away and left him all alone. He never loved Catherine.

D.S. — When Catherine finds herself in love with Bruno, their relationship is marked by affection and understanding. Is that perhaps the most important message in the novel, a sort of definition of love based on both passion and mutual respect?

A.H. — Yes, but I don't know whether Catherine will find happiness with Bruno. By being exposed to Michel and Lia, Catherine has become much more cultivated, much more open to all sorts of things — to poetry, for instance. In the long run she may find Bruno a little too rustic.

D.S. — I'd like to ask you a couple of questions about your writing for the theatre. *Le temps sauvage*, which was performed in 1966 by the Théâtre du Nouveau-Monde, presents a Québécois family in which everyone is suffocating; the mother has kept her many children isolated from the world, and they live in an environment marked by loneliness and dreams. Only the "primitive" poetry of the snow, the forest, the burst of growth and the scents of spring keep the play from sinking into the depths of pessimism. *Le temps sauvage* bears a close thematic resemblance to your other work, but what made you decide to write for the theatre?

A.H. — I've always enjoyed theatre. My mother liked it too. She obviously didn't write plays, since that would have caused a great scandal in her day. One of my brothers was involved in the theatre in Quebec City. They put on performances of plays in the parish hall in Sainte-Catherine, with Saint-Denys Garneau and Jean Lemoyne.

D.S. — I'm fascinated by the character of the mother in *Le temps sauvage*. Agnès tries to rebel against the Church's humiliation of women and a moral system based on resignation; at the same time, she seems to retain religious values that are overly simplistic and Manichean, so that in the end she seeks solace in a martyrdom of solitude, the "savage time" of the title.

A.H. — Agnès blames the priests for their attitude toward women but she adopts exactly the same attitude toward her children. She becomes a despot, slipping into the role of a priest and becoming just as authoritarian herself.

D.S. — A new Anne Hébert was revealed with the publication of *Kamouraska* in 1970. It is an historical novel based on historical fact: in 1838 a woman who felt trapped in a pre-arranged marriage with the sensual, drunken *Seigneur* of Kamouraska, goads her lover into killing her husband. *Kamouraska* is presented as a sort of conscious dream, an hallucinating film of the mind. It's perhaps my favourite among all your writings: a marvellous combination of poetic images, dramatic tension and philosophical reflections. *Kamouraska* is a real *tour de force*; its poetical structure is both surrealistic and mythological, yet at the same time it is firmly grounded in reality. It took you four years, I believe, to write the novel, and you did a lot of research into the period. What was it that interested you so much about the 19th century in Quebec?

A.H. — The 19th century was perhaps the most tormented and political period in Quebec history, and also the most Jansenistic. Yet, on the surface, everything seemed perfect; there didn't appear to be anything amiss in all those impeccable upper-town families in Quebec City. Now I said to myself that this wasn't normal, that in fact something must have been going on with those people. When I was a child, my mother used to tell me about the history of Kamouraska. You can imagine what a dramatic event that murder must have been at the time, the scandal it must have caused; there was my mother telling me about it four or five generations later. It must have blown that self-righteous smugness in Quebec City wide open. Of course, my mother didn't tell me the story the same way I told it. The women she was talking about was named Eléonore, not Elisabeth, and she hadn't aided or abetted her husband's murder; she wasn't the doctor's accomplice, she wasn't his mistress, she was absolutely not involved in it.

D.S. — *Kamouraska* strikes me in a number of ways as a novel of manners. Your descriptions of the clothes worn by the ladies of the former aristocracy are brilliantly realistic and evocative: lace, silk, cambric, muslin, velvet, satin, cashmere, ruched bonnets, little veils and necklaces all come to life before the reader's eyes. At the same time you satirize the people's idleness, their mastery of gossip, rosaries and fashion magazines. You refer to these ladies as "daughters of derision" in an "enormous circus."

A.H. — I did want to show the ridiculous side of it all, certainly.

D.S. — There are a lot of reflections upon marriage in *Kamouraska*. The woman who marries for glory (Elisabeth, as she appears in the beginning)[7], and the woman who sells her body to men (Mary Fletcher, the prostitute who became such a subject of fascination for Elisabeth), are practically twin sisters. Both of them are victims of a society that exploits women.

A.H. — In certain marriages, there's a type of woman who lets herself be kept legally.

D.S. — My impression is that the murder in *Kamouraska* is as much a symbolic murder as a real one. This would make it the expression in literary terms of a revolt against the *ennui* of a world without love.

A.H. — It's the story of a murder, but why a murder? It was the period that made the murder virtually necessary; in our time, if a woman can't bear her husband, if her husband's really detestable like Tassy, and if she's in love with another man, she gets a divorce. At that time this was so unthinkable that it induced a kind of extreme exasperation, a kind of convulsion that ended in violence.

D.S. — I'd like to ask you a question about the narrative technique used in *Kamouraska*. You usually move from one interior monologue to another and one character to another; into this living world of the dialogues, you insert the commentaries of a narrator who maintains an ironic detachment from the events being described. Did you give a great deal of thought to the different narrative stances, or was the technique a completely natural one?

A.H. — I began *Kamouraska* several times. The first time I told the story completely in the third person, like a news item. It was quite flat, exactly like an item from the newspaper. I then realized I had to try to understand Elisabeth from the inside, so that the story could come to life a bit and be more real.

D.S. — You talked about getting inside your characters. That reminds me that there's something rather Proustian in *Kamouraska*. The characters live on their memories; it's as though they were locked into an hour-glass with dreams and snow whirling around them.

A.H. — I like Proust a great deal, and it's true that the role of memories is very important in *Kamouraska*.

D.S. — I think you would agree that snow is the most important symbol in *Kamouraska*. Elisabeth is haunted by snow. It was in the snow that her husband was killed, down by the cove in Kamouraska — the same cove that Lemieux has captured so well in the painting on the wall across from us. The snow will always remain stained with blood. The descriptions of snow take on a poetic dimension. There's the red snow of violence. And there's the white snow that covers everything and seems to prevent the arrival of spring and love.

A.H. — Snow is very important in that novel. And when Elisabeth relives the whole tragic experience, the whole crime of Kamouraska, she relives it through the snow. She says, "No, there's nothing to get upset about; it's only snow," but the snow brings the story back to her. The fact that she's thinking of snow, recalling the snow, brings back the whole terrible drama in Kamouraska. At first the snow is something clean; then it's something white that's been stained and ruined.

D.S. — Five years after *Kamouraska*, you published *Les enfants du sabbat*, a novel that required an enormous amount of research. In *Kamouraska* there was a character who anticipated the subject of *Les enfants du sabbat*: the servant girl who had the gift of healing and the powers of a witch. In *Les enfants* you provide a detailed exploration of witchcraft and magic, which are inevitable components in a society immersed in morality and Catholic ritual. We might remind our readers that the character we're talking about is Sister Julie-de-la-Trinité, the daughter of primitive, diabolical parents who practiced, on B. Mountain not far from Quebec City, a religion based on animal sacrifices, orgies and drunkenness. You have read several works dealing with witchcraft as practised in Quebec and France. You quote textually, and in Latin, excerpts from the ritual of exorcism. What is it that interests you so much in witchcraft?

A.H. — What interested me so much in witchcraft was precisely the fact that life, and everything that was due to us, took on a kind of magical quality because of the workings of guilt. Life was not something that was given to you; you practically had to steal it. You practically had to commit a sacrilege to gain a hold on it.

D.S. — To what extent were you inspired by the stories told by Robert-Lionel Séguin in *La sorcellerie au Québec du XVIIIe au XIXe* or by the biographies of the first nuns in New France?

Quebec is always just beneath the surface in *Les enfants du sabbat*. The stigmata of Sister Julie, for instance, made me think of Rose Ferron, the Quebec woman who was famous for her stigmata and who was said to have the ability to be in several places at the same time, just like Sister Julie. At one point you say that Father Flageole dreams of "performing an exorcism with great ceremony, according to the rites of the Province of Quebec."

A.H. — I discovered, in a library in Montreal, a book about exorcism as practised in New France in the 18th century. It was in that book I found the words for the exorcism. Also, Catherine-de-Saint-Augustin, who was a nun at the Hôtel-Dieu in Quebec City, wrote that there were male witches who used to hold black sabbaths in Cap-Tourmente and would come to the Hôtel-Dieu to steal consecrated communion wafers for their revels. There was a girl named Barbe Hallé who was born about 1645 — as a matter of fact I used the same name for one of Sister Julie's ancestors — and she was accused of being a witch. A sorcerer may actually have been burned to death in Quebec City, but no one is really sure about this since there are no archives.

D.S. — What do the forces on B. Mountain, that mountain of spruce and birch swept by the winds of malediction, represent for you?

A.H. — Actually, there are two worlds, with a constant shifting between the convent and the mountain. The world of the convent is immutable, conservative and deeply fearful, while the world of the mountain — even if terribly cruel things take place there — is also full of life and movement. For example, the love that unites Philomène and Abélard (or rather Adélard, which is a name found in the area around Sainte-Catherine) has to be recognized as a love without constraints. B. Mountain is a mountain that is quite close to Sainte-Catherine; I didn't want to give its real name, so the name has something mysterious about it. The mountain no longer exists; it's been completely levelled. The mountains in Quebec are not all that big, but when I was a child they seemed like real mountains. Since the roads were poor and very bumpy when I went with my older cousins to get moonshine, I always thought we'd gone very far into the mountain and I found it quite frightening and unnerving.

D.S. — I'd like to talk a little about the religious symbolism that helps bring the Sisters of the Precious Blood back into the fold. In its pagan form, on B. Mountain, this symbolism seems to have a liberating effect: water is erotic, not divine; three days of lovemaking provide a meaning for life; the "precious blood" of Christ as a symbol of transcendence is replaced by the blood of a sacrificed pig. Could you comment further on this "world in which the usual order has been inverted" and those pagan ceremonies which bear some resemblance to Church rituals, except that good has been replaced by evil?

A.H. — In witchcraft, everything is inverted, including Church ceremonies and good and evil. The mountain is the opposite side of the world. When Julie is raped by her father, she's both terror-stricken and proud.

D.S. — The rituals of life and death as performed by Philomène hearken back to certain poems in *Le tombeau des rois*. Apparently you're still fascinated by "the night of the dead, their inordinate coldness, all shadowy with hidden horror and terror" (*Les enfants du sabbat*).

A.H. — That must be true, since you find the same rituals in *Héloïse* as well.

D.S. — There's something quite mediaeval about *Les enfants du sabbat*. God and the Devil are present in both the popular imagery of the mountain dwellers and the nuns' imaginations. There's a world of ogres and ogresses. There's the chaplain who is tormented by dreams of the Middle Ages and "succumbs with terror and rapture" to the complete disorientation of all his faculties — and who also knows the works of several demonologists almost by heart.

A.H. — Exorcists still exist, at least in France. I don't know about Quebec. There are still priests who are appointed as exorcists and who perform exorcisms. Very often it is people who are hysterical or insane who are brought to them, and it probably has a calming effect on the sufferers to hear a priest praying over them.

D.S. — The madness and perversion in the novel are construed as being the results of witchcraft. I wonder to what extent they can also be considered inverted symbols of Quebec society before the Quiet Revolution, of the ever-present choirboy, the curly blond St John the Baptist, pure in body and soul? Marie-Claire Blais painted a picture similar to yours, where the brothel and the convent are interchangeable in *Une saison dans la vie d'Emmanuel*. In *Les enfants du sabbat* you set evil loose in the midst of a Quebec society that sees itself as a model of moderation. You created a vision of Quebec turned upside down.

A.H. — It's Quebec turned upside down if you will, but it's the dream side of Quebec too, everything that people repressed, all their deep fears. We'd seen enough of the pretty dreams. I wanted to show the nightmares.

D.S. — The story of Sister Julie, whose pupils are slit horizontally like the eyes of a wolf, anticipated the strange, supernatural vampire story of *Héloïse* (published in 1980 and made into a film by Roger Fournier in 1982, entitled *Les chemins de l'imaginaire*). This novel describes the "slow eroding away" of Bernard, a future lawyer who lets himself succumb to dangerous dreams influenced above all by Héloïse, a vampire in the Paris Métro. You have thus gradually orientated your work in the direction of supernatural mysteries and possession by the Devil, and in this sense *Héloïse* can be seen as a sort of culmination of this tendency.

A.H. — I've always been interested in the supernatural, but it's simply more obvious in *Héloïse*. It's very difficult to find any explanation other than the supernatural, since Christine and Bernard die at the end and you can't say that dreams play any part in that. In *Les enfants du sabbat*, you can say that perhaps Sister Julie is crazy or hysterical and she's imagining it all.

D.S. — Even if the supernatural is omnipresent in *Héloïse*, there's also a very strong presence of the real world. You create all sorts of Parisian characters: newspaper vendors, small shopkeepers, gypsies, Krishna converts. In the end, though, the Métro dominates everything else:

> The rush of air...the same feeling as falling into a void. My old fear of the Métro sweeps back over me. I plunge into the bowels of the earth, its heart of fire and ice. At the level of corpses. The grey walls fly past in the darkness. The stations light up the night for an instant. Then darkness again, grey walls, pipe-like things that are red and blue. Now and then there's a Dubonnet ad, half torn away, like a lost fresco. (*Héloïse*)

A.H. — When I came to Paris, I was very frightened by the Métro. I had the feeling that all of us were going to sink into the earth and that we wouldn't be able to breathe. Little by little I got used to it, since the Métro is a very convenient way to move about. But I think my initial apprehensiveness has remained with me. When we went through stations that were closed, I was quite intrigued. There's also the fact that I'm fascinated by all forms of transportation: trains, planes, buses, cars. In the Métro I often used to think of the time when the first Métro was invented and filled with women in floor-length dresses and men in bowlers or top-hats. I used to imagine them mingling with people from our own time. *Héloïse* came out of a long period of giving in to my dreams of the Métro. It could have turned out differently. It could have been realistic, since you meet some extraordinary people in the Métro, but gradually the supernatural took over.

D.S. — Perhaps we could talk a bit about Bernard. The impulsive force of his emotions and the attraction of a beautiful, mysterious woman throw his life into confusion. Your novel seems to suggest that the lives of sensitive people are always threatened by the unexpected appearance of seductive individuals; because of some attractive stranger, the person dearest to us can suddenly become almost hideous.

A.H. — Happiness is very fragile. As an epigraph to the book, there is an excerpt from a poem: "The world is in order/ The dead below/ The living above." This is meant to indicate that the world seems to be in order but that a small event can completely upset everything. The world appears exceptionally well-ordered for Christine and Bernard. They're both young, beautiful, pleasant people. Even their parents are nice. Life is all set out for them, but a single meeting is enough to shake everything up. The world is never in order.

D.S. — Bernard and Héloïse's first apartment is described as being "primordial." It's presented as a space and time "from before the protozoa and plankton. From before the creation of the world." Why did you create this primitive decor?

A.H. — It's not primitive. It's a new house, all white and enamelled, without any soul or atmosphere. There's no trace of life. It's a place as enamelled as a bath-tub. And for Bernard, who is particularly attracted to the past, it's all the more insufferable than it would be for anyone else. Bernard is trying to write poems and he must have a fear of the blank page. For him, looking at all that white is terrible.

D.S. — Talking about *Héloïse* always brings us back to the Métro. Here's how you describe the crowd in the Métro perpetually surging back and forth:

> Men and women with a precise goal. Above all, not to be late...The death of each one immured in the secrecy of blood and bone. Fate. It can be heard sometimes rapping against the walls of the heart. Or is it the din of the Métro and the incredulity everyone feels in the face of such mysteries?
> (trans. Sheila Fischman)

Death is omnipresent in your work. But for me that doesn't arouse any feeling of tragedy or powerlessness. My impression is that it's rather a question of learning how to live with imminent death, or even living happily with the death we carry within ourselves.

A.H. — I believe you're right. There are brief moments in life, perhaps when we're experiencing pain or sorrow, when we have a presentiment of how ephemeral and fragile our own fate is, and others' too. Most of the time we don't hear the fate that has come knocking at our heart; we don't want to hear it because we have to go on living, and if we listen too carefully to those voices, we end up spoiling the time we do have.

D.S. — When I discovered about half-way through the novel that Héloïse is a vampire, I wondered why you had included horror fiction in a novel that was otherwise quite convincingly realistic. I finally came to the conclusion that the vampire element must be a symbol or a dream—perhaps Bernard was having a nightmare? It could be a symbol of the death or dissolution of the self caused by a love that is mad and impossible. In this sense the vampire element would be the literary expression of a destructive, devouring love in which one person is draining away another's blood, another's identity.

A.H. — I must say that it bothered me too. I don't know why I made Héloïse a vampire. I could have told the story without her being a vampire. Of course, Héloïse represents death itself, and Bernard is fascinated by death. It's a novel that isn't very fully developed; it's quite thrown together, never explained. In the beginning when he's talking about his childhood, Bernard says that his mother, who used to sew, probably sewed a lot of threads onto him to prevent him from living, to keep him close to her. At the engagement dinner, he has a vision of his mother at the table. He moves closer to Christine who chases the ghost away. He was always fascinated by death, and death finally meets up with him in the form of Héloïse. A person who drinks the blood of others is a person who wants to come to life again. But it's all still something of a mystery to me.

[1] In a letter dated September 20th, 1980, Anne Hébert reacted as follows to the connection I made between her early poetry and the writings of Nelligan: "You mention

that my poetry provides a link between Nelligan and the 'liberated' poets of the Sixties. This seems to me a bit far-fetched. I have no connection with Nelligan either in time or generation, and I was not influenced by him in a literary sense. And you seem to forget that between Nelligan and me there were two great poets: Saint-Denys Garneau and Alain Grandbois. The chronological order of a writer's work is not necessarily the same as his or her life. *Le tombeau des rois* was published in 1953 and *Mystère de la parole* in 1960. As for *Les songes en équilibre*, those were nothing but childish stammerings and are best forgotten. I thus claim my place among the poets of the Sixties 'who were able to reach beyond their solitude,' as you put it, and I do so because of *Mystère de la parole*, which is a kind of hymn to the world."

2 "I don't think my first collection expressed a sense of being absent from the world, but rather a presence of nature and an openness to the full joy and suffering of life." (Reaction in a letter from Anne Hébert.)

3 "The word mystified strikes me as very strange. I really don't know what you mean. Hands are totally real." (Anne Hébert.)

4 "Readers don't only speak about what one has written; they also talk about themselves, their own life experiences, the things they have in common with us. That's what communication is — it goes in both directions." (Anne Hébert.)

5 "I don't see what is fantastic about the short stories in *Le torrent*, except 'L'ange de Dominique.' They're rather poetic, and some of them, like 'Un grand mariage,' are more realistic." (Anne Hébert.)

6 "For me, writing is not an experience akin to dreaming but rather an experience I have lived, in images and rhymes." (Anne Hébert.)

7 "What do you mean when you say 'Elisabeth, who marries for glory'? Elisabeth marries Antoine because she wants to make love with him, which in that milieu and that time meant that they had to be married. Later when Elisabeth has been abandoned by her lover who has fled to the United States, she bows to family and social pressure and marries Jérôme; at the same time she's attracted, in spite of herself, by the settled life offered to her by Jérôme." (Anne Hébert)

Yves Thériault, Storyteller

Yves Thériault wrote twenty-five novels, nine collections of tales and short-stories, three plays, a hundred or so "dime-store novels," a film script and more than 1300 scripts for radio, some of which have already been published. The most prolific writer in Quebec, he is also the most widely read, studied and translated. The list of prizes he has won is impressive: the "Prix du Gouvernement du Québec" three times (including the "Prix David" in 1979), first prize in the Radio-Canada Drama Competition, the France-Canada Prize and the Governor General's Award for Literature.

Who was the man behind all this work? Born in Quebec City in 1915, Yves Thériault grew up in the N.D.G. area of Montreal. Since his family was poor, he had to leave school at the age of fifteen. Then began a bewildering succession of jobs, which exposed the future writer to a tremendous variety of different milieux: trapper, bush-pilot, bouncer in a night-

club, boxer; cheese salesman and tractor dealer; public relations officer, artistic director, journalist, script-writer, radio
announcer in Rimouski, Hull, Quebec City and Montreal;
Director of Cultural Affairs for the Quebec Ministry of Indian
and Northern Affairs; and co-director, in 1977, of a film
company (with his wife, Lorraine Boisvenue, author of a
best-seller, *Le guide de la cuisine traditionnelle québécoise*).

Before I started working on this interview, my knowledge of Thériault was largely limited to his most popular
novels: *Agaguk, Ashini* and *Aaron*. Thus I thought of him
primarily as an interpretor of various ethnic minorities: Inuit,
Amerindians and Orthodox Jews. After reading his entire
production, however, I became aware that my "anthologized"
impression of his work was both incomplete and inaccurate.
Thériault's writings are rich and diversified, and I was able
to detect a number of different currents in his work. One
cycle is basically Québécois or Canadian, its main subjects
being small-town people, fishermen, Italian and Jewish
immigrants, Westerners, and the amusing sexual or culinary
habits of certain parts of our population. Another cycle takes
place in settings that are difficult to identify, while still
another deals with the Inuit, Indians and Quebeckers in the
far North. Rather than simply portraying the primitivism of
native peoples, then, it is obvious that Thériault's work covers
a much broader spectrum. Since many readers are not aware
of the full range of his writings, Thériault had reason to be
wary of critics who stubbornly kept associating him with
Agaguk and other ethnic subjects; as he pointed out in *Textes
et documents*, at least half his work deals with altogether different themes. He became completely exasperated by critics
who would ask him such questions as: "Since Agaguk and
Ashini are both persecuted by Whites, does this mean they
represent the Québécois who are fighting for their survival?"

Of all Quebec writers, Yves Thériault was the most
wide-ranging and the most difficult to categorize. Beginning
in 1944 he published some forty books written in a captivating, simple, spare and lyrical style. His themes are such that
they appeal to many different sorts of readers. One of the
strongest impressions I got from his work is that Thériault
could not stand any form of exploitation: the weak by the

strong, the poor by the capitalists, the underprivileged by the privileged, or, as he puts it, the "mountain people" by people from more settled areas. It became equally clear to me that the author did not want the oral traditions of the various peoples to disappear, and that he was opposed to all the different races blending into a single, undifferentiated community.

Thériault's philosophical outlook is often pessimistic or even tragic: there is an endless succession of happiness and sadness, sickness and death, success and failure. We try in vain to reach beyond solitude and emptiness through dreams, emotions, stimulants, ambition and work: it is rare that we can ever be "in charge" (a key phrase) of our lives. And thus it is normal that the cult of the hero, the endless battles of man against man and man against nature — which we see as heroic or primordial or "almost erotic" — should all end in failure.

The most prominent and mysterious theme in Thériault's work is clearly his presentation of sex. At first glance, his attitudes seem contradictory: often the male dominates the female, but men are also very frequently dominated by women: Agaguk by Iriook, Agoak by Judith, Henri by Lisette in *L'appelante*, and the father by the mother in *Le marcheur*. Egotism plays a central role in Thériault's view of things; he clearly disapproves of excessive selfishness, since it turns love into a game of dominance in which men and women are motivated by lust and dreams of grandeur. And although love is often characterized by its animalistic impulses, it can also be gentle, noble, romantic or even chaste. Despite what certain critics have written on the subject, male dominance in Thériault's work is much more a symbol than a fact or desire: the "male" is the man or woman attempting to control their lives (the myth of Sisyphus coming into play): to be faithful to their origins, close to nature, and fighting the pernicious effects of capitalism. In this way, Iriook in the novel *Tayaout* becomes "a man": whereas Agaguk is blinded by "the magic of money," Iriook refuses to sell the ancestral stone to the Whites. Thus she replaces her husband and orders Tayaout to kill his father as punishment for his betrayal.

It is far from my intention to portray Yves Thériault as a writer of didactic novels or *romans à thèse*. Above all he is a storyteller; he speaks to us indirectly by creating fabulous characters and situations, and by using settings that say as much about the human condition as any speech could. He is almost never moralistic. His various landscapes contain hidden meanings. They are wild, primitive and extreme: high mountains, jagged peaks, rocky ridges and summits are contrasted with the flatness of the plains. Stark forests (especially of pines), thorny shrubs, thick underbrush, leaf-mould, scruffy mosses and lichens, sterile expanses of ice, tundra, steppes and rocky wastelands, all help make his settings evocative of the primitive instincts and passions that govern the lives of men and women.

As a storyteller, Thériault presents an impressive number of wounds and disfigurements; these are highly religious symbols, a sort of redemption through suffering, an allegory of men and women being cured of their pride. Another obsession that has symbolic overtones is the predominance of majestic animals; whether as faithful friends or fearsome enemies, these are the personification of various human characteristics. Caribou, deer, bears, wolves, husky dogs, foxes, stallions, hawks, mink, beavers, weasels, martens and others: all are included in Thériault's bestiary.

With my mind steeped in his work, I went off to my meeting with the author. Since 1978 Monsieur and Madame Thériault had been living in Rawdon, a picturesque little village about ten miles from Joliette. I was given a warm welcome to their home, part of which had been remodelled into a study for the writer and a sculpture studio for his wife. I also found myself fascinated by the intriguing statues she had created of monks with tortured, diabolical faces.

While tasting the stew and *tourtières* (meat pies) made by Madame Thériault, who is a specialist in traditional Quebec cuisine, and not overlooking the green ketchup that is Monsieur Thériault's specialty, I noticed their dog Louki had the annoying habit of barking at the Anglicans who were promenading ceremoniously up the street. Rawdon in fact is a rather bizarre, theatrical village, inhabited by Anglicans and Russian Orthodox, devotees of the United Church and of course an increasing number of French-speaking Quebeckers. It occured to me that Yves Thériault, with his penchant for interiorizing and reinventing his surroundings, might well come up with a short-story or even a film about the characters living in this little Laurentian village.

I turned on the microphone and recorded our conversation, which dealt at first with general topics and later with certain books I felt were particularly important. The reader should in no way be surprised if Thériault doesn't always reply to my questions directly. He's a man who likes to take detours, and after all, he *is* a storyteller. The interview has also been supplemented by excerpts I have added from a talk he gave to my students in 1980.

With Yves Thériault's death in October, 1983, Quebec lost not only one of its most brilliant storytellers, but also the writer who, out of love and conviction, made the greatest effort to explain literature both to students and to the public at large.

* * *

D.S. — You used to be a professional athlete, which I gather has contributed to your health problems. What can you tell us about this?

Y.T. — It's true, quite true. I played tennis as a semi-pro, since there weren't many pros in those years, and I was also a boxer. The training that this required weakened me and I ended up in the sanatorium, although in fact I didn't have tuberculosis, strictly speaking. There was something wrong with my lungs, but it wasn't really serious. In the "san," I met a couple of terrific guys: Floyd, a former game warden from Ontario, and a French-Canadian trapper whose name I've forgotten. It was near the end of the summer. We spent the winter talking about trapping, which was something I knew absolutely nothing about. I had no idea what the forest was like. We got permission to leave and we spent the summer exploring the surroundings, the lakes and rivers. Dr. Couillard, who was the Director of the Centre, considered that my two friends were pretty well cured, so I asked him if we

could get a trap-line from the Government. We got our permission and were allowed to go out mornings to check our
trap-line and come back in the evening. After a few months,
I said this is stupid, having a line only three or four miles
long. So then we had a line that went for 27 miles and we
would sleep outside, up above the dangerous passes, the Hell's
Gates, beyond Péribonka. The first year we took out $4,000
worth of pelts: mink, otter, beaver, weasel and marten. We
kept on like that for three years. It was very hard work. We
used to do ten miles a day on snowshoes. You had to dig the
traps out from under the snow, and if there was anything in
them you had to haul the carcass until you stopped for the
night.

D.S. − Could you tell us about the time you spent in Europe,
in Italy, Greece and Yugoslavia, when you went around the
world on an Italian freighter?

Y.T. − My wife and I set out on that trip but we had to
interrupt it because my wife took sick. In all we spent a year
in Italy. Then we went back to Florence for a year and a half.
Then there was a break for a year or two. We feel completely
at home in Florence. We don't even feel like we're living in a
foreign city there.

D.S. − Even if you don't like to talk too much about influences,
I'd like to ask you two or three questions about your favourite
writers. You've already said that Giono and Ramuz had a
lot of influence on you. What did you like about these two
writers?

Y.T. − I think we shared the same vision of nature, the same
way of seeing things—especially Giono. I could see Giono's
world all around me in my own country, even if we didn't
have the same way of expressing ourselves. My farmers and
Giono's farmers have the same wild temper, for instance. I
think that if there was some influence, it's strictly limited to
one book, or two at the most. There's one part in the *Contes
pour un homme seul* where you could say there was some
influence, and in *La fille laide* I think I even borrowed the

scenery, the setting. Obviously there's the style, the way of writing, which is very simple. Since I left school in the eighth grade, I had to write in a simple way because I wasn't very sure of my grammar, so I was always paraphrasing things and avoiding complicated structures.

D.S. — You're also very fond of Steinbeck, if I'm not mistaken.

Y.T. — That can be explained by my being bilingual, which meant that I read American writers before I read French writers. If there's anybody I should be compared to, it would be someone like Hemingway; I like his precise, simple sentences. Even if I quit school very young, I used to do an enormous amount of reading. I was a kind of paradox. I was a sporty little guy, a bit on the rough side, a bit of a fighter, but I was also an avid reader. I used to go through all the libraries. In those days the libraries weren't worth much. But one day my mother had a present for me which came from a coroner who was tidying up his library and who had cases and cases full of books: Zola, Balzac, Pierre Loti. So that meant by the time I was fifteen, unlike all my friends, even the ones who came from good families, I had read Loti and all of Zola. My mother, who obviously had some doubts about the moral value of what I was reading, had asked the coroner in question whether they were good books. He had understood good in the sense of quality, and so he replied "of course, Madame." So that way I was able to discover a whole world I knew nothing about. There was even some Pierre Louÿs, *Les chansons de Bilitis*, that I read when I was fifteen; I'll bet there wasn't another French Canadian at the time who had read that.

D.S. — You've previously said that you are basically a storyteller. Could you explain this idea a little further?

Y.T. — I'm a storyteller in the tradition of popular storytelling that goes back thousands of years, like the storytellers that accompanied the tribes wandering in the desert. They were the ones who handed down history, and at the same time they made up all sorts of characters and stories on the spot. Those kinds of storytellers cropped up here in Quebec at the time when the logging companies had their camps in the bush. They always hired a fellow who had a reputation as a good storyteller, in the style of the classic serial novel; that is, the fellow would start telling his story on Monday and he'd finish it on Friday. There are recordings that still exist of those storytellers; I have some myself because I met some of those guys in the Gaspé and taped the sessions.

I've never tried to make anybody believe I'm a great thinker. To the best of my knowledge, I've never written a novel that advances a particular thesis. I'm first and foremost simply a guy who has a story to tell, a drawn-out tale if you prefer.

D.S. — I read somewhere that you led a very protected childhood, that your parents were strict and you rebelled against them in your writing. How does that strike you?

Y.T. — Statements like that are sometimes a bit exaggerated. Let's say there's some truth in it. I was *very* protected as a child. As for whatever revenge I might have taken, it might be true of one or two books, and of my play *Le marcheur*, but it's not an underlying theme that you can find everywhere. There's another circumstance that influenced my writing, or rather my motivation to write, and that's the fact that I was brought up by parents who were basically poor but who lived in a middle-class neighbourhood. My father was an ordinary carpenter. We lived in N.D.G. because my mother was something of a snob. I didn't always find it easy to be accepted by some of the richer people in the area. When you get to be 16 or 17, you'd like to be able to go out with the girls you knew from school. But when you realize that you're *persona non grata* with the girl's family, for reasons that are never made clear, you end up understanding that it's basically because your father's not rich. At one point I rebelled against that and wanted to tell them, "Don't you see that if your daughter was married to me, she'd be the wife of Yves Thériault." That sort of rebellious pride lasted a while and then it disappeared totally.

D.S. — Is it true you're part Indian?

Y.T. — My father was a Montagnais. His father was named Ternish, Thériault being the name he borrowed. There are still a lot of Thériaults of Montagnais background on the North Shore. My grandfather, Charles, married a white Thériault. That explains how I got to be Adrien Thério's cousin. But to get back to my father, he married a white woman. My parents didn't get along at all, which may be proof that marriages of that kind run the risk of not being successful. My mother wanted to be completely urbanized; I wouldn't say civilized, because the Indians are a lot more civilized than people care to think.

My mother believed in that other concept of civilization known as the bourgeoisie, which is a rejection of all natural values. My father, on the contrary, wanted to hang on to his identity as an Amerindian. When I was young, to my mother's great despair, I wanted to learn how to speak Montagnais. My father taught me. It's an easy language for me. Later, when I was a bush-pilot, I met Indian guides and I was able to talk to them. After that I spent three years trapping with Indians who were distant relatives of mine. With them I learned about the bush and how to survive in it, and about the habits of the different animals. This means that when I'm writing novels about Indians, I know what I'm talking about. I can speak 11 of the 17 dialects in the greater Cree language.

D.S. — I still have one last general question to ask. As a writer, do you react in a particular way to the idea of independence? In other words, do you feel a sense of solidarity with the creative artists and performers who publicly opt for independence?

Y.T. — Yes indeed! I said so one day in Hamilton, in front of a group of anglophones. Now that we're finally having a good time in Quebec, finally having fun and making the English question themselves, for once it's really quite pleasant. Personally, I don't believe all that much in the economic consequences. It'll all work out on its own because North America can't afford to lose Quebec. Quebec has too many natural resources, it's too centrally located, the St. Lawrence is too vital for transportation. And I refuse to believe that an independent Quebec would ever block traffic through its territory. That's not at all what Jacques Parizeau, the Minister of Finance, has in mind.

D.S. — In *Contes pour un homme seul*, you depict in your own way rural Quebec as it was in the Forties. As the title indicates, these are tales for a man who is truly alone: he has no God, and he indulges both his worst instincts and his highly fertile imagination. The surrealistic atmosphere underlines the violence that seems to be inherent in all human beings. Is this the way you see the world?

Y.T. — Yes, and I make no bones about it. You just have to look at the violence that exists in the big cities, the number of absolutely sordid murders. I hardly scratched the surface of the subject.

D.S. — In 1945 it must have been a risky business, considering what the establishment was like in those years, to publish tales that showed the hideous, cruel side of farm life and that suggested either that God didn't exist or that he had created a world which had prostituted itself. Your stories describe families that are decaying, cuckolded, and you come to the defense of the longshoremen who were being exploited. Did your first book cause you any trouble?

Y.T. — None! Not for a moment! Other writers, such as Jean-Charles Harvey, suffered from censorship, but not because there were objectionable scenes in his novel but because of its political implications. Harvey's *Les demi-civilisés* is a *roman à clef*. My stories weren't deliberately written in that way, and they certainly didn't implicate people who might have been identifiable in them. The censorship came from the bourgeois, the bishops, and I never wrote about bourgeois characters; I was always talking about rural people and people nobody bothers about.

D.S. — *La fille laide* (1950) is one of the novels in which you take violence and jealousy to their greatest extremes; no doubt you magnify these feelings in order to show what all men have within them. The people from the hamlet of Karnac, located on a mountain, and the people down below on the plain share a mutual contempt for one another. I see this as a satire on racism, and prejudice in general. In your mind, do Karnac and the plain represent real places?

Y.T. — Maybe. Perhaps something as simple as Montreal and Quebec City, since people from Quebec City have always detested people from Montreal and people from Montreal have always made fun of people from Quebec City. In the abstract, this becomes Karnac and the plain, or any other place. I live in Rawdon myself, and you should hear what the people of Rawdon say about the people from Chertsey, which is only eight kilometers from here.

D.S. — In *La fille laide*, Big-Headed Vincent, who is insane but very much in tune with the poetry of people and things, expresses the opinion that the music, colours, forms and smells of nature are what give life its true value. My impression is that nature is actually the most important value in your work. Do you agree?

Y.T. — Yes, because for me it is nature which provides the real joys in life: the joys of seeing and hearing, and the joys of well-being. A beautiful spring day isn't only beautiful — it also makes you feel good. I respect nature.

D.S. — Precisely. In *Le dompteur d'ours* (1951) there is a character, Hermann, who loves plants and animals; he comes to a little village and, a bit like the novelist Germaine Guevremont's "Survenant," he upsets the inhabitants' moral hypocrisy and narrow-mindedness. Another thing that intrigues me in your second novel is the extreme landscapes. You often place your characters either up on a mountain or down on the plains. How do you explain your penchant for settings of this sort?

Y.T. — I'm very fond of opposites and antitheses. I like the kinds of landscapes that have caused me to feel either serenity or torment. I like all landscapes, but at times I've put them into opposition with one another.

In the main story of *Le dompteur d'ours* (literally *The Bear Tamer*), a stranger arrives in a small village. I saw this happen once in Saint-Denis-sur-Richelieu with someone whose name actually was Hermann. He came with a sort of little travelling circus, and I particularly remember his old bear, "Mangy Bear." Hermann had a head like Yul Brynner, and I saw all the women in the village literally go crazy over him, even though he was ugly and coarse; there was nothing special about him, but he was masculine. He'd wear a pair of little satin pants for performing with his bear, and he had this enormous contraption in his pants. I want to make a film of that novel soon. My wife and I have already chosen the actors, but nobody's been approached yet. The only actor in Quebec who could play Hermann and make a masterpiece out of it would be Jacques Godin.

D.S. — The teenager in *Le dompteur d'ours*, Clément, is a completely honest person. Hermann admires his frankness, his gift for fantasy and his love of animals. Even in 1950 there were signs that one day you would write books for children. *Le dompteur d'ours* often resembles a children's story.

Y.T. — Yes. I might as well be honest with you. My specific inspiration for writing hasn't always been completely virginal. Because of the fact that I quit school in eighth grade and later decided to make my living as a writer, the things I've written have actually stemmed from two impulses: on the one hand there are literary considerations, the love of writing; on the other hand there's the crassly commercial considerations. The commercial side meant that I had to give publishers what they wanted — not necessarily made-to-measure, mind you — but one sort of novel rather than another, and so on. After *La fille laide* I never had to submit a manuscript. I start with a contract, a title, a sizable advance on royalties, and then I write the novel.

D.S. — Let's get back to your penchant for children's literature. From 1962 to 1967 you wrote nine books for young people. They include stories of marvels and fantasies, secret agents (Volpe, accompanied by Barbara and Bason), science fiction and international politics. The books are very deftly written. You have a talent for concocting plots that are quite complex, and you keep your readers on their toes. In these novels, however, it is almost always the good that triumphs, which is far from being the case with your writings for adults. How were you able to change your perspective to such a degree?

Y.T. — Again, it's a question of adaptation, this time to the needs of children's literature, which is almost always written in the same manner, and to the publishers who want it to be that way. I have plans for children's books that will be different. I've found a publisher, La Courte Echelle, which wants to go off the beaten path, so I won't necessarily be faced with the same kind of moral obligation for the good always to win out in the end. I hope to go beyond that. I'm going to have fun. The illustrator, Louise Pommainville, wants to work with me on it.

D.S. — *Les vendeurs du temple* was published in 1951. In it you describe Saint-Léonide, a village that supported the Quebec Patriots in the old days. In your books, Saint-Léonide is a sad, monotonous place, filled with pseudo-political and religious "patriots." This was the time of Premier Duplessis, and Quebec was coming under foreign control. It is the most political of your novels, the most heavily ironic and caricatural. What prompted you to write it?

Y.T. — Before *Les vendeurs du temple* came out, I had already published quite a lot, even if they were things that don't appear in a list of my writings: things like dime-store novels and radio scripts. Since all these were sober, serious pieces, I wanted to write something funny. Now, I'd just moved away from Saint-Denis-sur-Richelieu, so I came up with *Les vendeurs du temple*; for all intents and purposes it takes place in that village using characters I'd known there, although the names have been changed. I was frightened of being sued, but in fact even the people who recognized themselves in the book thought it was very funny.

D.S. — We've spoken a lot about nature, but in 1957 you published your first urban novel, *Aaron*. It tells the story of a young Jew who has grown up in the streets and back-yards of the city, and who denies his race so that he can be successful in business. Together with *Saint-Urbain's Horseman*, by the English-Canadian novelist Mordecai Richler, *Aaron* is one of the most powerful literary portraits of orthodox Jewish life. But let's get back to the idea of the city and the country. In *Aaron* there's the following passage: "The real Canada exists in the North, with its forests and tundra, oil deposits covering an area as large as a country, its mountains and torrents, its rivers broad as estuaries and its estuaries wide as a gulf." My impression is that your writing is at its most poetic when you're describing, if not the North then a least the natural world in its unspoiled, primitive state. You're not primarily an urban writer, are you?

Y.T. — I'm not able to appreciate the poetry of cities, wherever they are. I've lived in Paris, Rome, New York, London, but for me cities remain impersonal. Even in Paris, after living there for a year, I had to get out. I went to Florence, but there again I couldn't breathe and I moved to Settignano, which is in the country, about ten kilometers away. There were farmers there. The only thing that has ever really grabbed me is the wilderness. I don't like nature close to the city either, nature that's been modified and ordered. In my soul I'm still a bush pilot.

D.S. — We must talk about the trilogy you wrote around the character of Agaguk. The first installment was published in 1958 with *Agaguk*, an action novel that contains scenes that are both mythical and morbidly realistic. Here, as elsewhere in your work, disfigurements and mutilations play an important role. For example, the disfigurement of Agaguk changes his character and introduces the theme of the loss of beauty as a source of happiness. When you were writing the novel, were you aware of the symbolic aspects of mutilation?

Y.T. — (loud laughter)…Oh shit, here we go, the wolf symbol and all that! I had a problem in the story I wanted to tell, a very serious problem. I had to have Agaguk disfigured because it was the only way I could get my story to move in the right direction, so that he wouldn't be recognized by the police and could go on living with Iriook. Now, there aren't a lot of animals that cause disfigurement in the Arctic. There are bears. If a polar bear's claws attack a man's face, that's the end of the man. There are wolves, too, except that wolves never attack humans unless it's an albino wolf, and they're completely crazy. By using a white wolf with yellow eyes, I was able to have Agaguk attacked and disfigured in a believable way. That's all (loud laughter). It's as simple as that.

D.S. — What does *Agaguk* mean to you: is it a novel about the way Eskimos live, a critique of White imperialism, or is it something else?

Y.T. — (tremendous burst of laughter)...My publisher in Quebec, the Institut littéraire du Québec, had managed to get *Aaron* republished by Grasset in Paris. At the same time I signed a contract with Grasset and they gave me a fairly large advance in American dollars. While I was in Paris for *Aaron*, Monsieur Privat asked me, "Do you still have problems with the Indians in the West?" "Do you still have to send armies to fight them?" This was in '55 and I said to myself that the guy had obviously seen too many cowboy films. So, time went by and eventually I got a cablegram from Paris asking me either to send them a manuscript or return the advance. So I decided to write something that the Frenchmen would find informative. I had often gone back to the Arctic. I had my own plane and I spoke Eskimo. But in the end I wrote *Agaguk* because of the Frenchmen. It took me a couple of weeks.

D.S. — How did you learn Eskimo?

Y.T. — When I was a pilot, I crashed in the Arctic. I was rescued by some Eskimos, and I spent six months with them before I was taken out. The Eskimos were still living in igloos at that time. Cramped into a small space, with ten or so Eskimos, I had no choice but to learn the language. It's a very difficult language; the infixes you insert in the middle of words change their meaning. It takes a hell of a smart people to speak a language like that. It's a rich language, beautiful. You can invent words just like that. You take a root, you add prefixes, infixes or suffixes, and you have a new word. Eskimo is an extraordinarily flexible language, with 35 verb tenses and 43 different root words for snow. If you add the whole range of prefixes-infixes-suffixes, you get incredible numbers of words to describe snow: its textures, temperatures, colours. Snow is an element that's extremely varied and the Eskimos have found a way to describe it.

D.S. — The second installment of your Inuit stories, *Tayaout*, is an even more mythological and epic novel than *Agaguk*. Here the Eskimos become craftsmen, artisans and miners, but they also become unemployed. What did you want to show by this?

Y.T. — The business of Eskimo sculptures disgusted me. And there was also *Agoak*, six years later. Stanké was the publisher who commissioned that one. He gave me three weeks to write a manuscript of 250 pages, and I did it.

D.S. — I found the conclusion of *Agoak* quite astonishing. At the end of the novel, Agoak is a kind of Agaguk who hasn't evolved, or rather he's evolved in the opposite direction from Agaguk: he's gone from being a civilized man to being a monster who kills his own useless daughter. How do you explain such an unexpected transformation?

Y.T. — The damned problem is that I have to give an answer that will deflate the whole business. It was absolutely necessary for me to keep the character alive, which is why he didn't die at the end. He's still running around in the Arctic. I don't know what I'll do with him one of these days. I may send him off to Japan, I'm not sure. He could meet some Laplanders in the Bering Straits. I didn't want to kill him. His backward evolution may have been a way of keeping the character alive. It's all got to do with my method and structure and doesn't have any connection to purely Eskimo considerations.

D.S. — You often refer to the Eskimos' religious beliefs. Tayaout, for example, believes that the spirits governing the Inuit religious rituals all live in the stones of the sea.

Y.T. — I believe in God, myself, because there certainly has to be some power that's superior to us. As for the Eskimos, I didn't transfer my personal beliefs to them; I simply took their religious ideas, which are very rudimentary, and embellished them a bit.

D.S. — Now let's talk about the Indians. The poetry of Amerindian speech, with its close connections to plants and animals, seems to be the one you're nearest to. Ashini is proud of his language, "rhythmical, passionate, whispering like the wind in the leaves, a language in harmony with the simplest things." The language you use in your books is no doubt influenced by the Amerindian languages you speak.

Y.T. — At the level of metaphors and symbols, yes. Sometimes even at the level of rhythm, as in *Ashini*, for instance. There are two languages in Amerindian: an everyday language and a noble language. The true art of the Indians is eloquence, and they developed a language parallel to their everyday speech in order to be able to express this eloquence. *Ashini* was virtually written in Montagnais and translated in my head as I went along. The rhythm of incantation in *Ashini* comes from the language of eloquence, the great, noble language of the Crees and the Montagnais. If you read *Ashini* closely, you'll see that there's a very precise rhythm, almost a biblical one. It's a novel I wrote with a great deal of care, so that I could remain faithful to the noble language. A lot of Montagnais I know read it — the tribal chiefs and the more educated people, such as a nurse and a young engineer who studied at Laval University. They find it contains the language of the really old people; it has the rhythm of the elders, of the orators at the feast of the "macousham" or caribou.

D.S. — You talk as though you'd almost have preferred to write it in Montagnais rather than French.

Y.T. — Not really! I like writing in French. It imposes a certain way of thinking, a certain outlook. A language's lack of logic, and this is certainly the case with French, which is totally illogical, makes for a lack of logic in thinking. If you want to have a good time, take a look at a book called *Plumons l'oiseau*, by Hervé Bazin. The author really demonstrates the lack of logic in French. That, by the way, is what makes it a beautiful language. Women who are illogical are also the most beautiful and the most fascinating. I myself wouldn't want a logical woman in my life.

D.S. — Since you suggest in *Ashini* that the Indians should once again have control over their own territories, did you run into any trouble with the Indian Affairs people after the book was published?

Y.T. — No, none at all. It was actually at that time that Indian Affairs approached me to direct their cultural affairs section. When I first began working in the Ministry, I wanted to help the native people. There are 250,000 to 300,000 Indians. And also there are 330,000 non-status Indians who live off the reservations. How can anybody believe they're going to survive? There are 11 major Indian languages, 11 different civilizations, and the 11 languages are divided into 218 sub-languages and dialects. Ethnic survival outside the reservations is going to be very difficult. When Indians leave the reservations, they tend to lose their language and become assimilated. I'm assimilated myself. As a writer, I've used the North as a source of inspiration. It's my own personal resource.

D.S. — In *Ashini*, human ambition is represented by the struggle for power between two wolves: the fable of Huala, a legendary wolf and hero to the Indians, shows how man must join into groups to ensure his collective survival. Do you personally believe that animals and humans are as similar as your writings seem to suggest?

Y.T. — Of all the animals in the forest, the wolves are the ones who behave most like a human society. Wolves have their leader, and when the leader loses his efficiency, they replace him with other leaders.

D.S. — *N'Tsuk*, which was published in 1968, eight years after *Ashini*, is nevertheless very closely linked to *Ashini*.

Y.T. — That's true. I wrote *N'Tsuk* as a counterpart to what Ashini had to say as a man. Since I'm not a male chauvinist, I wanted to give a woman a chance to express her vision of the world. I once knew a Montagnais woman who really seemed very much a female counterpart to Ashini. She was a woman who, with her husband, had spent her whole life trapping, from the time she was fourteen. She was really an exceptional woman. So, I created a character based on her, as a way of having an Indian woman say, "You white women just don't understand. You don't know what nature's like. You think you've lived and suffered. You haven't." *N'Tsuk* is one of the rare novels I've written where there's a character based quite closely on an actual person. Usually I don't do that.

When I reread *N'Tsuk*, it reminded me of one day when I was with some young Crees. One of them was a girl of about 16 who was studying at Roberval. I recorded our conversation. The girl told me something I found quite moving. "The hardest thing is when the girls at the convent call me a savage." She was a pretty girl, a real thoroughbred on the inside. It was so incredibly pitiful that anybody could have called that girl a "damned savage."

I wrote *N'Tsuk* after a trip in the bush — a hunting trip that ended up being a photography trip. I had gone with a white girl. We spent three weeks in the bush. One day we were out in a canoe and we came across a dead-head, a big floating tree trunk. The crazy girl decided to play log-driver and got out on the trunk. The dead-head fell to pieces. The girl didn't know how to swim; she sank to the bottom of the lake. I jumped out of the canoe with all my clothes on and rescued her.

In the evening the girl was frightened of blackflies and also of the dark. She was crazy enough to insist on having a light in the tent. We kept getting eaten by blackflies. *N'Tsuk* came from a kind of suppressed, hidden anger that had lasted ever since my trip with the white woman. I had spent money so that girl would be happy in the forest, and she'd ruined everything.

D.S. — The literary critics have written a lot about the theme of combat in your work. In *Les commettants de Caridad*, Héron is fascinated by the *corrida*, the "marvellous ballet": the bull, the arena, the sun, the crowd, and the "poetry of combat." Have you gone to bull-fights?

Y.T. — (suppressed laughter)...I had a record about bull-fights and I'd read a lot about them. So I invented a *corrida* of my own. You could say that *Les commettants* took the place of a trip I wanted to go on. I wanted to get away from my usual surroundings for a while. But I didn't go to Spain until after I'd written the novel. In spite of that, a Spaniard I met in Madrid, who reads French perfectly, said to me that my description of a *corrida* was extraordinarily accurate and that I must have gone to a lot of them. I wasn't about to tell him I'd never seen one.

D.S. — You've said previously that *Les commettants* is your favourite book. I was very taken with it too. You managed to present a very clear picture of the kind of wandering Spanish storytellers who go around telling their tales of vengeance, combats, rapes, murders and lusty priests. Why do you prefer this novel to the others?

Y.T. — Because it's a three-tiered structure; the same story is told by three different characters. Of all the books I've written, it's the most complex and the most highly structured; also the structure is not absolutely logical compared to my other novels, in which the dramatic development is very unified, starting from one point and going on to another. *Les commettants* starts at one point, moves backwards, goes on a bit more, and then moves backwards again.

D.S. — In *Le ru d'Ikoué (Ikoué's Stream*, 1963), you use the symbol of water more than in any other novel: "To know all there is of water: its source, its goal, its loyalty to the bed it lies in... I can sense water's desires, its forms; I understand what it is saying." Ikoué, a young Algonquin, tells us that his stream is a science which introduces man to the notions of freedom, slavery and imagination, and which teaches us the love of nature. *Le ru d'Ikoué*, which is a sort of Quebec version of *The Little Prince*, made a very positive impression on me. Has water, in all its forms, played a special role in your life?

Y.T. — The sea, fresh water, salt water: without water, I wouldn't have an inner, spiritual life.

D.S. — I mustn't forget to ask about your writing for theatre. Like Anne Hébert's *Le torrent* (1950), Gélinas' *Tit-Coq* (1948) and Loranger's *Mathieu* (1949), your play *Le marcheur* (1950) attacks the French-Canadian family. It seems as though the Quebec writers of that period all felt a need to rid themselves of their smothering family surroundings.

Y.T. — It's quite true. I think that the combination of circumstances came from the fact that, to varying degrees, we had all experienced the same kind of family pressures. I don't mean that *Le marcheur* deals with my own life, but rather with the way it could have been if my father had become the man he wanted to be. He could have been a real despot. He had a cousin who was the bully in the family and who served as a model for the *marcheur* ("the walker"). Of course I stylized him a fair bit.

D.S. — The critics have been almost unanimous in their praise of the theatrical qualities and the dramatic power of all your plays. I wonder why this positive reception didn't encourage you to pursue your activities further in this area.

Y.T. — I didn't feel that it was quite my own juices that were flowing when I wrote my plays. I'm not comfortable with it. I know I can do a good job of it, but it doesn't give me any pleasure.

D.S. — *La rose de pierre* (1964) is a collection of short stories that look at the world through the eyes of a child and an Amerindian. Here you make the point that people who have no formal education are often more intelligent and more sensitive to human truths than people who have had a lot of schooling.

Y.T. — I'm really just standing up for my own cause.

D.S. — In *Antoine et sa montagne* (1969), you make an association between yourself and Antoine, a character who is completely self-taught. Antoine, a farmer, is always looking at the
mountain at the end of his land, and the mountain evokes
dreams, poetry, as well as the desire to put an end to fear
and apathy. The mountain is also connected with Papineau,
who led an armed rebellion against the political establishment. Is this your way of briefly taking sides in favour of
independence?

Y.T. — At the time I wrote the novel, I wasn't particularly
thinking of that. I was quite simply dealing with a landscape
I knew very well. In Saint-Denis I had seen guys who wanted
very badly to have things they couldn't possess. There was a
guy I'd have a beer or two with every Sunday morning while
Mass was going on — he was hiding from his wife — and his
whole dream was centred on owning a piece of land covered
with grass and shrubs out on the fifth sideroad; it was completely unproductive land, but he wanted to turn it into a
camping ground. He never had enough money to buy it. I
transformed that guy's dream — he was a disorganized fellow,
not much of a go-getter. It's the old story of the desire for
possession that can happen to any man.

D.S. — Let us now talk about a book that really is an exception to the rest of your writings. *Oeuvres de chair* (1975) is a
collection of short stories I really enjoyed. In it, you give
expression to a *joie de vivre* that is at the same time sexual,
gustatory and gastronomical, and you also provide a satire
of our dissolute lifestyles. It's a sort of combination of *The
Joy of Sex* with *The Joy of Cooking* — an unforgettable feast of
all the appetites.

Y.T. — The general spirit of the book was supposed to be
erotic, and in fact its first title was *Oeuvre de chère* (an untranslatable pun on *chair*, "flesh," and *chère*, "great food and good
living"). My publisher prefered the other title. The book is
basically my recipe book, since each story contains a gas-

tronomical or culinary recipe. I personally saw the whole business as follows: old Thériault dies, goes up to heaven and tells St Peter, "I'm a writer." St Peter replies, "Yes, well now, we don't really have any spots in Paradise reserved for writers. The only one I could offer you, and you don't really belong there, is the corner of Paradise where Janette Bertrand, Jehane Benoît, Sister Berthe and all the other food specialists are ensconced in all their purity." So that's when I decided to write a book of recipes.

D.S. — In 1976 you published *Moi, Pierre Huneau*, the story of a ninety-year-old fisherman who has taken refuge in the Lower North Shore. Pierre Huneau looks back over the major events in his life, his beautiful, sincere love for his wife Geneviève (no sexual violence here), and his friendship with the hired hand, Florent. It's a dense, vivid story, written in a highly colloqual style: a genuine folk tale. Pierre Huneau is the Quebec counterpart of Gapi, La Sagouine's husband. Why, after 32 years of writing, did you decide for the first time, at least in such a complete way, to use all the resources of popular Quebec French, which is a highly colourful language?

Y.T. — I had a lot of documentation at home dealing with the language as it was spoken in Pierre Huneau's time. I wrote the first page using these words from this documentation. I'm a fanatic about words, I'm viscerally affected by the beauty of words, and before I set about writing any novel whatsoever, I always have a list of words I've picked up here and there so that I can integrate them into my book. I didn't have any preconceived ideas about writing one novel in particular, and two or three words in this old way of talking fascinated me so much that I said to myself, "How could I place them in a sentence?" And so, starting with those few words, a story suddenly took form. By the way, I have a sequel to *Moi, Pierre Huneau*. At the end of the novel, the old guy is left all alone, since his entire family has been killed in the explosion. I want to go on with his story. I have quite a fantastic amount of information about the Lower North Shore. It's going to be called *Cette année-là, vingt-six goélettes accosteront*, (literally, *That Year the Small Boats Came Ashore*).

D.S. — 1980 was the year you published your longest novel, *La quête de l'ourse* (literally *The Quest for the She-Bear*).

Y.T. — I put twenty years into writing that novel. It's almost 400 pages long. It's the novel in which I go deepest into my vision of the forest. I look at nature in detail, and the forest is seen as an actual character. It's also the story of an Indian man who marries a White woman. They are very much in love, but by marrying a White the Indian has gone against the dictates of the Manitous. More than anything else, it's a tender novel. Yes, for once there's tenderness in a book by Thériault! The Indian's name is Antoine and his wife is called Julie, which was the name of my neighbour when I was small. Julie is the one who taught me what tenderness is all about. The quest for the she-bear is quite encyclopaedic in terms of animal behaviour and the life of the forest itself. I really opened the flood-gates. There's something legendary about it.

D.S. — Is it the same Antoine as in *Antoine et sa montagne*?

Y.T. — No, not at all! But when there's a name I like, one I dream about for years, I tend to use it often.

D.S. — You've published or are about to publish a great many of your stories (approximately 1,000) that have appeared in magazines and newspapers. *Valère et le grand canot* contains stories that bring back the myth of the traditional Quebec village centred around the blacksmith's shop; *La femme Anne et autres contes* is a series of stories that take us into "the vast regions of Quebec, from the Gaspé to the North Shore, by way of Montreal and Quebec City;" and *L'herbe de tendresse* is a collection of "Amerindian" and "Eskimo" stories. Knowing you as I do, however, I'm not sure you'll be satisfied publishing old material.

Y.T. — Right now I'm thinking of a book of short-stories in which each story would deal with some subject related to cooking, and at the end, as a sort of final send-off, you would find recipes related to a particular subject. To give you an example, there is "La bière de Zuma" ("Zuma's Beer"). Zuma is a nun who works in the kitchen of her convent, where there are recipes for beer. She grew up in a very strict family, with a temperance cross on every wall. She makes beer, gets drunk as a skunk and goes to a parish priest to confess. She realizes he's a man, she leaves the confessional, she goes over to the priest and grabs him by the prick. The priest, who is wearing a pair of long woollen underwear, is terrified. This has never happened in his whole life. He runs away down the main aisle of the church. The girl chases after him. Once they're outside, he in his priest's robe and she in her habit, they roll up their clothes. She's wearing nun's underpants, slit in the front. He sees the hair, runs away and hides in a hotel. On the second floor he goes tearing into a room where there's a travelling salesman in bed with the daughter of the owner of the hotel. And that takes us to the end, the send-off, where there are recipes for making beer.

Then there's "La colle des frères" ("The Friars' Glue"). The brothers in a little college would very much like to spend a weekend in Quebec City visiting the other friars in their order. The superior doesn't want them to because they don't have any money to pay for the train. So they decide to find a way of making a little money on the side. By accident, one of the brothers discovers a recipe in which you mix pure albumen with quicklime to make an unbelievable glue. He doesn't think of egg-white at that point because he wants really pure albumen, so he uses sperm. At seven o'clock every night, the friars masturbate. They use their sperm to make little one-ounce pots of glue that they sell to the women in the area, who discover that not only is it a superb glue but that it also gets them all hot and bothered when they start touching and licking it. At the end of the story, you have all the recipes for household glue.

Jacques Ferron:
The Marvellous Folly
of Writing

When Jacques Ferron died of a heart attack on Monday, April 22, 1985, Quebec lost one of its most prolific and original novelists and short-story writers. Some have even claimed Ferron to be the greatest French-language storyteller of the century. What follows is a version of my 1983 interview with him, unrevised, since Ferron didn't publish anything after that year. It comes as a shock to realize that in the less than three years since this work was begun, no fewer than five of the writers interviewed in this book have died: Félix-Antoine Savard, Yves Thériault, Jacques Ferron, Gatien Lapointe and Gilbert La Rocque.

* * *

Interviewing Jacques Ferron seemed at first to be something of a Mission Impossible. I had been told several times that Ferron almost never granted interviews and that, although he was not a complete recluse like Réjean Ducharme, the good doctor was not very fond of talking about his writing. However, I was not about to let myself become discouraged. I had just spent five years working on a doctoral dissertation dealing with Ferron, and my head was teeming with his work: 16 plays, 12 novels, two collections of short stories, two books of fictionalized biography, two volumes of polemical writings and a book of historical tales. So I sat down with a blank piece of paper and wrote as follows:

Cher Monsieur Ferron,

I am not Scott Ewen in your play *La tête du roi*, a paternalistic Englishman if ever there was one; nor am I that enemy of the Québécois, Frank Archibald Campbell, whom you poison in *La nuit*. And I'm certainly not one of those Englishmen from Ontario in *Les contes anglais*, fanatics for the Red Ensign and that belligerent anthem "The Maple Leaf Forever." On the other hand, I must admit to being rather kindly disposed towards Frank-Anacharsis Scot[1] in your novel *Le ciel de Québec*. Frank, a poor Scot who sold his soul to the imperialist English, finally came to his senses and turned into François Sicotte. This is what you refer to as Jaxonization, in memory of Henry Jackson, Louis Riel's secretary from Toronto, who quite naturally spoke French when he took up the cause of the Métis. All that to say I'd be delighted if you would grant me an interview.

A few weeks later, Monsieur Ferron replied:

Your request for a meeting has been lying here in front of me for several weeks now, and I haven't been able to reply. I found you terribly naive. I had nothing to say to you. I could only disappoint you and I had no wish to do that, being incapable of acting like Msgr Savard in your interview with him. And also, I liked what you had to say about *La tête du roi* in your article in *Études françaises*. It's a play I wrote with affection and I still have a soft spot for it; it's my "Riel," my reality, at least indirectly…It seems to me I could manage to see you.

Before going off to meet Monsieur Ferron, I mentioned in a letter what a unique and unforgettable pleasure it had been for me to read *Le ciel de Québec*. I said in particular that I'd been fascinated by the Frenchman, Monseigneur

Turquetil, a character based on Arsène Turquetil, a former Superior of the Oblate missions in the Hudson Bay area, an imperious miracle-worker on the great ice-floes of the North, author of one of the first grammar books of the Eskimo language and a friend of the canonical visitor to the missions in the north of Saskatchewan, Gabriel Breynat, who was known as the flying bishop, the bishop of wind (he travelled by plane, since skidoos didn't exist at the time) and occasionally the lousy bishop (an appellation the reader can interpret as he/she wishes). Obviously Jacques Ferron is not the historian of the Oblate Fathers, but he does have a gift for satire, changing his "Borgia prelates" into strutting pigeons, into "turtle-preachers" with three wisps of hair on their skulls. In any case, it is thanks to Jacques Ferron that, in my mind, an Oblate is no longer an Oblate. I wanted Monsieur Ferron to know just how powerfully evocative his words are, and also to thank him for creating all those images that keep constantly recurring in my mind. The best way to do this, it seemed to me, was to describe the Ferronesque scene that lay before me that day as I looked through my living-room window. After all, it was Jacques Ferron who had taught me about the metaphorical possibilities inherent in our surroundings. Thus I wrote as follows:

> Your Turquetil from the Land of Aurélie reminds me of the Mennonite neighbours of my sister June who, far from your amélanchiers/Juneberry trees, lives in typical Ontario — or in other words Mennonite territory. Everything there is tinged with black: the car-hearses, the buggies, the clothes, even the bread. June, who happens to be an excellent painter although in no way similar to your overly theoretical Borduas, does marvellous sketches of the Ontario landscape.
>
> As for me, although my ancestors came from the Far-Ouest where they were familiar with the amélanchier/saskatoon berry, I myself live on Nelson Street in Ottawa. Often when I close my eyes I imagine I live on the same street as your famous patriot, Wolfred Nelson, but that must be an illusion, since this is

quite clearly Bytown, where Viscount Horatio Nelson lives on.

Also, just across from my place, at 305 Nelson, there are 168 air conditioners sticking out from the windows of the Oblate Monastery; 168 black suits — I haven't actually counted them — eat, sleep and distribute their pamphlet about the beatification of their founder, Monsignor de Mazenod, a friend of the second bishop of Montreal, Ignace Bourget. At 307 Nelson there are 17 white-robed Sisters of the Holy Family who cook in the cafeteria. The black suits are always crossing through the tunnel that connects 305 to 307. The trap-door opens and closes. The scandal-mongers say that the mouse-trap is getting emptier and emptier.

What fascinates me the most about this scene, however, is the majestic, black, skeletal oak tree on which someone has written in large white letters: PQ. The tree is located on the left side of 305 and is thus at the half-way point between the middle of the Oblate Monastery and the entranceway of the white nuns.

There's nothing literary about this description. I see the same scene every day and I'm only a simple spectator. You, however, living in the Land of Long-ueuil, must be able to contemplate scenes of equal significance at the Nunnery of the Sisters of the Holy Names of Jesus and Mary.

Several days later Monsieur Ferron sent me the following reply:

One of my distant Oblate cousins, who is a supply teacher and thus always travelling, came to see me one day and spoke about the Mennonites with some envy and a great deal of respect. At the end of his career, it was almost as if he'd found a new vocation.

On the other hand, I know a fellow named Schneider who was banished from the Mennonite community because he wanted to get an education. The first time I saw him he was hoping to get back into the good graces of his father. The last time, he was sad and a lot less sure.

Those Mennonites are one of our fascinating minorities in the West. The French spoken outside Quebec reminds me of the Flemish dialect that the Belgian missionaries wanted to impose on the Congo.

I thought to myself ahead of time that Jacques Ferron, whose letters are written as metaphorically as his books, would certainly not enjoy playing the traditional analytic game of interviewer-interviewee. And so it occurred to me that I would probably end up having to reconstruct a good part of the interview and fill in the gaps between certain sentences myself.

Jacques Ferron is a medical doctor; however, he's not the sort of doctor for whom a *portuna* (as a doctor's bag is called in the Gaspé) and an office are a sign of prestige, a barrier that sets him apart from the rest of society. Ferron is a "misbeliever," in the sense that he does not possess the ordinary "faith" in medicine, writing or the Quebec nation. And although he does not follow the beaten paths, he has beaten some very strange ones of his own in his creative writing. The path of medicine, for example, leads him to asylums, those lugubrious prisons for the insane, where Coco the Misunderstood in *L'amélanchier* waits blindly for death and where the doctors, locked into their individual worlds, avoid any thought of social considerations and hold fast to the established rules — which Ferron suggests is the cause of most illnesses. As for the various pathways the nation has taken or will take, Ferron claims that these get dangerously muddled and lost in the "Labyrinth of Progress," whereas the nation's people, suffering all too often from a lack of hereditary memory, perish in the wastelands of unconsciousness and anonymity. The literary language Ferron uses is like a living tree that grows in every little corner of the land of Quebec. According to Ferron, the reader learns in his own "Bible" that "The space that surrounds us plays a good joke on time by constantly replanting itself like wheat." As a writer, his references constantly move in the direction of local reality, whether that be Longueuil, Trois-Rivières, Louisville, the Gaspé, Quebec City or Montreal. Ferron interiorizes the landscapes of his country so that by recreating them, he can foster a deeper sense of belonging.

Jacques Ferron had little use for what he called the "parasites of literary criticism" — critics with their graphs in hand, ready to tear works of literature apart and deform their meaning. I wondered whether he'd see me as yet another academic, a discipline of Bachelard and Freud or member of some literary "coterie."

Before setting off to meet him, I finally decided that I would take Jacques Ferron for what he is: a doctor who cares for the working-class people in Longueuil, a man who clearly sets out his own positions in life, and above all a writer with a tremendous gift for storytelling. I was prepared to react to what he said, since I suspected he would talk more or less as he wrote, using images as anecdotes. This was certainly the case; blessed with an extraordinarily fine memory, Ferron sometimes unconsciously repeated complete sentences from his published work.

I finally got into the taxi which was to take me to Dr. Ferron's office. "1285 Chambly Road, please," I said to the driver; "1285, oh yeah, that's close to the shopping centre," he replied, flicking on the metre. Deep in Ferron's home territory, which had become almost mythological in my mind, I discovered that the phrase "shopping centre" recalled for me the marvellous passages Ferron had written about Longueuil — especially about Old Longueuil, when there were still animals and fields and swamps. And I realized that Old Longueuil had definitely been taken over by what Ferron in his novels calls the "terrible sameness of urban, suburban, gas-station, American banality." We drove by an immense and appropriately filthy grain elevator, which paradoxically looked like a gigantic castle. A few minutes later Ferron would refer to the elevator as an "urban castle," and at that point I realized the same elevator must be the source, in *La nuit*, of the malevolent castle of Montreal. After almost running into a young man who was no doubt suffering from a hangover and whose car was stopped in the middle of the road, the taxi driver yelled out "maudit flo!" ("damned kid"), and there I was again, right back in the middle of Ferron's work, since it was in his *Contes du pays incertain* that I had first discovered the Quebec word *flo* — apparently derived in the Gaspé region from the English "fellow." I got out of the taxi and found myself in front of an ordinary little red-brick house, which reminded me of *Papa Boss* and the "nice red-brick row houses, the achievement of a lifetime" for low-income workers and the unemployed. I entered the house. Monsieur Ferron, wearing a dark-blue suit and powder-blue turtleneck, greeted me warmly in an office filled with a curious mixture of books, paintings and bottles of medicine. We chatted for a few minutes about *flos* and grain elevators and gradually our conversation turned into an interview.

My first question dealt with the act of writing. Some writers build up a collection of filing cards and construct their books brick by brick, letting themselves go only occasionally, when inspiration strikes. If Ferron had worked in this way, I could have asked him precise questions about such and such a theme or the development of a particular symbol. However, this is how he explained the way he writes:

Sometimes after seeing something that has caught my attention, I put it into a book without even being aware of it. That's what happened with the nighthawks, those poor insect-eating birds that have trouble walking and that hovered over Montreal. They symbolize the City, but they've disappeared since then, I think, since the City doesn't even tolerate insects any more.

In the act of writing, images simply emerge. You don't actually know what you're doing. Just inventing things gives you pleasure. It's an accomplishment. You reveal yourself. When I have my historical character Chénier drink rubbing alcohol in *Les grands soleils*, for example, I added an unexpected dimension to the character, turning him into a beggar for a moment or two. This was a surprise. Writing makes time stand still. The hours go by and you're not even aware of it.

I did my apprenticeship as a writer with my plays. I learned how to create places, how to provide a setting. It appears that Jean-Marie Lemieux is going to produce *Les grands soleils* this fall, which will be sort of like taking up nationalism where Louis Fréchette left off in the 19th century with his *La légende d'un peuple.* I wanted to write a play entitled *Riel* but I wasn't able to do it. The situation around the character was utterly crazy! There was nothing crazy about Riel himself, proudly declaring that the Métis nation existed: "Here we are, established as a nation!" He was brilliant in both his words and his intelligence.

In *La nuit*, Ferron states that "reality is hidden behind reality." The critic Jean Marcel has previously underlined the importance of this phrase. Ferron, however, tells me that it is simply the "phrase of a madman," and since I know that madness in his work is often a sign of profundity, fantasy and illumination, I conclude that literary madness and the symbolic dimension hidden behind external reality are equivalents. From this perspective a nighthawk is not a nighthawk, but the macabre bird of Ferron's urban castle. In a similar way the magnificent canvas "Le bout du monde" ("The World's End"), painted by Ferron's mother, Adrienne Caron, is not simply a landscape of Maskinongé County; through the reality of a sinuous, black river and leafless trees in an autumnal evocation of the end of the world, it expresses a certain anguish caused by the dying natural world. Hung directly opposite Dr Ferron's desk, "Le bout du monde," because of its sinister atmosphere, seems to have strange connections to the novels and short stories — and to the sad, dull suburbs "flattened out so they spread wider, and spreading wider so they can drink more oil, the new blood of Christ and the milk of the new civilization" *(La nuit)*.

I've always been fascinated by rivers in Ferron's work. I remember a passage from *La nuit*:

> My own childhood was a river, and all along this river there was a succession of little compartmentalized countries marked off from one another by the bends in the river. After each bend comes another, and in this way my childhood reaches back into the past — at least a century or two, and perhaps more. My childhood includes a beginning of the world and an end of the world. It is my Genesis.

I had imagined Ferron's river of childhood to be sunny and surrounded by vegetation. I was mistaken, at least as far as the maternal river of "Le bout du monde" is concerned.

If a river isn't a river in Ferron's novel, then an animal is rarely an animal, but rather the incarnation of an individual or group of human beings. Cows, horses, pigs and wild boars, dogs, nighthawks and martins — all these are used as images through which Ferron speaks to us. When he was a young child in Louiseville, he told me, he often used to go to look at the cows that belonged to a neighbouring farmer, and *"every cow had its own name."*

Jacques Ferron has published almost nothing recently and this silence troubles him a great deal:

I wanted to do a book about madness, based on my experiences as a doctor, but I botched it...I had writer's block. Not being able to write any more has taken away my power.

Madness interests me. The insane are often more serene than the rest of us. All this goes back to my childhood. In Louiseville people talked about the ones who had escaped from the asylum in Beauport. They also used to say someone "was ready for Mastaï," for the Saint-Michel Archange Hospital named after Pius IX, Cardinal of Mastaï. Mastaï was a "very classy" place to be locked away, like Shakespeare's "Bedlam," a corruption of Bethlehem. Speaking of Shakespeare, British novels are among my favourite books. I really liked Dickens' *Hard Times*, and *The Mill on the Floss* and *Silas Marner* by George Eliot. The British countryside resembles our own more than France does. The French countryside is foreign to me.

Jacques Ferron's "English readings" seem to me rather significant. Dickens' *Oliver Twist*, with its elements of the traditional British "tale" and a sense of fantasy both light-hearted and nightmarish, is not unlike Ferron's own stories or tales. Like Ferron's young character Tinamer, Oliver Twist struggles against social injustice, "hard times," corrupt police officers and the evil personified in Fagin, who in turn is not unlike Ferron's Bélial, a *gripette* or devil in Quebec French. Furthermore, in *L'amélanchier*, the marvellous story of Hubert Robson of Tingwick in Arthabaska County is reminiscent of Mr Pickwick in *The Pickwick Papers*, although this would appear to be simply a coincidence since Ferron took the episode almost word-for-word from *Les bois-francs* by Abbé Mailhot. In any case Mr Pickwick shares Ferron's revolt against the inhumanity of our institutions. With regard to George Eliot, it was through her realistic nineteenth-century novels that Ferron first made acquaintance with the English countryside. Also, in Eliot's *Silas Marner* as in the works of

Ferron, childhood serves as a "humanitarian orientation." As far as the reference to Shakespeare's Bedlam is concerned, the insane asylum Saint Mary of Bethlehem, founded in 1247 by a group of nuns in London and infamous for its "Bedlam Beggars," is in much the same league as Ferron's "madmen's prisons"; his Mont-Thabor, Mont-Providence and Saint-Jean-de-Dieu, all sanctioned by the Church, are described as mediaeval "institutions of torture."[2]

Jacques Ferron attaches a great deal of importance to Quebec's history. He demythifies almost the entire group of Quebec heroes glorified in the schoolbooks published by the Christian Brothers and the Clercs de Saint-Viateur. Jacques Cartier, for example, is transformed into an apostle of free enterprise, coming to America in the name of "extraction" and "plunder." The "handsome but good-for-nothing Dollard de Zoro" (Dollard des Ormeaux) becomes the "bandit of the Long Sault" and not the pious hero depicted by the Church. For Jacques Ferron, however, the *historiette* (historical tale) is a good deal more than simply a collection of anecdotes. Here is what the author has to say on the subject:

> The *historiette* is true history without any window-dressing or prettifying. Too many of our historians have glorified men who were in fact bandits. Those who falsified our national history had to be silenced.
>
> The title *historiette* occurred to me because of the *Historiettes* written by Tallemant des Réaux. In his work, as in the witty memoirs of Hamilton, history becomes a series of picturesque and racy military escapades. One of my Polish friends said that the *historiette* is a "madman's paper."

The expression "a madman's paper" strikes me as being a very appropriate description of the way Ferron approaches history. He sets out to dispel certain myths and it is only in that sense that he sees himself as an historian. Moving from history to the historical tale, he "disenhaloes" events or characters that have been falsely acclaimed in the past and then moves on to the "picturesque," the colourful and the comic (satire, irony, puns and off-colour jokes). Emile Nelligan is a case in point. Ferron does not agree with the

nebulous fame of the poet described by some literary critics
as condemned, insane, castrated, mother-repressed, father-
repressed or even martyred:

**Nelligan couldn't do any better than he did. He wrote some
remarkable poems in a very short period of time, but then he
started pounding his head against the wall and he was declared
insane, which was normal at Saint-Jean-de-Dieu. That was it for
Nelligan. I met his nephew recently. He told me that Nelligan's
father, an Irishman who repudiated his country of origin in the
name of the civil service, was earning $8,000 a year, which was a
considerable amount for the time.**

In the case of the poet Saint-Denys Garneau, Dr Ferron
diagnoses a "swelling of celebrity" and he assigns this first of
Quebec's modern poets, changed into Orpheus for the occasion, to the hell of those Québécois who can't make up their
minds. Orpheus, the aristocratic "little brown-haired boy" in
Le ciel de Québec is condemned for having disavowed his
patriotic ancestor, François-Xavier Garneau, and for having
written "intimist poetry" based on a rejection of the space,
colour and games of his native land. According to Ferron,
the critic Jean Lemoyne also lacks a "collective memory" and
an "internal river." Lonesome for the "track of Confederation" and carrying a C.N. lantern, Ferron's "Pope" of the
magazine *La relève*, a veritable choir-boy "hung up" on the
Jesuits, accompanies Orpheus to hell.

Monsieur de La Barre is another example of an actual
historical figure viewed through the deforming lens of the
historical tale. After being sent out to Ville-Marie by Anne
of Austria, La Barre took command of a group of 60 men
fighting the "wicked Iroquois." In Ferron's view La Barre is
another of those historical bandits who need to be given a
"picturesque" and "racy" metamorphosis in the historical
tale. Thus Ferron's version has Monsieur de La Barre, an
extremely devout man with a crucifix hanging from his belt,
being discovered by Maisonneuve stretched out in the underbrush beside a pregnant Indian woman. Ferron's achievement is to be able to take various historical realities and
blend them into an original concoction of fact and fiction.

Ferron talked to me about the *Mémoires du Comte de Gramont* by Anthony Hamilton, an Irishman who wrote in French. Hamilton too was a writer of historical tales who always managed to find just the right combination of "picturesque" images and significant abbreviations to describe the vices and virtues of England at the time of the Restoration. The "francization" of Hamilton reminds me of all the Irishmen in Ferron's work, including his novel *Le salut de l'Irlande* (literally *The Salvation of Ireland*), who are "in the process of Quebecification" and thus contributing to the "Salvation of Quebec" in French-speaking North America. In Ferron's writings there are a certain number of English-speaking characters who break free of their minority/majority attitudes. Such was the case, in *Le ciel de Québec*, with Frank-Anacharsis Scot, who Ferron assured me "may one day become François-Anacharsis Sicotte, nicknamed Pit." In *Le salut de l'Irlande*, Connie Haffigan sets out on the same rocky road to "Quebecification" when he sympathizes with certain aspirations of the F.L.Q. As Ferron put it:

English people who have been assimilated make the best Québécois. At the beginning some of them were only here for industry. But there are always a few who come to understand that money is less important than identity. They start seeing themselves as an oppressive minority, they're ashamed of it, and they become nationalized. In Louiseville (the village Ferron grew up in) I had my first contacts with assimilated English people, Hamiltons and Lindsays. Later, in the Gaspé, I knew a British woman who became as Gaspesian as you can get.

In Ferron's writings names and nicknames are extremely significant. The author, like country people generally, is a "nominalist" (the term is defined in the *Appendice aux confitures de coings ou le congédiement de Frank Archibald Campbell*). He likes the way names sound, the senses and images they evoke. The character Papa Boss, who represents the "bonus value" and net profit of the American Way of Life, as the Commanding General of all the G.I. Joes, the new Eternal Father and the principal director of "Asshold Finance," was, Ferron explained, originally based on the Haitian dictator

Papa Doc Duvalier. The "nominalist" power of the key words in Ferron's work is so great and so fascinating that, for me, one night in Montreal, Papa Boss took on the altogether different nominal form of a unilingual English-speaking waitress in a restaurant called Papa Joe's. That night Papa Boss or Papa Joe became my own "reality behind reality."

The same family names frequently recur in a variety of forms in Ferron's writings, often in connection with Quebec history. These historical references are not always easily identifiable, however, and the reader may take a great deal of pleasure in discovering their origins. Perhaps the most flagrant example is that of "Frank Scott." Ferron's Frank Scot (not to mention George Scott, who goes hunting for Acadians in *Les roses sauvages*, the paternalistic Scott Ewen character in *La tête du roi*, and the Métis Henry Scott, who becomes Henri Sicotte) points the reader towards a whole family of Canadian and Quebec Scotts, some of whom, Ferron pointed out, were not terribly sympathetic to the Quebec cause. There is, to be sure, the English-Canadian poet Frank Scott, translator of Anne Hébert and son of an Anglican Bishop of Quebec City. That particular Frank is a social-democrat, a staunch federalist and a champion of bilingualism — in short, as "Hughmaclennenesque as they come," in Ferron's opinion. A rapid glance through the country's history, however, reveals a number of other important Scotts who have become part of Ferron's mythology: Thomas Scott, a young Ontario Orangeman who was executed by the Riel tribunal in 1870; Alfred H. Scott, representative of the English settlers in the official Métis delegation sent to Ottawa in 1870 to negotiate Manitoba's entry into Confederation, whom Ferron depicts quite positively; William Henry Scott, the patriot elected in Deux-Montagnes, a friend of Chénier and Girod and a supporter of Papineau, although he was in league with the Curé Paquin and thus opposed to the use of arms; and William Henry Scott's brother, the merchant Neil Scott from Sainte-Thérèse, who was also a peace-seeking patriot. Ferron's Scotts and Scots oscillate between the Quebecified Sicottes and the Scots along the line of the Anglican Bishop of Quebec City, who stands admiring the monument to Wolfe. It might be noted that even the name Sicotte is taken from Quebec history, since a farmer from Mascouche named Toussaint Sicotte was a minister in the Union government and a patriot charged with high treason in 1837. Jacques Ferron has an obsession with names. The same name or nickname may pop up in a number of different works, with or without changes in spelling. And in the course of our conversation that Sunday morning in the month of March, he spontaneously referred to a number of names that appear in his writings. At first these names may seem somewhat random, but it gradually emerges that they inevitably refer to four major thematic thrusts in Ferron's work: political, social, medical or religious betrayals and injustices. In *L'amélanchier*, Mr Northrop, for example, is an Englishman by birth and by choice, his compass firmly pointed in the direction of London. In this case the reference is obviously to the English-Canadian critic Northrop Frye, ironically described to me by Ferron as "a former Quebecker who prefers the anatomy of criticism and of the University of Toronto to the anatomy of Quebec." This is followed by one of Ferron's wry little smiles, an endearing gesture that manages to be almost childlike and at the same time reminiscent of the fox in *Le salut de l'Irlande*.

Ferron then goes on to explain that his character Rédempteur Fauché, the son of Papa Boss and a Québécoise virgin in *Papa Boss*, is somewhat closer to the criminal of the same name, who settled his accounts by setting fire to a house (although he got the wrong house by mistake), than to any real Redeemer *(Rédempteur)*. "With my Rédempteur," Ferron continues, "I intended to make some annunciations. That wasn't what happened. Young Rédempteur, the little bum, became a sacrilege." Sacrilege does not seem too strong an expression, in fact, since in the world of Rédempteur Fauché, the Almighty Dollar replaces the sacristy, soldiers replace the Messiah, and "Asshold Finance" replaces church collections and tithes. "I use names to conquer, to nationalize," says Ferron. I ask him if Abbé Surprenant in *Le ciel de Québec*, a pleasant local ethnologist, a "pilgrim" who is more interested in the unemployed than in holy places, who admires the communists, actually existed. "Not at all," laughs Ferron, happy at having led me down the garden path. The Abbé is a fictional charac-

ter who is *surprenant* (surprising) in comparison to the prestigious, plutocratic clergy of the establishment in the novel.
He is at the bottom end of the Catholic hierarchy, close to
the people. Ferron himself was once a communist, but he left
the movement because he found it too theoretical, full of
contradictions and corrupted by "that strange talent so many
reformed communists have for property speculation," (*La
charrette*, p. 22). Still, in *Le ciel de Québec* Abbé Surprenant
can claim, like Ferron, that communism

> takes account of historical reality and gives people in
> distress something that will save them quicker than
> bread and board — I mean an understanding of their
> situation...In [the Church's] abstract philosophy,
> we've bet our money on the absolute; in the concrete
> world we offer nothing but cheap escape, such as pil-
> grimages to fight unemployment; bowls of soup to
> people starved for justice.

(trans. Ray Ellenwood, *The Penniless Redeemer*, p. 279)

For anyone who plunges into the nominalist world of
Jacques Ferron, it is clearly interesting and perhaps even
useful to know whether such-and-such character actually
existed, but it is not essential. I had understood the significance of Abbé Surprenant, and that's what really matters.
Nominalist that he is, however, and whatever the degree of
consciousness or unconsciousness involved, Ferron's Surprenant reminded me of the Lorenzo Surprenant in *Maria
Chapdelaine*, a character who was much more a man than his
eunuch-like rival, Gagnon. Jacques Ferron is fascinated by
the religious history of nineteenth-century Quebec:

> **The most baroque and flamboyant manner of preaching
> was taught to us by Msgr Forbin-Janson, the Bishop-Prince of
> Nancy. His two-week retreat, as reported in *Les mélanges re-
> ligieux*, was very useful for me in *Le ciel de Québec*; I only had
> to arrange his sermons and put them into the mouth of Msgr
> Cyrille Gagnon. I don't believe Msgr Bourget was one of our
> great religious tenors, who like Chiniquy were all students of**

Forbin-Janson; nor was Msgr Lartigue, who must have preached in the serious, sober style of the Sulpicians.

The Sulpicians of Montreal, in close collaboration with their counterparts in Paris, sent the first Bishop of Montreal, Msgr Lartique, into retirement in Longueuil. In actual fact the first Bishop was the second, Msgr Bourget, who came from Quebec City. Without going so far into the past, I can quote from my own experience: in Louiseville, my first teachers, the Frères de l'Instruction chrétienne, were Canadians at the bottom of the ladder, Bretons in the hierarchy. But an even stranger thing was that in the kindergarten in Trois-Rivières, the Filles de Jésus, who were referred to as the French Nuns, were under the authority of two British ladies, who were in fact remarkable creatures.

Forbin-Janson had been an Ultra and it was after the Revolution in 1830 that he went into exile in America.

Brother Marie-Victorin is another religious "tenor" in whom Ferron shows an interest. Marie-Victorin is famous for identifying the plant-life of the Laurentian shield, and in his own way Jacques Ferron has identified the places and families of Quebec. The "family history" of Quebec, Ferron affirms, has its roots in the legend of the three brothers (which is told in *L'amélanchier* and in an article published in *La revue de l'Université de Moncton*, vol. 8, no 2, May 1975).

My father used to talk about the three brothers. People with other family names have also told me the same story. At the very beginning, there were three brothers. There's always one who turns out badly, a famous rascal named, in my case, Jean Ferron. When I went to Shippigan in New Brunswick, the Acadian Ferrons were amazed to learn there were Ferrons in Quebec.

In Acadian mythology it's the women who dominate: they dream of Evangeline, they know about Ave Maris Stella, they have their great Saint Anne. For us, the woman is an element of reunion and confidence who comes after the three brothers. The Acadians and the Québécois have different archetypes.

Popular legends are scattered throughout Ferron's writings. Their authenticity is less important than their unifying effect and their amusing, liberating qualities. Léon de Portanqueu in *L'amélanchier* claims that every family should "make itself into the stuff of tales so as to give new vitality to an old heritage and revive the tales and songs that are part of life's necessities." The cart, which Ferron uses as a symbol of capitalist corruption, human stupidity and the hard labour of the working people, has its origins in the legendary past of the Ferron family:

"La charrette" ("The Cart") was my father's favourite song. It's a song about a peasant farmer who runs into trouble with the middlemen. The Devil picks up the whole lot of them, except him. At the end he's a free man.

Jacques Ferron has a reputation for being deeply involved in nationalist causes. He tells me that he hasn't always been a nationalist and that when he was at classical college, even Pierre Laporte, who wore the little green beret of the Action française, was more nationalistic than he. "The situation was pretty well reversed in October, 1970," he remarks thoughtfully, perhaps recalling his role as intermediary between the police and the F.L.Q. after Laporte had been kidnapped and killed. It was well before the Quiet Revolution that Ferron first began to regard himself as Québécois and not French Canadian. This is already apparent in *La barbe de François Hertel*, written in 1947. The nationalist orientation began to take hold when Ferron thought back to his childhood, especially to that distant night the village church burned down (Ferron assures one that the fire Léon de Portanqueu talks about really did take place); this revealed to Ferron that, even without a church, the village could still exist. Quite independently from his father, who was somewhat infatuated with his own success as a lawyer, and his mother, an artistic woman who had a nationalistic streak but who died of tuberculosis, Ferron started thinking on his own about the problems of existence and the splendours and miseries of Quebec. From that time on he became his own saviour and considered any other messiah as "worthless."

Jacques Ferron's earliest memory of his childhood in Louiseville contains, in capsule form, the basic structure of his future work as a writer:

In Louiseville the overall structure was completely Manichean: lower and upper, good and evil, the big village of the important people, and the little village of the proletariat. Don't forget that today's Lachine used to be the little village of Montreal. The "little villages," no doubt of Indian origin, only had paths for streets. I saw the same thing in 1946 in the Micmac village in New Brunswick — an Indian reservation where there were Chinese men and Black women working. Micmac and Fredericton: little village and big village. Sydney and Montreal: little village and big village. The Black women in Sydney and the French Canadians: two little villages.

This obsession with villages should in no way be construed to mean, as the critic Gilles Marcotte has claimed, that Ferron, true to the old "agriculturalist" complex of French Canadians, is advocating a return to the land. The little village compared to the big village is simply one way of representing the small versus the large, Quebec versus the United States and Canada, the working man versus the boss. Ferron is, of course, fascinated by the parish structure, but this is how he explains it:

What more did the French settlers do than set up parishes? That's where the meaning of those little communities comes from — little communities in a larger community. That's why the main subject of *Le ciel de Québec* is the founding of a parish. In the old days they used to put a curse on the grasshoppers to drive them into other parishes, which were considered "foreign."

In an article entitled "Jacques Ferron et l'histoire de la formation sociale québécoise" (*Études françaises*, 12/3-4), Robert Mignier takes issue with Ferron, who sees the beginnings of Quebec's national history as emerging about 1837. Mignier claims that Ferron confuses history with nationalism, and that after the conquest, the French-Canadian people, contrary to what the author of the *Historiettes* states, did have a sense of patriotism, which came mainly from the fact that they were populating the country. Ferron objects to this, as follows:

There were barely 60,000 French Canadians after the Conquest. There weren't enough people to develop any real national awareness until the 1830's. A nation's history has a starting point. It's important to establish when it was.

In the writings of Jacques Ferron, the leading figures in the emergence of a national spirit are Papineau, the patriots Chénier and Bonaventure "le Beau" Viger, and the historian François-Xavier Garneau. The author confides to me that the episode in *Les grands soleils*, where Chénier collapses in a cemetery, was taken from a tale called "Petite scène d'un grand drame" by Pamphile Le May. In the case of Viger, a number of historians have told the story of the patriots' first encounter with the British soldiers on Chambly Road at the corner of Coteau-Rouge. Ferron was able to point out the exact spot to me: three blocks from his office, where a traffic light flashes anonymously at a busy highway intersection. The beautiful fields of Longueuil are gone forever.

They were there on November 17, 1837, however, when Bonaventure Viger, a farmer from Longueuil and captain of the militia, captured the colours from Colborne, Dr Davignon and the notary Demaray. I point out to Ferron that the man nicknamed "le beau Viger" was not Bonaventure, but rather Louis-Michel Viger, a lawyer, first cousin to Papineau, and founder of the People's Bank, a sort of precurser to today's Caisses populaires. I add, however, that in my opinion an "error" of this sort is not really an error, since Ferron's "beau Viger" and the historical "beau Viger" do not necessarily have to be the same person. For Ferron the expression "le beau Viger" acts as a leitmotif. And through a marvellous "coincidence," "le beau Viger" who is missing part of his thumb is related to the good-for-nothing brother in the legend of the three brothers: a strange beggar who also lost the end of his thumb, in this case in a battle against the English at Fort Maskinongé. In Ferron's world the history of the nation and the history of the family are never entirely distinct.

It was already the noon-hour and Monsieur Ferron and I had been chatting back and forth for three hours. Not wanting to impose upon him, I glanced at my watch and

Monsieur Ferron offered to drive me to the Métro station. Since we were driving in a yellow Renault, I remarked that Dr Ferron, unlike some of the more pretentious characters in his work, didn't drive the black "hearse" favoured by his doctors, prelates and incompetent honourable ministers. We drove past the house that formerly belonged to the Ferron family. "It was a lot more shaded by trees when we sold it two years ago," Ferron sighed. Behind the house I was amazed to see how far the woods extended; here was the origin of the "airy, chattering and enchanted" second-growth forest where the Ferrons' little girl, named Tinamer in *L'amélanchier*, used to spend her afternoons. There was no Minotaur stalking down Bellerive Street, as in Ferron's supernatural tale, but the street was as subdivided and asphalt-covered as I had imagined. The Juneberry tree *(l'amélanchier)* that young Tinamer refers to as "rakish and mocking, in league with the birds," is enormous for a shrub of that species. "It's the size of a small tree," Ferron remarks, "but it doesn't flower every spring." What does matter, I thought, is that it flowers and acquires new meaning in the minds of Ferron's readers.

The Renault drove past a shopping centre. I looked out at the huge parking lot with horror and heard Ferron remark:

I once saw Marie-Victorin give a lecture at the College in Longueuil. Did you know that in one of his tales ("Ne vends pas la terre") he tells the story of a proud and admirable farmer who refused to sell his land to the speculators swarming over here after the Jacques-Cartier Bridge was built? He sold it a few years ago, for a higher price.

Does the lust for money always win out in the end? How is it possible to resist the "urban sprawl" that Ferron depicts so effectively in his writings? These were the questions I was asking myself, and I couldn't help thinking of *Le salut de l'Irlande* and Major Bellow, a former land speculator in Quebec now living in Victoria, a city Ferron amusingly transforms into "a plastic English place" of retired "golden-agers" and American tourists from Seattle. If the Major "bellows," it must be out of contentment, although "sneer" might be a more appropriate expression, considering how he exploited the people of Quebec. As for the shopping centre,

the only thing left grazing there is the Steinberg super-
market. I left Monsieur Ferron with a firm handshake and
thanked him for the images he had awakened in me. A few
minutes later the Métro was whisking me under the St. Lawrence, under what Tinamer refers to so marvellously and so
"anachronistically" — after all, writing does make time stand
still — as the "majestic St. Lawrence, filled with greasy dish-
water," the most impressive "of all the sewers of Upper and
Lower Canada."

1 "The name Anacharcis comes from one of my patients who
  was called that because his father spoke Greek." (note from
  Jacques Ferron)

2 Regarding his readings in Quebec literature, Ferron con-
  fesses to being particularly fond of the writings of Hubert
  Aquin.

Gérard Bessette: Social Irony and Subconscious Impulses

Gérard Bessette is a professor, critic and novelist. His earlier novels are distinguished by a particular gift for social satire, irony and "realistic" characterization. In *La bagarre*, for instance, the protagonist Jules Leboeuf turns his back on the common people; in *Les pédagogues*, Sarto Pellerin exposes and denounces the prejudices of teachers; and in *Le libraire*, Jodoin, looking through the three little holes of his visor, observes the mean, narrow world of Quebec in the Fifties. Although these novels are rather traditional in terms of form and expression, the originality and innovative qualities of Gérard Bessette's more recent works set him apart from the majority of Quebec writers.

L'incubation, which has often been described as a Québécois equivalent to the French "nouveau roman," is a fascinating novel in which Ontario and England become intertwined through the confused workings of memory. In the "intestinal meanderings" of the London subway system, the author describes a "happy return to horizontality," with man crawling through the "underground" of his imagination, somewhat akin to the primitive people squatting in the labyrinth of their cave in *Les anthropoïdes*. As early as 1965, Gérard Bessette discovered that the primordial thrust of his creativity was to remember, to piece together fragments of the past. "Memory," he claims, "is a blender, a monstrous apparatus for digestion." In *Le cycle* (1971), Bessette adapts the techniques of memory to a subject more deeply connected with the Quebec experience: the break-up of the French-Canadian family. The seven interior monologues, with their dazzling verbal inventiveness and hallucinatory rhythms, plunge the reader into a world of tragic implications. *La commensale*, a novel written prior to *L'incubation* but not published until 1975, is more in keeping with the "realistic" vein of Bessette's earlier writings. The narrator in *La commensale*, a jaded accountant working for the "Plumbing Supply Company," emerges as a kind of urban counterpart to Jodoin in *Le Libraire*; both are highly lucid intellectually, yet neither can escape from his intolerable situation except through alcohol or obsessive meticulousness.

Like *L'incubation* and *Le cycle*, *Les anthropoïdes* is less concerned with describing the external world than with faithfully reproducing the world of inner experience. Here, however, the extraordinary and apparently "exotic" subject is strikingly original. The Anthropoids of the Kalahoum horde, a primitive race that has barely evolved from the apes, are caught in a struggle against nature, evil manes (ancestral spirits), and enemy tribes. The narrator is a "jato" or adolescent, an apprentice "worder" (*paroleur*) with a healthy mind in a crippled body; by subtly sharing the narration with other "worders," he tells of the history of three neighbouring tribes. Through the "caverns" of their mind, the different narrators convey images of the history of their race, thus revealing the "saturated paddocks" of their guardian memories. Gérard Bessette believes in the virtue of the word as the only source of possible harmony among men:

How can the relative position of the three hordes be determined without recourse to force and bloodshed? "Through the word," replied Duracoudi-the-Shaman (just as Salaloudi-the-Trismegistus would have replied before him), "through our future word-sessions we will be able to bring harmony to the disagreements and set the common imagery for the new horde."

Simultaneously an authentic documentary on the life of primitive peoples, a marvellous portrayal of unusual landscapes, and a succession of little adventure "stories," *Les anthropoïdes* is not quite as prehistoric as it may appear to be at first glance. One of its themes, for instance, is absolutely contemporary: women's liberation, with Salaloudi expressing a wish for women to be less submissive. In addition, the motto of the "worders," *Je me souviens*, is not only the motto of Quebec but also a reminder that a collective memory must be maintained. The landscapes, the key events from the past, and the "power of the hordic bonds" must all be preserved. On the last page of the novel we learn that the ancestral river is named "Kébékouâ": "a giant muscular river that the sorcerers Duracoudi-Sinaloké invoke using the guttural word Kébékouâ, and on whose fertile shores was born the unknown ancient forefather." It would be a mistake, however, to lay too much stress on the novel's connections with Quebec, since the themes it conveys deal with such universal concerns as sex, violence, history and the word.

Les anthropoïdes is a strange book, and I must confess it took some fifty pages before I began to lower my defenses and succumb to the charms of a narration and style that are without precedent in Quebec literature. For me it was like the first time I read *L'incubation*, or the works of the French novelist Alain Robbe-Grillet; I felt myself lost, exploring a landscape that was totally unfamiliar to me. Once I got used to the apparent disorder, however, I was able to discover an unexpected unity, rich in both beauty and meaning. If, after reading the first few pages of *Les anthropoïdes*, you start to wonder what's happening, whether you're reading anthropology or literature, continue reading and you will find a series of unforgettable "interviews" with the primitive people we all have within us. You'll find yourself propelled into a literary world which prompted the critic Ronald Sutherland to write that "*Les anthropoïdes* is on a level with such classics as *Gulliver's Travels* and *Brave New World*, a triumph of the imagination and a work of profound implications" (*The Globe and Mail*, June 3, 1978). I too was impressed by the originality of *Les anthropoïdes* and by its imaginative and metaphorical dimensions. Bessette presents the natural world in human terms: phosphorescent caves become the homes of our ancestors, and at the same time are associated with the "cave" of the skull, the source of fabulous images; the tortuous mountains are described as "bowels" through which the orators "imagine themselves creeping;" thickets of locust trees become "strewers of imagery." The novelist involves us in psychological descents into the "belly" of the subconscious. The story of a prehistoric nation seeking to protect itself is conveyed through the symbol of the "spacious belly" of time. Another dimension of the novel is the physical environment described in sexual terms and deformed by phantasies similar to the ones analyzed in the novels of Victor-Lévy Beaulieu. Even the ritual of the wounded penis, an ancestral form of initiation, recalls the trauma suffered by Jos Connaissant, one of Beaulieu's characters. It would be well worth examining the way Bessette turns sexuality, whether its orientation be anal, vaginal or olfactory, into a meaningful personal theme. In this work, one could delve into any number of symbols, but at this point it is perhaps best to turn to Gérard Bessette himself, twice winner of both the Prix du Gouvernement du Québec and the Governor General's Award for fiction.

* * *

D.S. — In *Mes romans et moi*, you talk about growing up in the village of Saint-Alexandre, in Iberville County; you mention your quiet childhood years, your father's dreams of travelling, your religious, over-protective mother, and the predominant role of the Church. With regard to your own novels, you adopt the same sort of psychoanalytic approach as you used, in *Une littérature en ébullition* and *Trois roman-*

ciers québécois, to analyse the work of Victor-Lévy Beaulieu, Anne Hébert, Émile Nelligan, Yves Thériault, Gabrielle Roy and Gilbert La Rocque. It seems to me that, in *Mes romans et moi*, you become one of the characters in your own writings. Just as *Le semestre* turns out to be more a novel than an autobiography, *Mes romans et moi* strikes me as more a work of literature than of self-analysis.

G.B. — *Mes romans et moi* is primarily an analysis of my writings; there's also a lot of self-analysis, so to speak, but it's *always* based on my writings. In any case, *Mes romans et moi* is not a novel, whereas *Le semestre* is.

D.S. — Since I know you're an avid reader of literature and criticism, I'm a bit hesitant about asking who your favourite writers are. I'm sure there are a lot of them, but are there one or two in particular who have influenced you?

G.B. — A great many writers have influenced me. Bergson and Freud have affected my work in a general sense, at least the greater part of it. Other influences have been more limited, sometimes restricted to a single novel. For example, Claude Simon's *La route des Flandres* influenced *L'incubation*, and the opening chapter of *War and Peace* had an effect on *Les pédagogues*. With *Le cycle*, various critics talked about Faulkner's techniques in *As I Lay Dying*, which I hadn't read at that point. With *Les anthropoïdes*, one book that had a remote influence on it — I say "remote" because it's a book I read as a child — is *La guerre du feu* by Rosny. There are certain echoes of it in my novel.

D.S. — As a writer, have your interest in poetry and your studies of form made you attach greater importance to the structure of your writings, to the rhythm and orchestration of your sentences, to the symbolic dimensions — in short, to meaning created through form?

G.B. — All that is more instinctive than deliberate. My writings are structured by "creative evolution," as it were. As for "orchestration" or harmony, those come from my highly developed auditory capacities: I hear the sentences I write. In the old days, we used to talk about three types of physical make-up: visual, auditory, and verbal-motor. I'm a cross between the auditory and the verbal (or written).

D.S. — In 1940, your one-act play *Hasard* won first prize in the Gala Competition for French-Canadian Drama at the Théâtre Saint-Sulpice. Have you ever thought of writing other plays?

G.S. — Yes, there's one filed away in my papers. I also used to write the occasional radio sketch. "La garden-party de Christophine" is practically a dialogue for the theatre.

D.S. — You began your writing career mostly as a poet. *Poèmes temporels*, the collection you published in 1954, is reminiscent of Paul Valéry; the poems seem to have very little in common with your work as a novelist.

G.B. — There were ten years between the time I wrote my poems and *La bagarre*. A person changes a lot between the ages of 26 and 36.

D.S. — Your Master's thesis deals with Nelligan's imagery, and your doctoral dissertation studies the imagery in French-Canadian poetry. You were one of the first critics in French Canada to stress the intrinsic value of works of literature, rather than their social "acceptability" or their biographical interest.

G.B. — Yes, I believed very strongly in that distinction at a time when clerical morality was trying to dominate everything else.

D.S. — You began to write literary criticism in the mid-Forties, and you believed from the start in formal criticism based on the structures of the literature itself, as opposed to external, historical or impressionistic criticism. Was that not rather a courageous position at that time?

G.B. — It came from my desire for freedom.

D.S. — In *La bagarre*, the critics were particularly impressed by your realistic description of the working class and their drinking places. In your opinion, is that realism the main achievement in your first published fiction, this so-called "working-class" novel?

G.B. — I have no idea. André Belleau felt that the language, or rather the different levels of language, were the distinguishing characteristics in *La bagarre*. After reading *Le romancier fictif*, which is one of Quebec's best books of criticism, I'm inclined to think Belleau was right. He spoke of "language as event" (I'm quoting from memory), which seemed to me a very astute observation. Belleau is an extremely perceptive critic.

D.S. — *Le libraire* quickly became one of the classics in Quebec literature. It must surely be the most successful of your novels of social realism.

G.B. — According to the critic Pierre Gobin, the realism is refined and "distanced" through the language, the often indirect style. He claims the character Jodoin reacts against the figurative use of words, diminishing rather than magnifying their intensity. Some critics have noted a propensity for ironic understatement.

D.S. — Where do you place *Les pédagogues* in the evolution of your fiction?

G.B. — If I remember correctly, I tried to present each chapter from the point-of-view of one character. No one seems to have noticed this. Apparently I wasn't able to get that across.

D.S. — Immediately upon the publication of *L'incubation*, Réjean Robidoux, one of the best informed critics of your work, described it as an "innovating novel" and a "smashing success." Robidoux claims it was your interest in the working-class novels of Quebec — Laberge, for example — that caused you to write realistic novels; he further suggests that your passion for the "nouveau roman" and for psychoanalytic criticism forced you, shall we say, to change styles. What are your thoughts on this?

G.B. — Robidoux is no doubt right. However, there's something else that brought about my change in style; I talk about this in *Mes romans et moi*.

D.S. — I assume you're referring to your bout with polio in 1963, when you were given hallucinogenic drugs that brought on fantastic dreams and spatial hallucinations. You had the impression the bed was vertical and the doctors were walking on the walls. After that, your narrative technique exploded; linear chronology gave way to hallucinatory images, and the verticality of your symbolic settings led to the hidden corners of the subconscious. In *Mes romans et moi*, you state that *L'incubation* was a crisis you actually experienced "both as reality and as mental phantasies." With reference to the setting, why does *L'incubation* take place in London and Narcotown (Kingston, Ontario)? Why did those two places seem so appropriate for that trip into our own depths, which forms the basis of the novel?

G.B. — In London and Narcotown, I happened to find myself in "secondary states," which no doubt explains the "trip" you mention.

D.S. — Several of your characters reveal a mania for precision, a need to analyse everything with a certain relentless cynicism. Could it be that this obsession with descriptive detail is something you yourself — and perhaps all writers — share?

G.B. — It may simply be a compensatory phenomenon; since I'm not a visual person, perhaps I multiply the details my memory fails to provide me with.

D.S. — Your use of punctuation in *Le cycle* is unique. Victor-Lévy Beaulieu is the only other writer I can think of who's been as innovative in this respect. How did you develop such a controlled yet natural way of manipulating all those endless sentences, dashes, single and double brackets — and all the other techniques that result in such a brilliant inter-weaving of interior monologues, subconscious images and narrative reflections?

G.B. — I was tremendously impressed by a sentence from Bergson (again I'm quoting from memory): "If we were able to write down our interior monologues, the immediate data of our consciousness, there might be commas but certainly not any periods."

D.S. — The belly is an important symbol in your work. To give only a few examples from *Le cycle*, the belly appears in the guise of the maternal breast, the subway and the arena. I would even suggest that these hollow spaces are the predominant symbol in most of your novels.

G.B. — No doubt you're right. I recently reread *Poèmes temporels*, which I hadn't done for more than 20 years. Even as early as that in my work, the intra-uterine phantasy was apparent, especially in the poem "Hymne à l'esprit alcoolique."

D.S. — Some critics have suggested that *Le semestre* was written as a way of taking revenge against critics such as Jean-Éthier Blais and Naïm Kattan, or writers such as Victor-Lévy Beaulieu, André Langevin, Jean Basile and Anne Hébert. There was even talk of "morbid vindictiveness." However, the writers who appear in *Le semestre* are called Butor-Ali Nonlieu, André Laigrafin, Ane Chambredebois, Jean Achier-Laid and Naïf Quatrânes (all names containing untranslatable puns). In my opinion, this means that you're in no way attacking the actual people, but simply exploiting some of the humorous possibilities inherent in the Quebec cultural milieu.

G.B. — Yes. You're quite right.

D.S. — The sexual dimension of your writings — masochism, sadism, anal and scatological fixations, off-colour jokes — have not gone unnoticed by many of your readers, particularly various women who have accused you of misogyny. It seems to me, however, that it's important to distinguish between a work of the imagination that takes existing realities into account, and writings that actually come out in favour of such realities. You never tell your readers that your characters are models whose examples should be followed; what you do, rather, is simply to delve into the subconscious, without making any attempt to hide what you find there.

G.B. — There's one critic I never fail to scandalize: Ben Shek, from the University of Toronto. No doubt it's because of his puritanical upbringing. Sometimes he reminds me of the early Quebec critic and priest, Camille Roy. Well, enough of that! The distinction you make is quite just. I never address my readers directly, nor do I present my characters as models of behaviour.

D.S. — The first five short stories in *La garden-party de Christophine* reveal a talented story-teller who knows how to write in a way that is condensed, ironic and spontaneous. You seem to have been very interested in the short story during the Sixties, when you published an anthology of short fiction entitled *De Québec à Saint-Boniface*. On the whole, though, you seem to prefer the novel.

G.B. — I feel confined in the short story.

D.S. — Your short stories are very light-hearted. What impressed me in *La garden-party* were the puns and the humour. I wonder whether the short story isn't something you amuse yourself with, whereas you see the novel as a serious look into some of the great questions confronting mankind.

G.B. — Are you referring to the whole collection or just the title story? I don't think all my short stories are "light-hearted." The last one in the collection certainly is, at least on first reading, I think. However, the two men who are "dialoguing" let themselves go more and more as the story continues. Their Freudian self-restraint and their super-egos disappear. By getting drunk, they demonstrate the accuracy of the following definition: "The super-ego is the only part of the psyche that can be dissolved in alcohol."

D.S. — Of all your novels, *Les anthropoïdes* is the one I find most intriguing. When did you write that novel?

G.B. — When I was rustling through my papers recently, I realized to my great surprise that I began *Les anthropoïdes* in 1971. I put that fragment of the manuscript aside for a few years, since I published *Trois romanciers québécois* in the meantime. Then I spent a whole year working in London. Later I had a sabbatical, and then a leave of absence. On the whole, I figure I spent two and a half years working full-time on that novel.

D.S. — Does this mean it was the most difficult of your novels to write?

G.B. — None of my other novels required as much work. *Le cycle* took me two years, whereas with *Les anthropoïdes* it was two and a half.

D.S. — Did it take that long because of the subject matter, or was it the actual writing that made it so difficult?

G.B. — I spent a lot of time fumbling around. At first I wanted to describe the events directly. I even considered having characters who didn't have the gift of speech. Naturally, that didn't work.

D.S. — Characters unable to speak would be the complete opposite of the "word-sessions" that are one of the basic themes in the novel.

G.B. — Yes, it's sort of an antithesis. Actually, the original opening was written "directly." Later, I realized that didn't work and I would have to use some form of "distanciation." I finally decided to present the plot as well as the descriptions from the point-of-view of a "worder," using interior monologues. The scene where the leopard is killed, for example, was originally written without an "interpreter." Later, I had to have Guito tell it because that seemed to me more "real."

D.S. — It's almost possible to start reading *Les anthropoïdes* at the end or in the middle, except perhaps for the opening pages that serve as an introduction. I can't tell whether you wrote the novel in chronological order. Did you have much trouble organizing the different parts?

G.B. — Well, at one point, when I started working on it again after a few months or maybe a year or two, I reread what I could of the manuscript and then tried to write a summary of it, which was difficult because it wasn't typed. My sister used to type my manuscripts, but she's no longer able to do it. So, I wrote a summary for myself, and I may have changed the order of certain sequences; most of all, though, I cut a lot of passages out. The idea wasn't so much to make a plan as a "digest," so I could find my way around in it. Also, while I was in the process of making this summary, I'd sometimes find myself writing again, so I ended up with a rather bewildering mass of material. If ever some masochistic researcher decides to stick his nose into that manuscript, he'll get more than he bargained for!

D.S. — I'd like to get back to what I referred to as the strangeness of the subject — strange not only with respect to your other writings, but also in terms of Quebec literature in general.

G.B. — Well, there is a certain logic in it, a certain continuity; to some degree there's a movement from ontogenesis to phylogenesis. In plainer words, ontogenesis refers to the origins of an individual, whereas phylogenesis refers to the origins of the species. In *Le cycle* and *L'incubation*, for instance, the characters feel that their past or their childhood determines their actions and their phantasies. In this sense, the novels can be called "ontogenetic." On the other hand, *Les anthropoïdes* talks about the origins of a species, so therefore it's a "phylogenetic" novel.

D.S. — In terms of theme and style, how do you think this novel fits in with the others?

G.B. — Well, the title gives some indication. If you really want to go back to the very beginnings, it's quite natural that you should end up talking about humanity in general rather than any particular individual or specific observations. I read a great many books in what is now referred to as ethology, that is, the study of animals in their natural habitat. For example, there's a woman named Goodall who did a study of chimpanzees; she actually lived with them in Africa. Other people have made careful observations of baboons, and the Japanese have done the same with macacos, or Japanese apes. The social organization of the baboons and macacos turned out to be the most useful for my purposes, since chimpanzees have hardly any social structures.

D.S. — Did that help with your descriptions and understanding of the social organization of the tribe or horde in *Les anthropoïdes?*

G.B. — Well, yes, it helped me imagine what it was like.

D.S. — So, you started out on a fairly scientific footing.

G.B. — As a point of departure, yes. Then the plot and the characters gradually became clearer. One book that influenced me a lot was Desmond Morris' *The Naked Ape.* I learned from it that our prehistoric ancestors first lived in the forest, then as food gatherers, and finally moved to the grasslands, where they gradually became hunters. This brought about a transformation of their social organization, and also of the relationships among individuals. Nowadays we can look to the apes for proof of the extent to which habitat affects or alters habits. For example, chimpanzees and gorillas live in the forest, while baboons and macacos live in open terrain. The former have a very loose, undefined social organization, whereas with the baboons and macacos, their social hierarchy is quite rigid and powerful. A band of macacos is usually governed by a sort of triumvirate of large males: alpha (A), beta (B), and gamma (Y). Alpha, of course, is the strongest one, but if he becomes too autocratic or dictatorial, B and Y unite against him to assure a "balance of power."

These apes have actual social classes that endure from generation to generation. For example, the male offspring of an "aristocratic" female has a good chance of becoming part of the oligarchy, either as A, B or Y, while the descendant of a lower-class female has no chance of this at all. When I learned that our ape cousins sometimes have a "hereditary nobility," I was astonished and fascinated.

D.S. — *Les anthropoïdes* tells of a tribe that is struggling for its survival. Do you see any parallels between this and the struggle of the Quebec people? As you know, critics have made connections of this sort between the Jewish, Indian and Eskimo minorities in Yves Thériault's novels, and the French Canadians. I also seem to recall an article in a Montreal newspaper in which a journalist stated that *Les anthropoïdes* presents a transposition of the problems facing Quebec. How do you react to this sort of interpretation?

G.B. — I don't see it that way at all! You know, towards the end of the novel there's an allusion to a river that is called Kébékouâ. I was strongly tempted to suppress that allusion, to prevent my novel from being interpreted too narrowly. The only reason I left it in was because one of the readers at the Éditions La Presse told me he found the term "Kébékouâ" both interesting and amusing.

D.S. — But it's only a secondary allusion!

G.B. — It's completely secondary, I agree, but in light of the reactions I've had, I think it was a mistake to leave it in. I'll remove it if a second edition is ever published.

D.S. — Why did you place that allusion at the end?

G.B. — I thought of it as something akin to a signature, if you will, to show that my origins are in Quebec. It reminds me of *La chanson de Roland*, where there's no author but rather a scribe who writes at the end, "Such was the song that…"

D.S. — Do you mean it was a sort of hidden signature?

G.B. — That's right, but as for thinking about Quebec, I mean consciously, no! Not even unconsciously, because it comes at the end. It's rather mysterious; I think it's a good idea to leave the allusion in, but I don't really agree when people start basing their whole interpretation on it. It's precisely to avoid interpretations of this nature that I'm going to have it removed.

D.S. — When you were writing *Les anthropoïdes*, were you aware of any symbolic dimension to the work, a dimension that might have haunted you and made you want to explore it thoroughly?

G.B. — Well, you know, when you've read and written as much psychoanalytic criticism as I have, you can't avoid being conscious that the very long sequence that takes place deep within the mountain is somehow connected with the maternal womb. Of course I was aware of that.

D.S. — Were you particularly struck by the maternal images?

G.B. — Yes, and also by the story of the rite of passage that the circumcision represents; still, I tried to think of it as little as possible.

D.S. — The notion of what is sacred provides one of the most fascinating themes in the novel; I'm not thinking here of religion, but rather of everyday objects that take on mythological significance, like the cave of the ancestors. How do you perceive this notion, which you seem to admire a great deal? Is it something modern man has lost?

G.B. — Well, I don't admire it, but I think it was important to our ancestors. Over the centuries, the manes, the ancestral souls which constantly exerted a good or bad influence on the life of the tribe, took on an importance that I found astonishing.

D.S. — I sometimes had the impression that it wasn't a question of religion, but rather superstition; I gradually realized, however, that it went a lot deeper, that it was actually something sacred, apparently stemming from the very nature of man.

G.B. — Yes. Until recent times, man in general was a believer; he believed in a divinity. The agnostics and atheists are a relatively recent species, if you think in terms of a collection of individuals.

D.S. — Still, in *Les anthropoïdes* it's not a question of divinities, since the manes are ancestors.

G.B. — Ancestors, yes, but they become something akin to gods. They know everything and they constantly interfere with things. It was the Romans who called the souls of their ancestors "manes." They also had the household gods, the lares. Someone said on radio that my novel was set thirty thousand years ago; I think it was more like five hundred thousand years ago.

D.S. — Why did you decide to invent a new language and create neologisms to describe your Anthropoids? The invented words demand an extra effort on the part of the reader, especially in the first pages of the novel, when one has to get used to the vocabulary. I'm not saying this extra effort is necessarily a bad thing, but what do you think?

G.B. — I previously wrote an article on the internal reader, an article that was published in *Liberté*. I've never tried to define this internal reader in any precise way, but I feel he or she is a reader who is willing to make the necessary effort. Once that effort has been made, the lexicological displacement produces a chronological colouring; at least I hope it does. At first glance it's a bit bewildering, but there's nothing to prevent the reader from consulting the glossary before he or she starts reading the book. In any case, most of the invented words can be understood without consulting the glossary.

D.S. — Did people criticize you for this "lexicological displacement"?

G.B. — In certain provincial newspapers, a few critics found the novel overly difficult, but in general I haven't had all that many negative reactions.

D.S. — The sexual act, the "daily mounting" of odorous females, plays a mysterious role in your novel. The act of love is seen as something initiatory and healthy, something that allows man to purify himself. This is quite the opposite of the sex in *Le cycle*, where the characters are ashamed of their sexual impulses or view them as a means of escape. Do we have to go back to primitive man to find a purer form of sex?

G.B. — In an article in *Le Devoir*, the critic Robert Mélançon spoke of humanity before original sin. I wouldn't say original sin doesn't exist at all, but there's relatively little of it. Thus, the important thing in the sexual act is the primordial role of the sense of smell. It's almost certain that in early times, when man was just beginning to walk upright, the sense of smell was still crucial. It was thanks to his sense of smell that the male knew when the female was in heat. The sense of sight is much less "incarnate" than either smell or taste. Nowadays, man is attracted to women because of the beauty of their appearance. With animals, however, this role is played by the scent of the female in heat.

D.S. — The males are dominant in your novel; women are nothing more than vaginas.

G.B. — Not completely, but they do have a lower rank. The exception is the old woman, Vikna, who has gone through a sort of traumatic experience and is resentful towards the males, who are frightened of her. All the women participate in the birth of Bao, and they all help to ensure his survival, thus accepting a mixture of the "races." The males would have been more inclined to dispose of baby Bao, especially since it takes him a lot longer than the others to learn to walk upright.

D.S. — In *Les anthropoïdes*, the reader is mystified by some elements in the setting that seem to have a particular significance for the inhabitants of a primitive land. I'm thinking here of the inaccessible sea of sand, the cabalistic caves and the devouring sun, for example. Were you also aware of the importance of these elements? Could you become a critic of your own novel for a few minutes and tell us how you interpret this setting?

G.B. — I'd have to think about it. One thing I can tell you is that the sea of sand and the desert came to me automatically, perhaps because I had been reading about the drought in the countries south of the Sahara. However, before I wrote the novel, I had no idea I was going to talk about crossing the desert.

D.S. — You show the horde searching for a new land in order to renew and preserve the race. Is this your way of describing in your own terms a theme that is universal and mythological?

G.B. — No doubt, since we used to be nomads. We still are: we move around in cars, constantly coming and going, on the move for the sake of being on the move, or out of curiosity. We're restless nomads, always wanting to go beyond what we know. At the beginning we looked farther in the external sense; now we try to look farther inward as well.

D.S. — *Les anthropoïdes* describes the rituals of speech and the cutting of the foreskin, which are a sort of initiation into life for the Kalahoums. Was this strange link between a sexual wound and the art of speaking a major preoccupation for you?

G.B. — It's been said that "Happy is the people without history." The same could be said of individuals. The rite of passage is a movement into awareness caused by fear. All young males experience that fear, but the narrator has also had a wounded arm, which reinforces his ritual wound. Therefore it's completely normal for Guito to turn towards speech, since he's no longer able to do combat. His physical wound helps with the speech-session. I realized that after I'd finished writing the novel, when I was correcting the proofs.

I noticed that Salaloudi's teacher, who is named Salalou, didn't want to travel because he was going blind. Physical wounds are sublimated in speech. There's a very close connection between the two.

D.S. — You seem to be praising speech. In fact, the most important of the words you invented is *parolade*, translated as "speech-session," and all sorts of variants: *paroler, parolader, parolage, paroleur*. It's as if you were saying, "Listen, we no longer know how to talk; we've lost one of primitive man's most admirable qualities: speech, the art of oratory."

G.B. — There's no doubt that the great difference between us and animals in general is the power of speech. Speech provides us with a collective memory, whereas for the animals it's instinctive, though I'm not saying animals don't have memories. Thanks to the power of speech, we have a memory in the strict sense of the word, a collective memory. We can tell about things that have happened to us.

D.S. — You have a marvellous way of handling interior monologues, which you often indicate by the use of brackets. Is this stream of consciousness central to your conception of creativity in the novel?

G.B. — I more or less have the impression, at least for the time being, that there's no other way I can write effectively. I said earlier in the interview that I'd tried describing my subject directly and it didn't work. And so it became an interior monologue, or rather a series of monologues within one another, like those Russian dolls. Guito's "I" is fairly fluid, still in the process of taking form; therefore his monologue is complex and to some extent "multiple." As you know, the opening line of the novel goes as follows: *We're moving slowly across the broad savannah (says Guito says Guito to himself I Guito say to myself)*.

In the first expression, "says Guito," Guito is an ordinary "he"; in the second, the "he" becomes reflexive; the "I" emerges only in the third. Still, he's all three of them at once.

On the radio programme, *Bookclub*, the critic Jacques Allard put a great deal of emphasis on this, perhaps because he always thinks openings are particularly significant. A half-million years ago, the "ego" in its present form hadn't yet come into existence.

D.S. — I'm starting to have a better understanding of why you were fascinated by primitive peoples. Their "I" made it possible for you to experiment with several different perspectives and to bring your own forms of the "I" into play. What I find surprising, though, is that the theme of primitive man is hardly present in your other writings; *Les anthropoïdes* seems to stand apart from the rest of your novels.

G.B. — Yes, although there's a frequently quoted passage from *L'incubation* where the character says, "Little by little, we started walking upright through the ages." In that sense, it's not completely new. The older I get, the more I realize just how much, in spite of all our cerebral pretentions, we depend on our bodies. As you get older, unfortunately, you become increasingly aware of the weight of the body. With the primitive peoples, it wasn't a question of getting older, since the body was absolutely central for them. In any case, the psychoanalytic critic Melanie Klein, a disciple of Freud, insists that the ego is primarily a bodily ego. This is true of children, and it's also true of primitive peoples.

D.S. — Would you say that primitive man represents those things we always have within us but which we either don't recognize or don't want to accept?

G.B. — It's rather the things we repress or don't want to talk about. There are certain passages in *Les anthropoïdes* which shocked one of the readers at the publishing house. In the parts dealing with smells and "shit," he put question marks beside the passages where the hunters are sniffing the excrement. When you walk upright, you're less likely to be sensitive to smells that come from the rear; in a crawling position, you're at just the right level.

D.S. — I consider you to be one of the most original and perceptive critics in Quebec. Your analyses of the psychological complexes that can be found in the work of Anne Hébert, Émile Nelligan and Yves Thériault were a revelation for many readers; thanks to you, they finally became aware of the omnipresent phantasies that lie hidden in the images used by these three writers. The analysis in your *Trois romanciers québécois* is in much the same vein, showing the preponderance of sexual symbols in the Quebec imagination. Newspaper critics, however, generally didn't think very much of your interpretations, dismissing them as exaggerated. Personally, I don't agree with those critics at all. Obviously, your psychoanalytic approach is only one way of interpreting Quebec literature. It may be a partial form of criticism, but that doesn't mean it's not valid. In France, a critic like Roland Barthes has generally been spared emotional and biased attacks in the newspapers; here in Quebec, however, the newspapers have interpreted your critical interest in sexual images and interpretations as narrow and simplistic. How do you react to hostile commentary of this sort?

G.B. — I'm irritated and angered by them. Whenever I read that kind of pseudo-judgement, I explain it as the phenomenon of resistance in the Freudian sense, that is, unconscious resistance.[1] Those impulses bother them in an emotional sense, and therefore they attack them because unconsciously they don't want to admit that they too have phantasies of that sort. It's the same phenomenon you find when someone is being psychoanalyzed: resistance, an unwillingness to accept certain feelings that are deeply repressed. Unconsciously, they're shocked and appalled. I understand them perfectly; I shouldn't get annoyed, but it makes me angry all the same.

D.S. — These same critics say you put too much emphasis on the novelist, and not enough on the writings. In fact, though, all your commentary is based on an internal analysis of the novel itself.

G.B. — When you're talking about novels, you always end up talking about the novelist, even if you don't do so directly.

D.S. — I would like to thank you most sincerely for granting me this interview. I can't wait until your diary is published. The excerpts I've been able to read leave no doubt in my mind that we'll learn a great deal about your readings, your travels, your certainties and uncertainties. And I wouldn't be surprised if your diary is really more a work of literature than simply a diary.

[1] In their book, *Vocabulaire de la psychanalyse*, Laplanche and Pontalis define the word "resistance" as follows: "When a person is being treated through psychoanalysis, the word 'resistance' is used to describe any of the patient's actions or words which stand in the way of his gaining access to his unconscious. By extension, Freud spoke of resistance to psychoanalysis as meaning *an attitude of opposition to its discoveries in that they may reveal unconscious desires and cause the person 'psychological vexation.'*" (Note and emphasis by Gérard Bessette.)

Marie-Claire Blais:
Deliverance through Writing

In 1980 the novelist, playwright and poet Marie-Claire Blais celebrated the twentieth anniversary of her career as a writer. Born in Quebec City in 1939, she is now considered, with Gabrielle Roy and Anne Hébert, to be one of the most important women writers in Quebec. Since being "discovered" at the age of nineteen by Jeanne Lapointe and Father G.-H. Lévesque of Laval University, and also by the influential American critic, Edmund Wilson, Marie-Claire Blais has to date written some twenty works of incontestable literary value. The publication of a book by Marie-Claire Blais is always one of the major events in the literary season.

Marie-Claire Blais presents her themes in a symbolic atmosphere both delicately nuanced and rich in philosophical implications. Above all she is a poet, even in her prose: water (the sea, rain, springs, fog), mountains, trees, the seasons, the wind, and unforgettable Manichean images of

Biblical origin are recurring symbols throughout her work. Like most writers, Marie-Claire Blais is obsessed by a few central themes: broken families; middle-class marriages; children who are smothered by the capitalistic world of adults; ugliness, a source of suffering imposed by a restrictive society; love, either destructively egotistical, passionate and charitable, or tragically ephemeral; social inequalities; homosexuals and lesbians caught up in the problems of existence; sickness, seen as a symbol of the universal struggle against death; the temptation of suicide; criminals, with the revelation of both their appealing and reprehensible sides; the city, that marvellous theatre of existence; and the function and personality of the writer.

Marie-Claire Blais' talent became immediately apparent in her first novel, *La belle bête* (1959), which won the Prix de la langue française in France. Still one of the author's most successful books, *La belle bête* presents an unforgettable world of hate and ugliness, miraculously redeemed through the love shared by an ugly girl and a blind man. Her early works are those of an adolescent rebelling against injustice, and thus her second novel, *Tête blanche* (1960), is a surrealistic portrait of a nasty, sadistic juvenile delinquent, marked by moments of ineffable tenderness. Included in what Marie-Claire Blais calls the "writings of my youth" are: *Le jour est noir* (1962), a description of the joys and disappointments of a first love affair; *Les voyageurs sacrés* (1962), a poetic dialogue suggesting that the only victory over impossible love must come from art; and *Pays voilés et existence* (1964), poems that reveal to us the "inner country" of premature death, suicide and illness.

Besides *La belle bête*, the most outstanding book from this initial period in Marie-Claire Blais' career is *Une saison dans la vie d'Emmanuel* (1965) which won not only the Prix France-Québec but also the very prestigious Prix Médicis in France. Grandmother Antoinette and Jean-le-Maigre will always remain key characters in Quebec literature. Thanks to them, we plunge into a novel of remarkable power and depth, a haunting satire of the old messianic civilisation of French Canada. Here the novelist reveals her penchant for turning myths on their end: purity becomes impurity, chastity is transformed into onanism, piety into heresy, tolerance into alcoholism, and innocence into crime.

Succeeding chapters from Blais' "writings of youth" include: *L'insoumise* (1966), the diary of a broken family; *David Sterne* (1967), the story of a former seminary student who is struggling against urban violence and a terminal illness; and *L'exécution* (1968), a play in which three seminary students kill one of their classmates, thus revealing "the monster that lies within each of us, ready to awaken at any time" (p.85).

The publication of a trilogy dealing with the life of Pauline Archange indicated a new direction in Marie-Claire Blais' writings, as she turns increasingly towards the life of adults living in the city. The first volume, *Manuscrits de Pauline Archange*, which won the Governor General's Award, marks a transition from the world of childhood to the adult world. As a ten-year-old girl, Pauline Archange describes the atrocities of life in the convent, the cruelty of her parents, and her sexual awakening. In the two succeeding installments, *Vivre, vivre* (1969) and *Les apparences* (1970), Pauline is growing older. These are the years of the second World War, and *Vivre, vivre* can be viewed as a kind of sequel to Gabrielle Roy's *Bonheur d'occasion*, transformed by the violence of dreams. This marks an important step in the career of Marie-Claire Blais: for the first time, tenderness wins out over hate; the subject too changes, with the author going down into the street and painting striking portraits of ordinary people overwhelmed by work. *Vivre, vivre* is a superb novel; together with *La belle bête, Une saison dans la vie d'Emmanuel* and *Une liaison parisienne*, it is among my favourite of her books.

Le loup (1972) explores a side of city life with which Marie-Claire Blais shows an increasing fascination: the world of homosexuals, in this case the *loups* (wolves) — self-centred, narcissistic gay men. However, as with Michel Tremblay's play, *Hosanna*, what is really being analysed is the life of couples in general, their problems of non-communication, their unique "mythologies," and their "unfathomable needs and fantasies" (p.184).

Montreal again provides the backdrop for *Un Joualon-ais, sa joualonie* (1973), published in France under the title *A coeur joual*. Here Marie-Claire Blais shows her ability to write an adventure novel, although poetry and dream sequences also play an important role. The novel takes place in a variety of different milieux: taverns, gay bars, the world of transvestites, bourgeois society, Marxists, working-class people, separatists and federalists, strikers and feminists. *Fièvre et autres textes dramatiques* (1975), dealing with such familiar themes as social inequality and overweening ambition, also demonstrates the author's ability to write radio dramas involving a good deal of suspense.

Une liaison parisienne, published in 1975, is a captivating novel about a young Québécois novelist and his stay in Paris. A number of different elements serve to hold the reader's attention: an indictment of class consciousness and all forms of discrimination; a caricature of the French aristocracy; the light-hearted style; a cat, Victor, who is the incarnation of a snobbish school-mistress; and grandiose descriptions of life in Paris. Two plays written for television, *L'océan* and *Murmures* (1977), deal with the role of the writer and the omnipresence of death. In *Les nuits de l'underground* (1978), Marie-Claire Blais introduces the reader to "a whole group of women who are part of the homosexual community (and thus the community of all human beings, marked by the same universal forms of suffering)" (p.180). This agreeably Proustian novel, in which Paris is juxtaposed with Montreal, conveys the full flavour of both cities and at the same time presents the reader with a world based on the memories of profoundly human and sensual women. *Le sourd dans la ville* (1981) is a collage of tragic monologues in which the author comes to grips with death. *Visions d'Anna* (1982), a sequel or extension of *Le sourd dans la ville*, is a portrait of adolescents rebelling against injustice and tormented by imminent death caused by sickness, pollution, wars, crime and old age. Anna's thoughts and obsessions express a concern for social inequalities, whether these happen to be found in Thetford Mines, Asbestos or the Third World. Preoccupied with "the destructive mechanisms of our time," Marie-Claire Blais "confronts the solitude, the exasperation of destiny." Although *Visions d'Anna* is clearly the most socially engaged of Blais' novels, its success stems less from its metaphysical uneasiness than from its technique: the incantatory, natural rhythm of the sentences, and the "visions," flash-backs, obsessions and images that structure her characters' lives. *Visions d'Anna* is the "anarchy of the imagination in a momentary triumph over the empty values of society." In *Pierre ou la guerre du printemps 81* (1984), an adolescent rebels against the violence of our world by rejecting everything: family, Quebec, and social values. Pierre's response to the absurdity of existence is to join a motorcycle gang and flee.

With all the different facets of Marie-Claire Blais' literary world running through my mind (all those characters I'd come to know, all those situations I'd experienced), I went off to my scheduled interview with the author in a Montreal bar. Marie-Claire Blais does not like to give interviews, and this is not surprising: interviews are often intimidating and are always incomplete. My only intention was to try to share with her my experiences as a reader. I discovered her to be a warm, welcoming person, and thus began our conversation in a downtown bar.

* * *

D.S. — The characters in your novels like to read. They often refer to Balzac, Baudelaire, Dostoevsky, Hugo, Kafka, Nelligan, Proust, Rimbaud and Chekhov. Is there a particular French or Québécois author you're especially fond of?

M.-C. B. — Among the ones you've mentioned, I think Balzac has been enormously important for me, and also Proust. I've read a great deal of non-French literature as well. The whole of Russian literature is very impressive for Quebec writers, who share a very similar emotional outlook. I really enjoy reading. A writer has to be aware of literature. It's the source of our lives, the source of our inspiration, because we have to know how our ancestors, how previous generations, saw the world.

D.S. — Who are the Quebec writers you admire?

M.-C. B. — I'm very impressed by writers like Gabrielle Roy, Anne Hébert, Réjean Ducharme — people who have been able to keep up a steady production as the years go by. Actually, there are a number of them. I'm also fascinated by the work of Hubert Aquin. Our literature is very rich.

D.S. — Could you explain your own conception of literature?

M.-C. B. — For most people who write, writing is primarily a passion, something that is necessary to go on living. Also it's a way of expressing a vision of the world; it's a very intimate vision, but one that's quite real, since it deals with aspects of universal reality. I've been writing now for twenty years and I feel my way of writing has become increasingly intransigent, as has my way of discovering people. Writing is a need, a desire to communicate, punctuated by periods of reflection and silence. Writing isolates and torments you. Sometimes you have to put your pen aside, observe people and live among them.

D.S. — Your books must really cling to you. The act of writing must be an occupation that lasts almost 24 hours a day, because of the psychological preparation and the period of observation that are no doubt necessary before a book can be created.

M.-C. B. — Yes, that's the opinion of a number of writers I know. Writing causes me tremendous anxiety. It never leaves me with much inner peace. Since you have to be able to understand everything you're going to describe in a fictional universe, you also have to understand it in real life. You have to get close to it; you have to have that awareness of people and things. Sometimes it's very difficult. Musicians and painters have other ways of functioning. I have the impression their way of working leaves them a good deal more freedom.

D.S. — *La belle bête*, like a number of your novels, takes place in a setting that is not clearly specified. The family lives on a farm somewhere in Quebec. Why do you tend to like neutral settings, unconnected with any particular place?

M.-C. B. — Maybe that was a time in my life when I wanted most of all to be a poet. Also, as I told you, I was extremely influenced by the poetry of Anne Hébert, as well as by Cocteau's novels. Furthermore, I had a feeling that I knew life through knowledge. I had a sort of slightly crazy conception of the world and people, and I was describing them in story form, not in terms of pure reality. At the time, things were so explosive for me that I felt I had to describe this explosion of feelings and terror and all sorts of things I could see before me, even if it took the form of poetic echoes. However, it was a somewhat bastardized way of seeing the world.

D.S. — Do you think your novels are more realistic nowadays than they were ten or so years ago?

M.-C. B. — You might say that, although there's always lots of room for dreaming and relaxing a little. Poetry is part of the novel. I don't believe the two are all that different. Right now, for me there's no great separation or barrier between things that belong in poems and things having to do with analyzing people. However, for a long time I was bothered by the problem of trying to blend two literary genres into one. You can find examples of this combination of genres in the writings of Virginia Woolf, Cocteau, Anne Hébert, Réjean Ducharme and Monique Bosco. They're people who have worked with both poetry and the novel, combining them to such a degree that you find both genres at the same time.

D.S. — Your novels are more like long stories than novels. They're dominated by the forces of enchantment and nightmare. Even the plots have something allegorical or unreal about them. The atmosphere in your novels is often reminiscent of mediaeval paintings, like Hieronymus Bosch, for instance. In the final analysis, what fascinates me in your work is its impressionistic side.

M.-C. B. — I think what's involved is a sort of frenzied or upside-down realism, a mixture of all the different realities.

D.S. — In *La belle bête*, Louise's dandified lover, Lanz, is a personification of hypocritical love in which the woman is exploited. As early as 1959, then, you were interested in what happens to women-as-objects, which you refer to in the novel as "doll-women."

M.-C. B. — Yes, I was very much interested in that. In my first book, which has all the faults of adolescence — there's an abrupt, wild side to it, with everything seen in terms of black and white — the repressed woman is more an expression of feminine vanity than a real flesh-and-blood woman. On the other hand, what is important and real is her passion for her son's beauty. That part was very deeply felt: the passion between two people, involving both the soul and the body. It's this quest for the visible and the invisible that is constantly plaguing me.

D.S. — I wonder why there are so many marginal characters in your writings, so many people who are sick, insane, blind or epileptic, suffering from tuberculosis, cancer, and so on?

M.-C. B. — For me, that's the world as it is. It's not only literature; the world is like that. It's the human condition, and I don't think people should be afraid of talking and writing about it. Life and death are always with us in all sorts of forms. You can't say we're here on earth to be completely happy. There's nothing to prove that to us, except ourselves, our own personal attempts in which we're very much alone.

D.S. — Why do you like to give nicknames to your characters? I'm thinking of Tête Blanche (White Head), La Belle Bête (the Beautiful Beast), Jean-le-Maigre (Skinny John), etc. Is it to reinforce the unreal, symbolic atmosphere?

M.-C. B. — Sometimes it's by accident, as in the case of Jean-le-Maigre; there's something very seductive in his name, because he's perceived by others as being skinny, but not by himself. In the same book (*Une saison dans la vie d'Emmanuel*), Le Septième (The Seventh) is simply the seventh one in the family; something always puts him far down on the family ladder, even the human ladder.

D.S. — In *Tête blanche* you created a teenager who hopes to become a writer. You have an impressive list of writer characters: Stéphane (*L'exécution*), Josué (*Le jour est noir*), Paul (*L'insoumise*), Romaine (*Vivre, vivre*), Miguel (*Les voyageurs sacrés*), Ti-Pit and the whole group of writers in *Un Joualonais*, Mathieu and Madame d'Argenti in *Une liaison parisienne*, the father and François in *L'océan*, Louise in *Les nuits de l'underground*, and Alexandre in *Visions d'Anna*. For these characters, writing is a form of deliverance or salvation; thanks to words and the liberating power of speech, your writer characters can temporarily triumph over boredom and misery. Has that been your own experience with writing?

M.-C. B. — Yes, I think you're right. Writing is a salvation, a deliverance. The world of Dostoevsky is described as being written by an orderly madman, a lunatic who has put order into his ravings. However, the apocalypse he was carrying within him was enormous, and letting it out must have brought him unbelievable release.

D.S. — Writing is almost like therapy.

M.-C. B. — It's a violent form of therapy because you have to do violence to yourself; you have to learn a very hard craft. But there are moments when it's a tremendous joy, even if it only lasts for a few moments.

D.S. — The youngster Tête Blanche is preoccupied with God. He asks the following question: "Does He exist? If He does, why does He let people suffer?" What sort of religious attitude or message do you want to convey through your characters?

M.-C. B. — Once again, *Tête blanche* is a book I wrote when I was extremely young. The questions which were perhaps radical at that time are a lot more nuanced now. I don't think I want to convey any message whatsoever; I simply want to describe states of mind that, for me, change from one year to the next. Seeking God is certainly part of the adolescent experience. However, the problems of justice and injustice I see around me cause me a great deal more concern than any metaphysical or philosophical considerations.

D.S. — Your characters are fascinated by the play of light and shadow. These two images form the basis of your symbolism and seem to represent the human condition. Do you often think of this visual side in your writing?

M.-C. B. — Painting has played an important role in my life. I find that painters go perhaps further than writers, especially in portraits. That business about light and shadow is no doubt connected to the period when I was reading the Bible, in which it's often a question of the children of light and the children of darkness.

D.S. — As you know, beginning in the Fifties, Quebec poets became interested in the land, in political and social concerns, in other words what Paul Chamberland called "founding the territory." With the *Parti pris* writers in the Sixties, and writers like Jacques Godbout and Hubert Aquin, the novelists also started writing specifically about Quebec. In your case, however, you've chosen to speak in a different register, using inner voices. Was there even a time when you were tempted by what Jacques Brault, Gaston Miron and Paul Chamberland were doing?

M.-C. B. — I have a great deal of admiration for Miron, Brault and all those poets, but I'm not seeking the same things as they are. We're different, that's all. I think we have to be able to live together with our differences. In a land of writers, you have to support one another. I respect their struggles and their quests, which are every bit as valid as my own. On the other hand, although I don't present the notion of a country in the same way Miron does, I am very much interested in describing our big cities, and even the smaller cities. Seeking out people who have been crushed by the city interests me. The city keeps me alive and stimulated. I dream of translating this reality into words, of describing the extraordinary swarms of people moving around in our cities. Montreal is a city I find enormously fascinating. The more I know it, the more I'm attracted by the richness of its inhabitants.

For me, the land or country is the cosmos, the world. The land is a refuge, something familial, and for that reason

Quebec is very dear to me. But even if we became autonomous, we'd absolutely have to open our borders. We'd have to become a land for other peoples, welcoming all the lands of the world.

D.S. — When you were writing *Une saison dans la vie d'Emmanuel*, to what extent did you intend to create a satire of the repressive and hypocritical aspects of French-Canadian society?

M.-C. B. — I don't know if I was really attempting to do that. It's a book that was written very instinctively, without a great deal of intellectual awareness. It's a book I wrote because that's how I felt it and saw it; I was especially attracted by the problems of suffering and poverty, the struggle for survival. In any case, the family is one of my major preoccupations because it allows you, within a group like the one in *Une saison*, to study a number of different characters. Today I'm keeping on in the same vein; I study families and cities, since a city is also a family.

D.S. — In *L'insoumise*, Paul often talks of running to a mirror and looking at the reflection of his face. Why do you have this obsession with mirrors, which is apparent in your other novels as well?

M.-C. B. — With that character, I was describing a boy whose self-image is on the verge of disintegrating. He's trying very hard to discover himself through his body. He's a person you could find here in the street, or in a university. He's someone whose fate is very fragile, a young student who is just beginning to make the most important discoveries in his life. Perhaps the mirror acted as a revelation of the animal world within him.

D.S. — Why did you decide to write a play, *L'exécution*, after having had so much success with your novels?

M.-C. B. — I want to try everything. I don't want to be locked into a single literary genre, because writing is an occupation that requires you to develop your talents in every possible area. The theatre is very interesting because it puts me into contact with other people, with actors, and this draws me out from my isolation as a writer. I really enjoyed working with the people at the Théâtre du Rideau-Vert. The actors' world is so much more reassuring than our own. Writing is a much more solitary occupation.

D.S. — Why did you dedicate *Les manuscrits de Pauline Archange* to Réjean Ducharme?

M.-C. B. — He was kind enough to dedicate a book to me. I'm very fond of him. On a personal level he's quite exquisite and full of imagination, and he's also very loyal to the people he chooses as friends. As far as talent is concerned, he's in a class by himself.

D.S. — A number of critics have stated that snow is one of your favourite symbols. Some see it as a source of dreamlike happiness, while others view it as a sort of muck that drags your characters down into misery and poverty. What does snow suggest for you?

M.-C. B. — We live in a land where a regimen of cold followed by personal renewal at the end of the winter plays a central role in our lives. It could be said that the poetic imagery of all our writers has been tremendously influenced by this. It's very pronounced in Gabrielle Roy and Anne Hébert. I've noticed that in Russian literature the role of snow and cold is also very important.

D.S. — Reverend Father Benjamin Robert, on the whole a rather likeable man who has a strong social conscience — which proves that it's wrong to accuse you of being anti-clerical — expresses a thought that seems to me essential for understanding your work: "It's sometimes necessary to show a killer that he too is loved, to plunge in one stroke through to the durable centre of our prejudices, for we are prevented from understanding him by our distance, by the superiority of our pride over his humiliation...good and evil are now different things for me…They are life and suffering. Evil is our injustice towards life!" (*Vivre, vivre*, p.79, p.167). Is one of your goals to show your readers that criminals deserve attention, that in a sense we have all had a hand in creating them?

M.-C. B. — Benjamin Robert is not a conventional priest. He's a priest of the kind you might see nowadays, fairly involved in the world and confronted with the problems of life; he's a man who had lost control over what was good and evil in religious terms. That must be an impossible struggle for a man or woman of God. Benjamin Robert has a personality that really intrigues me. His affection for the young criminal is a bit like my uneasiness about the world of crime in general. It's true, as you said a while ago, that everything is part of us. We can't simply put aside the things that are bothering us, that cause us suffering and torment and fear. If someone robs us or tries to kill us, we are perhaps not responsible ourselves, but at some point someone *is* responsible. Those are moral problems that haunt me tremendously.

D.S. — The numerous homosexual relationships described in *Le loup* raise questions that concern everyone: the problem of loving, or what you refer to as "the doomed couple" (p.203). Is this how you would like readers to view the homosexual and lesbian couples so frequently found in your most recent novels?

M.-C. B. — Yes, I think so, especially in the case of *Le loup*, which was written before *Les nuits de l'underground*. It was a sort of moral portrayal of a number of different passions, but in a world that is so much a minority that people don't talk about it. They prefer to ignore it, but it seems to me absolutely inherent to all other forms of reality. Also, in the case of *Le loup*, there is the suffering of several generations of homosexuals. The young ones don't suffer too much, but the older generation, who were the pioneers and protesters, suffered a great deal just to exist. In that sense, all the struggles for personal rights and the rights of minorities are extremely important. We can't hope to create a society without harmony; it's vital.

D.S. — In *Une saison* you could have had your characters speak in *joual*. Even though it was a working-class family, you chose to have them speak a neutral kind of language, which in a sense removes them from any local sense of reality. In *Un Joualonais*, as well as in *Les nuits de l'underground*, you've clearly opted for colloquial Québécois French. Why did you make this change, and how did you find the experience of writing in *joual*?

M.-C. B. — I wrote *Un Joualonais* in France, and I was very nostalgic for Quebec. I used to go back to Montreal several times a year, and I'd spend a lot of time studying the characters described in the novel. I encountered almost all of them in one tavern or another, and I listened to them, but they didn't talk exactly as in the novel. Their way of talking was rougher, perhaps, and with my being in France, I found that there was so much colour and so much Rabelaisian charm that I wanted to do a sort of satire, an affectionate satire, of this race of people I could view from afar with greater objectivity. That's how the book was written.

D.S. — One of your characters in *Un Joualonais* makes fun of a professor, a literary critic who is looking for the principal (phallic) fixations in a writer's work. Does this mean that you yourself distrust literary criticism, or at least a certain kind of criticism?

M.-C. B. — There is a form of extremely brilliant, intelligent and penetrating criticism which inspires the reader to read. However, there's also the opposite kind, critics who rip things apart, who don't listen to the writer at all, and who make our lives more difficult. Criticism can play a very important role, especially in the case of a first novel, which is always the great hurdle for the writer.

Criticism is an art which can be very creative and which can create a new audience for works that are silent and difficult. Here I'm obviously speaking of gifted critics who have an intuition for literature. In Quebec, the criticism is very severe. You have to have the strength to resist it. You mustn't be like Virginia Woolf, whose spirit was destroyed each time one of her books was published because she found the criticism too cruel.

D.S. — Is writing radio drama the same thing as writing drama for the theatre? Was it largely the same experience?

M.-C. B. — Working for radio is very interesting because it lets you unite two different art forms. The incantation of the word and voice can produce results that are very successful artistically. It's a new form of writing. You can do immense numbers of things with it, especially here in Canada where we have such good facilities.

D.S. — In your writings for radio, one feels much more directly than in your novels a revolt against the rich and against social categories in general. Is this because you've evolved towards such an approach or is it because, as a medium of expression, radio is better suited to direct denunciations?

M.-C. B. — Radio is a very direct medium that makes such denunciations possible. Immediately — you can hear it — a radio script is more direct and substantial as a means of artistic communication. That's why you get the impression there are more denunciations. The word is there in the room with you.

   I was lucky enough to meet some very inventive television people, like Jean Faucher, for instance. We worked together on *L'océan*, a story about the difficulties an old writer has in living with his loneliness. My contacts with the actors were a very enriching experience for me. *La belle bête* was choreographed, and this too was a fusion of the arts, which is something I firmly believe in.

D.S. — The passage in *Une liaison parisienne* describing the reactions of a young Québécois living in France are hilarious. Such humour is rare in your work. Is the story of Mathieu Lelièvre also to some extent your own story, when you were living in Paris?

M.-C. B. — You could call it my own story, although it contains a great deal of self-criticism. It's a stupider version of me, but there is some truth in what you say.

D.S. — I was particularly struck by one passage in *Les nuits de l'underground:*

> She didn't love Lali; what she loved in her was beauty, the perfection of art. But what left her at a loss was the realization that art everywhere is living and carnal, that what she had seen from afar, out of danger, in the reassuring comfort of museums, was living and trembling right there beside her, in her very life...and that living work of art was Lali. (p.20)

Are writers destined to view people and things as if they were works of art?

M.-C. B. — They are very often prisoners of the creative world from which they take their inspiration. I think, however, that writers are often able to forget the problems of being a writer. They can have fun, even if their sensibilities are a bit too tender. It's quite difficult for them. Amusement isn't as simple for them because they can never completely forget their role as a writer. But there is also their freedom of imagination, which brings with it a tremendous amount of joy, even outside their work.

D.S. — Would you care to talk a bit about *Le sourd dans la ville* and *Visions d'Anna?*

M.-C. B. — *Le sourd dans la ville* is a fairly complex novel. It deals with a family in Montreal, and the poetic world plays an important role in it. The problems of crime, loneliness and death come up again, this time involving even greater violence. I spent four years thinking about the book and it took me a year to write it. It's a novel that may well determine the direction of my work in the future. The deaf person ("le sourd") in the title represents death itself.

   Visions d'Anna deals with crime in children. I tried to connect this particular problem with the crises and anguish of our society at large.

D.S. — What sorts of books can we look forward to in the future?

M.-C. B. — I'm working on a book which will talk about my life in the United States in the Sixties and Seventies. I want to revive the people I knew, the pacifists and the artists.

Jacques Godbout:
Transforming Reality

Distortions, the title of a film by Jacques Godbout, seems a particularly apt description of his entire literary output. Both as a writer and as a film-maker, Godbout shows a penchant for transforming and transmuting reality — for "distorting" it. This is readily apparent in his film work. His suspense movies, for instance, focus on the sensationalistic and melodramatic sides of Quebec culture, while his documentary films provide a highly personal, contentious view of artistic and journalistic circles.

As a writer, Jacques Godbout first emerged as a poet; here we see him perfecting his favourite weapons of irony and fantasy. His six novels, with all the hallucinatory, dizzying effects of distorting mirrors, have had a profound influence on Quebec literature. The transformations began as early as 1962, with the publication of his first novel, *L'aquarium*. This was the time of Quebec's "Quiet Revolution," and in many ways the whole world seemed to be in a state of turmoil. In these circumstances, Godbout's choice of setting was a highly unusual one for a Quebec writer: a tropical land where the bored Whites spend their time drinking while a revolution rumbles about them, as the Blacks prepare to set their country free from the shackles of colonialism. Algeria had just won its independence, the Black countries were working towards it, and Quebec was seeking its own solutions. All these images and realities are blurred together in *L'aquarium*, where the reader discovers not only a new set of themes in Quebec literature, but also a highly original style.

With *Le couteau sur la table*, in 1965, another "distortion" takes form. English Canada has a name, an identity. For Godbout, its name is Patricia, a young Americanized woman who sings "Eeny, meeny, miney, moe, catch a Nigger by the toe." However, appearances are deceiving. Quebec still hasn't found a name; it is as anonymous as the "Narrator" himself. The title, *Knife on the Table*, is a sign that Godbout wants to lacerate the name "French Canadian" and replace it by "Québécois." Thus, finally, begins the slow process of creating a genuine name for his people.

By 1967, Jacques Godbout has had his fill of politics. *Salut Galarneau!* shows him in the company of a true friend, François Galarneau, owner of a hot dog and French-fries stand. Godbout, who admires Galarneau's vitality, lets him talk, learning in the process that the use of "Ban Roll-on" and "Florient" disinfectant spray doesn't necessarily turn a person into an American. A new image starts to take shape in the mirror of the imagination: the image of a Quebec writer who accepts his identity as a North American and uses it as the basis for both his life and his writings.

Then followed five years of silence. There were still people who hadn't understood, who hadn't assumed their own identity, who tended to confuse themselves with the French from France. Pierre Beaudry, who wrote a language column in *La Presse*, went so far as to claim that Félix-Antoine Savard's classic novel, *Menaud, Maître-Draveur*, should actually have been entitled *Menaud, Maître-Flotteur*, to respect the "purity" of the French language.[1] This was more than Godbout could take. *D'amour, P.Q.*, in 1972, shows how a snobbish writer gets put in his place by a witty, clever secretary. Enough is enough!

In 1976, Jacques Godbout turns into a story-teller, and the distortions he produces are very beautiful indeed. Quebec is an island, *L'isle au Dragon* or *Dragon Island*. The Americans are buying it up in bits and pieces, and the Québécois just sit back and do nothing about it. If Uncle Sam wants to build an atomic dump site, let's just take the money and leave him to it! Not Godbout, though; he unsheathes his sword and saves the island from the clutches of the ogre.

In 1981, the Parti Québécois is in power, having won two elections and lost the Referendum. This time the distortion takes a comic turn. Do the Québécois have two heads, one French-Canadian and the other Québécois? One English-speaking and one French-speaking? Has a bicephalous monster landed in the very centre of Quebec? On November 4, 1981, an invitation showed Charles-et-François, the two-headed protagonist of *Les têtes à Papineau*, inviting Godbout's friends and fans to the launching of his latest novel. I was there, and so were the actors: an elderly man was pushing a baby carriage through the crowd of bewildered guests. Needless to say, it made a rather bizarre family: two old parents wheeling around a plastic baby. Was the doll, by any chance, a reincarnation of the two-headed Papineau?

On December 23, 1981, I visited Jacques Godbout at his home in Outremont, where he had been living for 15 years. Going into the living room, I noticed a magnificent collection of porcelain dolls. As Godbout picked up one or two of them to show me, I thought of the doll at the launching: another distortion. Since I couldn't film the image before me, I filed it away in my mind. Then I turned on the tape recorder and the interview began.[2]

* * *

D.S. — You have never talked very much about your childhood, your parents, or the area you grew up in.

J.G. — I do talk about that in *Souvenir-Shop*, which was recently published by the Éditions de l'Hexagone. As for the rest, I think there are large swatches of it in *Les têtes à Papineau* as well as in my other novels, especially in *Salut Galarneau!* However, I've always wanted to keep a certain distance between my family, parents, childhood, and my writings. I'm not a journalist; I write novels. That I was born in Côte-des-Neiges, that I lived in the city of Joliette when my father was the director of a tobacco cooperative, that I came back to Montreal during the war and that because of the war we lived in the east end of Montreal, that I knew the territory of Claude Jasmin, Hubert Aquin and Michel Tremblay because I lived on the same streets as they did, that later I went back to Côte-des-Neiges and studied with the Jesuits at Brébeuf College, which was the most prestigious private school in French Canada, that right now I live in Outremont and also the Eastern Townships or the Lower St. Lawrence in the summer — all this indicates a certain level of freedom in my life. However, I don't think it has any relation whatsoever to my writing. If there is a connection, it's only as a background.

D.S. — It's true your childhood isn't very apparent in your writings. It's only after your adolescence that you start taking your inspiration from actual life experiences.

J.G. — Not really! I think I take my inspiration — the term is always a bit vague or suspect — from my surroundings in the two or three years before I write a novel. From one year to another and one book to another, I'm inspired by the situation I find myself in at that particular moment, although this obviously takes me back to things I've actually experienced, things from my adolescence or childhood, or even from my adult life. If I think about *Les têtes à Papineau*, for example, it talks not only about myself but also about my father and my son, or my wife and daughter. At the same time, though, it's neither I nor they; it's the people of Quebec, especially as I saw them at the time of the Referendum: torn apart, not knowing what they wanted, rightly or wrongly.

I don't talk about my life. If I'd chosen to tell the story of my life, I'd have done so in my first novel, *L'aquarium*, but it's quite the opposite. At that time I decided to tell a story I'd experienced and reacted to, but which took place somewhere else and had no connections with my own life.

D.S. — It came from your experience at that particular moment.

J.G. — Yes, and it was also my memories of a few months spent in Mexico and the Caribbean, a long three-year stint in Africa, and 20 years of living under Maurice Duplessis. In the end, these things formed a book, but the book made no claim of being a biography. Any attempt at writing is an attempt to mask, transform and transmute things, not to tell them as they are. For example, in *Le couteau sur la table*, the description of the big house where Patricia and the narrator are going to live together, bears no resemblance whatsoever to any house I've ever lived in myself; actually, it comes from a picture of a house pasted inside the lid of a cedar chest, in which my mother used to store bedspreads with mothballs every spring and take them out again in the fall. The whole process of suddenly opening that cedar chest, with all its smells and that pen drawing of a Victorian house, helped me to write about Patricia. In that sense, the house doesn't have anything to do with an actual house but has everything to do with the business of transforming memories: sounds, smells and people. For me, writing means changing things.

D.S. — That must imply a break in chronology.

J.G. — It means breaking up the chronology and breaking up the representation. I don't write abstract, non-figurative novels because that bores me. But I don't write realistic novels, either. I keep one foot in each camp, as it were.

D.S. — You did your M.A. thesis on Rimbaud. Does that mean you were more interested in poetry than in the novel? In fact, your first four books are collections of poetry.

J.G. — The first thesis topic I proposed was Jean-Paul Sartre, but Canon Sideleau, who at that time was Dean of the Faculty of Arts at the University of Montreal, rejected it with the pretext that Sartre wasn't a Catholic. So, I asked myself, "Okay, who can I get them to swallow?" I thought that perhaps

Rimbaud, who was a poet I liked and who may possibly have converted on his death-bed in the hospital at Marseille, might be acceptable to Canon Sideleau.

The poetry I was familiar with at that time was more or less narrative, ironic poetry, like that of Queneau or Prévert. I wasn't much attracted by, shall we say, the poetry of René Char or other such poets who inspired my classmates. Basically, I had turned to poetry as a school of writing. I learned to write through my poems. Writing a poem is like writing a song or a short narrative.

D.S. — After finishing your M.A., you and your wife went off to Ethiopia, and then the Sudan, Greece, Egypt, France, and so on. Did these travels have a determining effect on your decision to become a novelist and film-maker?

J.G. — I don't know. I think, for me, travelling has always provided the most beautiful moments in my life; if I'd had the choice, I think I'd have become a pilot or a sailor so I could keep going around the world. I like to go away, travel, discover other people and live in other places. I'm a born traveller. There are people who like to stay put, people who say they have roots; like carrots, potatoes, turnips and cabbages, they probably are better off in their own garden. Personally, I don't have any roots in that sense. It's more as if I had roller skates on my feet; I get tremendous pleasure from moving around the world. It's incredible how much I enjoy being abroad; I enjoy being at home, too, but always on the move. No doubt I'm frightened that if I ever stop moving, I'll grow roots or be killed by somebody.

D.S. — After living in Africa, you worked first for an advertising agency and then as a translator. Your writings show an obsession with advertising, which you seem to view as a world that is rich in hidden meanings and information about our civilisation.

J.G. — Yes, because for me advertising is basically a perversion of poetry. It's very much a twentieth-century phenomenon, although obviously it began in the nineteenth. There are a lot of great creators in advertising. Speaking of things in a metaphoric way is a literary activity, and advertising speaks of things metaphorically. Therefore, there's no basic difference between a literary writer and an advertising writer. Advertising is the dominant form of literature.

D.S. — But you don't like the message it conveys.

J.G. — Advertising is literature in the service of the priest, the prince, the Church or the object. Basically, it's the most servile form of literature imaginable. Even when I was involved in it, I perceived it as that. When I was working for an advertising agency, I used to suffer every day from being forced to think up ads that would sell General Electric appliances, natural gas, Maxwell House coffee or Five Roses flour. Every day for a whole year I made up a two-minute ad for Five Roses flour; that's the equivalent of a book! You can't imagine the unbelievable amount of energy and imagination I spent selling flour. I was writing wholesome literature in the most literal sense of the word, and I don't think I've ever forgiven advertising for taking up all that space. There's also the fact that nowadays advertising takes up so much imaginative space. What the children of all social classes have in common is not certain literary stories, not certain songs or even children's books, but simply jingles, little ditties, advertising images. At least when we were small, we had the fables of Hans Christian Anderson; now all they share is "Bud-Bud-Bud-Weiser" and "Snap, Crackle and Pop."

D.S. — In the case of Budweiser, the ad-makers have managed to change the Québécois' taste.

J.G. — It's because the Québécois are Americans. That ad was very crafty, coming right after the Referendum.

D.S. — In 1960 you began working for the National Film Board as a script-writer and producer, and in 1969 you became the NFB's director of French-language productions. What attracted you to the world of film?

J.G. — Nothing! Or rather, it was a question of luck, accident, a job offer. I got into film because I was with the magazine

Liberté, and André Belleau was with both *Liberté* and the NFB, in the personnel department. They were looking for someone to do French adaptations of English films. I remember that the poets Fernand Ouellette, Michel van Schendel and Gilles Hénault had also applied. Since I was the only one of the four who didn't really want the job, of course I ended up getting it.

D.S. – The more than 20 important films you've made can be divided into three categories: the detective movies, the most famous being *IXE-13* and *La gammick*; the "engaged" or "political" films, including *Feu l'objectivité*, which deals with journalistic objectivity, *Distortions*, which compares the news media in Africa and Quebec, *Le monologue Nord-Sud*, which looks at rich countries and poor countries, and *Comme en Californie*, which shows the influence the American West Coast has had on lifestyles in Quebec; and the cultural films, including *Paul-Émile Borduas* and *Deux épisodes dans la vie d'Hubert Aquin*. Your films have won prizes in a number of international film festivals, including Chicago, Italy, Argentina, France, and Toronto. As a film-maker, you are deeply marked by your temperament as a writer. Your films are highly stylized. *La gammick* could have been a novel; the film on Aquin would have made a great short story or novella.

J.G. – It's very generous of you to talk about "important" films. My films are all acceptable, and when you put them all together they may make a certain amount of sense. When you're a writer, you know to what extent you can influence writing and keep changing a manuscript until it becomes the most you can possibly give, materially speaking, in a literary sense. When it comes to films, however, you have to keep in mind that this involves teamwork. Each of my films has depended on the work of a certain number of very important associates. Florian Sauvageau played an essential role in the films about the media, for example. In other cases, it was the editor, Werner Nold. Sometimes it's the co-producer, such as Pierre Turgeon with *La gammick*. In *IXE-13*, the set-designer, Claude Lafortune, played a key role, as did the musician François Dompierre. In that sense, there's no comparison with literature. In the one case, you're responsible for everything, including the stupidities; in the other case, you can't say "It's my work," except if you're a genius like Orson Welles or Fellini. Can you imagine where Francis Mankiewicz would be if he hadn't had Réjean Ducharme to work with?

D.S. — *Derrière l'image* (1977), *Feu l'objectivité* (1979) and *Distortions* (1981) form a triptych about the big guns in the media. *Distortions* is an indictment of the organizations that control the flow of news: AP, UPI, Reuters and AFP. You seem worried about the effects of media monopolies, both as a film-maker and as a novelist, since the false images propagated by the news indoctrinate us in spite of ourselves.

J.G. — I'm even more interested in the fact that information or news is a kind of transformation of reality, and also that I find in the news the same sorts of connections I make in my novels. The only thing I'd like people to be aware of — and that's why I made the three films you mentioned — is that there's almost no difference, except in terms of objectives, between writing a novel, that is transforming reality, and writing a news report, that is shedding light on some aspect of reality. In a certain way, it's all fiction. I'm so fascinated by people's capacities for mixing fiction and reality that I tried to play around with that in *Les têtes à Papineau*. On the back cover of the book, I spoke about the Dionne quintuplets, whom everybody knows about, and Charles and François Papineau, whom very few knew about. Because of that sort of presentation, there were a number of people who believed, at least for half the book and sometimes the whole thing, that Charles and François Papineau actually existed. I wasn't trying to play a trick on the reader, but rather I wanted to play along with him, by saying that there's a very fine line between fiction and reality. The experience of my Papineau is quite believable; he never existed, but he could have. Throughout the whole novel, I tried to write a book people would find convincing; I was talking about a two-headed monster, but it's a believable monster.

D.S. — As it happens, *Distortions* is a film in which we see that the so-called reality of news reports is actually closer to fiction, in that it's an interpretation or transformation of reality.

What was your initial reason for making *Distortions?* For example, what did you expect to discover by having African people talk about us?

J.G. – The same thing they blame us for, I think. They showed they had just as many preconceived ideas as we do. Cultural relations are difficult if you don't stop for a couple of minutes and try to understand another people's culture.

D.S. – That's true. The African reporters talked mostly about what characterizes us in a superficial sense: the MacDonalds, the sex industry, drug use, and homes for the elderly, which would be unthinkable in Africa, where old people are revered for their wisdom. It's the same way our Western journalists present a partial image of Africa: warlike tribes, the women dominated by the men, violence. You say in the film that "as civilisations come into contact, cultures come into conflict." Do you see that as good or bad?

J.G. – It's inevitable.

D.S. – As a creative artist, you've also been active in a number of related professions. I'm thinking here of your activities with the magazine *Liberté*, which you edited for a brief period, of the essential role you played in setting up the Union des écrivains québécois (the Quebec Writers' Union), of which you were the first president, and also of your essay on the deceptive appearance of democracy, *La participation contre la démocratie*.

J.G. – I'm a social animal, and at certain times I actually imagine that if I don't get involved – whether it be with the Lay Movement, the organisations you mentioned, or the Professional Association of Film-Makers in the Sixties – that if I'm not taking an active part in things, nothing will happen. I always need to write on a scrap of paper a constitution or the principal objectives for one thing or another, or a circular for this or that. That's the social animal side to me. It's my way of paying something back to the society which provides me with a fairly good living. I also get a lot of pleasure out of bringing people together around an idea, a goal, or a taste for living and doing things. There are different ways of building. You can build Place Ville-Marie, or you can build the Writers' Union. When we built the Union — I'm thinking of André Major, Pierre Morency, Hubert Aquin, Jacques Brault, Nicole Brossard and Jean-Yves Colette — we built our own building, our own Place Ville-Marie.

D.S. — In 1979-1980, you were writer-in-residence at Carleton University. I know you're rather critical of professors who tear literature apart, reduce it to equations, and decipher it using formalist concepts. What impressions have remained with you from your contacts with the students and professors at Carleton and other places?

J.G. — My impression is that in general the students are generous, open, admiring, occasionally naive, but always anxious to participate in something. It seems to me that the professors are also often generous, but that they're threatened by their colleagues and forced, because of these threats, which come from the institution itself, to structure their courses and organize their teaching in such a way that their particular area cannot be attacked. Thus the professors have developed systems of defense that move them increasingly away from literature, which is the primary object of their studies. I think the ones who are most to be pitied are not the literary critics who say, "My God, we're ending up with a literature ruined by professors who are killing all the poetry in it," but rather the professors themselves, who have been forced to defend themselves by using reductive conceptual tools, whether these be structuralism, Marxism, socio-critical analysis, or the Freudian approach.

D.S. — They move away from the true nature of literature, from spontaneous excursions into the imagination?

J.G. — It's not that. All conceptual tools are useful, but they mustn't be considered as being exclusive. Some people work with wood, others with stone. Personally, I have no wish to criticise the professors, although I do think it's a shame for them. In general, they lose the pleasure of reading, or else they only get pleasure from the critical games they play. Having said this, I should add that there are exceptions in the universities; some men and women there have kept their freedom.

D.S. — Before talking about your literary works, I'd like to ask you a question about your career with *Liberté, L'Actualité, Parti pris, Vie des arts, Lettres françaises,* the now defunct *Le Jour, Cinéma Québec,* and so on. Some 40 of your articles in these and other publications were reprinted in *Le réformiste,* published in 1975. Other articles, especially the ones from *Liberté,* were collected in *Le murmure marchand* (1984), which is an indictment of the "murmurs" of the present-day "Sirens" — the advertising industry. In the manner of an irreverent essayist, you come to the defense of Quebec culture, and at the same time denounce in no uncertain terms the religious and political dogmatism that has been so prevalent in Quebec. The most important article, one that caused considerable repercussions, is surely the essay entitled "Écrire," originally published in *Liberté* in 1971. This is where you define what you refer to as the "texte national," the "national discourse," where you proclaim the necessity, before independence is achieved, of a communal "text." I quote:

> It's all very fine for Quebec literature to spring into life one day in the pink or white pages of a textbook on the History of French Literature; we can munch "madeleine" cookies with Proust, enjoy the company of Gide, cast admiring glances at Michaud, and imitate Simon. Inevitably, however, our roots in Quebec will gradually turn into thick vines, and sooner or later we'll find ourselves locked up in the corral of "la Belle Province," milling around behind the Wailing Wall of Quebec like wild horses destined for Dr Ballard's dogs... Every young writer in Quebec has to realize that there's no way to escape being blackmailed by the Land. As soon as he loses his virginity, he discovers he's not the one who has authored the books bearing his name; in Quebec there's only one Writer: *The People...* A Quebec writer cannot hope to exist

outside the national discourse; he must either participate in our communal project or else find himself in
a void.

Do you think the message from "Écrire" is now dated, even if
independence hasn't been attained?

J.G. — I haven't made a "career" out of being controversial,
because polemics isn't really a career. I think a person is
quite simply endowed with a capacity for indignation which
means that at certain moments, when various things are said
or various things happen, you start to burn with an absolute
desire to respond to them or proclaim something. That's the
impulse behind all those articles, pamphlets, or letters. As
far as "Écrire" is concerned, I was describing the phenomenon of writing in a nationalistic environment, and that hasn't
changed. However, just because I described the phenomenon doesn't mean I approve of it. On the contrary, I seem to
remember saying that being drafted into literary service,
like being drafted for military service, is an idea that makes
me break out in a sweat. It matters very little what the individual decides; it's the readers in a collective sense who give
meaning to things. *Les têtes à Papineau*, which was published
in the fall of 1981, is a book that got caught up in the circumstances of a certain political context. I didn't write it with all
those political dimensions in mind. I did write it as a metaphor, of course; however, it was primarily a novel, and
suddenly it became a political piece. As it turned out, there
were some people — not very many, actually — who attacked
me for writing a pessimistic ending to the novel, as if I'd
been writing a pamphlet. But I wasn't suggesting it as something that would in fact happen! It's simply what happens in
the novel, period. The ideas advanced in "Écrire" haven't
changed a great deal; they're probably in the process of
changing, or will change when public sensibility moves on to
something else. Books that are successful, without necessarily being a literary success, are always those books that give
meaning to the life of the community.

D.S. — Are you saying the public reception of books has to change if we're ever to get beyond the idea of a national discourse?

J.G. — It's not that it *has* to change; it may change, it will change, but it's not the writers who decide, who set out to write a national, communal discourse. That decision belongs to the readers, the people who receive the discourse. If the readers rejected that discourse completely, writers would stop writing it. Only a small minority of writers are prepared to go on describing things that nobody wants to read.

D.S. — We've been talking for an hour already, and we absolutely have to get around to discussing your literary work. Your poetry is marked by a sense of both fantasy and irony, which anticipates the tone of the novels you would write later. Like your prose, your poetry is also engaged in a struggle against people's lethargy.

J.G. — Each of my poems is a sort of very short story. After I wrote poetry, I wrote short-stories, and after the short-stories, I wrote novels. In that sense, you can see a progression in the narrative. I'm not a psychological novelist. I'm an individual who tells stories, but who plays around the characters in order to create various atmospheres and unexpected dimensions in both the plot and the style of writing. I played in the same way in my poems.

D.S. — Well, then, let's talk about your first novel. As soon as *L'aquarium* was published, the critics proclaimed it Quebec's first "nouveau roman." With its blurred chronology and its, shall we say, depersonalized characters, *L'aquarium* does remind one of Robbe-Grillet, Nathalie Sarraute or Claude Simon. Were you influenced by these writers?

J.G. — Not at all, as far as *L'aquarium* is concerned. I must say that, if any modern novel had an influence on me, it was Anne Hébert's *Les chambres de bois*, which was probably the most modern novel I'd happened to have read at the time I was writing *L'aquarium*. I hadn't read any of the writers you mentioned before I finished *Le couteau sur la table*. After *Le couteau*, I wrote *Salut Galarneau!*, and there again, I wasn't influenced by anything similar. That doesn't mean *L'aquarium* didn't have a sort of "nouveau roman" atmosphere. That atmosphere, however, came much more from films than from literature. I'm thinking of Antonioni, for example, and especially Alain Resnais, whose *Hiroshima, mon amour*, based on a text by Marguerite Duras, and *Last Year in Marienbad*, from a script by Robbe-Grillet, had exposed us to modern literature in the form of images. That certainly permeated my way of looking at the world, especially since I was learning how to make films at the same time. My writing was nurtured on cinema.

D.S. — While we're on the subject of influences, do you have a favourite author?

J.G. — I have several of them, depending on the moment. Right now, for example, there's Milan Kundera and Philip Roth. *The Ghost Writer*, by Roth, is one of the most successful novels I've read in years. I was very deeply affected at one point by Gabriel Garcia Marquez' *One Hundred Years of Solitude*. Certain Quebec writers have adopted Latin-American writing as their special reserve. However, that's not true of me; I'm more sensitive to American literature.

D.S. — The majority of Quebec writers seem to prefer American literature to other literatures.

J.G. — Of course. Steinbeck, Faulkner, Hemingway, John Irving, Saul Bellow, Updike — I'm more familiar with all those writers than with Sartre, Camus, Tournier and the others. I get fiction from the former and ideas from the latter. With the Americans, it's the novel, cinema, and adventure. The ideas come from France.

D.S. — To what extent are the political and social history in *L'aquarium* a transposition of the situation in Quebec? You wrote the novel in 1960, which means that the Quiet Revolution had just begun in Quebec, and a few months later the first FLQ bombs would explode.

J.G. — *L'aquarium* was a description of recent experience. It was a time when Duplessis still kept a tight lid on things in Quebec; it was difficult to find air to breathe, and just about everyone had given up, except for a few little sparks of revolt. *L'aquarium* was a reflection of Quebec at that time, but it was also a reflection of the phenomenon of decolonisation all over the world, in Africa and elsewhere. The novel provides a faint echo of the decolonisation process. However, it's also a novel about the movement from adolescence into adulthood; it describes the sort of absence from existence that affects a lot of adolescents, and which ends up with the possibility of living, provided one goes somewhere else and does something.

D.S. — *Le couteau sur la table* (1965) is also an incitement to "do something." I've always thought the story of Patricia and the narrator acts as a sort of response to Hugh MacLennan's "Two Solitudes" myth.

J.G. — It's not a response, since I've never read *Two Solitudes*. I've heard a lot about it, however, and when I wrote *Le couteau sur la table*, I was in fact dealing with that same central theme. I obviously wanted to write a love story involving Patricia and the narrator, but the story got short-circuited because, while I was writing it, violence erupted in the form of the FLQ actions. Like all my books, *Le couteau* was helped along by current events. It wasn't a response to Hugh MacLennan, but rather a transposition of the mood and feeling of the time, which, by the way, haven't changed all that much.

D.S. — Is it true you knew a girl named Patricia who lived in Manitoba?

J.G. — No, I knew one named Patricia who lived in Côte-des-Neiges and who served as a model for the Patricia in the novel. As far as Manitoba is concerned, I did know some women there, but in the novel I used the Canadian West more as background, or atmosphere, as you say in filmscripts.

D.S. — A while ago, while we were eating in the restaurant, you were telling me about a woman from Brandon who broke up with you because you were French Canadian.

J.G. — True. That was the final split between the two solitudes.

D.S. — It seems to me there's something profoundly auto-biographical about *Le couteau sur la table*.

J.G. — Yes and no. There are always autobiographical elements in all my books; there are never any autobiographical elements in my books. They're total and complete transformations. I would defy anybody, except my wife, and I'm not even sure about her, to be capable of recognizing the factual origins of the things I write. My writings have always come from experience, but in a variety of different modes: things I've been told, things I've experienced, or things I've imagined. Thus, it's all actually happened, but not in such a consistent way. In any case, what difference does it make?

D.S. — Since it's literature.

J.G. — Right.

D.S. — In my opinion, *Le couteau* is your richest novel in terms of symbols and personal myths. For example, there's the setting associated with Patricia, a young English-Canadian woman who's superficial, Americanized and apolitical: the water and snow, which stultify or destroy consciousness; the treacherous quicksand, the blinding sun and the contaminating dust. You make a comparison between the Québécois, who are alert and aware, and some of the apathetic people in the West: the former look towards Mount Royal and the higher mountains, while the latter remain motionless on the Plains. What I'm trying to say is that I like *Le couteau sur la table* because in it you deal with political and social problems by creating a symbolic, pictural world.

J.G. — I'm delighted you like it.

D.S. — A number of critics have said the narrator murders Patricia at the end, which would indicated the national "split" you allude to in the novel. However, I'm not sure the murder actually takes place. At one point you say that the knife will remain on the table. As far as I'm concerned, the murder is only imagined; it takes the form of a divorce from the rest of the country.

J.G. — When I wrote the book, I didn't see the murder as a solution, but rather as a metaphor, a threat, a meridional figure of speech, shall we say, since people in southern countries often say, "Hold me back, I'm going to do something awful." The proof, I think, is that violence has had very little success with the Quebec public; in fact, it was probably only ever used as an imitation of what was happening in other countries. Violence isn't something we're familiar with. The Québécois are good people, sometimes too good, although I'm not sure you can be too good; in any case, they're nice, and they're certainly not a violent people. Far from it! I don't think there's a more gentle people in the world, except perhaps the Hawaiians before the arrival of the Americans, or the Tahitians before the arrival of the French. As things stand now, I'm convinced that if there was a worldwide competition for gentleness, the Québécois would have a good chance of winning. Thus, the knife will remain on the table, as I said at that point in the book. And it has remained on the table.

D.S. — In *Salut Galarneau!*, you leave behind the table of indifference and instead paint the portrait of a young man who sells hot dogs. *Salut Galarneau!* is by far your most popular novel. It was produced as a play; it's studied in colleges and universities; it's been printed in a deluxe edition illustrated by Quebec artists; and in English Canada, it's become a classic of "Quebec literature in translation."

J.G. — The success of that book is due to a social phenomenon. I was saying a while ago that some books are popular successes, others literary successes, and some are both. If *Galarneau* is a popular success, perhaps it's because it responded to the Québécois' desire for a positive, happy story that appealed to their appetite for life, not to their appetite for destruction or self-destruction. Even if the ending is a bit ambiguous, even if Galarneau shuts himself away so he'll be able to emerge a better man, those are all things that are heading in the right direction. Another thing that played in the book's favour is its use of the funny, ironic, colourful ways the Québécois have of speaking. There's also the fact that Galarneau is an appealing character. I think his character fits in with a myth, the myth of the sun. Perhaps one day the same thing will happen to Charles-François in *Les têtes à Papineau*. But that's not something you can programme. You can try to write the best book possible, but when it comes out, it's the public that decides whether it will be a success — or whether it will be anything at all.

D.S. — François Galarneau's brother, who has lived in France, is very critical of what he sees in Quebec. Do you think he represents you to some extent, since you, like Marie-Claire Blais, had to leave Quebec so you could get a clearer perspective, so you could actually write?

J.G. — By living in Kingston, Ontario, Gérard Bessette has left Quebec to a far greater extent than we ever did. I left, not for very long, and then I came back. Ever since then, I've had no trouble breathing.

D.S. — I have the impression that François is also a projection of yourself. Although he takes pleasure in it, he feels himself invaded by American culture: everything from James Bond to Florient air-freshener to *Readers Digest*.

J.G. — François and his brother Jacques are the two facets of what I am, or what I could have been.

D.S. — In *Salut Galarneau!* you present your view of the problem of writing in Quebec: what is the role of the French-language writer in a society living under the influence of a foreign culture? François' solution seems to be his famous *Vécrire*, a combination of *vivre*, to live, and *écrire*, to write. In other words, he takes his own life and surroundings as the subject of his novel and uses his creative faculties to bring the whole thing together, including the American elements that have taken hold of the Québécois imagination. Is that what you mean by *vécrire?*

J.G. — It means refusing to lock oneself up in writing for its own sake, as a sort of abstraction, and making it into an object distinct from reality. It means refusing to lock oneself up in living for its own sake, as the only reality, and refusing to turn it into an object to be transformed. It means both walking and knowing you're walking, eating and talking about what you're eating. It also means loving, and simultaneously transforming love. It's a manner of living; people may choose it, like it or reject it, but for me it's the only way.

D.S. — Do the American products with which Galarneau is surrounded make him into an American?

J.G. — Not necessarily, at least not in a cultural sense. Culture, you know, is just about everything you can think of: the way you brush your teeth, the way you go to bed in the evening. Everything we do is cultural, in an unconscious way, obviously. Culture is the way we use tools, whether they're bulldozers or automobiles. A Mustang, in the hands of a Smith from Ottawa, a Tremblay from Chicoutimi, or a Fellini from Rome, is not the same thing. It doesn't travel at the same speed, it doesn't roll through the streets in the same way, it doesn't make the same kind of noise, and yet it's the same machine. Culture's a bit like that; it's the way we use tools. When culture interacts with technology, we call that a civilisation. Unfortunately, in the West, our technologies are more and more similar, and therefore the differences between civilisations are slim. However, that's a definition of a culture experienced unconsciously. There's also conscious culture. When you take the trouble to read a book, performing an act that is conscious and lucid, you're at another level of culture. Conscious cultural production is essential. When a writer working for an advertising agency and looking for a slogan to promote the sale of beer happens to hear somebody in the street say "Can't you just taste it?" or "Go for it!", if he uses these expressions he's performing a conscious cultural act. For the thousands of people who read *Salut Galarneau!*, I'm an instigator of conscious culture.

D.S. — *Salut Galarneau!* played an important role in the acceptance of Quebec literature based on everyday experience. The Quebec writer who chooses to *vécrire* describes himself as he is, and above all he shows no disdain for a milieu that a whole generation of earlier writers considered too vulgar. Since the frequent cursing can be seen as an acceptance of Quebec's cultural identity, one critic has described *Galarneau* as a "nostie" novel (from *une hostie*, the communion wafer, and a favourite Quebec swear word). In your article, "Écrire", you commented on the necessity of sharing a generally accepted Quebec language. I quote:

> The *national discourse* requires formal research whose principal goal will be to invent a literary language which corresponds to the originality of the national group. It will be a language that reflects the way people talk on Saint-Denis Street in the same way as written French reflects the French language as it is spoken in France. After all, writing "good French" makes the writer a good Frenchman, probably, but certainly not a good Québécois.

J.G. — I don't think I've ever talked of the necessity of a Quebec language (*langue*); I've always spoken of a Quebec *langage*, a form or level of language which is our own particular way of expressing our linguistic heritage. In any case, as far as I was concerned, the swear words in *Galarneau* were nothing but an acoustic phenomenon. I discover things with my nose, since my sense of smell is more highly developed than any of my other senses, but when I write, I use my ears. The idea of ending a certain number of sentences with *stie* (an abbreviation of the curse *hostie*), as a sort of punctuation mark, seemed to me melodic. I never thought people would be angered by this, or turn it into a theory.

D.S. — For you, it was something musical.

J.G. — Yes.

D.S. — Does the fact that you publish in France mean you have to make concessions in your use of language?

J.G. — I'm careful to provide enough clues so that a French reader can understand it with a minimum of effort. After that, I don't give a damn; it's their problem. When I read books by French writers, I go the necessary distance to be able to tap into their culture. When I'm writing, I think first of all of my own surroundings, but I don't go so far as to cut myself off from people in other French-speaking countries. To take *Salut Galarneau!* as an example, every time I used a Quebec phrase that's perfectly comprehensible to the family — because Quebec is less a nation than a family — I arranged things so that, in the dialogue or elsewhere, the same information was quickly transmitted in another linguistic register.

D.S. — For you, and for François, writing is one of life's essential elements: love and words, whether spoken or written, form the two poles from which life takes its meaning. Love, however, is fragile and often ephemeral, whereas writing seems to be permanent and reliable. With reference to his brother, Jacques, who only believes in business success, François writes: "He doesn't know what it's like to have a notebook where you can sprawl yourself out as if you'd fallen on the ice, where you can roll around as if on a freshly planted lawn."

J.G. — The fascinating thing about writing is that it's a way of transforming the things you've experienced; it's like being able to live twice. When you're writing, of course, you find yourself — I know it's a cliché, but it's essential, I think — sitting alone at a table with the blank paper in front of you; you're cut off from sound, cut off from reality, cut off from everything, but in the process of writing, you live again. It's as though you'd died and been brought back to life, because you do bring things back to life. It's the power of magic, as magical as the power of the *Houngans* who perform voodoo ceremonies, and it's perhaps the only thing that makes writing possible. It really is fabulous: through the process of language, levels of language, writing, scribbling on a sheet of paper, you participate in the material act of being able to reinvent life, transform it and refashion it. It's better than any drug. People should get stoned on words, I think.

D.S. — Writing is also one of your major concerns in *D'amour, P.Q.*, your fourth novel, published in 1972. The definition of writing is at the centre of this novel. Mireille makes fun of Thomas' elitist style, and of all the professorial notations scattered through the manuscript she's typing. She suggests to Thomas that he should take his inspiration from *sloche* ("slush"), *stèques saignants* ("rare steaks"), and Coca Cola; she advises him not to lose sight of his fellow countrymen, and to open himself up to the spontaneous pleasures of writing.

J.G. — When Mireille is talking to Thomas d'Amour, she's also talking to me. She has a down-to-earth side to her that's quite worthwhile. In the end, Mireille says, "Don't be ashamed of the people around you, the people who've brought you up. Keep on trying to write literature, if that's really your thing." When you get right down to it, why bother trying to write a play based on Greek mythology, for example, when all around us there are enough characters and situations that can also be made into drama? It's a sermon I was preaching to myself at the same time as Mireille was laying it on all the writers and teachers. *D'amour, P.Q.* is first and foremost a history of Quebec literature in the form of a novel. The first version of Thomas' article resembles the things being written in Quebec about 1957 or 1958, and the last version resembles the writings of the Seventies. The history of this writing, its transformation and its assumption of reality, is presented in the form of a novel.

D.S. — Before we began the interview, you told me *D'amour, P.Q.* is a complex novel which received a superficial critical response.

J.G. — I've only met one person, a teacher from the Cégep in Saint-Hyacinthe, who had understood the full dimensions of *D'amour, P.Q.*, including the dimension I thought essential at the time; much more than the level of language, I felt the level of relations between men and women was significant, because I was already aware of the importance of feminism. I wrote *D'amour, P.Q.* as I did because I'm as deeply feminist as it's possible for a man to be. That dimension was overlooked by women, who on the whole wanted to be the only ones who could deal with feminist concerns, and it was totally ignored by the men, who probably had no intention of giving in to that sort of discourse.

D.S. — The political dimension is also important in *D'Amour, P.Q.* The FLQ is present throughout the novel. I believe you viewed the FLQ episode as a sort of literary document.

J.G. — Well, it was highly literary. Just think of the Manifesto that the FLQ managed to have read on CBC Television.

D.S. — I remember it quite clearly. Gaétan Montreuil was the one who read it.

J.G. — It was a literary document quite in keeping with the style of that period. It was like the articles in *Parti pris*, or like our novels; it almost looked like a collage of poems and novels or articles from *Liberté* or *Le quartier latin*. It was a literary adventure. It wasn't natural for Québécois to turn into terrorists, as is apparent from the way the whole thing ended; it was borrowed from the images we were receiving from other countries. It's the same thing as when a good part of our literary community behaves in the way they think people should behave in London, New York or Paris. It's a phenomenon of second-rate imitation, and in my opinion that's what influenced the thinking of the FLQ.

D.S. — Perhaps we could talk about how *D'Amour, P.Q.* was received by the critics. The French really liked the novel; the Académie française awarded it their Prix Dupau. They saw it as a sort of "nouveau roman"; however, unlike the "nouveau roman," which tends to be abstract and theoretical, *D'Amour, P.Q.* is very much a concrete novel, firmly anchored in reality. The French like Michel Tremblay for much the same reasons: he writes "nouveau théâtre" or theatre of the absurd, but he's also very much involved with everyday life.

J.G. — When we talk about "the French," we're making a generalisation that doesn't do justice to the individual French reader. I think it's fair to say a majority of French critics have their own way of interpreting books written in Quebec.

They make incredible mistakes from our point-of-view, but don't we make the same errors when we read French or American books? It's the right of every nation, when they come into contact with foreign works of literature, to transform them through their own vision. Let's take *One Hundred Years of Solitude*, for example. All the Québécois who have read that book — and there are a great many of them — and who have never set foot in Latin American, have constructed a Latin America made out of paper. They think Marquez invented a country, whereas his novel is almost always a documented lie. French documentaries turn into fiction in Quebec, and our own documentaries become fiction in France. Well, so much the better, or so much the worse. We can't change France, England or Romania so that everything will be crystal clear all the time.

D.S. — If we turn now to *L'isle au dragon*, it's clearly your most alarmist book. Our planet is threatened by capitalist technology. And Quebec, which is so close to the giant or the "American beast," as you symbolize it in your novel, is in particular danger.

J.G. — *L'isle au dragon* is the book I feel closest to because of its baroque side, and also because of its way of manipulating both American mythology and the classic tale. It's a book that was adored by certain people and violently rejected by others. It's a book that took a great deal from my childhood, my adolescence and my adult life. It came out of an adventure I had on Isle Verte, but it also owes a lot to the time I spent in the Canadian West when I was young. Somebody could have a lot of fun finding parallels between *Le couteau sur la table* and *L'isle au dragon*. It's a book I'm extremely fond of, even if — or perhaps because — it's not easy to read.

D.S. — At a certain point in the novel, you mention the Quebec patriots: "the white river, the green island, my red-hot anger — that could make a flag, with the same colours as the old patriots' flag." Does this imply a connection between the patriots' ideal of building themselves a country and the theme in *L'isle au dragon* of preserving our heritage?

J.G. — Absolutely! Protecting your island and building your country; taking charge of your world and no longer depending on others; choosing your poetry, experiencing, accepting and circulating it; these things are always things worth doing, in my opinion. It seems to me we should always be producing and creating rather than always consuming. *L'isle au dragon* is a book against consumption, but then *Salut Galarneau!* was too. In the one case, a dragon hunter goes off on a safari against the multinationals, while in the other case it's a hot-dog vendor who sets out to do battle against the stupidity of advertising. They're fighting against the same thing. The more we talk about them, the more I realize that it's always the same book in different forms. The concerns are always the same, and like a lot of writers, I must have two or three little obsessions that keep constantly cropping up. Since I haven't identified them too precisely, I can keep on having them appear in different forms. One fine day, if I happen to identify them quite clearly, well, I'll just have to stop writing.

D.S. — You've previously written somewhere that a book "is born out of confusion. By writing it, one wants to understand the world." What were you trying to understand when you wrote *Les têtes à Papineau* (1981)?[3]

J.G. — I wanted to understand why so many people around me couldn't manage to make a political choice about what they really wanted on a cultural level; why so many people couldn't decide in their life within a society what it is they want in an economic sense; why so many people were torn apart; why so many families sit around looking at one another like china dogs. Let's start with the hypothesis that we're French-Canadians; that's what we were until 20 years ago, if you forget the change in labels, and it may be what we still are — with a hyphen. And what's this hyphen if not the fact that we have two heads, two appendixes? I tried to describe this two-headed monster, live with him, suggest that he have an operation, and see how far the logic of the novel and the choices those heads would make might lead me. I was also curious about the family they lived in, which seemed to me as important as Charles and François themselves: the intelligent mother; the big-hearted father who wants to save the world; and the little sister who looks at the whole business and says to herself, "My God, where will they end up?" All these characters protect one another against the whole world, as much against the State as against the Church, and against their voyeuristic fellow citizens; as I kept on writing, these characters came to form a remarkable, admirable family who actually made it possible for the monster to go on living. However, once the monster decided to transform himself, the family couldn't prevent it from happening. The book ends the way it does because it follows its internal logic. You know, when you write, you do so using several hypotheses, and at times some of the hypotheses you believed in fall apart; this happens because they don't seem to move in the direction of the book or the direction of the characters, not necessarily in the sense of basic psychology, but in the sense of the direction the writing takes.

D.S. — Well, let's talk about the direction of the book. A number of critics have stated that *Les têtes à Papineau* implies a political status quo. Nevertheless, Charles-François "say" they're "ideologically separate... That's why this book can't be an attempt at reattachment, a mediation."

J.G. — It's not a question of reattaching anything whatsoever. The heads are fine just as they are on the body, and in that sense the status quo would consist of saying "let's not touch the heads and let the monster live as it is." If it were possible, that would probably be the solution. However, the monster is twenty-five years old. He's already begun to separate mentally, there are already two distinct tendencies within him, and he's already heading towards the beginning of the end. Therefore, the question isn't one of "status quo," or not "status quo." The novel describes the situation as it exists, and as it evolves after the arrival of an English-Canadian doctor. Thanks to American technology, the doctor (who could be a politician) proposes a solution — since it appears that for every problem there's a technical solution — which proves to be materially valid. He turns up with a laser, although it could just as easily be a television cable, or pay T.V. or a satellite, and what does he create? With the best intentions in the world, he creates a schizophrenic, another monster.

D.S. — But when he removes one of the two heads...

J.G. — He doesn't remove one of the heads; he cuts vertically through each of the heads and then joins them together.

D.S. — However, the one-headed person who emerges from this speaks English. Your readers are sure to interpret this conclusion in a number of different ways. What's your own interpretation of it?

J.G. — It's the fate that awaits the French-speaking people in North America, as things now stand. I think we're veering toward the American side full steam ahead, in spite of all the laws that have been passed and all the efforts made. The children are the ones who are veering, not the adults. One day the children are going to change allegiances, because they'll be caught up in the very powerful and very dynamic cultural context of the United States. It will happen whether we try to isolate them or try to drown them. Whichever way we choose, the United States is still going to swallow us up anyway. However, I'm not a prophet. I'm just one of many onlookers. I watch what's happening, I draw my conclusions, and I'm frightened. In any case, all that's not terribly important; the important thing is the struggle we put up. It's the permanent nature of this struggle that will enable us to go on living.

D.S. — We're talking about the political implications of *Les têtes à Papineau*, but the style of the novel seems to me a good deal more important. In a style that is droll and ironic, you provide some hilarious glimpses into the social realities of the country. To illustrate the assimilation of the Franco-Manitobans, for example, you have a woman give birth in a CN train car and then have her baby adopted by English people. I quote:

To begin with, she gave herself to the conductor of the Transcanadian. In a cattle car. On the straw. With the train still in the station at Winnipeg. While the railwaymen were washing down the steam locomotive. Her moans of pleasure blended in with the squealing of the brakes and the shrill wails of the train whistle. Later, she went to the local orphanage and deposited the fruit of her sins, enveloped in the sweet smell of baby powder. He was adopted by an Anglo-Catholic family, however. Even then, in Manitoba, Faith was no longer the protector of the language! Germaine Beaupré died of chagrin shortly thereafter.

J.G. — I think it's a novel that raises a great many questions, if you take the time to read it carefully. I put a lot of our defects in it, and a lot of our good qualities, too. However, that doesn't make the monster into something monstrous — quite the opposite. Charles-François is a likeable character, and I think once we've finished laughing at his predicament, he's worthy of some serious thought. You know, if the people of Quebec are monsters, in a certain sense, it's because we've always rejected outside influences. The question now is whether we're going to go on for a long time performing in the Quebec circus, or leave the tent and confront the outside world. The circus is very tempting.

[1] *Draveur* is Quebec French for "logger" or "raftsman." Since the word originally came from the English "driver," Beaudry condemned it and suggested *flotteur*. For the Québécois, however, *flotteur* means "float," and nothing else.

[2] The interview also contains some of the comments Monsieur Godbout made to my students at Carleton University in 1979.

[3] "Ce n'est pas une tête à Papineau" (literally, "He hasn't got Papineau's head") is a Québécois expression meaning "He's a real dummy."

Gatien Lapointe:
Rediscovering the Land and the Body

Gatien Lapointe, who was only 52 when he died of a heart attack in September 1983, was best known as the author of the *Ode au Saint-Laurent* (1963). Anticipating Paul Chamberland's *Terre Québec* and Jacques Brault's *Mémoire*, Lapointe's *Ode au Saint-Laurent* was one of the first collections in modern Quebec poetry to give full expression to a deep sense of *appartenance*, belonging, to both Quebec and America. For thousands of Québécois, passages from the *Ode au Saint-Laurent* are embedded in their memory:

> Mine is a language of America
> I was born of this landscape
> My first breaths came from the silt of the river...
> I am memory, I am future
> I am descended from the groin of the springs...
> My greatest hope is planted in the earth...
> Space and time oh most carnal phrase...
> From now on it is man that matters
> This is the land I shall inhabit

However, it is also well worth taking the time to read Lapointe's eight other collections of poetry and poetic prose. To
begin with, there are the books published in the Fifties. Here
the poet makes his painful discovery of the body, the senses
and the void; here too he discovers the importance of the
word, his only weapon against a dispossession complex inherited from a repressive society. *Le temps premier* is also worthy
of note. Published a year before the *Ode au Saint-Laurent*, this
collection marks the end of a Nelligan-like immobility and
the beginning of a plunge into the future. Springtime and
joy enter into Quebec poetry for the first time, signalling the
end of a long, suffocating winter, and an incipient harmony
of body, land and landscape. After the delirious cry of the
Ode au Saint-Laurent came a desperate moment of hesitation,
Le premier mot, with its traumatic reflections on fate and the
relative usefulness of writing. Some ten years later, Lapointe published *Corps et graphies*, radically different in style and
inspiration. As suggested by its punning title — both "Bodies
and Graphics" and "Choreographies" — the collection is a
celebration of the body, a dance of words, an ardent study of
the body in movement. Going back to the origins of time,
when human beings were "in a primitive state that is basically androgynous," Lapointe discovers the "instinctive gestures" and the "erotic rituals" of the human condition. Having
rediscovered the land, he now rediscovers the body. A retro-
spective of Gatien Lapointe's writings, to be published by
the Éditions de l'Hexagone, should provide a unique occasion to follow the evolution of one of the most important
craftsmen in contemporary Quebec poetry.

* * *

D.S. — You were born in Sainte-Justine-de-Dorchester, south
of Quebec City. I imagine the landscapes of this region must
have played an important role in the development of your
sensibilities as a poet.

G.L. — It's a land of mountains interspersed with small plains.
All year long there is the green and black of the coniferous
trees, and then brief flashes of red in October. The soil is
poor and rocky; only a basic minimum of things will grow in

it. Whenever a flower bursts into bloom or a clump of straw-berries starts to ripen, it's something very moving for us.

The horizon, all ragged and jagged, was itself a kind of marvellous script. The peaks and hollows, the hills falling away or piling up one on top of another, all this was a sort of beautiful syntax. Looking out from the hillside by the church, sometimes you could see a second, paler blue horizon, and if it was very clear, there would be a third, far off towards the north; I'd look at these and imagine vast spaces, the spaces of the world.

There was a sort of rough clearing where I felt happy, a circle that was out of time, immediate, without sickness or death. One day, however, coinciding with a sudden personal loss, a crack formed and all the negative forces came tum-bling through it. Eternity and happiness disappeared through the same breach, and it was then that my own history began.

D.S. — What did the Etchemin River mean to you?

G.L. — Geographically, the Etchemin was the first road that opened up the circle. At the end lay the plains, the St.Law-rence, and the tumult of the first city: Quebec.

D.S. — What's remained with you from these landscapes?

G.L. — Mountain paths in the July darkness or the winter storms, a certain mound of sand blanketed with everlastings, a half-exposed spruce trunk clinging to a boulder, glimpses of animals here and there, the inside of a buttercup — all these images of what is holy were lost in a flash when death struck. However, they've left their mark, their imprint on me, and their effect on my imaginative faculties still remains.

D.S. — Painting and poetry are art forms that have many points of similarity. In this regard it's interesting that, before you became a poet, you studied at the École des arts graphiques (Graphic Arts School) in Montreal.

G.L. — For me, painting is an ordering of coloured sounds. I used to take handfuls of red, green and yellow, and throw them onto a white canvas. It would make a nice splash in the centre, and then, spreading out from the core, there would be a fine, delicate network of grey or brown. It was as though I'd flung a handful of notes against a wall. It was as though I'd painted an extraordinary coat-of-arms in sounds. However, I never showed them to anyone.

Before studying literature, I went to the École des arts graphiques mainly to learn about typography, the various kinds of scripts, layout, and so on. At the end of the only year I spent there, I published *Jour malaisé*, the writings I'd been dragging around with me for some time. Since I was impatient and still not very adept at operating a typewriter, I was anxious to see how they'd look on a white page, to discover the shape of their music and the form of their rhythms.

D.S. — You worked on the writings of the surrealist poet Paul Éluard. Were you influenced by him?

G.L. — Éluard helped me make the transition from dreams to reality. I was fascinated by his use of light, the simplicity of his writing, his clearness, and the immediate textual quality of his words. It was simple and infinitely mysterious. I still find myself quite moved by "Pour vivre ici," "L'amoureuse" and "Liberté," for example.

D.S. — Are there other writers you are fond of?

G.L. — I like René Char's elliptical, concentrated, short-circuited way of writing. It's like "mountain writing": abrupt, always broken and breaking. I often reread Albert Camus' *Noces*. I also liked *Les nourritures terrestres* by André Gide, but it didn't really stay with me very long.

I wish I could have discovered Paul-Marie Lapointe's *Le vierge incendié* right at the beginning of my youth. At a meeting in Jean-Guy Pilon's house in March, '76, I was telling Laurent Mailhot how the beginning of the poem on page 26 of *Le vierge* completely overwhelmed me when I first read it in '71, and how it still kept coming back to me. Those words in particular, not to mention the whole book, would have pushed me ahead by leaps and bounds! I definitely intend to use that passage as an epigraph to the second volume of my collected poems that Hexagone is going to publish. There are also flashes of Rimbaud ("Your finger tapping on the drum releases every sound / The new harmony obtains"), and flashes of Nelligan (poems like "Je veux m'éluder" or "La romance du vin" or "Visions") that I often enjoy rereading. They're like black fire; they're new every time you look at them. I also discovered Roland Barthes about 1970 and Deleuze in '76; his *Rhizome* is an endless celebration. Walt Whitman also made a great impression on me, although I must point out for the benefit of various critics that I actually discovered him *after* I'd written the *Ode au Saint-Laurent.*

In Whitman's poetry, Robert Frost's deer come to resemble the torsos sculpted by Rodin or Michelangelo, although sometimes I associate them with the more breathless versions of Zadkine, or occasionally the highly stylized figures of Brancusi, Arp or Giacometti. They're the sun's horsemen, the ones who would come galloping in right after supper. The evening was the most important part of the day for me.

D.S. — Have you never been tempted to write novels or plays?

G.L. — Plays tempted me a bit, but only a bit. I've never had any urge at all to write novels, for reasons I explained in the magazine *Liberté*, number 42. My reasons haven't changed, even today; I want to be able to guess at things and imagine them, not to tell what I already know.

D.S. — You founded the Écrits des Forges, a publishing house that's already produced some thirty books. Do you like working as a publisher?

G.L. — I'm not a publisher in the real sense of the word. I haven't made it my profession or a full-time job. I do it freely, out of a love for it. I was the first one in Quebec — by a long shot, I think — to publish only poetry, and only very young writers. It means going out on a limb, and a shaky one at that, but this makes it all the more exciting. You have a first outpouring of talent and you're not sure how much water there is in the well. You wonder if the writer's inspiration runs deep or whether it will dry up after just one book. I think you have to have a nose for it. Somewhere in a first book there's a rumbling that usually rings true, but you have to be able to hear it. Sometimes you can also be wrong.

I don't intend to be a "publisher" all my life. The pressure to do my own things is increasingly strong. I have a whole pile of my own manuscripts that have been gathering dust for the past ten years, and I'll have to publish them soon if I don't want to fall behind in my own work.

D.S. — This year marks the tenth anniversary of the Forges. How can you sum up the experience?

G.L. — I'm happy that this rather small publishing house has, among other things, enabled some twenty poets to make their voices heard, to have their writings reach the hands and eyes of unknown readers with whom they've established a special rapport. They've managed to appeal to various audiences and they've gained the attention of the critics, some of whom have been fierce and some understanding. In short, they've tried their voices. Writing is not easy.

D.S. — Your first collection of poetry, *Jour malaisé*, goes back to 1953. The title, literally *Uneasy Day*, indicates your uncertainty in terms of the flesh, the burning sun, and the passage of time. Absence and impotence are the dominant themes in the book, and yet they bear little resemblance to you as you are now.

G.L. — Those are early drafts of poems that were published too soon. Everybody writes them, you have to begin somewhere, even Rimbaud and Nelligan wrote some, but you don't have to show them to the public at large. Some writers, like Alain Grandbois, are wise enough not to begin publishing until they've reached a more mature age. Others begin in a blaze of their own power, like Paul-Marie Lapointe, as though they'd already reached a summit.

Most writers, however, have the other privilege of tapping into a source of inspiration and then watching it flow gradually into a stream, then a river, and finally out into the depths.

Jour malaisé at least shows one thing: the uneasiness of living, of breaking out of the walls one has built up around oneself, and finally emerging into the world. In my own solitude, in the sort of desert that Quebec was in those days, trying to cry out even with a strangled voice was already an act of liberation.

D.S. — Was there a particular event that propelled you into writing *Jour malaisé?*

G.L. — Formed and conditioned as I was by all sorts of false absolutes, I used to regard time as a terrible kind of suffering. It not only strangled my sense of what was possible but it also consistently ruined the good moments in my life. I was caught up in the inescapable cogs of a wheel. I think I would even have been deaf to any offers of help. Either the pain in me had to come to a head or my determination had to become stronger than the obstacles I was facing. The only resolution is in extremes.

If there's anything to be salvaged in that collection, it's the fire I ignited with all those words and all those pages at the end of the book, at the same time burning away all those impossible ideals I'd had pounded into me. But that's something you can't just get over in one fell swoop.

D.S. — In *Jour malaisé* you use a surrealistic and symbolic style of writing, but the language itself is simple, a language "whose signs can be transmitted as a tool might be passed from hand to hand or fire carried from mouth to mouth" (*Le premier mot*, p.13). Thus you reject an esoteric or elitist form of poetry, preferring words that are simple and down-to-earth.

G.L. — As a farmer, a man of the earth, I speak with my hands, my eyes and my body. Simplicity has a depth to it that all the finery and flourishes of so-called "learned" discourse can never attain. The language of culture is *complicated*, but the language of life is *complex*. A cry is always naked and open-ended. The thunder of astonishment doesn't constitute a style. And if, in its accumulation of moments of real life, the body produces images, these will be made of the fire of its blood, a fire that is always immediate and yet impervious to analysis or completion. Writing is made complicated by its cerebral elements, and the cerebral elements are precisely the ones that fill in the spaces life has left empty. However, just as you can't always be burning at the stake, you don't always have the need to write either.

D.S. — In your second collection, *Otages de la joie*, (1955), you gradually evolve towards an acceptance of life without God. "Like a child who learns to walk/ To name bread, water, plants and sleep," you affirm the necessity of language as a means, if not of possessing life, at least of enjoying it.

G.L. — Language can give me life only to the extent I infuse it with desire. At that point, what was important was the act of naming and simultaneously appropriating what I named. I was coming out of an empty dream. People had filled my heart with illusions; my desire had been made into something dim and melancholy, almost a punishment. The body was getting ready to take its revenge.

I then began naming the things around me in order to know them, to provide myself with what I was lacking; with those first words and the reality behind them, I began constructing a world that I could use to oppose a world which denied me a place, left me on the margins. I had been made into a "hostage of joy," as in the title, and deep within myself I was getting ready for the challenge of attaining that joy, of claiming and possessing it as my right.

During my adolescence, I had tried my hand at music (piano and clarinet), I had done theatre for a year and dabbled in painting, but none of this satisfied me. Words came to my rescue. I'm not saying they saved me, or will save me, but they did bring me a joy that those other forms of expression didn't. I was gradually brought back to the world through the imagination, and the full weight of reality it contains. Language provided my opportunity for revenge.

D.S. — After everything that's been written about Nelligan, and as a teacher of Quebec poetry, how do you approach Nelligan's work?

G.L. — Nelligan is one of the poets I talk about, but I should make it clear right away that the Nelligan I like is not the one who weeps and moans, not the crêpe-hanger or the perfect little angel. My Nelligan — the unknown one, or almost unknown — is a poet who "blasphemes against his fate," transgresses against the prohibitions, welcomes the experience of hell, gives in to his instincts, accepts what is different about him (might that be one of the reasons he went mad?), and goes into his own inner depths to discover his real self, knowing full well that what he will discover is damned.

What I like about Nelligan is the imagination which, occasionally in his poems, starts to work towards building an autonomous world. I like it when the desire within him starts to lash out against all the forms of coercion he is subjected to. I also like it when there's nothing left of him except a sensation expressing its pain or its joy. The two stanzas in "La romance du vin," where he starts attacking society, strike me as moments of weakness in an otherwise great poem, a "hurricane of desire."

An adolescence like Nelligan's, with its lashing out, its impatience, its blazing flashes, has the saving grace of occasional moments of genius. That sort of adolescence doesn't explain; it affirms. It doesn't describe; it invents. And all this is beautiful in the sense of something springing out of nowhere, beyond the chain of cause and effect, a law into itself. It may bring pain or pleasure, or both at the same time, but it is raw, unexpected and unexplainable.

D.S. — The Quebec poets of the Sixties are often viewed as the prophets of a nation in the process of liberating itself from a past that was oppressive in a social, political and individual sense. You weren't the only Québécois who was a "hostage of joy," who had "uneasy days." I think it was Anne Hébert who remarked in her *Mystère de la parole* that by gaining a mastery over language, the writers were taking up the cause of a whole nation.

G.L. — I've never pretended to take upon myself the whole fate of this country. I've never made myself a spokesman for any cause. I haven't even been part of any group. I've quite simply tried to invent an "I" for myself.

Using words, I've tried to win back my body and my life. I've tried to escape the pitfalls of loneliness, death, and half steps. I've tried to regain my breath, rebaptize myself in my own manner, and to forge a language for myself.

I might add in passing that if writing, with all its mysteries and its apparent uselessness, could ever be defined, it may be that writing is the expression of imminent desire, a desire that will be constantly thwarted by political forces which are the expression of normality and mediocrity.

If it happens that the building of my "I" coincides with building a country, if my own plans correspond to the plans the country happens to have at that point in time, then so much the better: its energy can only supplement and coalesce with mine. One doesn't live in an ivory tower; we are all affected by everything going on around us. But I repeat: above all, I spoke for myself.

You mentioned being a prophet. To be a prophet might mean expressing the things you see and feel when you sense that the borders of your "I" have disintegrated and you're adrift in a sort of limitless "we" (as in my *Arbre-Radar).* On the other hand, being a prophet may simply mean seeing through your own blood.

D.S. — With the publication of *Le temps premier* in 1962, you entered into a new period, just as Quebec did about the same time.

G.L. — I had been living in France since October, 1956. I had crossed through those three reaches of blue I mentioned earlier. I'd been able to weigh in days and nights the time it takes to cross the ocean. I'd gained a sense of the vastness of space, and I was trying to live in a new land.

I was also trying to speak a new language, a language that had the same words as my own but which made me feel foreign. I was trying "to fit my feet into somebody else's footsteps," to use the words of a famous poem about alienation (is it entirely unconscious?), and I kept stumbling and stammering. In the best Cartesian fashion, I tried to adopt a cultivated Sorbonne manner to bring my impulses under control. I was working on the French poet, Paul Éluard, and he kept gradually seeping into my voice, to the point where it was already beginning to change without my being aware of it. People all around me were trying to change and even threaten everything I'd managed to achieve.

I was suffocating, and one day it dawned on me what was happening: I wasn't from or of that country, and I'd never be successful at setting down roots in any other land but my own. Exile must be one of the most painful experiences possible!

And so, on the inside, with a different stance and a different attitude, I started out on my second experience of France. It proved to be quite different from the first. I found it easier to breathe. Instead of continually trying to translate, I began affirming my own way of speaking, primarily in opposition to Éluard, whose language both fascinated and oppressed me. I found myself moving into a new beginning, the *temps premier* of the title; I was moving into my own time and my own space. At that point in time and space, Quebec started to be my *terra nova*.

I should add, though, that I'm still in France in some ways, in terms of binary thought and logic, and a hint of something foreign; the difference is that now I'm usually aware of it.

D.S. − Would you care to comment on the act of "naming" and its significance in *Le temps premier?* For example, I'm thinking of lines like "I am born in all I name," "Utterance is unity rediscovered," and "Remembering majestically."

G.L. − I would literally become the things I named. I found the flesh of words becoming part of my own flesh. To proffer, to pronounce a word, would make me actually quiver with the body of the word. I was building my own world. My imagination became my one and only reality. Utterance is the most powerful act possible. I believe in words in the same way I believe in people. All things are born in assemblages of sound. All victories too can come only from the effects of writing.

To utter is to invent. To utter is to create something new out of the unknown that pervades us. In a very deep sense, utterance is remembrance; it means giving voice to what is immemorial within us, to what has always existed in our blood and is now given form by some particular event. To imagine something is literally to remember it; it is expressed and experienced, not in any past or future tense, but in the present. There's also another way to explain this: to invent is to become oneself, to reach through to what one's always been, to discover the fundamental resemblance within oneself.

D.S. — Quebec poetry in the Fifties and Sixties has been called cosmogonical, a poetry of first beginnings. In *Le temps premier*, we find time and space awakening, ready to be inhabited.

G.L. — Having repossessed my own time and space, I found myself drunk with the possibilities of my new-found freedom. There's a line in a book I was reading by Éluard, "from the horizon of one man to the horizon of all," and what I could hear in this were the sounds and rhythms of my own world. Having realized that Eluard was in fact a foreign author, as far as I was concerned, I felt that the troubles he had been causing me were a thing of the past. Since I was in temporary exile, and knew it, I undertook to write in a way that would shelter me and provide me with a homeland — a true homeland, completely internalized. In the meantime, back in Quebec, the first sounds of the pickaxes and shovels could be heard building a new country, a country that unfortunately is still only a province: a bilingual province, which means an English province in an English country.

If a poetry of beginnings, of founding, consists first of all in creating an "I," then I agree with your definition. Since an "I" is centred on the power and reality of desire, a country can be founded only on the hunger and substance of that desire. Seeing the land in terms of a beloved or desired woman, or any number of similar conceits, does not seem to me a sufficient basis on which to establish a being, a language, or a country. Quebec won't be built on speeches or progaganda, but rather on the sustaining power of a thirst for freedom. When that happens, the impact of its birth will no longer be of interest only to a handful of people, but will send shockwaves of liberty throughout the world. The rest is only politics.

D.S. — The notion of time is central to your poetry: "At that time/ Time had no seasons / The space of my shelter was pure / I was a passenger dreaming of eternity" (*Le temps premier*, p.12). For you, what is the essence of this advancing time, this childhood you finally managed to create for yourself?

G.L. — As I said earlier, one night I touched the frightfully cold forehead of death, a dead body, and at that time a crevasse took form, a wound opened, and in one blow I was exiled from the great primeval unity. In one blow I discovered myself alone, solitary, and mortal. Expelled from the place where "real" time had now taken up residence, I took to the road and started trying — I still am — to get myself back into the world, to use words to create a world of my own.

In 1957 I wrote, "At that time, the space of my shelter was pure." I had only begun to understand that "the body too is an absolute," and I could barely conceive of the dimensions of the struggles that lay ahead of me.

However, I'm well into it and time is trembling to the very depths of space. I'm a pirate of fire, and I plunder pleasure with all my strength. As things go by, and the seasons pass, I take from them what I need to construct that other form of time and space: *une oeuvre*, a body of writing. What a big word to describe the two or three major upheavals in a human life!

D.S. — In poetry of birth and emergence, the tree is almost always a favourite symbol:

> I return to the threshold of my childhood
> I walk beside the returning sun
> My phrases are suffused with pure breath
> And the tree holding upright a whole forest
> *(Le temps premier).*

G.L. — In a context like that, arborescent forms are necessary or natural in that they provide a measure, an order, a hierarchy; they indicate the absolute referent, the total meaning. During that period, in spite of myself, my mind was working in binary time. Darkness and light were distinct. Pain wasn't mixed with pleasure. The world appeared to me dichotomous. I was severed in two by dualities. A little more of the Sorbonne, a few more discourses on knowledge and power, and I would have fallen completely programmed into the comforting compromise of dialectics.

D.S. — In "Lumière du monde," the second part of *Le temps premier*, the poet is haunted by the primeval landscape, by naked existence in a primitive land. This is what Paul Chamberland refers to as the theme of primitivism.

G.L. — I would see, or experience, or try to create, flashes of what is sacred. The raw, the primitive, the living, the organic: in other words, everything that was not yet organized produced in me a thunder of astonishment. This soil not yet polluted by logic and civilisation provides a glimpse of what is divine, of things greater than man, of what is above him, or perhaps below. In 1970, in response to a the *Questionnaire Marcel Proust* submitted to us by the VLB publishing house, I wrote that this was the soil of the time I had previously inhabited. To rediscover the primitive land of that time, I need only a melody by Mozart or Schubert, or a solo by Robert Fripp, Paul Kossoff, Chuck Berry, Roy Buchanan, Jimmy Page or Terje Rypdal.

    Gauguin went off to the Pacific Islands in search of the primitive and the sacred. Segalen did the same. Loranger came back to his new land. Why? Were they fleeing the impasses of reason? Searching for lost instincts? I think Europe represents time that marks out limits, whereas America, for instance, represents the instant that has the power to create the infinity of space. Once one is free of chronometric time, everything becomes possible. And that is when impulse overcomes moderation, dance denies process, motion wipes out trajectories, the flaming instant obliterates history — the sad history men make for themselves.

D.S. — Various critics have said that the *Ode au Saint-Laurent* was your first profoundly Québécois piece of writing. They like to recall that you wrote the collection while living in Paris, when you felt a need to recreate the land of your origins. However, there were symbols of birth in your previous collections, the difference being that in the *Ode* you place a greater importance on the land and brotherhood, and less on the emergence of the individual.

G.L. — First of all, it's a poem that was written in a period of two days and three nights. I also think it's essentially political because it disclaims any form of politics. For example, I didn't use the tools of dialectics, whose two-beat tempo can be found in almost all the writing of that time. I've never been fascinated by the tandem of denunciation and annunciation. I avoided that form of thought, leaving it completely aside; I used the clay of the earth to fashion a sort of man, and then I set him free in space.

It's a poem that doesn't talk about the Saint Lawrence or any form of patriotic nostalgia, and I hope there's no whiff in it of the old workboots of our folklore. The man in it, that "I," is talking about myself and the desire that motivated me. Outside and inside myself, it's the first morning of the world.

D.S. — How do you see the *Ode* as being structured?

G.L. — It's all expressed through a juxtaposition of declarations, and through specific moments that accumulate but are never articulated in rational terms, which would give them a precise meaning. It quite simply comes out of life. It's anarchical and apolitical, without any recourse to the tools of logic. Obviously it conveys all sorts of things that I'm more or less fond of; that's inherent to the very form of the poem. But there are also chunks of life in it.

At the same time as Quebec was experiencing the first contractions of its impending labour, and the most beautiful French garden was threatening to dazzle me permanently, I was there with a branch in my hand, tracing out on the new land of a leaf the rhizomatic, rebellious outline of a figure who perhaps resembles us a little. In any case, it was my own figure, and it set out what was different between me and a culture that didn't belong to me.

D.S. — You make an association between the universal and the particular, the crisis facing Quebec and the crisis any human being faces when he or she comes up against the great questions of existence. Is that why, as an epigraph to your *Ode*, you wrote, "All men bear the same name"?

G.L. — Yes, I think that's the only way to attain the universal. The opposite would soon have us deep in abstractions and generalizations, completely governed by the orders of the "general."

D.S. — Why did you choose the title *Ode au Saint-Laurent*?

G.L. — I originally called it *L'homme en marche* (literally *Man in Movement*), and that seemed to me a good title. Later, following the good advice of close friends, it became this horrible title which gave the book a nice little folksy touch. Now I don't know how I can get rid of the title. Next year when I'm preparing the first volume of my collected works for Hexagone, I may reduce the title to just *Ode*, or I may even give it back its original title.

D.S. — When you were writing the *Ode au Saint-Laurent*, did you spontaneously order your words around those "first words" — earth, water, fire, fauna and flora — or did you have to rework the internal organisation of the poems several times?

G.L. — As I said a moment ago, it all came to me in one spurt. I very quickly had a vision of the whole thing. It just organized itself. Its particular form comes from the fact that I started out on a specific beat and that rushes of emotion came washing over me at various moments. On the other hand, it did take me a lot of time to work out the architecture of *Arbre-Radar*. The vision came on its own, but my nerves were too frazzled to capture its full scope right away. Also, I was too tired, and it went on for three weeks: my body lacking sleep, my being assailed by squalls of emotion, images, rhythms, music. Oh, I was in agony! My senses were flaming with stabs of pleasure, I was gasping, it was fierce, my heart was a mess.

D.S. — Let's now turn to the collection that came after the *Ode: Le premier mot*, published in 1967. The land is present in *Le premier mot*: "Will this people live in vain?/ This land which muzzles itself like a shout/ This land where snow reverberates in mid-July." The rending of time, however, acts as an impediment to happiness. This may be the most tragic and devastating of your collections, especially compared to the *Ode au Saint-Laurent*, in which the sense of presence is occasionally so ecstatic that it becomes disquieting.

G.L. — The joy in the *Ode* is disquieting precisely because of the force of its affirmations, and this is all to the good: the joy reaches out towards other horizons and other desires. In *Le premier mot*, that joy is constantly short-circuited. The dream vision, the timeless song, the "wordless romance," as Verlaine would say, all appear only in fits and starts, in fragments.

I should add that it was perhaps normal for it to turn out this way, especially after the constant flowing of the *Ode*. If a door is opened too wide, one's immediate reaction is to close it or just leave it partly open.

D.S. — In "Le pari de ne pas mourir," a sort of preface to *Le premier mot*, you ask yourself what good it is to want to go on writing, since art is no solution to man's solitude or to the inevitability of fate. Neverthless, for you, "to write is to still have hope...Create, cry out, and for an instant the heart beats more smoothly. Lost and losing, man literally attempts the impossible...There are no satisfactory answers...The negative forces are a constant threat."

G.L. — At that time I was breathing in gulps, with great outbursts of enthusiasm that would die away immediately afterwards. The fear of death was strangling me, no matter what I did. It was such a heavy experience for me, and I was writing about my outbursts of terror so quickly, that I didn't have time to develop them, to turn them into poems in the real sense of the word. They were kernels or embers that I would throw onto the page. It all came out in gasps, like the moments of fright that would wrack my body. I had become an animal who was terrified by death.

I waited three years before publishing those writings, since I was apprehensive about the idea of revealing myself in such an extreme state of suffering. Rereading myself was like touching my own pain. How would others react to it?

D.S. — You write poetry that is *engagé*, committed to independence and struggle. Nevertheless you keep your distance in terms of political commitment:

> All poetry is committed; all poetry is social. I mean
> that poetry has a name, a date and a face that are
> both real and transfigured; I mean that the primary
> aim of poetry is to communicate with others...Thus,
> I don't want to politicize poetry, to make it prole-
> tarian or imperialistic. It's of no account to me
> whether a man is on the left or the right; if I know
> he's in a state of revolt, I'm sure he's on the side of
> life and active in the party of the humble and down-
> trodden.
>
> (*Le premier mot*, p.13)

There you're taking a position that Gaston Miron and other confirmed socialist poets would surely never accept.

G.L. — Of course the independence of Quebec is important to me. For Quebec to emerge and take its place in the world is an exact counterpart to my own emergence as a man. One can be born and live only in one's own difference, just as you can take sustenance from the world only if your "I" is supreme. The nuance of difference that we alone can bring to humanity is the nuance of each one of us. If we die as a people, the process of articulating the world in Québécois will come to an end as well. However, I think one or two of our literary works have made us universal, and in "Choré-graphie d'un pays," I questioned what sort of death could overtake us. At the same time, I tell myself that our desire for freedom perhaps still lacks music, and that perhaps we're not yet hungry or thirsty enough for freedom.

On the other hand, I'll state again that any ideology is a prison and always ends up in some sort of fanaticism or fascism. I would never die for any idea whatsoever. I don't have to run errands for anybody. I'm part of the struggle, and faithful to it in my fashion, but my only aim is to broaden my life — and indirectly, if my writing is contagious enough, other people's lives. My only intention is to burn with the brightest flame I can muster, and if it makes a nice fire, a good fire, so much the better if it can awaken the metaphorical and transmorphological faculties in all of us. The intensity of pleasure — blazing, lashing out, tearing apart — has its own way of bringing me out of the shadows and sharpening the thirst of liberty I share with my compatriots and all mankind. There's nothing political about the body, or blood, or muscles, but the writing a body produces is all the more political in that it is rebellious, random and free.

D.S. — Your writing changed radically in 1977, the year you wrote *Corps et graphies*, which came out of seeing a performance in Montreal of *Ocellus*, by the Pilobolus Dance Theatre. *Corps et graphies* was published by the Editions du Sextant in 1981 and contains an original etching by the artist Christiane Lemire. You've previously stated you were fascinated by the performance of *Ocellus* because in that dance, that "syntax of the body," you recognized your own preoccupations with "meaning and signs." What did you mean by that?

G.L. — *Ocellus* first revealed to me, in the flesh and in rhythms, the syntax of the body that would later be apparent in *Arbre-Radar*. I was fascinated by the choreography and the immediate sense in which the body could be made expressive. Those dancers didn't practice anything, didn't do anything they'd learned by heart, didn't get into any of those weird contortions that you often find in classical dance. They invented. They created flashes of light out of darkness. What radiated from them was live and new and raw, and I shared it, and that was what compelled me to start writing on the programme I had in my hands.

As for the "sign" and "meaning" you referred to, they come from a series of reflections on writing, of which one fragment was written and read on February 28, 1980, at L'Université du Québec à Montréal. This was at the end of a conference on "New Writing," and it came of course as a response to what I'd been listening to all day. Primarily, however, it's part of my compulsive dreaming about poetry, which I first wrote about in '76. Inspired by the French critics Blanchot and Barthes, the Sixties in Quebec had everyone full of the idea that writing had to be made into something less linear, something with a multiplication of meanings. However, even in the singular, meaning can still be detected and capitalized upon in one way or another. To take this further, and experiencing it as if for the first time, I would like to be able to produce nothing *but* meaning; I would like to convey nothing but presence, and I'd like that presence to depend on nothing but the life it contains: only people who are alive would be able to recognize it and gain something from it.

D.S. — *Corps et graphies* reveals a profound renewal in your writing. The images are jumbled and disjointed, like close-ups in a film: "astounded bodies, astounded bodies — *dance* — muscle writings cries gleam road never settled *beyond meaning*, incessant variation, the blood sparks without proof without design seeking only a thirst a mouth." Everything is fragmented; the collection itself is printed on loose sheets so that the reader can rearrange them over and over again. This strikes me as a radical departure from your previous poetry, as though you were attempting to invent a new form of writing, a "choreographics," in which poetry could be linked to dance.

G.L. — I think everything you've said can be found in *Arbre-Radar*, parts of which can also be traced back to my earlier writings, although not all of these have actually been published. I don't deny that there's been a major change in my writing: I'm a living creature, I change in spite of myself, and I also have the right to experience my own reality and my own being *differently*, with other intensities, *otherwise*. Basically it doesn't depend on me; in *Arbre-Radar* I wrote about what I was experiencing and how I was experiencing it. This book was *given* to me, just as the *Ode* was.

I think I was *myself* in that book, and whenever this happens to a person, whoever it may be, it always results in a new form of writing. Being oneself means necessarily being original, and alone as well. In a cultural sense, you're always a bit like others and like your previous selves. In the quick of the body, the raw instant, you can't help but write in a way that is new. You find within yourself other selves who no doubt go on saying the same sorts of things, but say them *differently*.

D.S. — Why did you choose the title *Corps et graphies?*

G.L. — In *Corps et graphies* I first tried to unfetter the body completely, to wrest it out of the grasp of time, history, fate and the limitations of its very name. Then, for a flaming instant, I let it dance, let it express mystery and meaning, which in this case is the joy of living without constantly having to drag around the ball and chain of death. The body dances for the pleasure of dancing. It expends its energy and its life without thinking of the past or future, without any preordained purpose. It is an instant in which the body can fulfil its desire to live. The resulting fire doesn't simply express *a* meaning, which is always limited and comprehensible; rather it is the free expression, in the fullest sense, of vitality, mystery and holiness.

D.S. — You are very enthusiastic about modern dance.

G.L. — Yes, I would have liked to be a dancer. The dance is man's most complete expression of himself. The body becomes its own writing, directly, without intermediaries.

D.S. — I believe you see poetry in sports as well.

G.L. — I find it tremendously exhilarating: Nettles or Brett running in the outfield, then stretched horizontal to catch the ball; Denis Potvin's way of snatching the puck from an attacker; Gilbert Perreault speeding up the ice from one net to the other; a pitch by Juan Marichal or Dick Ruthven. Players like that are artists, and in me they set off a series of beautiful but dangerous internal manoeuvres that one day will result in my producing something that is there within me, unknown and waiting to be born. Once again, it's primarily the writing of the body itself. I'm very little inclined to metaphysics. If divinity exists, it will manifest itself in the body. One always has the body of one's soul.

D.S. — The poetic language you use in describing the body is much more complex and specialized than the language of your earlier poetry. You seem to have moved away from your statements in *Le premier mot* about the necessity of keeping poetry simple and down-to-earth.

G.L. — In fact, what I'm heading for is even greater simplicity, a style that is more direct and immediate, poetry in which the syntactic forms are dictated by the energy of the body itself, its radar waves of nerves and muscles.

I write in lumps of emotion, fits and starts, zigzags of waves and muscles, slams of smells, and clots of fire. This has all been spelled out in *Arbre-Radar*, as well as in other places in my books.

I believe that within ourselves we often speak in isolated words, whereas with others it's either lumps of words or exclamations. That's what I mean by the syntax of the body. Moreover, that syntax is like a twin sister to the syntax of the instant which appears not to be articulated by any force from the past or future. The moment or instant, however, pushes both forward and backward; like the body, it establishes its connections and fulfils its potential, yet at the same time it renders words nomadic again, preventing them from coagulating into a precise meaning. The body/instant is mobile in the same way as Jack Kerouac in the trailer of a truck, rolling full-speed yet diagonally towards the Pacific.

D.S. — The prose poems in *Corps-transistor* were written in 1978 and published in 1981. Accompanied by reproductions of Etruscan paintings, these poems are in much the same vein as *Corps et graphies*; once again, dance provides the inspiration, and the somewhat cubist style — "I ellipse curves of pleasure" — reveals the body perceived in terms of separate elements.

G.L. — I'm not sure the body should always be considered a single unit, which is the traditional way of representing it.

The entire body may also be felt beating in the ankle or the back of the neck, even if these seem to be isolated from the rest of the body. In a certain context, each part of the body can be an absolute; each part is flesh that can create pleasure, emotion or pain. Every element in the body is part of a whole, of which we know neither the past or the future. The very name of the person may not be important. Pleasure or pain are hardly concerned with such things; a hand just wants to touch things that are warm, and has no need to connect this with a story, a name, an address or a soul. Life isn't necessarily experienced as a story or a tale or any other mental construct; there may be no sense of a beginning, a middle and an end (and a moral of course). I've had enough of all that.

I also have absolutely no need for others to provide me with learning or knowledge. What would I do with it: put it in a bank or a museum, for some hypothetical future? What I seek and need is to be touched directly, to be moved; I want to be thrown into vitality, propelled towards a continually different awareness, without knowing where it's going to take me, or even if it *will* lead somewhere. For me it's enough just to be on the move, with my whole body trembling.

Oh, I long for literature or films that would give me nothing but sudden, raw moments of living, variations of intensity, lumps of fire; I would want these to be devoid of history, without any sort of progression or explanation or definition. An example would be what Klaus Schulze and Brian Eno give us in their music: no repetition of the past, only a sense of my own being in the future present.

Experiences are all that count, and even mistakes are important. In this life, it's less likely to be some God than a person very much like ourselves who can rid us of our remorse and make us innocent. A work of literature breathes through the very openings of the wounds of which it is made.

D.S. — Even if *Corps-transistor* reflects this new vision of writing you call "inverted writing," the poetry you are now producing is not altogether different from your earlier work. We still find the "spiritual propulsion" of childhood, words which "risk your life," and time as the "mortal form of despair."

G.L. — One always says the same things, but one says them *otherwise*, with different modulations and intensities. How can I create that world of sounds to oppose this world that is unacceptable to me? How can I reach, outside history and its inherent despair, through to that eternally "beginning beginning" that so fascinates me? How can I recreate a childhood for this ruined man and his ruined world? A long time ago, I wrote "I am advancing towards my childhood." That initial time is something I move forward towards, not back. I have to plough through the whole bulk of human experience — and language — to be able to make that time something real and inhabitable. It's like an optical illusion that makes me feel as though I were reading myself backwards. I'd also like to be able to write myself backwards, or inside out, or even all crooked or sideways, so long as it's living and vital.

D.S. — There's a phrase in *Corps-transistor* that really set me thinking: "origin I inhabit green onomatopoeias." What is this language of origins, this "universe that extends back to its kernel of sound"?

G.L. — "Origin I inhabit green onomatopoeias." What I mean by these words is that, for at least the space of an instant, I reached that beginning I just spoke about; and that instant, having escaped from the prison of time, is no longer a slave to its undeviating trajectory through history — nor to the poor tools such a trajectory borrows from logic. I would even say that reality then transformed itself into words, which themselves escaped from their meanings and became nothing but sounds of pain or pleasure. It is thus natural that in certain poems there are only syllables or murmured vowels. Poetry can be nothing more than a painful series of questions without answers, or raw astonishment causing a joy that is sometimes as intolerable as suffering.

D.S. — Together with *Corps et graphies* and *Corps-transistor*, *Arbre-Radar*, published in 1980, forms what might be called your triptych of the body. To quote your press release:

Through bursts of emotion, through lumps of words in a *body-distillery* — a sort of firmamentary egg —

mixing all kinds of atoms and molecules of all sorts, I
listened to the germination of this *initial body* from
before the time of history, culture, or any form of
destruction. Might it also have been, at the same time,
in the audacity of fire, a sketch of that *future body*
already dreaming its way into existence within us?

Could you explain how you conceive of the initial body and
the future body?

G.L. — To begin with, I'd like to make it clear that *Corps et
graphies, Corps-transistor* and *Barbare inouï* are each separate
pieces of work and complete unto themselves. I intend to
collect them, along with other writings, in a book which as
early as 1977 I entitled *Instant-phénix*.

It may be that the civilisation which produced Capital-
istic/ Christian/ Cartesian man is now nearing its end. Man
has produced palpable threats of self-destruction, and there's
not much room left for hope. In "Le pari de ne pas mourir,"
I said that history does not really progress and that the only
inalienable thing we're given is the instant itself. The exploiters are happy that history exists because it works to their
advantage. Politics also makes use of it. The body, however,
can only live in the instant, just as life can be received only
by the same body in the same instant. You don't reach a
climax either in the future or the past.

It is thus necessary for this body to be given back its
primitive powers. In that initial man, reinvested with all his
instincts, I see the man of the future who, keeping himself
warm by burning old objects from our museums, will create
new values. Sometimes it seems to me that we're already enter-
ing another reality, that some mutation is already affecting
us. If we stop impeding it, the energy we're made of will be
enough for us to make the leap.

D.S. — In *Arbre-Radar*, one senses that writing, for you, is an
erotic activity, an act of love.

G.L. — It's body-to-body, both in flesh and in words, with
the body in pawn to language which gives expression to the
experience.

D.S. — In *Arbre-Radar*, as in *Corps et graphies* and *Corps-transistor*, you systematically reject the use of the first-person "I." Everything is depersonalized. Even the act of love takes place in the abstract. Do you intend to start writing in the first person again, as you did in your poems of collective belonging, and adapt the "I" to your present investigations of the body and words?

G.L. — Nothing is depersonalized here. There's always an "I" which produces its particular forms of "your," "his" and "her." And if it happens or operates in the style of "cubism," that is no doubt because life isn't offered as a whole, but rather in fragments, piecemeal. Any consideration of a person or a thing in a total sense can only be an abstraction. In concrete terms, a whole is perceived in bits and pieces, in separate manifestations: a foot moves forward, a heart beats faster, and so on.

There's nothing abstract in the book, either. At an initial level, poetry has to be a language of signs: you write with words. However, poetry may also be a language of gestures, by which I mean writing that is done by movements of the body. I would like poetry to be even more concrete: I would like the bodies themselves to dance and write without any intermediaries.

As far as the "I" is concerned, although in fact I've never given it up, it's true that I'd like it to appear as little as possible. In a way, just saying "I" already indicates a *reaction*, which means one is no longer in the *action* itself. The "I" is in itself a conjugation, a step towards a sort of metalanguage. From now on, I would like to write only raw flashes of holiness and newness, without narration or commentary. I would like my "I," when facing those epiphanies of the origins, to be only a sort of cathode screen on which signs would flash into being. And that screen is still the body and skin of my "I."

D.S. — In "Choréographie d'un pays" ("Choreography of a Land"), which is a long introduction to *Québec*, a book of photographs by Mia and Klaus, you make a connection for the first time between modern writing, in which sounds and images stick to the movements of the body, and cosmogonical writing based on symbol and myth. Here the land of Quebec becomes for you a perpetual dance whose forms and steps you map out. Rivers are "bodies of water" which become enamoured, extended and exhausted, like an overcharged dancer. The whole of nature dances before your eyes. A stag leaps into a waterway; a bird splashes in the wind. "Chorégraphie d'un pays" reveals you in the process of reconciliation with your former self. It's a fascinating piece of writing.

G.L. — Having accomplished what I view as basic and essential, I think that now, in 1981, we can take possession of this space through the dancing body, making Quebec a source of pleasure, a dance in the true sense of the word. This land is possessed through the body and in the instant, as I've said repeatedly. I'll also repeat that what cleaves me to this land is the very substance of its soil, and not some spiritual quest or patriotic credo. When I was asked to write an introductory piece for Mia and Klaus' book of photographs, I looked at this land *again* as a body, as my own body fused with the body of the land.

D.S. — In 1981 you published a series of poems entitled *Barbare inouï*, with an original drawing by Louis Desaulniers.

G.L. — Those are *raw new noises* that were written in October '76, that is, six months after *Arbre-Radar*. I can't really talk about it. I'm not about to try rationalizing something that can't be rationalized. It's a book that has to be read, experienced and lived.

Michel Tremblay and the Collective Memory

Selected as the most important Quebec writer of the Seventies in a survey conducted by *Le Devoir*, the playwright, novelist and story-teller Michel Tremblay has produced a prodigious body of work since 1966. Born in 1942, the author of *Les belles-soeurs* first gained recognition primarily for his talents as a playwright. Increasingly, however, he has turned toward the novel, and those who wondered if he would be able to move successfully from one genre to another now have their answer: the "Chronicles of the Plateau Mont-Royal" have established Tremblay as one of Quebec's most prominent novelists. In addition, he has recently published *Albertine en cinq temps* (1984), a play in which a seventy-year-old woman comments on the various decades of her life. Acclaimed by the critics as one of Tremblay's most dramatic creations, *Albertine* proves that the Outremont writer is one of the few in Quebec who have managed to establish parallel careers as both playwright and novelist.

In his literary work, Michel Tremblay constantly draws his characters from the working-class surroundings of his childhood, and at the same time invests them with symbolic and mythical qualities of universal significance. Fabre Street and St.Lawrence Boulevard are thus transformed into an immense theatre of the absurd where men and women desperately seek out happiness in a repressive, unjust society.

Michel Tremblay's writing can be divided into six parts: the early works with no fixed locale (one book of tales and one novel); his translations and adaptations (five); three musicals; the St.Lawrence Blvd — or "The Main" — series (five plays featuring homosexuals and transvestites, prostitutes, female country singers and the tawdry "stars" in local night spots); the family series (five plays, of which four are focused on working-class women and one on a son's revolt); the chronicles of the Forties in the Plateau Mont-Royal area (four novels); and various works that are difficult to categorize *(Les héros de mon enfance, L'impromptu d'Outremont* and *Les grandes vacances).*

Michel Tremblay has lived in Outremont since 1974. He gave me a very warm welcome to his home one stormy afternoon in the month of June. And, as I somehow suspected, the electricity wasn't limited to the skies overhead. Confronting a writer with his work is enough to unleash conversational storms as well.

* * *

D.S. — In what way has your childhood served as a setting or background for your literary work? I'm thinking here of your characters and even the places you reconstruct in your writings.

M.T. — I think I always create retrospectively. It's fairly obvious when you read my books or go to see my plays that I do use my childhood and adolescence almost exclusively, although it's not so much my personal life as the world that surrounded me. I made myself the bard — not the bawd! — of one street, Fabre Street, and since I only knew that street until I was twenty-one or twenty-two, I've described it only up to the time I became an adult.

D.S. — You've already said that your childhood was influenced mostly by women, and there are a lot more women than men in your work. Does that mean you feel closer to the psychology of women than of men?

M.T. — In a normal society that question would hardly be relevant because there wouldn't be all that much distinction between men and women. But since we live in a sick society, those distinctions have to be made; and as a matter of fact, my first flashes of awareness did come from women, from the day I started writing in Québécois. Until I was twenty-three years old I was writing what I would term a kind of provincial literature of France; in other words, I was writing in the way I'd been told I had to write. But as soon as I started writing in Québécois and describing the surroundings I'd grown up in, I wrote about women and used women characters. The first human beings I ever heard speak and the first ones I observed — because I was born with a gift for observation, which isn't my fault — were women talking about their husbands, their problems or about society. It was completely natural for me to feel closer to women.

D.S. — Your first book dates from 1966: *Contes pour buveurs attardés*. These are stories told by men who are out drinking; they're mystical tales with occasional sadistic or masochistic overtones, and they're surprisingly violent. It's hard to recognize today's Michel Tremblay in these Hitchcockian horror stories. Why did you write these tales, and not plays or even poetry?

M.T. — I've never been close to poetry. There's something elitist about it that has always escaped me. Since I didn't go to school — I went all the way to grade eleven! — I never had a natural tendency for poetry because I had the impression that it wasn't something addressed to me. So the first things I actually wrote, when I was a teen-ager, were plays. I wrote my first plays when I was fourteen or fifteen. For example, *Le train*, a play that was performed in the little theatre in Place Ville-Marie in 1964, comes from exactly the same period as the stories.

And so my first writings were plays, but when I discovered fantasy literature, it stirred my imagination for a time. I began to write the provincial literature of a foreign country. When you read my tales, you see that they're written very much in the style of Jean Ray or Edgar Allan Poe, Balzac, Maupassant, you name it.

D.S. — Precisely! Even if the title of your first collection (translated as *Stories for Late Night Drinkers*) gives the impression that the setting is our local taverns, the *Contes pour buveurs attardés* aren't at all inspired by Quebec. The places are difficult to identify and the characters come from foreign countries, whereas everything you've written since takes place in the kitchens, living-rooms, streets, bars or taverns of Quebec.

M.T. — I don't find anything so surprising about that! Since we were brought up to feel a bit ashamed of our own literature and taught to write as they did elsewhere, and since we were forced to turn ourselves into colonials, it was normal for a little seventeen-year-old to turn towards other countries. For instance, I remember writing a play called *Le bûcher* (literally "The Pyre") just after I'd seen *Les visiteurs du soir*, a film by Marcel Carné that is set in a dungeon in medieval France. I'd watched it on television. I must admit part of my education came from television. One thing is sure, my first models were all foreign ones.

D.S. — In *Contes pour buveurs attardés* you quote Poe: "I offer this book to those who have put their faith in dreams as the only realities." Do you still believe in the central importance of dreams in literature?

M.T. — Yes, because when I came back to the novel with *La grosse femme* in 1977, I tried for the first time to combine the two forms of literature that interest me: fantasy and realism. That was even the main goal of the novel.

D.S. — We mentioned Edgar Allan Poe. Who are the other authors who have influenced you? I know, for instance, that you read ten or fifteen thousand pages a year.

M.T. — In drama, it's the Greek classics above all, and also Beckett, Ionesco and Genet. It was through them that I started to educate myself in a literary sense. I also like Racine, Shakespeare, Zola, Julien Green and Le Clézio. I haven't been influenced by any Quebec writers. It was in the Sixties that I started reading our own writers, but they didn't really influence me because I'd already started writing literature myself. You know, I wrote *Les belles-soeurs* in 1965, and at that time it was difficult to detect any influences. Even if the *joual* novel *Le cassé* was published in 1964, I read it after I'd written *Les belles-soeurs*.

In drama, obviously, I was never influenced by Gratien Gélinas, because when *Tit-Coq* came out I was maybe three or four years old, and I was probably about fifteen at the time of *Bousille*. But even if I don't like to admit it, I must have been influenced by Dubé, in his earlier style, if only in the sense of a delayed reaction. It's quite obvious that I've seen all Dubé's plays on television.

D.S. — And you reacted against Dubé's drama?

M.T. — I mean I didn't react against Dubé as a writer but I reacted against him on the level of language. I decided that, rather than perpetuating a generation of writers who came out of the classical colleges and then deigned to lower their gaze upon the common folk — it was all very well to forget that's where they'd come from and had managed to escape from — it was necessary to write drama that took place on the inside, plays that didn't feel like they came from the outside.

D.S. — ...and doing it without deforming the way people speak.

M.T. — Right, by using language almost as a political weapon, by transposing it — without changing it — into a language of the theatre, by keeping all the words and making them take off in a very theatrical way.

D.S. — It's obvious that you have a tremendous sense of observation. Do you take notes before you write a book?

M.T. — In the beginning, I used to work from my subconscious and it would all come out in a gush. Now I look over the manuscript at the end but I never write two versions of the same work.

D.S. — Let's now talk about *Les belles-soeurs*, which I think is the greatest play ever written in Quebec, because of its theatrical qualities and its enormous influence. The story of these fifteen women shows how they are exploited by the world of capitalism, how they all fall prey to dreams of instant happiness symbolized by winning a jackpot of trading stamps. It's also an original meditation on human existence since the "belles-soeurs" of the title talk to us about the major events in their lives: birth, death, love, marriage. The controversy surrounding the first performance of the play aroused a great deal of commentary, with a whole flock of insecure, French-oriented purists claiming you weren't even capable of writing in so-called standard French. Yet *Contes pour buveurs attardés* is written in a form of French that is completely neutral.

M.T. — That's because my *Contes* were relatively unknown, and since *Les belles-soeurs* was such a shocking success, it was normal for the purists to fall upon it like vultures and to forget, or decide to forget, that I had previously written other things in French. It was a lot more convenient for them to stab me in the back, calling me on the one hand an opportunist and on the other — God, what was it that Victor Barbeau called me? — a vulgar literary piece-worker. It was easy for them to say that since I hadn't gone to school I didn't know how to write, rather than taking a close look at what I was up to, which was a bit more complex.

D.S. — There's been a lot of emphasis on the realism of your drama, and it's true that you do describe the surroundings of the "belles-soeurs" in a realistic way. However, it's your talent as a playwright that explains why *Les belles-soeurs* will still be performed a hundred years from now; it's the theatricality of the play: the allegorical sequences, the monologues in the form of flash-backs, those choruses reminiscent of Greek drama. Did this mastery of the craft come to you naturally?

M.T. — I've seen a lot of theatre. I started going to the Théâtre du Nouveau-Monde when I was fourteen, and the first show I saw there was *Le temps des lilas* by Dubé. I also saw Anouilh's *L'alouette* at the opening of the Comédie canadienne. I really used to get off on the kind of plays I saw as a child, and I thought that was the only kind of theatre there was. As far as my way of writing is concerned, it more or less just came to me, apart from the influence of the Greeks, Beckett and Ionesco. You can find all that in *Les belles-soeurs*, that kind of absurdity. The reason *Les belles-soeurs* has lasted twenty years is not the fact that it's realistic, because it's not; it does say things that are true, but primarily it's theatre. Even if Quebec has changed incredibly in the past twenty years — amazingly and luckily — if a new production of *Les belles-soeurs* were performed today, it would still be a play that would be exciting and, I hope, never boring. It may become an interesting historical play because it presents Quebec as it was in April 1965, but it does this within a theatrical context and a structure that I hope will remain exciting.

D.S. — What significance is there to the fact that the "belles-soeurs" steal Germaine's trading stamps? It's much more than just jealousy, I think.

M.T. — We live in a society in which, when something nice happens to others, we've got to take it away from them. We're in a competitive society and when somebody gets something for free, something he hasn't worked for, society teaches us to take it away from him. People always say that the Québécois do a lot of back-biting. I was a victim of that for a long time. Other Québécois or other writers couldn't accept my being successful. A little of what happened to Germaine happened to me in my career. I got some of my trading stamps stolen too in the sense that I was slandered and stabbed in the back a few times. In our society other people's success is seen as a bad thing.

D.S. — I have another question about a bizarre incident in *Les belles-soeurs*. Why did you have them sing "O Canada" at the end of the play?

M.T. — Because for me, "O Canada" in French is an anthem of submission. It's pretty ironic to have a woman who's collapsed, and who's been robbed of everything, get up and join everyone else in the last two verses — in the French version, the words are literally "And your greatness, forged by faith / Will protect our homes and our rights" — especially since both her home and her rights have just been trampled upon. It was a political move, having a woman like that resign herself completely when she should have revolted against it all. In *Les belles-soeurs* every monologue is a sort of attempted revolution or rebellion, but unfortunately it's taking place in 1965; the end of Rose Ouimet's monologue is quite explicit when she says "Women can't do that; women are just going to stay stuck." They're women who should have rebelled but it was still too early in our history for that to happen. They know why they're unhappy and they'd like it to change, but they still don't have the means to do it. All they can do is give in and go on accepting it. As a matter of fact, when *Les belles-soeurs* is performed again, that's what's going to stand out the most; people haven't noticed it so much up until now because we were still too much involved in the play. *Les belles-soeurs* is the last time women accept what's being done to them.

D.S. — But *Les belles-soeurs* is still a play about rebellion. You take a very strong position in that play, even if Jean-Claude Germain claims that you wrote *Les belles-soeurs* from the outside, "as if you'd been looking at Germaine through a window."

M.T. — I think Jean-Claude said that at a time when all he knew of my work was *Les belles-soeurs*. Since it's a sort of a saga or a group portrait, the first thing that comes to mind is to say that it was done from the outside, but I don't think that's the case. Just because the author doesn't have a spokesperson on stage doesn't mean that his play was written from the outside. My dramas are inner dramas as well. If you take a close look at each of the characters, you'll realize they've all been created from the inside. Of course when you're talking about other people you're doing it from the outside, but when you write you're on the inside nonetheless.

D.S. — One last question about *Les belles-soeurs*. Writing a play as important as that one must surely have some disadvantages, especially at the beginning of a career. How do you reconcile yourself nowadays to the almost excessive influence this play still has on people's perception of you as a writer?

M.T. — Luckily for me, *Les belles-soeurs* wasn't performed immediately after I'd written it. By the time it did hit the stage, I'd already written two other plays. I didn't have the problem a writer has when his initial success makes it a hard act to follow. But I did have problems because it created a sort of social scandal.

D.S. — A year after *Les belles-soeurs* was first performed, you published your first novel. *La cité dans l'oeuf* is a tale of the supernatural inspired by one of the episodes in *Contes pour buveurs attardés*. The narrator in *La cité* has a mysterious African egg that plunges him into the monstrous world of the gods from the green planet. You seem to be very interested in the occult. Do you intend to get back into writing bizarre stories like the ones in *La cité dans l'oeuf?*

M.T. — No, not for the moment. *La cité dans l'oeuf* arose out of my own needs. I'd just written a series of plays dealing with the local situation, with my own surroundings, and I'd put aside the supernatural for a few years. I wanted to write a supernatural novel, but even at that, it's set in Montreal — in Outremont. When I was rereading *La cité* several years after it had been published, I was surprised to realise that its setting is right here where I ended up living. It was set in my future. It's all quite amazing: a supernatural novel that was set in the author's future!

D.S. — You might be a bit surprised if I told you that *La cité dans l'oeuf* is not unconnected to two of your more recent novels. In *La cité* the gods are in the process of killing one another off. In that sense you are settling your accounts with a hierarchical religion based on fear. It's the form of religion that prevailed in Quebec for more than two centuries, and you also denounce it in *Thérèse et Pierrette à l'école des Saints-Anges.*

M.T. — *La cité dans l'oeuf* is very much a Judeo-Christian novel. It's a novel full of guilt and sin, presented in black and white. All the patterns or conventions of Judeo-Christianity are there, but I probably needed to write about them in an indirect way before hitting *Marie-Lou* and *La grosse femme* and talking about them openly. I needed to take an indirect route and write out of my imagination.

D.S. — The year you published *La cité dans l'oeuf* was the same year you did your first adaptation, *Lysistrata*, based on the play by Aristophanes. Basically you stuck to the same story as Aristophanes: in the fourth century B.C. the women managed to banish war by threatening not to make love with their husbands any more. Why did you write this adaptation?

M.T. — Because I'd been commissioned to! The Théâtre du Nouveau-Monde already had an adaptation that Jean-Louis Roux didn't like. No one wanted to stage the play until one day they called up André Brassard, who must certainly have been the last name on Jean-Louis Roux's list. Finally, as a last resort, Jean-Louis agreed to the idea of an adaptation by Tremblay and Brassard, which left me only a month to write the script.

D.S. — André Brassard has staged the majority of your plays. What does working in collaboration with the same director mean for you?

M.T. — I wouldn't be the author I am now if Brassard hadn't been there. I hope that if he was here he'd say that he wouldn't be the director he now is if he hadn't known me! We've worked together for a long time and the thing that's saved us is that we've never worked at the same time. I'd start working first and discuss things with him while I was writing, and then he'd get to work later. In the same way that he'd let me work while I was writing away in my bedroom, I'd let him go ahead while he was creating my plays on stage, and that made for shows that were a good deal more complete than when a director sticks too closely to the author. One of the interesting things about the various productions Brassard has done is that, with each one, his personality comes through more and more clearly. If you'd seen *L'impromptu d'Outremont* as he staged it in 1981, with an all-male cast and in English, you'd see that it was much more a Brassard show than when he first directed it in French.

D.S. — And you agree with the liberties Brassard takes?

M.T. — I agree completely! As a creator he's as important as I am, if not more important, because I consider him to be infinitely more intelligent than I. I think I'm very, very lucky to have him. He gives me an enormous amount of help in writing my plays, in making them what they are on the stage.

D.S. — Coming back to your adaptation of *Lysistrata*, Aristophanes believed, no doubt a bit naively, in the possibility of universal peace. In your adaptation, however, you don't take that idea seriously. That's also the main point on which you differ from the Greek author.

M.T. — I have twenty-five hundred more years of history behind me than Aristophanes did. It would have been too easy to trot out the rather simplistic message of *Lysistrata*, especially since it's almost an anti-feminist play in which the women's revolt doesn't lead anywhere. What I wanted to say in *Lysistrata* was actually that the women's revolt doesn't lead anywhere — because of the men. In the final scene when you see projections of all the wars from Aristophanes' time right up to the present, they're still all wars that have been caused by men in spite of the good intentions of the women.

D.S. — You spoke of the play as anti-feminist. But in your *Lysistrata*, the women attack the males who treat them as sexual objects. The last words Lysistrata replies to the men who want an orgy are quite revealing in this sense: "I am a woman, true, but I'm a woman with a head on my shoulders! I want that to be understood and never forgotten."

M.T. — It's exactly the same reply as Aristophanes used and I put it as an epigraph in the book. Denise Filiatrault even learned this reply in classical Greek and Jean-Louis Roux wanted to include it in the script, but in the end we gave up on the idea because it sounded a bit corny. However, it's obviously the key phrase in Aristophanes' play.

D.S. — You spoke of signs of incipient feminism in Aristophanes. You still seem to be interested in feminism, because for its summer season in 1981, the Théâtre du Nouveau-Monde featured another of your feminist adaptations: *J'ramasse mes p'tits pis j'pars en tournée*, a translation of the American musical *I'm Getting my Act Together and Taking it on the Road*, by Gretchen Cryer and Nancy Ford. Again it starred Denise Filiatrault in the role of Louise, a singer who decides, a bit like some of the singers in your own work, to put together a show in which she can poke fun at some of the stereotypes imposed by men.

M.T. — Cryer and Ford are two American feminists who decided to write a musical about feminist subjects without it being too heavy. The play had a lot of affinities to Denise and the period she was going through in her life at that time.

D.S. — You've also translated and adapted two plays by another American writer, Paul Zindel.

M.T. — Yes. And there again it was women's rights that interested me in Zindel's work. I'd seen *The Effect of Gamma Rays on Man-in-the-Moon Marigolds* off Broadway, with Sada Thomson, and I'd really fallen in love with the play. For a year or two Brassard and I had been wanting to work with Denise Pelletier and we didn't know quite what to propose to her. I knew that Zindel's play was just made for her. *L'effet des rayons gamma* advances a very interesting theme, since there are two generations of women. One of them is the kind of woman who's always been fairly independent but who's been completely spoiled by society, as often actually happened in the past, and instead of rebelling she's destroyed herself. However, through her youngest daughter, you realize that women can manage to do whatever they want. It's through science in the play, but it could be anything at all. That's the message of the play. The girl, whom everyone laughs at, is a real scientific genius. At the end of the play she pulls off a miracle with the marigolds — which I called *vieux garçons* in French — and this makes her extremely valuable to science.

D.S. — Your adaptations of Zindel go back to 1970 and 1971. In 1975 you translated and adapted a play by the Brazilian author, Roberto Athayde.

M.T. — *Mlle Marguerite* by Athayde is a highly original play about fascism and education. Here it's a school-mistress who represents the manipulations of fascism, and in my adaptation she has three different levels of language. When she's really a school-mistress, she speaks perfect French. When she wants to be herself and speak person to person with her students, she speaks Québécois. And when she gets angry, she speaks *joual*. She's quite a martinet, full of old-fashioned ideas, but she's also a great actress, just as education itself has always depended on great acting. We see education doing a seduction number on us and then Mademoiselle Marguerite, who you hate and despise all through the play, pretends that she's having a heart attack. You find her touching. You want to help her. Which means that she's screwed us again. In the end she takes off, leaving a gun on the stage for her students. She hasn't changed a bit. She's had us again. It's an absolutely extraordinary play.

D.S. — It's interesting to talk about your translations since it would appear that you translate writers who resemble you a bit. However, let's return to your creative writing. We're now back in 1970, a year in which two plays came out, *En pièces détachées* and *La Duchesse de Langeais*. The former presents a series of sketches about the trials and tribulations of workers and waitresses in the east end of Montreal; it's about people stuck in their jobs, whose only pleasure in life seems to come from alcohol. I really liked the gripping, mesmerizing, colourful style in which these "odes" are written: *ordres de smoked meat lean avec pickles pis d'la moutarde*, as you put it.

And, as with all of your plays, there's someone who's out to raise people's consciousness. Hélène, for example, rebels every time a customer insults her. Your characters are always getting themselves involved in causes.

M.T. — Not in that play! Besides, Hélène really did exist. She was a cousin of mine and she was very important in my life. What was terrific about her, as I said in the dedication of *La grosse femme d'à côté est enceinte*, was that she's a woman who rebelled twenty years before everyone else and who suffered the consequences. That was the fate of women who rebelled: they suffered the consequences and died for it. Society put so many obstacles in the way of women who wanted to do things. But it didn't prevent them from expressing themselves. Women often expressed themselves, but always within the framework established by men; when a woman tried to get out, really tried physically, she was considered either a slut or a saint, which was the only way of reclaiming her. That's what happened to Hélène. In the Fifties usually the only way to get out, and not only for women, was to live on the fringes, at least in the milieu I grew up in. Either you let yourself be totally reclaimed through education — then you got out of your surroundings and became a doctor or a lawyer and started dumping on your origins — or you ended up on the Main and became completely marginal, which is what's happened to most of my characters. They're characters who are aware of the fact that they've destroyed themselves rather than let themselves be reclaimed. Hélène is a waitress but you sense that she's already done the sidewalks. *En pièces détachées* is a competition to see who's suffered the most, as shown in the scene between the mother and daughter. We were brought up to suffer more than others. When you stage that scene in a way that's tragic without being melodramatic, it's extraordinary to see two generations of Québécois engaged in a competition to see who's suffered more. It's a scene of incipient rebellion. Since we were brought up to be individualistic — because there was a fear of people joining together, a fear of imagination — we never learned to speak to one another. All my early plays are about the inability to communicate. The fifteen women called "belles-soeurs" would have started a revolution if they'd really talked with one another. What causes the revolution to abort is that, when they need to say something, they come to the front of the stage and say it under the spotlights rather than saying to the women who are their neighbours: "We should get together and rip the whole damn place apart." They're individuals who are trying to escape from any kind of revolutionary act.

D.S. — You illustrate the problems of living too much as individuals, but at the centre of everything there's still the family. As you know, the family has long been a central concern in Quebec drama, from Gélinas to Dubé, and you're hardly an exception!

M.T. — No, I'm certainly not! My own intention was to put a bomb in the Quebec family, to fill it full of explosives and blow it to bits — "once and for all," to use a good French expression. It was in *Marie-Lou* that I really tried to blow apart this Quebec version of a prison cell that I and everybody else resented so much.

D.S. — In *En pièces détachées*, the most tragic victim of the family prison cell seems to me to be Claude. Having escaped from an asylum, he's a pathetic victim of a stingy, brutal world which is almost completely devoid of love.

M.T. — I'm in the process of coming back to Claude. He's the Marcel character in *La grosse femme* and *Thérèse et Pierrette*, and now I want to explain what became of him — that is, how he became crazy. I want to make him a sort of chosen person, a person who could have changed things but who was refused and rejected by society because he had imagination. Claude represents the imaginative element that's so important in a revolution. A revolution with nothing but revolutionaries is boring. Even in *Thérèse et Pierrette à l'école des Saints-Anges*, Marcel's mother says, "I've given birth to either a lunatic or a poet. If he's a lunatic, it's not serious; there are ways of treating that. But I'm really afraid if he's a poet, there won't be any cure." In the third novel Marcel is nine and the fat lady's kid is five; it's the fat lady's kid, who is

me to some extent, who's going to have to take up where
Marcel left off since Marcel goes completely crazy. Society
drives him crazy because he's an imaginative genius. He knows
how to play the piano without ever having learned to, and he'll
probably be writing poetry at the age of nine. He could have
become a revolutionary later on, but society — the first form
of society we come into contact with is the family, once again —
rejects him. The fat lady's kid, who is not a chosen person,
asks permission to become one, and is rejected. Thus he's
forced to reconstruct his whole family through writing, by
becoming a writer who invents everything.

D.S. — Claude isn't the only person who's rejected in *En pièces
détachées*. In *La Duchesse de Langeais* you focus on the Duchess of the title: he's the uncle of one of the families in the
previous play, a "sixty-year-old faggot" who at the end of his
life finds himself alone and worn out. Is it true that you got
the idea for the Duchess after meeting someone in Mexico
who was just like him?

M.T. — Yes. I was in Acapulco, writing *La cité dans l'oeuf* on
my first Canada Council grant. I used to go to the Zocalo
every evening. There was a bar next to the cathedral. One
night I saw a guy from Quebec who was completely smashed
and who stood up on a chair and said something like, "Tonight's not for making love. Tonight's for getting drunk." I
went over and listened to him talk and I immediately wanted
to make a character out of him. At that time I was looking for a
way to speak about the duality of Quebec, our man and woman
side, this sort of mixture we are, our self-colonization. I
wanted to write a play to say that when we wanted to get out
of our situation in Quebec, we'd either have to become sluts
or start speaking French. I decided to create a man-woman
character who speaks French when he's a woman and, according to the standards of society speaks *joual* when he's a man.

D.S. — The   Duchess is a transvestite. You've previously
claimed that transvestitism is a symbol for the masquerade
that we all take part in, whatever role we play.

M.T. — Culturally we're all transvestites like Hosanna. Quebec was a "Duchesse de Langeais" for three hundred years. There have always been some people who rebelled, who wrote in Québécois, but they've rarely been given any recognition. The singer Madame Bolduc from the Thirties was rehabilitated only after her death. We submitted to a foreign culture and this turned us into transvestites. That's why I wrote *Hosanna*, a play that's presented as a sort of psychological strip-tease. Deep inside Hosanna there's a completely ordinary man who's decked himself out in rhinestones and feathers so that he'll look like something else. It's a strip-tease that's been turned inside out. He comes on stage dressed like Elizabeth Taylor and he ends up completely naked. That's what culture has done to him. A few years ago, Quebec culture was like Elizabeth Taylor in *Cleopatra*. Quebec culture had all sorts of disguises to keep its heart and roots from being seen. And there was also an elite that wanted to forget that Quebec's roots were rather vulgar. Finally, in the Sixties, we began taking off our foreign clothes and trying to rediscover the centre of our Quebec reality, with Quebec laws, Quebec myths and a Quebec language.

D.S. — *Hosanna* had tremendous success abroad after its premiere in 1973. The play deals with a crisis in the life of a homosexual couple: Hosanna, a hairdresser in St. Hubert Plaza, who's a tacky drag-queen dressed up as Cleopatra; and Cuirette (literally "Leatherette"), who's dressed up like a biker. After four years of living together, Hosanna and Cuirette's love for one another has changed. This is a crisis that almost all couples go through, whether they're heterosexual or homosexual.

M.T. — That's true, and I took up that idea again in *Les anciennes odeurs*, where I deal with a couple a few years after they've split up. But it's not true that Hosanna and Cuirette don't love one another, because Cuirette says three times in the play that he does love Hosanna. The two of them are also prisoners of society and the roles they have to play. They form a couple, they feel they have to be a man and a woman, and after a while a man and a women don't get along any more, sexually or otherwise. They're prisoners of the images that they're forced to project. But the play ends with a recon- ciliation. You don't know what sort of shape Hosanna and Cuirette are going to be in when they wake up the next morning, but you can speculate that they'll get along with one another, that they'll try to build something together rather than go on perpetuating an image that's been forced on them — the image of man and woman.

D.S. — There's another side to the crisis Hosanna and Cuirette are going through. They're horribly frightened of growing old. Growing old is a problem for everybody, but trans- vestites seem to fear it more than others.

M.T. — Because again they're projecting the image of what men think women should be like. It's doubly dramatic now that feminism has become so powerful. A transvestite is a man disguised as a woman and the problems he has are the problems men think women should have; for example, they think a woman shouldn't grow older. I'm in the process of rereading Balzac and every page is enough to make a femi- nist shudder. He compares women to anything at all — a city, a piece of furniture. The woman is always an image that the man projects upon himself. They're always objects that men would like to love or hate. By turning themselves into sexual objects for men, transvestites play a double game as women; it's a game that's bound to make them unhappy one day or another. They disguise themselves as objects that women hate as much as men.

D.S. — When Hosanna is ridiculed by the other transvestites in a drag-show, she finally decides not to be a transvestite any more, to stop disguising herself. She becomes a "he" and she'll be a man who lives openly as a homosexual. Is that the way you explain what goes on with tranvestites: that they're individuals who don't dare to come to terms with their con- dition in life?

M.T. — No, not at all! I don't know very many transvestites. I wrote *Hosanna* completely in the dark. None of my plays, and especially not that one, should be interpreted strictly on a psychological or realistic level. Hosanna represents much more than just a transvestite. I've never wanted simply to tell realistic stories. They should never be interpreted simply on the level of what you see on stage. Take *Sainte Carmen*. If *Sainte Carmen* is nothing but the story of a country singer who wants to change her style, then it's a bad play. It's the same thing for *Hosanna*. I didn't intend to write a play about homosexuality. I've never used homosexuality just in itself; I've always used it to say something else. It's a shame that a number of homosexuals have criticized me for the image I project of homosexuality, saying they're always transvestites, because I've never used transvestites simply as transvestites but rather as images of a culture that's disguised as something else.

D.S. — I know what you mean, especially since for me Hosanna is not really a transvestite. Hosanna is a part of me, a part of everyone. Today, for example, I'm wearing a khaki shirt and by doing that I change my appearance. You could say I'm hosannifying myself!

M.T. — All fashion is a form of transvestitism. Every fashion is imposed by someone else who decides how you're going to be dressed so they can make money at your expense. And as a matter of fact, although I don't mean any offense, I find that military fashion you're wearing very dangerous. It's been the most dangerous fashion through all time. It's basically a very fascist, very militaristic fashion that goes together with disco music, which is also a form of military music with a military rhythm. Fashion is an extraordinary way that society has found for regimenting homosexuals in particular, since homosexuals are very fashion-conscious, and now they're being turned into little soliders, alas!

D.S. — It's obvious that you've made a tremendous contribution towards creating a Quebec mythology in the field of literature. As an example, let's take the part of your work that deals with "The Main": a cycle of five plays, one musical and two full-length films about the nightclub stars, transvestites and call-girls of St. Lawrence Boulevard. One of the most famous plays in this series, *A toi, pour toujours, ta Marie-Lou,* first performed in 1971, presents a family of "losers": a violent, alcoholic father; a mother addicted to rosaries; one daughter, a country singer, who's always on "The Main;" and another daughter who's so religious she's practically a nun. Thanks to the effectiveness of your stagecraft and the clever contrapuntal construction of the play, you were able to keep the audience on the edge of their seats from beginning to end. The character who intrigues me the most is Carmen. Would you say she's another example of transvestitism, all decked out in her country singer's outfit?

M.T. — Of course, and at the end of *Sainte Carmen de la Main* she says that someday she may not only manage to write her own lyrics but also her own music. She'd like to go on stage without any disguise. However, in *Marie-Lou* she can only express herself through someone else's culture.

D.S. — Marie-Lou is haunted by madness. Perhaps it's the only way she can escape from her surroundings.

M.T. — She reminds me of Claude in *En pièces détachées.* It's also the main way out all through the series. *Damnée Manon, sacrée Sandra* ends up in total schizophrenia. The only means of escape for everybody is through madness. It's the only way we have for solving all our problems. If we don't choose to go mad, we cause revolutions or we get together to accomplish things. For Marie-Lou, who's caught in the web of her awful little life, madness is a dream of escape because at least then she could take pills that would make her happy all the time.

D.S. — In *Sainte Carmen de la Main,* published in 1976, Carmen says something very important to Bec-de-Lièvre (literally "Harelip"), a lesbian transvestite whose childhood you described in *Thérèse et Pierrette à l'école des Saints-Anges.* I quote:

> Harelip: Everybody always told me that I was ugly!
> Sandra: That I was vulgar!
> Rose-Beef: That I didn't talk good!

Choruses I and II: That I was dirty!
Everyone: Everybody was always ashamed of me.
    But Carmen said I was pretty and could go outside
    the tavern!
Chorus I: Wake up! she said.
Chorus II: Get up! she said.

You seem to be suggesting that your characters on the fringes of society should get out of their miserable surroundings and start considering themselves beautiful. And at the same time you're telling everyone not to let themselves be exploited by a money-grubbing society, not to let themselves be disguised by a society that forces roles upon us. Carmen realizes this. She's tired of disguising herself as a cowgirl. She wants to find her own style.

M.T. — But that's why she dies. The only way Carmen can remain pure is by getting herself murdered. Any sincere process of creation always includes the possibility of being reclaimed. What I mean by that is, if Carmen had gone on living and singing, she would have let herself be reclaimed — like me ending up on Davaar Street in Outremont! I hope I'll go on being effective, but I'm a lot less pure than I was fifteen years ago. To keep Carmen pure, I killed her. Carmen has a message — my message — and it's almost revolutionary. She tells people to try to rebel. In order for her to remain pure, she has to die. At least, at the end of *Sainte Carmen*, the Chorus is starting to know Carmen's songs by heart. What Carmen has sown can therefore bear fruit, even if she's dead. Some people have said that the end of the play is botched. On the contrary: someone who dies immediately after sowing their seed, someone who remains pure, leaves seed that is pure.

D.S. — We've been talking almost exclusively about women, which is normal since there aren't many men in your drama. But let's talk a bit about the father in *Marie-Lou*. I have the impression that the father is the real scapegoat in the play. Everyone attacks him. Nevertheless, he's as much a victim as his wife and children. Carmen realizes this to some degree. She knows her mother has always played the martyr.

M.T. — Since my writing is — my God, dare I say it? — women's writing, writing seen through the eyes of women, it's normal for the women to dump on the men a bit. I didn't rehabilitate the men until *Bonjour là, bonjour*. In *Marie-Lou*, however, Léopold is a very touching character. He's a man I like a lot. He's not a loser; he's the one who finds the solution, which is to die. In any case, since society has always been separated into men and women, it's normal for men and women to get into fights with one another. That's another myth, that men and women can't get along because they're too different. It's completely wrong.

D.S. — In the sequel to *Marie-Lou*, *Damnée Manon, sacrée Sandra*, published in 1977, you juxtapose two monologues: there's the recluse Manon, who seeks the answer to existence in her rosary, and there's the transvestite Sandra, who seeks it in sex.

M.T. — *Damnée Manon* is a play about the two great needs of every human being, God and sex. They're the two great themes of every civilization. They're separate, alas! They could very well not be separate. I wanted to bring the "belles-soeurs" series to a close on these two basic needs.

D.S. — It's interesting that you said "bring the series to a close" because the play *Surprise! Surprise!* that comes after *Damnée Manon* bears little resemblance to your other plays. It's a light comedy based on a telephone misunderstanding.

M.T. — *Surprise! Surprise!* was a show for the noon-time theatre at the Théâtre du Nouveau-Monde, for people who wanted to have some fun during their lunch hour. The wager was to create a very funny play by caricaturizing my own plays. It's a play that's absolutely stationary, using the same structure as *Marie-Lou*. Instead of having two plots, there are three. It's what I'd call a French farce without doors, a Feydeau play in which everyone remains seated. Instead of having doors slamming, you have the telephone ringing. It's really a self-caricature. I wanted to laugh at myself and the highly stationary way I have of writing my drama.

D.S. — You like setting your characters in confined, closed-off spaces. In *Trois petits tours*, which was telecast on "Les beaux dimanches" in 1969 and published in 1971, Berthe is a disillusioned ticket-seller who works in a glass cage. It seems there's always a "glass cage" in your plays: a kitchen, a nightclub or a living-room that closes your characters in.

M.T. — We're a civilization of prisoners. Any setting at all can be the image of a prison. You can be imprisoned in the middle of a crowd just as well as in a glass cage. Since we live in an individualistic civilization, our own body becomes a prison, and since anything good that happens to others is outside our prison, we want to take over other people's prisons.

D.S. — You indirectly denounce the passivity inherent in the naive, impossible dreams of several of your characters. Germaine dreams of trading stamps as an escape from poverty. Berthe dreams of getting rich like the Hollywood stars; she dreams of the glory of stardom, which is effectively conveyed in the name Gloria Star, a character in one of your "trois petits tours" (literally "three little tricks").

M.T. — *Trois petits tours* is first and foremost a play about social success. It begins with a piece about someone who has always wanted to be a star but has never done anything about it, who's settled for just getting fat in a glass cage. Then we move to people who have tried to succeed socially but who are so pitiful and who have so little talent that they've chosen the wrong way of going about it and they end up standing behind trained dogs in a nightclub. They appear in a number in which the dogs are more important than they are. And finally there's the story of a woman who pretends to be "glorious" but who's settled for selling human bodies. She's been rendered completely insensitive by an insensitive society. She's looking for something new and she finds it in the "go-go boys," which showed a good deal of foresight in 1969. At the end of *Gloria Star*, Gloria chooses a guy to go on stage and take off his clothes. It's her new way of finding social success.

D.S. — *Bonjour là, bonjour*, which was published in 1974, is the play in which you move furthest away from this obsession with social success. Serge, who has returned home after travelling for three months in Europe, develops a close friendship with his father, an admirable man who wants to reach out beyond the limits of his stifling surroundings. Serge has an incestuous love relationship with his sister Nicole, and in this he resembles the other marginal characters we've become used to seeing in your writings. Here you take the incest myth and turn it upside down, since unlike Oedipus, the incest here doesn't lead to tragedy; rather it marks the beginning of a victory over the type of character who is closed in upon himself, neurotic, constantly complaining about his "goddamn boring life" and "goddamn sex." The critics put a lot of emphasis on the fact that *Bonjour là, bonjour* marks the arrival of happy people in your plays and that it's the first time tenderness and optimism are the dominant sentiments. What do you think?

M.T. — Actually it's true that there are three marginal characters in *Bonjour là, bonjour:* the incestuous brother and sister, and the accomplice father who may have chosen to be deaf, since we're never sure whether he can hear or not. Suddenly, at the end of the play, Serge doesn't have to repeat what he says to him.

Tenderness can also be written and spoken about, but once again it's done through society's image of women, through the sorts of women's gossip that put a barrier between the father and son so that they can't talk to one another. There's been a lot of talk about the latent misogyny in *Bonjour là, bonjour.* In my opinion, however, the women are exactly what society wants women to be like. They're perfect products of a society that consumes women. The father and son attempt to show their affection for one another, as do Nicole and Serge — they're three characters who are trying to communicate — but they always have to communicate with one another through the filters of society, because they're marginal people and because the son has to shout to his father, over his two gossiping aunts, to say that he loves him.

D.S. — I was struck by the fact that Serge's first experience of physical love is through incest.

M.T. — I can't explain that myself... They're people living on the fringes of society, and probably at the time I wanted to say that the only way we can be happy in society is to be marginal, to experience our happiness on the borders of society. Within society, happiness is impossible. The three characters who are the heroes in *Bonjour là, bonjour* go off at the end of the play to set up a new cell on the fringes of society. The father accepts his children's incest and will thus be rejected by the five other women. But at least this new threesome will attempt to be happy on the fringes since they can't be happy within society itself.

D.S. — Your marginal characters appear not only in your plays and novels, but also in your musicals and films. Your most impressive musical so far is clearly *Demain matin, Montréal m'attend*, which was performed in 1972. It brings to life a deeply tragic universe in which the characters (singers, transvestites, waitresses and prostitutes) disguise themselves in an attempt to find success in the world of nightclubs. They're jealous and destructive of one another, and like some of your other characters, they're ashamed of their real names. Everything falls apart in this mad race for happiness. I'd be interested in knowing why you're so fascinated by the world of cheap entertainment. Is it partly because this sort of nightclub is beginning to disappear and you want to write about it before it's too late?

M.T. — My interest in nightclubs is that they're an integral part of The Main and one of the few means of escape. Becoming a performer on The Main in the fifties meant either doing a show with trained dogs or else trying to sing when you didn't have any talent. It was a way of getting out of our prison, of attaining a kind of social success. For the people on The Main, being a star on The Main was as important as being an international star in Paris. Lola Lee is a star to her sister, whereas for anyone outside The Main she's an absolute nobody. It's a little bit like our culture. For a long time we thought that being a somebody here was nothing; it didn't mean a thing. Now we're in the process of proving that's not true, that you can very nicely go on creating things here for the people here and still become known in other places; in fact you may be less scorned and more respected precisely because you haven't succumbed to other people's dictates. The French-speaking cultural world needs us as long as we stick to the way we really are. It was by subjecting themselves to the French from France that the older generations ended up getting shit upon, looked down upon. It was by trying to look like Frenchmen that they made themselves ridiculous. Our generation makes itself respected by saying what we have to say to one another and not bothering about Paris. Paris takes an interest in us because we're not interested in them.

D.S. — In 1976 you presented a second musical, *Les héros de mon enfance*. This involved a demythification of fairy tales, with sexuality and malice replacing the eternal triumph of good over evil. What were you trying to do here? Was it a revenge on all those heroes that we serve up to our children, with idyllic visions and happy endings?

M.T. — Yes, and I also wanted to bring the characters back to how the original author, Perrault, intended them to be. Perrault wrote moral tales. When the big bad wolf appeared in one of Perrault's tales, it was obvious that it was Louis XIV. Little Red Riding-Hood was also Louis XIV running after the little shepherdesses. That particular tale only becomes interesting when you're aware of its social implications. I wanted to demolish a bit of the sugary image those heroes had in my childhood, return them to their original meaning and add my own irony; I wanted to ridicule them a bit because they were overly important in my childhood culture. I'd be a better Québécois if I'd had Quebec heroes when I was young. It should be added that Perrault's characters had also been "purified" by the Quebec elite, who completely twisted and distorted them, just like those characters by Marivaux and Molière that people tried to prettify so that they wouldn't be too offensive. I wanted to make fun of Perrault for all these reasons, unfortunately perhaps.

D.S. — The film version of a major part of your work, a full-length feature produced by André Brassard entitled *Il était une fois dans l'est,* had a tremendous success. Were you closely involved in making the film and do you have any further plans for projecting your characters onto the movie screen?

M.T. — No, I wasn't involved in it. I did follow the shooting but, as in the theatre, I let Brassard do what he wanted. In any case, in the cinema a film is much more the work of the director than the script-writer.

The great quality I find in Quebec cinema — it's been called filmed theatre, but I say why not! — is that it's one of the rare forms of cinema that is lyrical in a verbal sense. *Il était une fois dans l'est* is a very lyrical film, and its verbal elements are very important. Just because it's cinema doesn't mean that it doesn't have things to say. It's not garrulous cinema, it's lyrical, and I make a clear distinction between the two. People talk in it, but they do so in a very lyrical way that is well adapted to the screen, with the help of the camera.

D.S. — Your second screenplay for a film is entitled *Parlez-nous d'amour.* Directed by Jean-Claude Lord, the film denounces the corruption in various areas of the Quebec television, newspaper and recording industries. Were you the one who had the idea of making this film?

M.T. — No! I'd been commissioned to do it, and as was the case with *Lysistrata,* I had to write it in a month. It was a project Jean-Claude had come up with and he needed a script-writer, so he asked me. Unfortunately we didn't have time to get to the bottom of the subject, and this resulted in a sort of hodgepodge of intentions that I find interesting, but far from perfect. Unfortunately it's not a finished piece of work.

D.S. — Your first novel dealing with a Quebec subject is entitled *C't'à ton tour, Laura Cadieux* and was published in 1973. It's set mainly in the waiting room of a doctor's office where fat Laura gives us a straightforward presentation of her views — including her prejudices and her insights — on a variety of subjects: immigrants, rich people, nuns and sex. It's a novel that's both funny and touching. You have no hesitation at all in showing Laura's narrow-mindedness about immigrants, who she says are dirty, strange and suspicious.

M.T. — The same subject exists in *L'impromptu* except that there the woman is bourgeois, not working class. I think everybody is racist and xenophobic. We live in closed societies. It's all very nice to tell ourselves that we're a nation of fine, generous people, but that's no reason to close in upon ourselves completely and hate everything that comes from outside. All over the world people mistrust anything different from themselves. It's rare for me to talk about it very much, although even in *Les belles-soeurs* there were cracks about the damned Frenchmen and the smelly Italians. Those are the kind of gross prejudices we were brought up with and we absolutely have to laugh at them now.

D.S. — That's a bit like the philosophy of the comedian Yvon Deschamps.

M.T. — Sure it is, but Deschamps got into the subject a lot more deeply than I have. In my plays it comes up sporadically but it's never the main thing I'm talking about. Unfortunately there are Québécois who went to see Deschamps and thought he was a racist himself, which is not at all the case.

D.S. — Why does most of the action in *C't'à ton tour* take place in the waiting room of a "guy necrologist," a sort of social club for a "bunch of crazy women who don't know what to do with their afternoons so they decide they're sick with something"?

M.T. — It had been a long time since I'd written a novel when I began *Laura Cadieux*. I was working in theatre, so I used a theatrical approach to help me. At that time I was also overweight and I wanted to write a novel about obesity, about the misfortune of being fat. That was a period when I was going to a doctor's office every week to get needles that would make me urinate. I actually heard all the conversations I put into *Laura Cadieux*. It's almost an ethnological study. Practically everything in the novel is true, even the absurd story of the woman's husband who died with a nail in his forehead, because someone had been playing with a revolver that shot nails. It's a sort of documentary report and at the same time an inside view of the torments of being fat.

D.S. — Before we start talking about the novels that come after *Laura Cadieux*, let's say a few words about a play that is distinct in both its subject and its language: *L'impromptu d'Outremont*, which was performed in 1980. Four bored and lonely sisters share an upper-middle-class house. Through them you satirize the social-climbing aspirations of the French-Canadian elite: one of the sisters has even married a Drapeau! Included in the satire are their misplaced values, their linguistic complexes and their social insecurities. *L'impromptu* is the only one of your plays that isn't written in *joual* and the only one set in a non-working-class milieu, a bit like the work of Dubé. It's a humorous commentary on the ridiculous pretensions of those Québécois who look down on the language and culture of their own people and who would be ashamed to have a common name like Tremblay! Harking back to Molière, who took revenge on his detractors with his play *L'impromptu de Versailles*, you get your digs in at those who claim you're too close to the common, "vulgar" people. Your *Impromptu* marks an important change of subject and setting in your work, does it not?

M.T. — Since I moved to Outremont seven years ago and since I've met people from Outremont who've said some rather peculiar things to me, after five years I began wanting to write a play about all the idiotic nonsense I'd heard said about the new Quebec culture. The character Fernande, for instance, doesn't only repeat things I'd heard. I'd reached the stage where, as a writer, I wanted to do an impromptu of my own. But instead of having the author on stage talking about his work with the director and the actors, I did a double impromptu: that is, instead of the author, I gathered together some women who talk about culture and who often say exactly the opposite of what the author thinks. Fernande, for example, is my own version of Madame Bovary, since Flaubert wrote *Madame Bovary* to prove that a writer is able, through one of his characters, to say the opposite of what he thinks. But I missed my chance a bit in that I let myself start liking Fernande, even if I really hate what's inside her. I'm not capable of describing characters that I don't like at all. And so I weakened Fernande by giving her feelings and sometimes even my own ideas.

D.S. — One of the Beaugrand sisters says something that reflects one of your major concerns: "There's nothing worse than knowing you won't leave any trace of yourself after you're dead." This worries several of your characters, whether they're country singers, transvestites or staunch members of the middle class.

M.T. — It's the great worry of my life. It's fine for me to say that I'm not ambitious and not "on the make," but I think if I'd gone through my life without knowing that I'm going to leave some trace of myself, some little mark on the world, I'd have considered my life a complete failure. I can't conceive of going through life without leaving some sort of trace behind. It's the major theme of my life, even if I don't give a damn about posterity since when I'm dead, I'm dead. But while I'm still living, the world will have become aware of my existence. That doesn't happen only at the level of culture or fame, but even within a family. It's always imperative to be important for someone else or to be important in one's surroundings, whatever they might be. There are a million ways of leaving traces of yourself, but what really counts is that you do leave some. I look down on people who just give up and become vegetables. You must always have enough courage to tell yourself that you can be important for someone else.

D.S. — You were born in the Plateau Mont-Royal district and to date you've written four novels or "Chronicles" about this area, the first being *La grosse femme d'à côté est enceinte*, published in 1978. The action takes place on a certain Saturday in 1942 and is set in two different places: a row of houses on Fabre Street and Lafontaine Park. This allows you to maintain the unity of time and place that is so important to you as a playwright. The women are almost all pregnant and the fathers are away at war. The characters in the novel are extremely authentic and engaging. How could one forget Marie-Sylvia, who runs the restaurant, or her dog Duplessis, an important character with a role in the narration, or Betty and Mercedes, the gentle, kindhearted prostitutes! And then there's the fat lady of the title, weighted down with the burden of procreation; she fantasizes about far-off Mexico and dreams of her children: merry, vivacious Thérèse and sad, serious Richard. I was very impressed by the poetic descriptions of nature in *La grosse femme*, particularly since they didn't play a very prominent part in your writing until you started publishing the "Chronicles." For me your *Grosse femme* will remain a striking portrait of the fortunes and misfortunes "trailed along in the wake of a people smothered in poverty and ignorance." My first question is an obvious one: why go back to the Forties?

M.T. — Because I wanted to take my characters back twenty-five years and create a "genesis" for my drama. I had written one series between 1965 and 1976 and I needed to describe to people how the characters ended up as they did. When the four novels of the "Chronicles" are finished, my next work, chronologically speaking, will be *Les belles-soeurs*. I'm in the process of explaining how my characters became the "belles-soeurs," how they became Marie-Lou, Carmen and so on. Also, I'm very much interested in the Forties. They were the years before people began thinking about rebelling.

D.S. — You've previously stated that with *La grosse femme d'à côté est enceinte* you wanted to renew your writing. What did you mean by that?

M.T. — The biggest change is in the level of tone. I was initially a theatre writer which meant that I shouted a lot. My drama was full of shouts and despair. Now I'm interested in talking about tenderness. The only way I found of doing this was to write a novel in which the narrator could say to the reader how much he likes his characters. In theatre, the author is never there — at least that's my theory — even if

you can find fragments of his personality in various characters. However, the author is never on stage. Therefore I
wrote a novel so that I could talk to people myself, without
doing it through my characters. One of the great discoveries
of my life is that I've been able to establish a fundamental
distinction between the novel and drama. Until now I've
always written plays when I wanted to sound off at people.
Now I'm writing novels because I want to whisper stories
into the ear of my best friend. In *Les anciennes odeurs* I tried
for the first time to combine both techniques.

D.S. — Does that mean that *Les anciennes odeurs*, one of your
most recent plays, is quite special for you?

M.T. — Absolutely! It's a play about the intimate knowledge
and the tenderness that remain after a couple has split up. It
deals with two guys who used to be together and who broke
up four years previously; they meet and they talk together.
When you're no longer with someone, what you loved about
them still remains. I still share that kind of intimate knowledge with my former lovers. It's not always easy, but you
manage. There are problems that are easier to discuss with
someone you've known for twenty years than with someone
you've only been with for six months. Anyway, in *Les anciennes
odeurs* I tried to combine the tenderness I use in my novels
with the shouts of despair that I used to put in my plays.

D.S. — Before we finish I'd like to ask you a question about
Les grandes vacances. It's a puppet show, is it not?

M.T. — Yes. It's a play I wrote in 1980 for Olivier Reichenbach at the Théâtre de l'Oeil. I amused myself making fun of
the social rituals connected with death, embalming and
funeral parlours. Death has to be demystified and undrama-
tized. The puppets allowed a certain exaggeration and car-
icaturization. Reichenbach did a wonderful piece of work on
it, making the very most of all the special effects: shadow
theatre, masks, and puppets using both sticks and strings.
And just for fun I put two of my "belles-soeurs" in it, Angé-
line and Rhéauna. I hope by now they've learned to laugh at
themselves.

D.S. — Let's now talk about *Thérèse et Pierrette à l'école des Saints-Anges*, a novel that won the France-Québec Prize. The second installment of the "Plateau Mont-Royal Chronicles," *Thérèse et Pierrette* recreates the repressive convent world previously described by a number of writers, usually women, including Marie-Claire Blais in *Une saison dans la vie d'Emmanuel* and Claire Martin in *Dans un gant de fer*. I must say I prefer *Thérèse et Pierrette* to *La grosse femme* because of the natural ease with which you put yourself in your characters' shoes and also because of the humour and the various "symphonic movements" that act as a musical background to the novel. It's a book both gentle and cruel in that it gives expression to the repressed violence of the nuns and girls who are subconsciously taking their revenge on the tyrannical, hypocritical society around them. Nevertheless, *Thérèse et Pierrette* aroused some negative reactions. Here again, though, it was the use of Quebec French that was at stake, not the intrinsic value of the novel. Madeleine Ouellette-Michalska even wrote the following in *Le Devoir*: "Setting out to promote and institutionalize the lowest register of the spoken language is to encourage the morbid complacency binding us to that which is most likely to kill our collective body and our common language." You'd think we were back in the days of *Les belles-soeurs!*

M.T. — After sixteen years I no longer know what to reply to those people; I don't know where their duplicity leaves off and where mine starts! There's even some question of double duplicity in that story. When I read Madame Ouellette-Michalska's article, I thought she was being totally insincere; I thought she was a feminist who had read the book hoping to prove once and for all that I was a misogynist and that what pissed her off was that she found it good, so the only way she could attack me was by lashing out at the language I wrote in.

D.S. — But I think Madeleine Ouellette-Michalska would say that, since *Thérèse et Pierrette* is written at least partly in Quebec French, and since the French language is threatened in Quebec, it's a dangerous book for students who have a poor knowledge of French.

M.T. — What I find alarming is that a woman who's a critic for as important a newspaper as *Le Devoir* isn't even aware that the novel isn't written in *québécois*. I don't want to defend my writing and I don't mean that I've never written in *joual*, but in my Plateau Mont-Royal novels I deliberately never let myself get inside the dialogues. There are no interpolations in my dialogues. There's a narrator who is telling a story in a language that's his own version of French. I'm certainly not about to start writing as they write in Paris simply because our language is threatened. In any case, it's not true that the French language is threatened in Quebec! I've no right, on the pretext that I'm an intellectual and no longer part of the working class, to change the language as it's spoken by a community. It would be vulgar, contemptuous, ugly and dangerous to change the language of the people just because I'm writing a novel. That would be completely ridiculous. My characters speak in a language and I write in a language. The two of them aren't all that different. Above all I didn't want to look like an intellectual condescending to write about the poor people and using a different language from theirs. That's why my novels are written in big chunks, with no paragraphs. I want people to forget there are two kinds of French in my novels; I wanted them to move from one to the other without really being aware of it. The descriptions are mixed in with the dialogues and there's no cut-off point between the two. I never say "She said this" followed by a colon and quotation marks.

D.S. — But what would you say to someone who thinks that, because of certain passages written in *joual*, *Les belles-soeurs* and *Thérèse et Pierrette* are dangerous for students who speak badly and write badly?

M.T. — In any case, students who speak and write badly don't need *Les belles-soeurs* to teach them how. People go crazy and tear their hair out because French is apparently in a bad state in the schools. I remember that in 1949, there wasn't a student in the class who was interested in the French language, except me. I got off on French, I came first in French, I was the class sissy because I liked French. There's nothing new about the Québécois not being interested in French. We were brought up thinking that French was for girls. Of course that sort of thing shouldn't be perpetuated; it has to be fought against, but there's no need to start tearing your hair out right now, because it's always been like that. It's too bad the young Québébois aren't interested in the French language, but the young people in France aren't interested in it either. The French have an accent that sounds very pretty to our ears and we think they speak better than we do, but if you read the articles on the state of French in France, you see that it's just as pitiful as here.

D.S. – And often it's not a question of speaking badly but rather of speaking different levels of language. The Québécois have the right to their slang, their *joual*. The French have their own slang and the English too. I wonder whether your detractors aren't simply trying to make all French the same. For them there's only one way of writing French.

M.T. – In Quebec, unfortunately, there's always been a breed of people who want to sterilize everything, to remove any trace of dirt in favour of Beauty with a capital B. There's nothing as dull in the world as a language perfectly spoken by someone who's perfect. There's nothing more boring than the accent you hear on Radio-Canada. As a matter of fact a French linguist who came to Quebec said that there's nothing more ridiculous than the accent affected by the people at Radio-Canada. He said they were the only people in the French-speaking world who didn't have an accent. It's unbelievable. Personally, I'm much more ashamed of that than I am of my characters who roll their "r"s. We're the laughing-stock of French linguists when we try to speak "properly." People who try to speak a written language are ridiculous. From the very beginning, in every country, in every civilization there's always been a spoken language and a written language. And there have always been writers who transcribed the spoken language.

D.S. – Well now, I think we've talked enough about the problem of the role of Quebec French in literature. I have some other questions to ask you about *Thérèse et Pierrette à l'école des Saints-Anges*. You put yourself in the position of three little girls living through the terror of the School of the Holy Angels. You're very much at ease with this viewpoint, and yet it seems so distant from the perspective you adopted when you brought to life the world of the "belles-soeurs" housewives or the transvestites.

M.T. — It's not more distant; it may seem more distant to you because you've just finished reading it or because it's new. In any case, ever since I've been writing I've been inventing things that I don't know much about. That's why as an epigraph to *Thérèse et Pierrette* I used a sentence by John Irving, the author of *The World According to Garp*, who says, "Imagining something is better than remembering something." That sentence explains everything I've written since '65. I wrote my plays about transvestites, for example, without knowing what it's like to get dressed up in drag. I've often spoken about things I don't know from my own experience but that I can very well imagine because everyone has a collective memory and a shared cultural baggage. In our lives we collect baggage without being aware of it, especially if we have a sense of observation. We pack little inner suitcases which become bigger and bigger as we gradually get older. When I described the lives of the nuns and the little girls, I used my collective memory — things I had heard about — and then I invented from within myself. I never really put a pane of glass between myself and what I'm writing. The pane may seem to be there because it's in the form of a drama or novel, but I end up becoming all my characters and even the objects I describe.

D.S. — That's why Thérèse and Pierrette ring so true.

M.T. — It all goes back to the collective memory. You hear so much talk about things by the people involved in them that you can end up imagining them as they really are. My nicest compliments about *La grosse femme* came from women who had children and were absolutely astonished to see how far I could get into the mind of a pregnant woman. But by using their imaginations, everybody can imagine what it's like. I could have made a mistake but I didn't — luckily for me. One thing for sure is that it wasn't difficult; it was all quite natural. Maybe that's what they call talent!

D.S. — Let's talk a bit abut the structure of your novels. *Thérèse et Pierrette* takes place over a period of four days. You like to concentrate the action within a limited time and space. Was this a technique you learned from the theatre?

M.T. — Yes, certainly. When I started writing *La grosse femme*, I hadn't yet decided it would take place in a single day. It was while I was writing the novel that I realized I wasn't capable of spreading myself out; that's just not the way I work. So I decided very early on that it would all happen in one day and that really relieved me. It's like with *Thérèse et Pierrette*. I decided months in advance that it would take place in four days because of Brahms' Fourth. I have to latch on to certain laws of the theatre in order to write novels because that's where I came from, where I got my first taste of success. *La duchesse et le roturier*, the third installment of the "Chronicles," takes place over a whole winter. I wanted to explain how Edouard, Victoire's son in *La grosse femme*, had come to be the Duchess of Langeais. It's a great romantic love story about two guys joined by their feet: that is, one's a shoe salesman and the other's a dancer. I was really getting off on feet!

Antonine Maillet:
Acadia, Land of Tales and Cunning

Nineteen seventy-nine was quite a year for the Acadians: it marked the 375th anniversary of the founding of Acadia by Champlain and M. de Monts; Antonine Maillet won the Prix Goncourt for literature; and the Acadian singer Zachary Richard was awarded the "Grand Prix de la chanson française" by the French President. With regard to fame and commercial success, Antonine Maillet has had a spectacular career unprecedented in the annals of Acadian and Quebec literature. Born in the village of Bouctouche, 40 kilometers from Moncton, Antonine Maillet studied in Memramcook, Moncton, at the University of Montreal, and finally at Laval University, where she completed a doctorate in French literature. She has worked as both a script-writer and programme announcer for Radio-Canada, and she has also been a professor of literature. It would be a mistake to think that her success as a writer started only when the successful play *La Sagouine* was published in 1971. Far from it! In fact she has been winning prizes since the very beginnings of her career: in 1960, the Quebec Government's Prix Champlain and the Canada Council Prize for her first novel; the Governor-General's Award in 1972; in 1974 the "Grand Prix littéraire de la Ville de Montréal;" the Prix France-Canada in 1975; and in France, the "Prix des Volcans" (1975) as well as the Goncourt. The author of *La Sagouine* and *Pélagie-la-charrette* lives for writing. Even in a conversation she remains very much the story-teller: *une radoteuse*, as they say in Acadia for a woman with "the gift of the gab." Antonine Maillet's writings contain a wealth of themes that are captivating, subtly nuanced, and typically Acadian. "Genealogy" is a good example here, since almost all her characters are amateur genealogists or, as the Acadians put it, *défricheteux de parenté* ("relative-finders"). They like to discover their common ancestors, untangle family connections and "make their roots extend all the way back to the Deportation" (*Evangéline Deusse*).

Madame Maillet has done for her land what Jacques Ferron has done for Quebec: transcribing and transforming its history in both popular and monumental terms, and in-jecting new life into its oral traditions. She celebrates Acadia in the rough, gurgling sounds of the sea and the myriad songs of her people: Acadian versions of ballads, ditties, sea shanties, jingles, fiddle tunes and *frolics* (evening get-togethers). Just as Jacques Ferron wrote his tales "of the uncertain country" inspired by the folklore of Gaspé and the Beauce, Antonine Maillet writes the legends and folktales of a newly awakened Acadia. Captain Beausoleil-Broussard's ghost ship is an outlaw vessel which roams the high seas picking up Acadians from whatever port they have been languishing in. The cart of death or the Devil's cart (a land-bound equivalent of the Québécois *chasse-galerie* which flies through the skies) provides transportation for a "cart people" who have been dispersed from their homeland. Acadia lives in its legends of horses whose manes have been braided by elves, *marionnettes* (the Northern Lights, in Acadian), were-wolves, monstrous turtles, *fi-follets* (Acadian will-o'-the-wisps) and mythological whales. In the land of Acadia, people read the future in cards or the stars, in the call of a Canada goose or the motion of the sea. There are supernatural appearances as impressive as the one at Lourdes or the vision of Fatima. In addition, Antonine Maillet is a sort of literary "map-maker," exploring the different "lands" of Acadia. The action in her books takes place mostly in the areas around the bays of Bouctouche and Cocagne. Sometimes, though, the reader is transported to the landscapes of the northeast, to Shippigan, Lamèque, Miscou and Treasure Isle. And occasionally we are led into other "Acadias": Nova Scotia, Louisiana, the Gaspé, the Magdalen Islands and Prince Edward Island. Yet however Acadian her themes and landscapes may be, they are always connected with a problem that is universal: the exploitation of the weak by the powerful.

Luckily, as with any good writer, the value of Antonine Maillet's work is not essentially ideological or documentary; rather it lies in the power of her imagination and the poetry of her perception. The sea is a thing of wonder. La Sagouine claims to have eyes that are deep and blue from staring at her reflection in the water; she says she has high cheek-bones and knitted eyebrows from so often watching for fish at the bottom of the ocean; her voice is hoarse from breathing in so much salt air. And for Pélagie, water is the stuff of dreams, whence comes the fertility of the race. Her Acadians remember their "spawning grounds" and their heritage, and like the salmon of their land, they stubbornly fight their way back up against the current. For Antonine Maillet, landscape is not simply landscape but an emblematic setting. In a land of sand-dunes, *buttereaux* (mounds of sand in Acadian French), *barachois* and *aboiteaux* (dikes or embankments), smelt huts, oyster barrels and rail fences, her characters tell the poetic story of their lives. The "moaning" of sea-cows, whales, cachalots, cod-fish and seals is transformed into an unforgettable music. This is an ancient, primitive land, the cemetery of Viking explorers. It is also a land of epic dramas with a flora and fauna nothing short of fabulous.

My meeting with Madame Maillet took place in Outremont, and I approached it with excitement and enthusiasm. I knew in advance that the interview would be lively, for in *Pélagie* Antonine Maillet makes it abundantly clear that the Acadians stem from a people of story-tellers and chroniclers, a people who four centuries ago produced Gargantua and his noble son Pantagruel. I had no need to worry: the conversation would flow freely.

* * *

D.S. — You were born in the Thirties, at the beginning of the Depression. It's a period that has often inspired you, has it not?

A.M. — Yes, because I believe that, essentially, a writer just keeps going back to his early childhood over and over again. You know, a novelist's first heroes are the first heroes in his life. I've been surrounded and marked by a whole series of characters and events from the Depression years: historical facts and people's actions. However, it's only later that you go looking for all that in your subconscious, and then you magnify it, transform it, enlarge upon it.

D.S. — It was a period that was quite extraordinary.

A.M. — It was extraordinary for several reasons, the principal one being economic, of course. Only, for us, the Depression had a very strong impact because at the same time it created the whole smuggling business. And that was really an adventure. It's quite exciting for a novelist.

D.S. — You wrote your M.A. thesis on the role of mothers and children in the work of Gabrielle Roy. I wonder to what extent the author of *Bonheur d'occasion* encouraged you to discover Acadia and to write about it, since in your thesis you often emphasize the national qualities of Gabrielle Roy's writing.

A.M. — I hadn't realized I'd emphasized the national qualities of Gabrielle Roy's writing; you're the one who's pointing it out to me. But it's clear that Gabrielle Roy did influence me. It was while I was teaching Quebec literature that I realized just how much she had stimulated me. I wanted to be able to write like her. I finally discovered Gabrielle Roy was the one who could open the door for me because in her work you find both a convincing form of realism and at the same time an extraordinary level of poetry. That was precisely what I was looking for in literature. There is realism in *Trente arpents* but not the same level of poetry as in Gabrielle Roy. On the other hand, there's an extraordinary level of poetry in *Le Survenant* by Germaine Guèvremont, but there's no story. And for the first time, there was Gabrielle Roy with both! I'd found the connection I was looking for.

D.S. — Were you influenced by other Quebec writers? For example, I've noticed a lot of similarities between your work and Jacques Ferron's: the folktale atmosphere, social concerns, the ancestor theme.

A.M. — Ferron is the writer I feel closest to, with whom I identify the most completely. I really think he's the most talented Quebec writer.

D.S. — In your doctoral dissertation, *Rabelais et les traditions populaires en Acadie* (PUL, 1971), you study the Acadian people's loyalty to traditions that go back to the Middle Ages in France. Your *Aventures de Panurge, ami de Pantagruel*, a play performed at the Rideau Vert in 1984, is inspired by Rabelais' *Tiers livre* and *Quart livre*. Like Rabelais, the first Acadians had heard the tale of the great Gargantua, not to mention other moral, mocking or bawdy stories. Acadia has kept alive more than 700 words and expressions and some 50 games as well as countless songs, legends and *fêtes* from Renaissance France. Have your doctoral studies had an important influence on your writing?

A.M. — They've been more than simply an influence on my writing; they were a discovery of the value of our heritage. By studying Rabelais, I first came to understand literature, since for me Rabelais is the most complete author in the French language — in the way I perceive literature, of course. And at the same time I discovered to what extent Acadia still had the rudiments of everything you find in Rabelais. So I said to myself, not that I was going to be an Acadian Rabelais, but that there were no longer any bounds to our imagination, no limits to our ambitions. In Acadia, everything was possible in literature. Rabelais was more than an influence. He was a kick in the "derrière."

D.S. — In your dissertation you discuss both the origins and the originality of the Acadian language. As you know, an identification with popular language in Quebec has played an important role in the development of Quebec literature, song-writing and cinema. Will the Acadian language have a similar influence?

A.M. — The Acadian language should, and in fact does, play a very important role in expressing its culture in all forms. And when I say the Acadian language, I have to be specific since there are several different levels in the Acadian language. One level of the Acadian language is simply the French language, period. Many people such as teachers and civil servants speak that kind of French, although they obviously have their own intonation and accent. There's also the Acadian language of the man in the street or the young people, and this is what's known as *chiac*, which is yet another form of Acadian French. And finally there's the Acadian language that I myself chose for my literary works — not that I chose it — but which chose itself because I had decided to evoke the past. For me, the oldest form of the language is the one that was preserved for three centuries in North America through natural force of habit; this was the old French language, chafed by our local climate and chafed also by our English-speaking surroundings, but still spoken in Acadia almost in its pure form right up to the present generation. This is the language of Acadia's national heritage. In saying that, I'm not suggesting that the language spoken by the little guy in the street isn't Acadian. I accept all the Acadian languages. For example, it doesn't bother me if people write poems in *chiac*.

D.S. — As far as I know, there haven't been any huge protests against the use of Acadian French in literature. However, as you're well aware, a number of Quebec novelists, playwrights and poets who have used colloquial forms of Quebec French have met with fierce criticism from the purists. How can you explain the fact that you haven't had problems of this sort?

A.M. — First of all because Acadia has a lot fewer purists than Quebec, a lot fewer cliques and Academies. So it's normal that Acadia should react less to innovations in literature. But the real reason is that some levels of language in Quebec are richer than others. Now, there may have been some attempts to identify the Quebec language with a certain level that wasn't necessarily the richest. However, the language I use, among all the levels of the Acadian language, is perhaps the richest one from my point of view — although others might challenge me on that.

D.S. — Still, you know, even Savard's use of Canadian words and expressions in *Menaud* was criticized at the time, and yet he wrote the Quebec equivalent of the Acadian French that you use.

A.M. — Right, but that's because it was in the Thirties. If I had happened along with *La Sagouine* at that time, I would have caused the same uproar. Acadians have a good sense of timing; they always know when to arrive. (Followed by Sagouinical and Pelagiac laughter!)

D.S. — Let's now take a look at your literary work. In your first novel, *Pointe-aux-coques* (1958), you created the character of Mademoiselle Cormier, a young school-teacher who leaves the United States to go back to her native village in New Brunswick. Surely there must be something autobiographical in that novel?

A.M. — The adventure part that happens in Richibouctou Village, which became *Pointe-aux-coques*, was something I experienced. The part that isn't autobiographical is that I never had a father who went off to the United States. But the descriptions of the village are very real.

D.S. — In this novel, there's some question of a new kind of economic organization for the Acadians. I'm thinking of Jean, for example, who wants to set up fishing cooperatives. Even in your first novel, then, it appears to me that there is a clear social commitment.

A.M. — Well, it's a little artificial, I must confess. At that time I didn't know anything about problems like that. I could have told the story a lot more truthfully and realistically. Jean is a person who's been invented. He's a character who's a bit false and his mission is rather artificial. It lacks substance. I was twenty years old and that's the way I perceived society. The novel proves I wanted to be socially commited, but it's very embryonic.

D.S. — The sea has a magic power over Jean and the school-teacher. What, for you, is the meaning of this sea that you portray so well?

A.M. — I'm going to be a bit pedantic, but I would say that the sea is a feminine symbol. There are all sorts of sea symbols, so I'm not making anything up. The sea is some-thing visceral, with its storms, its movements, its spherical side. When I look at the sea from my lighthouse, it always looks round, like a ball. It's the horizon. The sea is almost always moving. And when it's not in motion, I know there are extraordinary currents and eddies going on beneath the surface. And then the sea is smooth and calm, dangerously calm. It has the character of Racine's Phaedra, who calls herself "daughter of Minos and Pasiphaë" — the most beauti-ful phrase in French literature. That comes at the time when Phaedra has reached her greatest level of inner turmoil. There's something complex, nocturnal and lunar about the sea; it's a synonym of the "anima" world as compared to the "animus." The sea's feminine side is of particular interest to me because Acadia is like that. Acadia is not solar or cerebral. It's visceral, instinctive and intuitive, and for me the sea is like that. As La Sagouine says, we end up looking like the country that we were born in. So there you have it!

D.S. — In your second novel, *On a mangé la dune* (1962), you put yourself in the place of Radi, a little girl who transforms the world by seeing it through the eyes of fantasy. When Radi looks at the sand-dune, there's an entire painting presented to the reader. Tell me a bit about those dunes and mounds of white sand, those *buttereaux* that keep cropping up in your landscapes.

A.M. — They were the first landscapes I ever knew. When I was very small, I don't know at what age, I went to play in the sand-dunes. I was pitched into the dunes when I was born. I was living in a little village called Bouctouche. But seven miles away there was a place called "Fond de la Baie" (the "Cove"), and at that time it was all sand-dunes, although the sea has eaten away at the dunes since then. One dune was seven miles long, like a finger sticking out into the sea. My great grandfather had built a house by the seaside in the Cove, and that house is still there. My father was born in it. Every year during my father's holidays we would go to spend a few days at my grandfather's place or my uncle's, with our cousins and all the other relatives. This was a tremendous time for us, a real free-for-all, and I'd spend the whole day rolling down those dunes. Don't ask what a dune was for me. It was a place for rolling around, for getting drunk on nature. I'll never be able to get the sand-dunes out of my nostrils or my ears or my belly-button. The sand got into every orifice of my body. I have the impression that my mind, my stomach and my soul all got filled up with sand; certainly my heart and my backside did. For the rest of my life, sand-dunes will always be a symbol of both nature and communion with nature, of celebration, love of life and childhood.

D.S. — The children you have created in your work almost all have an active knowledge of Acadian history. They play patriotic games and get themselves ready to defend their land.

A.M. — I wouldn't say they're children. They're myself: me and the little group that I hung around with. I had a prose-lytizing and apostolic mind in those days and I dragged everyone else into this patriotism. I think it was something peculiar to my family; both my father and mother were school-teachers and they were both very deeply committed to their country, not politically, but in their way of thinking, their way of seeing things. Basically, they were very nationalistic and they were especially drawn to the French culture. They were absolutely determined that we would hold on to our roots. So I inherited that and I passed it on to my neighbours and my girlfriends. In my village I formed a sort of group along the lines of the Order of the Garter and we would talk about socking it to the English — except that the English in Bouctouche spoke French. They didn't have any choice. In actual fact we were very good friends with them. We all went to the same school, since there wasn't a separate school system in New Brunswick.

D.S. — Let's move away from the world of children to talk a bit about the adult world you portray in *Les crasseux* (1968). You describe the revolt of the people "from down below" (Don L'Orignal and his son, La Sagouine and her daughter), who steal molasses from the people "above" and who become *soldars* (soldiers, in Acadian) in the fight for greater social justice. Is this to some extent your own revolt against the *godêches*, the "bigwigs" and prominent people in Acadia and elsewhere who exploit the underprivileged classes and other people who have been symbolically "deported"?

A.M. — You know, at the time of *Les crasseux* there was, and there still is today, a kind of duality in my way of describing the world. It's not so much a duality between good and evil — my mind isn't as Manichean as that. It's more a duality between those who are well provided for and the others, and paradoxically the better-off are more unhappy than the others. In my books — and it's not something I set out to do, it just came by itself — the "happy good old fellows" are the ones who aren't well-off, the "have-nots." *Les crasseux* doesn't represent a struggle I had against the prominent people because actually, from that perspective, I would have been on the prominent side. It's more the ones who are happy against the others, the ones who are free against the others.

Perhaps instinctively and unconsciously it was the Acadians against the others. In *Les crasseux* the real symbolism behind it all isn't between two classes of Acadians, but rather the Acadians against the English. But I wasn't looking for symbolism.

D.S. — In *Les crasseux* your character Citrouille, overwhelmed by social injustice, commits suicide. This is a tragic ending that is rarely found in your work. What explains this suicide?

A.M. — Well, the proof that it's very rare indeed is that I rewrote *Les crasseux* with Citrouille coming back to life. That proves that I'm not at all inclined towards suicide, and when I had Citrouille die, it was probably against my nature. Actually, there are moments when a writer does go off on the wrong track, especially when it's the head that takes over, when it becomes cerebral, when you draw up a nice plan in order to be able to prove a point.

D.S. — It's certainly not the head that takes over in *La Sagouine* (1971). Your character is utterly spontaneous. In the preface you say that La Sagouine is not aware of being exploited, that she naively thinks she's a "full-fledged citizen." But she's not all that naïve; she knows she's less privileged than the others and she's not really completely taken in by it all.

A.M. — No, you're quite right. *La Sagouine* is an ambiguous work. That's why people may keep on studying it. If *La Sagouine* is rich, it's because of the truth of its ambiguities and its paradoxes. The world is full of paradoxes. So is La Sagouine, and so is Acadia. On the one hand, it's true that La Sagouine is naïve — it's almost as if she asked pardon for stealing a breath of air from someone else who might need it. But while she's doing this, she's also winking at us — not at her neighbours, but at the readers and the author, as if to say "I know darn well it isn't true." It's as though she were making a public confession, and that's what makes her interesting. There's nothing crazy about La Sagouine. When she's describing the nicest Christmas possible, she describes it with sen-

suousness and pungency and pleasure, and when she ends
up saying "A nice Christmas like that ain't for poor people,"
the paradox is enormous. Christ died on the cross and was
born in a manger for the poor people, but the nativity scenes
they've built are so beautiful that it's no longer something
for the poor. So, when La Sagouine is throwing barbs at
other people, she's quite aware of what she's doing. But if she
was aware to the point where she broke out laughing, it
wouldn't be as funny. The naivety comes from the fact that
she's saying it without appearing to be saying it. The Acadians are people who describe intelligence in this way: they
say "he's crafty." It's strange, but Acadians identify intelligence with craftiness; this means that for an Acadian, to be
intelligent is to be sharp, to be crafty. He's perfectly aware of
when he's making fun of something, but he looks so naive
that you think he isn't conscious of it.

D.S. — Apparently most of the characters in *La Sagouine*
actually existed: La Sagouine, Gapi, La Cruche, La Sainte,
Don L'Orignal and the others are real names.

A.M. — *La Sagouine* isn't a real name, although there are some
real names behind her. La Sagouine is a common name, the
feminine form of *sagouin* (literally a "slovenly fellow"). La
Cruche isn't a real name. Gapi isn't either; even if there was
a man in Bouctouche called Gapi, it's not the same Gapi at
all. On the other hand, there are some real names. There's a
whole series of them that I didn't want to change because
they're too beautiful, especially the nicknames like Don
L'Orignal, Noume, Michel-Archange and La Sainte.

D.S. — I'm very interested by the role of religion in your
play. La Sagouine says that we mustn't question the workings
of "the good Lord," but she questions them anyway. She
wants to know why we have to "hope to be carried to the
other side" before we can be happy. She seems to call into
question a certain form of religion that offers "the hereafter"
as an answer to everything. What do you think of this?

A.M. — La Sagouine questions religion a great deal. One
day a critic told me that *La Sagouine* was the most anticlerical

work that had ever been written in Canada. He might be right. But what is meant by anticlerical? It doesn't mean antireligious. Anticlerical means to be against the clericalism of the priests, and in this sense La Sagouine is anticlerical. She's against the structuring and regimentation of religion and faith. It's not that she's against religious principles; she has no religious ideas. She just looks at the facts and she questions the results. She says, "Come on, how is it that I have the right to sleep with my husband but not the right to dance with him in the kitchen on a Saturday night and then go take communion with him the next day?" She has no idea of morality. Her instinct tells her that it's not logical. La Sagouine questions God with such overwhelmingly obvious and natural commonsense that God the Father must be laughing along with her. A theologian like La Sagouine starts to have doubts in God's goodness when God isn't good. When the priests make God into a monster, you have to ask questions about the goodness of God.

D.S. — Apart from the matter of religion, there's the problem of politics that comes into play in *La Sagouine*. La Sagouine calls herself an Acadian, but she deplores the fact that there's no established country or nationality. Do you have any precise ideas about the kind of collective organization Acadia will need to survive?

A.M. — The political question is very complex and very difficult to deal with. It would require a great many parentheses and qualifiers to answer it properly. The way I see it goes something like this. I tell myself that the survival of a people doesn't necessarily depend, or at least not in a basic sense, on frameworks, whether they be political, geographical or territorial. Acadia is proof of this. Acadia has proved that it has an inner need to exist and an inner quality of existence. We need to exist and we exist as such-and-such a thing, and there's no destroying that. If you like to eat codfish in a certain way at a certain time, three generations after you've left the place where the codfish are, then it's because there's something very profound in that manner of existence. There's a culture, in the most general sense of culture, which is the expression of one's selfhood. There is a tradition, a whole background of heritage, which comes from very deep roots, and this means that you don't sing or pray or sneeze or walk in the same way as your neighbours. For me, that's what defines an ethnic group. By giving it a framework, you may make a nation out of it but you don't necessarily make a people. The soul is what makes a people. Now, political struggles are never waged to make a people but to make a nation. And the danger in that is that you end up making nations which fight against one another. It's not the peoples who fight against one another but the nations, and that's why there are sometimes wars in which brothers are fighting against brothers. I'm not saying that the present struggle of the Québécois or the Acadians or the Basques or the Bretons is useless. And I'm not saying it shouldn't be happening. But I do say that you have to be careful that the struggle is not for frameworks when in fact it should be for the soul. And I believe that the soul can sometimes go on without frameworks, but the framework can never do without the soul.

D.S. — In *Emmanuel à Joseph à Davit* (1975), the people living on the hillside don't want to leave their bit of land to go live in the village. This would mean a betrayal of their past and their heritage — their *hairage* as the old Acadians used to pronounce *héritage*. The people of Quebec, on the other hand, have cities where they can live in French alongside their traditions and their national inheritance. For the Acadians, however, things are different. Moncton presents the dangers of assimilation. What solution can you see for this dilemma of moving from the country to the city?

A.M. — It worries me, but I think the solution will either come of itself or won't come at all. I'm perhaps being dangerously Acadian in what I'm going to say, but I've always trusted in time, and I know that in the past the Acadians found themselves on the edge of the precipice much more often than now, and in much more dangerous circumstances too. The present danger is of being assimilated. However, assimilation — ah, even if there was only one chance in a thousand, maybe the Acadian would even take that one chance — assimilation can happen in the opposite direction. They might be able to assimilate the others. Last year in Moncton there was the three hundred and seventy-fifth anniversary of the Acadians and there were eight thousand people in the Coliseum to celebrate it. The English could not ignore that. At the anniversary of the City of Moncton, I doubt if there were even three hundred people. What does that prove? It proves that there's a vitality in the Acadians that the English people in Moncton no longer have. There's a French university in Moncton but there's no English university. If you look at Moncton through the eyes of a foreigner, it's an Acadian city. If you look at it through the eyes of an Acadian, it's an English city. What interests the tourists who now go to Moncton — or to New Brunswick, period — is the Acadians. Even from an economic point-of-view, we're an important consideration. So, just wait a while! We'll be able to assimilate the others. When Rome conquered Greece, it was Greece that assimilated Rome!

D.S. — La Sagouine and Mariaagélas have led us into some timely topics. But now let's turn to your other books. In 1972 you published *Don L'Orignal*, which you described as a "Puciade," a sort of Acadian *Iliad*; in it Don L'Orignal tries to protect his poverty-stricken people against the "big bosses." The *Puçois* (literally the "Fleas") have been living on their land for generations but they've never signed a lease. The *Crasseux* (literally the "Crass") have no lease either. Might this be an allegory about the present situation of the Acadians who are living in a territory that is not a country?

A.M. — To reply to that I'll have to put the cart before the horse. What I mean to say, strangely enough, is that reality has begun to imitate my books. I never thought at all that I was creating a symbol of people who had lost their lands. I simply saw people like Citrouille and Noume. Usually if a writer turns to his primary source of reality — that is, his source of inspiration — if he describes his surroundings, they often reflect the reality of an entire people. In my case, I simply told the story of someone who had experienced something. Don L'Orignal existed, and so did his son Noume, and Citrouille — and they didn't have any land. All that is true, in the small sense. However, because it's true, it's also true in the large sense.

D.S. — I wondered if the Ile-aux-Puces, which we find in *On a mangé la dune* and *Don L'Orignal*, is a real place.

A.M. — It's a real place that has the proportions of the Ile-aux-Puces in *On a mangé la dune*, but in *Don L'Orignal* it takes on Rabelesian dimensions. The real Ile-aux-Puces is about as big as my house here. The island is not inhabited. There is poison ivy (*l'herbe à puces*, in Quebec and Acadian French), and that's where its name comes from, not from any fleas (*puces*, in French) that might have been found there. I enlarged it to the dimensions of the imagination.

D.S. — You know, of all your novels, in my opinion *Don L'Orignal* is the one that most closely resembles a fairy-tale. A flea turns into a man, an island defends itself against invaders, a fisherman is changed into a knight. Do you intend to write other tales for adults or, why not, perhaps even tales for children?

A.M. — I'm quite intent on writing other tales. As a matter of fact, the publishers are after me to do so. I did write some children's tales when I was a girl. However, I know — and there's nothing to do about it — that my children's tales will very quickly become tales for adults. *Christophe Cartier de la Noisette dit Nounours*, which was published in 1981, was my first children's book. The first tale that I ever heard was the one about the three bears. As for Nounours (an equivalent for "Teddy Bear" in French), that is truly an archetype for children's legends as they've been translated in Acadia.

D.S. — Your only collection of tales for adults is *Par derrière chez mon père*, which was published in 1972. In it you take a trip through time, starting from Touraine in France and continuing on through the villages of your childhood. In that book, as well as in others you have written, the Indians are brothers to the Acadians.

A.M. — There's an Indian reservation close to Bouctouche. In *Pélagie*, Jean marries an Indian named Katerina. Historically, such marriages often took place. We had frequent contacts with the Indians. They used to come down to our place to sell their baskets. In *Par derrière chez mon père* there's the story of the Indian who cast a spell on my Uncle Marc. My Aunt Evangéline told me this story. She's convinced that my Uncle Marc, who is epileptic, has been sick all his life because the Indian cast a spell on him. Indians were rather mysterious characters for us. They lent themselves to that. When the Indians would come to sell us things, if we refused to give them what they wanted, they'd say, "I'm going to cast a spell on you." They played with their power over us and we were really frightened of them.

D.S. — The characters in your tales are as frightened of diseases as they are of Indians. They have very superstitious attitudes towards sicknesses: epilepsy, mumps, colic attacks, burning lungs. Was there a lot of death in your childhood?

A.M. — It's not so much that there was a lot of it in my childhood, but whenever we talked of illnesses, it was always made into something enormous. For example, if someone had the burning lungs, it was understood that he wouldn't recover from it. That particular disease was absolutely terrifying. The sick person would spit and drool. I never saw it myself, but I imagined it. It was quite something for a four-year-old girl, really appalling. I was very much impressed by the diseases people would tell me about.

D.S. — In *Par derrière chez mon père* there's a story that's essential to an understanding of your perception of Acadian history. It's called "Fanie" and in it you reproach Longfellow for having created an Evangeline that doesn't bear much resemblance to the real Acadian Evangélines. She's too pure, too passive, too lacey — in other words too tragic, too literary and romantic. The real Evangélines must therefore have been more along the lines of the women in "J'ai du grain de mil" (a traditional folksong made popular by Edith Butler, which serves as a refrain in *Pélagie*); they're solid supporters of their husbands who have gone off to war, they're cheerful creatures and there's nothing idyllic or sombre about them.

A.M. — For me the women in *Pélagie-la-charrette* are in fact a good deal closer to what the Acadian women were like than Longfellow's famous Evangeline. So I had my little revenge on that Evangeline that everybody always found a bit too delicate. There's a paragraph in "Fanie" that explains it all:

> There you have her, the real Evangéline! A courageous, wily, loud-mouthed mother with eleven kids. Let her loose in the middle of a poem and she'll manage to make an epic out of it. An epic that's not crammed with symbolic virgins and eternal women, but full of Tante Zélica, Godmother Maude, Mariaagélas and Fanie. If Longfellow had placed just one of those women opposite the English soldiers, I'm not saying he'd have saved Acadia from exile, but he'd have given the *Grand Dérangement* (the Deportation) a certain tone of truth that would have made it more real and, who knows, perhaps less tragic. (p.70)

D.S. — In *Evangeline Deusse*, performed at the Rideau-Vert in 1976, what does the meeting between the eighty-two-year-olds, Evangéline and the Breton, represent for you?

A.M. — It's not the meeting as such that may have symbolic overtones. It's the play itself, which may be a kind of eulogy or song I wrote about old age and exile. Those are two themes I put together to see what would emerge. Evangéline and the Breton, who meet one another in a park in Montreal, represent different degrees of exile. There's also the Jewish rabbi, and he represents eternal exile. The Breton is a voluntary exile, a man who came over here in search of adventure; he's the eternal sailor, and he ends up being an exile. He'll never set foot in his native Brittany again. Evangéline Deusse is an exile in her own country. She's Acadia as it's experienced here in Quebec. In that sense she's an exile wherever she goes, since she has no land of her own. No matter where they live, the Acadians are exiles. And Le Stop, who in one sense is an exile from the Lac St-Jean region, is also a rural exile who pitches up in the city. So there you have three degrees of exile, although the Breton and Evangéline are more symbolic in the sense that they come from the same source: a people that was separated three centuries ago now finds itself together again, and deep down they have the same way of seeing things, the same desires.

D.S. — Your character Mariaagélas is a commited woman. She refuses to be just another worker on an assembly line, shelling lobsters under the eye of a foreign boss. That's why she gets involved in the "epic of smuggling." Where does this fascination you have for "bootleggers" come from?

A.M. — Thanks to the famous bootleggers or smugglers, Acadia had a great moment of glory. Don't forget we're right beside the sea, right on the maritime border between the islands of St-Pierre and Miquelon — with wine from France and rum from Jamaica — and the United States and Quebec. Thus we were at the crossroads of the world, a world that was thirsty and had nothing to drink. And since the Acadians had always more or less been outlaws — because at the beginning they didn't even have the right to vote — they said to themselves, "since we're outlaws, we may as well take advantage of it." And at the same time, since the Church was against it and the Sunday sermons spoke out against smuggling, there was also the taste of forbidden fruit. It was marvellous because it was also a sin. There were some sensational adventures. Bouctouche is considered nowadays as being the bootlegging capital of the Twenties and Thirties. There are still a lot of caches even today, and lots of eyewitnesses from that time. Recently I interviewed some of them.

D.S. — Was it based on those interviews that you wrote *La contrebandière*, which was performed at the Rideau-Vert in 1981? Or the novel *Crache à pic*, published in 1984?

A.M. — Yes, in part, but *La contrebandière* was mostly a new version of *Mariaagélas* written for the theatre. It tells the story of Mariaagélas, a legendary heroine who defies the law and keeps up the traditions of the Gélas family, in which smuggling was something handed down from father to son. I also included the rivalry between the Gélas and the Basiles. It's a sort of saga of the people living there.

D.S. — The critics claim it's your best play since *La Sagouine*.

A.M. — Possibly. I put a lot of emphasis on Mariaagélas' dreams, the call of the open sea and the secrets of the deep.

D.S. — In *Les cordes-de-bois* (1977) you paint a historical scene that keeps reappearing in your work: foreign sailors, petticoat pirates, prince charmings and legendary heroes.

A.M. — There's no time when I'm closer to reality than when I'm talking of sailors. Bouctouche is a small seaport, but the water is deep enough for foreign ships to enter. Every year there were ships from Norway, Holland, Ireland, France, Italy and so on. The result was that we were flooded with foreign sailors. And a sailor is a sailor. That meant terror for the mothers of families, joy for the girls, and joy for me as a future writer. I gradually became aware of the excitement that would come over the village whenever a ship arrived. The village was transformed. It would trigger a certain sense of celebration. That's why I'll always have sailors in my work: lighthearted sailors who like to tell stories and lies.

D.S. — Is the tradition of *défricheteux de parenté*, the amateur genealogists, as important as your writings seem to suggest?

A.M. — I think it is that important. I'm going to advance an idea that's rather bold and you can be the first to hear it: Acadia exists because of its storytellers. Take *Pélagie-la-charrette*; the most important character is Bélonie, who forces the others to go back to their native land by telling them about their history. And they return to the land in order not to forget — it's the phenomenon of the collective memory, and thus culture. They come back to Acadia because of culture. Then once they are back, it's the storytellers of 1880 who describe the whole long journey and Pélagie's entire experience so that they won't forget what their ancestors had done. That's another phenomenon of culture. It was the storytellers who brought Pélagie back to Acadia and it was the storytellers who saved Pélagie from oblivion; in other words, they were the ones who literally made the history. The oral tradition is really that important. Perhaps the most significant line in *Pélagie* is the following: "And then she had the nerve to tell me that a people who can't read can't have any history."

D.S. — The blacksmith's shop was the village centre, the place where "the guys hanging around the blacksmith's" got together to *radoter* ("shoot the breeze") and *jongler* ("daydream"). In this sense it seems that most of the village gossip took place around the anvil.

A.M. — In every country each village has a centre, a soul, a focal point. And in Acadia the centre was usually a blacksmith's shop. It could have been a general store or a barbershop. But what struck me most when I was a child was that the blacksmith's shop was a rather dark place, and also the fire and the anvil were quite mysterious — almost like an alchemist doing his experiments. There were only men in the blacksmith's shop. Any time a little girl like me poked her head in to see what was happening, they'd all shut their mouths and not say a word. It was the world of alchemy. I was tremendously impressed by the blacksmith's shop.

D.S. — I have another question related to your tales. In *Les cordes-de-bois* the character called Tom Thumb, an Irish storyteller who's becoming Acadianized, shows that there's an enormous similarity between Acadian and Irish folktales (in this novel, the stories of St Brendan, the "holy navigator" and the Blarney Stone). In *Le salut de l'Irlande*, Jacques Ferron also shows the affinities between the Irish and the Québécois. And you yourself claim that Ireland is a beautiful land, "an Ireland transposed and transfigured" through Acadia's own spirit of liveliness.

A.M. — There have always been tremendous relations between the Irish and the Acadians. There's an affinity in temperament. The Irish have the same visceral side and the same influence of the sea. Irishmen are not primarily cerebral; they're dreamers, adventurers, people whose roots are very deep. We were rivals, but at the same time we were rivals who sought one another out. We were attracted to one another. I knew a character named Sullivan, and he got put into *Gapi et Sullivan*. He was the one who gave me the inspiration for Tom Thumb.

D.S. — In the Acadian and Irish folktales that inspired you, the devil is certainly the most important character. There are individuals accused of selling their soul to the devil or of performing black sabbaths with the witches; the devil also appears in such typically Québécois and Acadian guises as the *chasse-galerie* and the *fi-follets*.

A.M. — The devil was as important as God. In Acadian society there was this old medieval notion of the devil being an incarnation of evil. The devil was a character who was terrifying, funny, dreadful and marvellous — and there was no doing without him. There was a need to dramatize evil and give it a form. There was God and the Holy Family and the saints in heaven and all those white robes. Gapi's not so sure about all this; as a matter of fact he says, "if I'm going to resurrect just to put on a white dress, I won't do it, no damn way." And then there's La Sagouine who claims that there's nothing that says Gapi couldn't keep on wearing his "coveralls." The number of funny stories the Acadians have about heaven and hell is incredible. Our bellies were so full of them we had to find some way to get rid of a few.

D.S. — In 1978 you published *Le bourgeois gentleman*, a play presented by the Rideau-Vert Theatre in Montreal. You dedicated this play to Tit-Louis, a childhood hero who apparently introduced you to the theatre. Who in fact was he?

A.M. — He's a man who actually cried when he saw the play, an extraordinary character. Right now he's a hairdresser in Boston. He lived in my village. If I had to name an Acadian who's a genius, I'd say it's Tit-Louis. He's an exceptional person, both for the quality of his intelligence and for his talent. He's got a talent for everything — painting, dramatic novels, music — and above all he has no equal as a storyteller. He absolutely dominated my childhood, much more than the parish priest. He lived through the Depression in a way that was extraordinary. He was completely alone in the world and he managed to get through it. He left my village when I was still a little girl but he dominated my childhood in the sense that when there was a play, it was Tit-Louis who directed it, and when there was organ music in the church, it was Tit-Louis who played it. He was the parish priest's assistant. His presence was felt everywhere in the village. He was the artistic soul of the village, even if he's practically illiterate. That's why I say he's a genius. I still get together with him once in a while. He comes to Bouctouche every summer. I spend time talking with him, and he's as rich a source of material as La Sagouine.

D.S. — Even if *Le bourgeois gentleman* is dedicated to Tit-Louis, the characters in your play, except the servant girl, are all Québécois. Does this mean you're starting to become a bit of a Québécoise yourself, or at least becoming more and more interested in the things you see around you in Montreal?

A.M. — I'm always very interested in the things I see around me here. Since the play *Le bourgeois gentleman* is a comedy and a take-off on another comic play by Molière, I didn't necessarily have to take my characters from the depths of the oral tradition, since comedy takes its inspiration from everyday life. I was inspired by the people I'd known here. I knew a "bourgeois gentleman" man and his "bourgeois gentleman" wife. It's probably that little nationalistic side to me that had me make the servant girl an Acadian. In Molière, it's always the maid who represents the author; she's the one who represents common sense and who puts up with all the ridicule. However, it wasn't directed against the Québécois but rather against the bourgeois.

D.S. — I'm sure your readers would like to hear you speak of *Pélagie-la-charrette* (the story of Pélagie bringing the scattered Acadians back to Acadia) and *Cent ans dans les bois* (a sequel to *Pélagie*, which doesn't tell of a hundred years living hidden in the woods, as the title might seem to indicate, but rather the process of coming out of the woods). The two novels, interspersed with legends and folktales, are both bouncing with Rabelesian humour and cushioned with scenes of poignant tenderness.

I'd be interested to know to what extent you adapted the legend of Captain Beausoleil-Broussard and his ghost ship — the former Pembrooke now known by the very Acadian name of "Grand' Goule".

A.M. — The only character I really took from history is Beausoleil-Broussard. Beausoleil was the name of a village located quite close to Moncton, and that's where he came from. He's an historical character who developed into a legend and who did on a small scale what I had him do on a large scale. He really did save a ship with Acadians in it, or at least that's what the legend says. So I took the legend and I put it into my book and that's the reason it may seem a little less real than the others. Since I took as much of him from legend as from history, I stuck to the legendary Robin Hood part of his character. He seems like a character who is "out of this world" in that he's already enshrined before the end of the story.

D.S. — Still, there's a whole historical background underlining *Pélagie* and *Cent ans dans les bois*, a whole series of historical and geographical references. What kind of research did you do while you were getting ready to write these novels?

A.M. — No research at all. I never do research with the idea of writing a novel. That is, I never write a novel because my research has been completed. Without my noticing it, though, my whole life is involved in research: every time I go to Acadia, I talk with the old people, chat with my cousins; I root around and I register things in my memory. And I sense that these little scattered facts gradually come to form a complete history. However, it may happen that I'll be stuck with a problem, and then, instead of rummaging around in libraries, I telephone my friends. Once I wanted to know what sort of oil they used to grease the wheels of the carts. I called up a friend: "Well, they oiled them with garter-snakes." "What! That's terrific!"

D.S. — I've noticed that women tend to play the principal roles in Acadian literature. Often it's the opposite in Quebec literature, where you have not only the Maria Chapdelaines and the Belles-Soeurs but also male protagonists like Savard's Menaud and Victor-Lévy Beaulieu's Jos Connaissant.

A.M. — As I said when I was talking about the sea, Acadia is feminine both in its symbolic temperament and its symbolic qualities. If you look at the symbols of various ethnic groups, some of them are rather masculine and some come more under the feminine sign. A tree is a masculine symbol; the sea is a feminine symbol. Now, the Québécois are more a people of the forest than a people of the sea. Suppose that you undertook an analysis of the Québécois; I think that, in comparison with the Acadians, the Québécois would lean more towards the masculine symbols.

D.S. — Their most prominent symbols are the forest, the mountain and the earth?

A.M. — Yes, and so it's normal for their writers to move instinctively towards their symbols, and for me to move towards mine. But there are exceptions to this. After all, there's Gabrielle Roy, and her main heroes are heroines.

D.S. — Even the name Pélagie is feminine since it evokes the sea — *pélagique* meaning "of the high seas" in Greek.

A.M. — That's another one of those nice tricks that God plays on us from time to time — and that I love. I discovered the symbol of Pélagie only after my book had been written and published. Before that, I hadn't even remembered that it came from *pélage* — since it had been a long time since I'd studied Greek — from *pélagos*, which means "beach" and therefore "the sea." Imagine, I chose the Acadian symbol *pélagie* from a name which meant the sea, and I didn't even know it! I chose the name for the way it sounded and for the memories it recalled. I remember several women called Pélagie, and the name has such a rich sound to it.

D.S. — That's incredible! When I asked Félix-Antoine Savard if he knew that *menaud* means "of the mountain" in Breton, he didn't know what the name of his character meant either. It's amazing how literature can play tricks on us!

You fitted two folktales into *Pélagie*: the tale of the White Whale and the tale of the Giant Lady of the Night. Are these real folktales?

A.M. — In part. They exist as important leitmotifs. The story of the White Whale is based on an actual tale — the man who runs after the hen, who runs after the fox, etc. — but I doctored it up to my own taste. The story of the Giant Lady of the Night is based on three or four tales, so I put them all together and turned them into one.

D.S. — Would you tell us a bit about the film of *Pélagie-la-charrette*? I gather it's the most impressive film project ever undertaken in Canada.

A.M. — It's being produced by Nielsen and Ferns, the biggest production company in Canada. The director is René Bonnière. The film will be shot partly on location in Georgia, Pennsylvania and Acadia, and they'll be making a six-programme television series as well as a full-length film that will last about two hours. Most of the actors will be from Quebec and a lot of the studio shooting will be done here in Montreal. I've already prepared the script for the first six hours of television and I've remained quite faithful to the book. Of course for the film, where we've only got two hours, there will have to be another screenplay that will concentrate on the main events.

Adrien Thério:
A Passion for Literature

Because of his myriad activities as a writer, promoter, organizer and teacher, Adrien Thério is one of the most important figures in Quebec literature. Without Thério such essential Quebec magazines as *Livres et auteurs québécois* and *Lettres québécoises* would never have existed. Without Thério, the journalist Jules Fournier would certainly be less known to the public and the literary talents of Ignace Bourget, the second Bishop of Montreal and founder of the old French-Canadian theocratic society, would perhaps have gone unrecognized. Without Thério, innumerable teachers and students would have a lesser degree of enthusiasm for and interest in their own literature. And without him, Quebec would have been deprived of a talented, prolific and fascinating writer. I have no hesitation in talking about the "Thério phenomenon," since in terms of Quebec writing he has virtually become a literary institution. And his work is far from being finished.

* * *

D.S. — You were born in Saint-Modeste in the County of Rivière-du-Loup, which emerges in your work as the Chemin Taché region. You seem to be very attached to this area.

A.T. — I was born in Saint-Modeste, just beside Rivière-du-Loup, but I wasn't brought up there. When I was five, my family moved to the Chemin Taché, which is a rural route and part of Saint-Cyprien, located about 30 miles inland from Rivière-du-Loup. So it wasn't Saint-Modeste that became the Chemin Taché, because the Chemin Taché actually exists. I didn't call it Saint-Cyprien because that's a name I don't like, but Saint-Cyprien and the Chemin Taché are really one and the same place. In my last story, Saint-Cyprien becomes St-Amable. It took me many years to realize just how much that barren piece of land had left its mark on me.

D.S. — The father and mother characters play an important role in your novels. There must certainly be something autobiographical in that.

A.T. — I was brought up in a patriarchal kind of family where all authority belonged to the father. I've always resented this a bit, sometimes too much. It's clear that my mother was closer to her children than my father was, and that she provided most of the understanding. My father never really dared to show any affection; you had to guess what his feelings were.

D.S. — Was it your parents who encouraged you to go to school and developed your taste for learning?

A.T. — Perhaps my mother did, a little, since she'd been a school-teacher for a few months before she got married, although it wasn't the kind of work she liked. She must have gone to the sixth or seventh grade, which wasn't too bad for the time. In any case, I remember she used to give us lots of ideas when we were doing our homework around the big kitchen table after supper. She hadn't forgotten her grammar rules. As for my father, how could he have ever given us a taste for studying? He didn't know how to read or write.

Unlike his brothers and sisters who had gone to school for a few years, he apparently refused to. We never found out exactly what had happened, but he did insist on our going to school. I think he was sorry he hadn't gone himself. Of course my older brothers quit school after grade three. I repeated grade four because the school-mistress couldn't teach grade five. The next year a new teacher had me do grade five, and then six and seven. But I was the first kid from the Chemin Taché to reach grades five, six and seven. I was the only one in my class. There was someone else in my family who gave me a taste for learning: my father's younger sister, who had a fairly advanced diploma that allowed her to teach in the model school in Saint-Epiphane. She had students in grades ten and eleven. There weren't many villages fortunate enough to have grades ten and eleven at that time. I was very fond of this aunt, and she was fond of me too. I think that, unconsciously, she was the one who made me want to get an education.

D.S. — When you were a student at Laval University, you were very sick. It seems that your convalescence played an important role in your decision to become a writer.

A.T. — The first time I got sick wasn't at Laval University. It was at the Seminary in Rimouski, when I was in first year philosophy. In October 1947, I think, I left for the sanatorium in Mont-Joli, where I stayed for three years. They treated the patients like dogs. One day, after a fight with the head doctor, I decided to leave for the sanatorium in Sherbrooke, where I stayed for yet another year. In Sherbrooke, the patients were treated like human beings. I was 19 when I went into the sanatorium and almost 24 when I got out. It was very difficult because I was never seriously ill. They'd tell me I'd be getting out, and at the last minute they'd say no, I had to stay for six more months. Having your hopes dashed like that ends up killing a person. I've never talked about this period in my life, probably because I have too many bad memories of the time I spent in Mont-Joli. However, I did do a great deal of reading in those years and I decided to write a novel along the lines of Savard's *Menaud*, although I later destroyed it. It was during my time in Mont-Joli that I

wrote my first published pieces: a tale in *XXe Siècle*, a literary magazine published in Ottawa, and a dramatic sketch
that was performed on Radio-Canada in 1949, I think. It was
through this sketch that I got to know Yves Thériault, who
wrote me a letter after the play had been aired. We discovered
we were related.

D.S. — Was Thério originally an Acadian name?

A.T. — Yes, my family is of Acadian origin. Our ancestor
landed in Grand Pré, Nova Scotia, in 1637, which may not
have been true for Yves Thériault's family, because there's
also a French-Canadian family named Thériault.

D.S. — But you just said you were related to Yves Thériault!

A.T. — That's right, but not necessarily through the same
family of Thériaults. His grandfather Thériault was married
to a Thériault who was my grandfather Thériault's sister. So
we're related through his grandmother. His father and my
father are first cousins.

D.S. — You have written three books about Jules Fournier,
the journalist and pamphleteer. First of all there was your
doctoral dissertation, *Jules Fournier, journaliste de combat* (1955),
then *Jules Fournier*, published by Fides in 1957, and finally
Mon encrier de Jules Fournier, also published by Fides, in 1964.
What was it you found so fascinating about Fournier: his version of nationalism based on economic concepts not unrelated
to the social-democratic policies of the Parti Québécois, his
desire for social justice, the encouragement he gave to local
writers, or perhaps his clear, ironic, mannered style of writing?

A.T. — I don't really know how to reply to that question. It
was Luc Lacourcière who first put me on to Fournier and
suggested I write my dissertation on him. What I can say is
that I found Fournier's work as congenial as someone with
whom you get along marvellously well from the very start.
His direct way of saying things, his desire for justice and his
denunciations of injustice, his humour, his irony, his way of

setting himself up as a target and risking public scorn in order to pound some sense into the heads of certain people who had become dizzy with power — these were all things I liked about him. I wrote my dissertation on Fournier when I was 26 or 27. I didn't have much experience at that time and I thought I could probably do a better book with a few more years of experience and exposure to literature. However, I had to earn a living and I went off to teach French at Bellarmin College in Louisville, Kentucky, since there were virtually no openings in the classical colleges at that time. Two years later, in 1956, I switched to Notre Dame University in Indiana, where I gave courses in French literature and language. I spent three years at Notre Dame and one year at the University of Toronto before going to the Military College in Kingston. I stayed there for nine years and was director of the French Department for seven years. It was when I got to Kingston that I had the idea of founding *Livres et auteurs*; it must have been floating around in my head for several years.

D.S. — You have a passionate belief in Quebec civilization. Exactly like the narrator in your *Soliloque en hommage à une femme*, you want to make it known to the public. For more than 30 years you've been publishing reviews and anthologies dealing with our writers and journalists, and even political and Church figures. You have made an enormous contribution to the dissemination of Quebec civilization.

A.T. — Every nation has its own civilization. And here I make a distinction between civilization and culture. Civilization is what we get from our parents, our surroundings, our environment, our lifestyles, our forms of behaviour and so on. In North America, our own civilization is quite special, and in order to understand it, I would say it's absolutely necessary to go back especially to the 19th century, and even to the 18th or earlier. We have inherited a way of thinking that comes to us directly from the 19th century. As a people, we might have been very different from what we were in 1960 if nineteenth-century liberalism had won out. It didn't and that's unfortunate. However, even if our origins were humble, even if our ancestors were repressed by the authorities, that doesn't mean we should close the door on our past. Quite the contrary. And it's too late to lay any blame. We have to accept ourselves as we are and try to become something else, to transform ourselves.

D.S. — You've been interested in figures of controversy such as Fournier and Asselin. And I know as a teacher you often refer to the critical spirit of Arthur Buies, the outstanding pamphleteer of the 19th century. It's therefore quite normal that you yourself are a polemicist and a figure of controversy. Your editorials contain pertinent attacks on everyone and everything that plays against the full flowering of Quebec culture: publishers who have no national conscience; a Canada Council that has been much more international than national in outlook; and the neglect of local writers by Radio-Canada.

A.T. — I think I attack mainly people who are pretending to promote literature and culture when they are really just trying to get public recognition for themselves, and also people and institutions that could be doing something for the arts in general but just aren't. As for the Canada Council, all its policies should be reviewed. The best way of doing this without the government getting involved would be to make sure that, from now on, anyone holding an important position in the Council should be limited to a three- or four-year term.

D.S. — You founded your own publishing house, Les éditions Jumonville. Since 1973 several of your novels have been published by Jumonville.

A.T. — The reason I set up Jumonville about 1966 was so that *Livres et auteurs* would be connected to a publishing house. Later, I decided to have Jumonville publish my own novels. It may not have been such a good idea because literary commentators in general pay very little attention to anything produced by that sort of publisher. My latest novel, *C'est ici que le monde a commencé*, is proof of this. I've only seen two reviews of this book, and I'm convinced it deserves better treatment than that.

D.S. — Do you still have a certain bitterness or disappointment or even anger left over from all your struggles to promote Quebec literature?

A.T. — What do you expect me to say? You're asking me that question at the very time the authorities reigning over the Canada Council are stubbornly refusing to give *Lettres québécoises* grants on an equal footing with other magazines. I'm persuaded that they've done everything possible, indirectly, to scuttle our magazine. I know there are some people who think I'm imagining all sorts of things. There should be an inquiry into the whole business. Then people might have a clearer idea of what's going on.

D.S. — You've sometimes been accused of exaggeration, of seeing plots behind everything and too often attacking individuals rather than blaming institutions. What do you have to say about that?

A.T. — I have never talked about plots myself, and I've never been a witness to any. But I have seen injustices. For example, between 1961 and 1981 only one of my stories or novels was ever reviewed in *Le Devoir*, and that was André Major writing about *Soliloque*. And what was the reason for all that? I published an article in *Le Devoir* in 1961, in which I took issue with some opinions expressed by Jean Ethier-Blais about four or five books he had discussed. And so they decided — I heard about it from others — to act as if I didn't exist. The two other house critics at the time, Jean Basile and Jean Hamelin, must have agreed with this since they never reviewed my books. It's quite possible that Jean Basile was simply never interested in my novels and it was his right not to be. But Jean Hamelin, whom I happened to meet several months after the publication of *Mes beaux meurtres* and whom I asked if he was going to write about it, told me that it was too late, and also, since I'd attacked one of his colleagues.... These reviewers could have refused to write about my books themselves, but why didn't they get someone on the outside to do it?

That's what I did with *Livres et auteurs*. I took the trouble of finding good critics to write about books by Hamelin, Basile and Éthier-Blais. For me the individual and the writer are two different things.

The policy at *Le Devoir* can't have changed very much because, since 1974, they haven't seen fit to speak about *La colère du père*, *La tête en fête* or *C'est ici que le monde a commencé*.

* * *

Adrien Thério has already published some 15 works of fiction, including short stories and tales, novellas, plays and novels. His favourite subjects can be divided into two categories. First there are the stories, novels and diaries which bring to life either rural Quebec in the Thirties (six works in all) or the world of the cloisters (two works) or of teachers (five). Then there is a series of tales that are supernatural, macabre and nightmarish, and which often include great explosions of violence (two collections). Thus we see two basic tendencies in Thério's work, two currents or styles: either he tells stories that take the form of diaries or short fictions, or else he makes himself the interpreter of the subconscious and the inner workings of the mind. These two tendencies blend together; the storyteller inevitably drifts off into daydreams or visions of striking intensity (called "phantasms," "inner movies" or simply "dreams") in which the author's foremost obsessions — the erotic, any form of anger, and a love of nature — all come into play.

There are two predominant landscapes or settings in Thério's work. One is made up of a dreamscape of hallucinations and the "strange spectacles of our dreams" (*Mes beaux meurtres*, p.148); the other is the descriptive, basically realistic landscape of the Chemin Taché and its surroundings. Here is how he describes the Chemin Taché:

> The Chemin Taché surrounded me with its great fields of snow occasionally broken by a protruding stump. The top of the north hill was covered in forest, and there lay all the houses built of big squared timbers piled one upon the other; most of them were

flanked by a tiny barn awaiting the addition they kept promising themselves to build summer after summer. At regular intervals, fence-posts would disappear into the distant outskirts of the forest. The whole horizon surrounding me, north, south and west, was blocked by the forest that would be pushed back a few acres every year. Here and there a sort of clearing would allow you to see further. But the road was bordered by houses on both sides and gave the impression of wanting to become a village. A general store, a school, a blacksmith, a carpentry shop, a post-office, a sawmill on the Saint-Hubert side — was there anything we lacked? I knew that each house was alive, with a big, double-bellied stove spreading heat throughout it. I was seeing all these things with new eyes, I was touching it all with my gaze and, probably happy to be feeling myself alive in the middle of all the living things around me, I began to imagine that the Chemin Taché was only a little patch of land that I could hold up in my hand and spin about in the dry air as if it were some casual object I was playing with. (*La colère du père*, pp.69-70.)

It's obvious that the Thério speaking in this passage has a love for rural landscapes and people. Nevertheless, he doesn't advocate a return to the land. On the contrary, he says it is necessary to leave the hamlet behind in order to live in a world of intellectual stimulation; yet, paradoxically, you must always "return to the clan," to the family and landscapes of your childhood. For Thério, you should never deny your small-town origins. You end up, however, being torn between the city and the country.

Adrien Thério excels in presenting three types of characters. Above all, there's the adolescent; almost always an unhappy individual misunderstood by parents and friends, he wants to learn everything there is to know about life, from the beauties of nature to the joys and sorrows of love. Secondly, there's the father, an insensitive and authoritarian figure. And finally there are the various professors: the one who feels ill-at-ease in the pretentious world of the intellectuals, the one who is lacking in imagination and never questions anything, and the other one who aspires to break free from the ordinary world:

> Colour, above all, colour. Everything is so bland. It's all so boring. The students go to class to get a piece of paper so they can go out and make money. The professors go to class so they'll be able to spend the cheque they get every month. Researchers do a doctoral dissertation so they can get more money and then keep quiet. No one ever thinks of putting a bit of colour into their lives. (*Un païen chez les pingouins*, p.123.)

The narrators in Thério's work have several points in common. They are opposed to bourgeois values, to religious or capitalistic fanaticism, and to apathy. They advocate, for both men and women, equality in the family and in the workplace. The world according to Adrien Thério is devoid of absolute values. Selfishness proves to be man's constant and perhaps inevitable enemy. Still, all is not black — far from it! There are those special moments, however ephemeral, of love, friendship, and a sensual attachment to the land of one's childhood. The love of nature, the marvellous mystery of the woods, the call of the rivers and mountains, all provide, if not a meaning to life, at least a reason not to give up completely. Actually, Thério is a poet in whose work the tree becomes a symbol for rootedness and rapture. Characters "feel the need to cling to the earth" (*Les fous d'amour*, p.46) and to let themselves be lulled by the magical powers of the snow.

Adrien Thério knows how to tell a story, to describe people and places realistically. Luckily, he also knows how to dream, to portray in an original, personal manner both a sensual attachment to the land and a panoply of fantasies, whether they be erotic or traumatic, gentle or painful. Now let us ask him some questions about his work, a considerable body of writing that holds some pleasant surprises for those not already familiar with it.

D.S. — Let me begin with a quote from *Un païen chez les pingouins*: "Does literature serve any purpose? I could answer no, and no doubt not be entirely wrong. I could also say that, without literature, life would be lacking in colour. Colour is the power of transformation, the power to make things more vivid and lively." Could you comment further on how you conceive of literature?

A.T. — Good Lord! Literature is passion in all its forms! It's the entire human being struggling against the forces of injustice and the power of nature. That's what must come through in all writing. It's life itself being brought to life. Literature doesn't make anyone a better person, or more moral. It does enable a person to live a better life, however; it lets us invent for ourselves a world of our own to help us escape from a world which leaves us unsatisfied. And that's as true for the person doing the writing as for the one reading it. People who read detective novels are simply searching through book after book for the kind of life they dream about living and which they are unable to find in the world they live in.

D.S. — Together with Victor-Lévy Beaulieu, who comes from Saint-Jean-de-Dieu, and Roger Fournier, who was born in Saint-Anaclet, you are one of the most important literary spokesmen for the Lower St Lawrence region. Perhaps you could tell us a bit about some of the characters you took as models for your Chemin Taché.

A.T. — It never occurred to me to model my characters on people I knew. I made up stories and then, afterwards, I suppose I instinctively moulded people I knew into the forms of my characters. I've become aware that in doing this, I have used a large number of individuals from the Chemin Taché, and from the surrounding area as well. Let me give you an example. In *La colère du père* there are three brothers who more or less run things in the Chemin Taché; the twelve-year-old narrator's father is the head of the clan. Well now, I had invented my story and I needed this clan, these three brothers, to work it all out. To make them more believable, I based their physical appearance on three of my uncles. I changed the family name from Lebel to Martel, but I kept the same first names. In the end, the three brothers in *La colère du père* have nothing to do with my three uncles. They bear some resemblance to them morally and physically, but that's all. So what I do to make my job easier is to put people I know into the skins of the characters I invent. Let's take another example: none of the characters in *Ceux du Chemin Taché* have ever really existed. However, I think the way these characters act and the way they live their lives make them all people from the Chemin Taché. A few of my characters resemble my father to some degree, but in the end they're not him.

D.S. — *Les brèves années*, published by Fides, is a novel in which the central characters are adolescents, although it's not a novel for adolescents.

A.T. — No, I don't think so either. It's a story in which fiction and reality are so intermingled that I myself couldn't say which parts come from my own life and which are fiction. This novel obviously hearkens back to perhaps the best French novel for adolescents ever written, *Le grand Meaulnes*, which I read when I was 17 or 18. I was 25 when I wrote *Les brèves années*. In both books the characters are adolescents, and therefore it's easy to say I'd been influenced by Fournier's book. It's also possible that, without being aware of it, I adopted some of his ideas and techniques. But it's the second part of my story that recalls *Le grand Meaulnes*, because of the Big Forest, the Unknown Road and the natural wilderness. However, I didn't need Alain Fournier to come up with places like these. They're right out there in the fourth concession in Saint-Hubert, where we used to have our woodlot. I went back there two years ago and took some beautiful pictures. The land is even more a wilderness than it was when I was young.

D.S. — In *Les brèves années*, Clair Martin worries about what's going to become of Quebec's heritage. *Menaud, maître draveur* is his favourite book. Félix-Antoine Savard was one of your teachers. Did the author of *Menaud* have an important influence on you?

A.T. — A few months ago I reread two chapters of *Les brèves années* and I had the surprise of my life to hear Clair Martin talking about Menaud. I'd completely forgotten that. *Menaud* in fact did get me quite worked up when I first read it. I mentioned earlier that I'd written a story in the same vein, which luckily I destroyed.

D.S. — Who are the other writers, Québécois, French or American, who have influenced you?

A.T. — I really couldn't say if there are writers who have actually influenced me. There are a good number of writers I like a lot, both here and elsewhere: for example, Gabrielle Roy, Yves Thériault and Marie-Claire Blais. Among the foreign writers, I could name Marcel Proust, Albert Camus, Julien Green and Dostoïevsky. You can see that there's a world of difference between them and that there's nothing in my work that really resembles them very much, so you'll have to draw your own conclusions.

D.S. — *Les brèves années* is only the first installment in the Chemin Taché chronicles, the others being "Le chat sauvage" (in *Mes beaux meurtres*), *Le printemps qui pleure*, *Ceux du Chemin Taché*, *La colère du père* and *C'est ici que le monde a commencé*. With the exception of *Le printemps qui pleure*, which strikes me as perhaps the weakest of these novels, all these works contain convincing dialogues, accurate, vivid descriptions and fascinating dream sequences or hallucinations. We could take as examples the tales in *Ceux du Chemin Taché*, with their strange stories of a magic fiddler, madmen, ghosts and women who read fortunes in teacups. Did the tales you write emerge from the oral tradition, from stories you heard as a child, or were the yarns you spin in *Ceux du Chemin Taché* mostly your own inventions?

A.T. — I never had stories told to me when I was young. I remember when I was about 12 or 13 I loved to spend the evenings in the winter reading pirate stories I had discovered in magazines I'd found someplace or other. I've racked my brains trying to remember where I got hold of those magazines, which were superbly illustrated in brown, I think, but I can't figure it out.

Actually, I got the urge to tell stories myself immediately after I'd read my first short story; it was when I was 10 or 11, in a book I'd received as a prize at the end of the school year, entitled *Le petit violon de la grande demoiselle*. So then I made up stories based on the things I saw around me. The episode of the fiddler who gets everybody dancing in *La colère du père*, even dancing through the air, came to me straight from our neighbour Alphonse Ouellet; he was an excellent fiddler (to my ten-year-old ears) and he used to play the violin on his porch in the evening and would often bring it over to our place. I must confess that I was quite enchanted by this. I couldn't understand how you could get such sounds out of an instrument like that. I needed someone to get the people dancing in *La colère du père*, since the people in the Chemin Taché had become Protestants and were not allowed to dance; so, since I knew him well, I invited him to play. And I even had him take a nice little sashay into the air above the Chemin Taché.

D.S. — In *La colère du père* (Jumonville, 1974) a crisis develops in the Chemin Taché: when church services are withdrawn by a bishop who is pompous and stubborn, the farmers in the region decide to become Protestants. I was quite taken with this novel. You have a talent for stringing out a good tale with lots of suspense and the genuine, direct sense of humour of the simple folk.

A.T. — When I got to the Chemin Taché at the age of five, there weren't any Protestants left. But some 20 years before, or maybe a bit earlier, they had all become Protestants for the reason I indicated in my story. At that time there were still a few vestiges of the schism, such as the Protestant cemetery and the house they had used as their church. And people would still talk about those troubles. Eventually, I got the urge to tell a similar story. I said to myself, how can you suddenly become a Protestant when you've been a Catholic for ever and ever? It must have bothered a lot of consciences. That was what I wanted to look at by recreating the main characters in the crisis and leaving them quite free to act as they wanted. At certain moments I myself was surprised by what they said and did.

D.S. — In several of your works, the father is "head of a clan," a curt, proud man who doesn't want his children to go beyond high-school. What counts for him is the land and manual labour. Is there anything autobiographical in this?

A.T. — I said earlier that there's something of my father in several of my characters. The curt, authoritarian father you just described does exist in certain of my books, but on the other hand I can tell you that my father never wanted to keep us from going to school. And he didn't put up any obstacles against my going on to college. I even remember that one day, he came to take my place when I was working at turning the grain in the fields, because my mother had just told him I didn't want to miss school. He took the pitch-fork out of my hands and said, "Go on, get off to your school."

D.S. — You're very fond of narratives. All your novels, or almost all of them, are written in the first person. *La colère du père* is no exception.

A.T. — I feel more comfortable when I write things using the "I." I think my first novel, *La soif et le mirage*, is written in the third person. It's not a very good novel. The important thing for me, before starting to work, is for me to be able to become, psychologically speaking, the character who will become the narrator. I turned myself into a cloistered monk for *Les fous d'amour*. Certain individuals found an easy explanation, since Thério, they said, had spent time in a monastery. I never lived in a religious order. I thought of it when I was about 15 but by the time I was 20 I'd forgotten all about it. Psychologically speaking, I entered a monastery a year before I began writing *Les fous d'amour* so that my narrator would be able to play his role properly.

D.S. — One of the chronicles of the Chemin Taché is entitled *C'est ici que le monde a commencé* (Jumonville, 1978). The title, literally "It's Here that the World Began", provides a clear indication of how important this little corner of the Lower St Lawrence is in your work.

A.T. — The world always begins in the place where you have your roots. And my roots are there, in the Chemin Taché region, which I enlarged a bit to include the whole parish of St-Cyprien, although I prefer to call it Saint-Amable. There's also the Big Forest which is located in Saint-Hubert, and there are also the parishes of Saint-Epiphane and Saint-Modeste, where my mother and father were born, just beside Rivière-du-Loup.

And at that time it was a very poor region, like a lot of other rural areas. It was the poverty, I think, that was at the root of a lot of the troubles I witnessed and that I still haven't finished writing about. From the time I was very young I could sense the effects of this poverty. I think I felt humiliated every time my father was humiliated, for all sorts of reasons.

D.S. — My feeling is that *C'est ici que le monde a commencé* is one of the best books in the Chemin Taché series. The world of your childhood is recalled, and of course transformed, with such apparent ease. Sex plays a leading role in *C'est ici que le monde a commencé*. The narrator is very sexually aware. He's an avowed hedonist (genital, oral and anal) and potentially bisexual. There are an enormous number of examples of sexual ambivalence in your work. When Clair takes a fancy to Solange in *Les brèves années*, Jacques becomes jealous and fights with him. The young professor in *La soif et le mirage* is equally smitten with Bill and Mary Lane. The mother-in-law in "Le chat sauvage" accuses her grandson of not being attracted to girls. And in *Soliloque en hommage à une femme* ("Soliloquy in honour of a Woman"), we can easily guess that, paradoxically, the narrator is bisexual. In *Un païen chez les pingouins* a student marries a girl out of a sense of familial duty, but secretly he's in love with a man. As well, there are all those masculine symbols in your work: the sun, trees, church steeples.

A.T. — I don't recall Clair fighting with Jacques, but it must be right if you say so. And several other facts you've mentioned have completely escaped my memory. On the whole, though, I think your remarks are accurate.

You know, all the religions have perverted love. They've made all sorts of rules and told us that, except for the union they've decided to sanction, all the rest is sin and blasphemy. When I think about it, I'm revolted that for thousands of years the majority of nations have accepted these stupid standards. All love is beautiful, and no one has the right to destroy or prohibit it. To believe that one form of love is normal while another is abnormal is a mental aberration. And what I'm trying to say about this in my books is that we have to get out of a straitjacket that's been fastened on us over the centuries by the most frustrated people who've ever existed. It's love and sexual desire that transform our entire lives. To repress these impulses is to repress what is most beautiful in us.

As for the symbols of the sun, trees and steeples, I've never thought about it. There must be other ones too.

D.S. — There's a scene that comes up over and over again in your novels and which is not without sexual overtones. In it there are young men who are fascinated by a river; when they swim in it, naked, they get a mysterious sexual pleasure from the soothing effects of the water.

A.T. — I don't know where that comes from. I remember that when I was young, I used to swim naked — even though I couldn't swim — in the river I call *La Blonde*, which has another, less poetic name in the Big Forest. I also remember that this same river, right beside the village of Saint-Amable, gave me a great deal of pleasure.

D.S. — Your adolescents are both naive and licentious. They marvel like children at such things as nature, horses or fishing. But then they make love like a bunch of wild animals.

A.T. — Where is it that they make love like a bunch of wild animals? I don't remember that. But whatever the case, it's completely normal. It's when you open yourself to the mystery of love that you have the greatest need to make love.

D.S. — *Marie-Eve, Marie-Eve* (1983) is perhaps your best book. At any rate, it's the most dense and the most aesthetically pleasing of your novels, the one in which you manage best to convey the vitality and originality of the people in the Chemin Taché and the Lower St Lawrence. How were you able to put yourself in the shoes of that old biddy, Carmélia, who's really an exceptional lady? The style is so natural.

A.T. — I must admit I didn't completely invent this character. She was actually a neighbour we had when I was young. I may have changed her a bit to my own liking, but I started out with this Carmélia in mind, although that obviously wasn't her real name. Put myself in her shoes? Any creator can enter into the skin of another person, and in a way become that person, if he has the right inspiration. I had gone off to Italy, four years ago. I had to make a stop in Paris and I was in the airport waiting for my plane to Rome. Suddenly I had a visit from Carmélia. She had read some of my books and scolded me for never talking about her. I had the impression I was being attacked by her for a good half-hour. It was later that I got the idea of letting her speak.

D.S. — You certainly do let her speak! Carmélia reads novels, and she says straight out that the women of Quebec weren't all submissive like Louis Hémon's Laura Chapdelaine and Grignon's Donalda. "I resent Laura," she says, "for letting herself be taken over by that idiot husband of hers... Donalda and Maria Chapdelaine were deprived of everything that life could and should normally have given them."

A.T. — What I can say is that Carmélia, my neighbour in the Chemin Taché, wasn't very much like Laura Chapdelaine and even less like Donalda. She wasn't a woman to be dominated by anybody, and it's understandable that she resents women who were submissive.

D.S. — In a way, folk-tales were a sort of salvation for Carmélia, who found life a bit too dull for her: "We were nurtured on fables... they have more effect on us than the ordinary things in our everyday lives." Fables and the ability to tell stories are one of the best forms of therapy in the world.

A.T. — Everybody needs imagination in his or her life. In my part of the country, not many people told folk-tales. I never knew any storytellers like the ones who were so prevalent everywhere else in the Province. I came into contact with the world of the imagination through those illustrated magazines that came from wherever. As for Carmélia, after having thought about literature and done a lot of reading, she tells herself that there must be some literature in the Chemin Taché. In the second part of the book she proves it to us. Then she decides to go even further and bring the dead back to life. Without really being aware of it, she actually moves into the literary world.

D.S. — Now let's take a look at your books in which the narrators are teachers. In 1960 there was *La soif et le mirage*, a comic novel based on observations of American culture in the Fifties. In 1965, with *Le mors aux flancs*, a drily humorous teacher in a classical college presents his observations of French-Canadian society. Finally, in 1970, a professor who is, according to the title, a "pagan among the penguins," describes the university professors as a "flock of black sheep with white fleece." All these narrators have a good sense of humour. There aren't many comic writers in Quebec, and in the preface to *Le mors aux flancs* you claim that the novel had been turned down by several publishers because "the French-Canadian public isn't used to laughing."

A.T. — Basically, *Le mors aux flancs* is not a very good novel. But there are certain chapters that I think are really quite funny. That's where most of the interest lies. I have no desire to reread *La soif et le mirage* because it's my worst book. There may be some humour in it, I don't know. In *Un païen chez les pingouins* there is perhaps a bit of humour, but mostly it's irony. I believe that, even if you do your work seriously, you should still be able to laugh at yourself once in a while. I wanted to take a little wind out of the sails of all those great intellectuals who think they're God's gift to the world. I can think of a number of other gifts that are a lot more interesting. That book didn't meet with much success. I'd be very happy if somebody decided to republish it one day. Maybe then it would be better received, especially since academics are less stuck-up now than they were 10 or 15 years ago.

D.S. — You published another work in which the narrator is a professor: *Soliloque en hommage à une femme* (Cercle du livre de France, 1960). I know that you think that *Soliloque* is one of your best books.

A.T. — I think the book is very well written. The stories of the two main characters are told in segments, using flash-backs, but by the end I think you're really able to sense the passion of what they're going through. Also, I think the book contains a portrait of those Québécois in the Forties who, although they started out pretty far behind, had the drive and the willpower to educate themselves and really start living. Towards the end of the book, when one of the charac-ters takes the trouble to define himself, the words and expres-sions he uses still impress me.

D.S. — I was completely captivated by the poetic dimension of *Soliloque*. Some of its passages are splendidly written:

> I want you to get to know an essential part of me: Saint-Hubert, my land, my mountains...I belong to this barren land even if there were days when I hated and dishonoured it. I belong to this poor hillside even if I had to let myself lie in the sun and be beaten by the wind, surrounded by the weeds that grew better than the oats and barley...I've been attracted by distant places and I've left this one behind. But I've never been able to pull up the roots that keep me tied to this soil. They've gone on nurturing me, bringing me those bitter juices that have become mixed with the salt of what is called civilization (pp.19-21).

A.T. — I really like the passage you've just quoted. Your question proves that you understand why I am so attached to the book.

D.S. — *Mes beaux meurtres*, a collection of short stories pub-lished by the Cercle du livre de France in 1961 and 1973, was very favourably received. The critics liked your compact style as well as the unusual and fantastic elements in the collection. Personally, I was struck by the violence. In the final story, you explain why so many of the characters turn to violence: "I'm like everyone else; I sometimes have thoughts that I try to bury in the depths of my consciousness, desires I would be ashamed to reveal in public, feelings that would sometimes make me blush if I had to show them. To be subject to these thoughts, desires and feelings only goes to show that I belong to the human race" (p.145).

A.T. — We are surrounded by violence. How could it be otherwise when there is so much injustice in the world? Everybody would like to rebel against injustice, but few people have the means to do so. The first strikers who rebelled against their bosses were considered to be destroyers of public order. The powerful always present the underdogs as being unscrupulous, immoral bastards, whereas it's the people with power who are the real bastards. It's a game they're forced to play if they want to hang on to their power for a certain time. But how is it that so few people really see what's going on with this game? If you don't denounce the bastards, with all the risks that involves, what's going to become of the world?

D.S. — In *La tête en fête*, a collection of "strange stories" which bear some resemblance to the short fiction in *Mes beaux meurtres*, madness is a synonym for the imagination. In *C'est ici que le monde a commencé* you write, "It's a good thing to be crazy once in a while. It would do everybody some good."

A.T. — You know, I had originally entitled *La tête en fête* (literally "a party in the head") *La folie en tête* (literally "craziness in the head" or "craziness ahead"). A month or two before the book came out, I saw a novel by Violette Leduc in a bookstore, and that was the very title she had chosen. I took the title from one of the stories entitled "La tête en fête." But this title was misleading in that it gave the reader the impression, even before he began reading, that it was a book of funny stories. Actually, if you look at them carefully, it's a book of dramatic stories in which madness plays a large part.

At certain moments in our lives we all find ourselves on the edge of madness and sometimes it takes an enormous effort not to be swallowed up by it. This is what I wanted to say, to express, in *La tête en fête*, which is in fact the story of a boy who ends up in an asylum. But *La tête en fête* wasn't an appropriate title to choose for the book. I did discover the right title for it, but only after it had already been published. It should have been *Le délire en tête* ("delirium in the head" or "delirium ahead"). That way there wouldn't have been any danger of misleading my readers right from the start.

When I say it would do everybody good to be crazy once in a while, I simply mean it would be good for people to listen to the inner impulses which rise to the surface of their consciousness, but which they immediately repress because the society we live in has imposed all sorts of barriers. Instinctively, most people refuse to take pleasure in this because of false moral values they accept as being true. When you say no to those false values, you're considered to be crazy. The powerful, the so-called upright people, take shelter in these true moral values and at the same time do all sorts of filthy things to those who don't have the means of defending themselves. It's terrifying!

D.S. — You have published two plays. In these works for the theatre you have moved some distance away from your Chemin Taché and your "strange stories." As a playwright you've been interested in Quebec under Duplessis (*Les renégats*, Jumonville, 1964) and the phenomenon of Quebec's English-speaking millionaires (*Le roi d'Aragon*, Jumonville, 1979). Why do you deal with contemporary questions in these plays, whereas in your novels and stories you focused mainly on the past (your childhood in Saint-Justin) or the world of inner impulses?

A.T. — When I wrote *Les renégats* (literally "The Renegades"), the first title I gave it was *Les jouets mécaniques* ("The Mechanical Toys"). This was in 1959 when I was at Notre Dame University. I talked about it with the director of the University theatre who would have liked to be able to read my play in English. But I never thought of the Duplessis regime while I was writing it. The powerful people like the rich family father — the main character — who force others around them to be their slaves, these people have existed since the beginnings of mankind. Duplessis is neither here nor there.

In *Le roi D'Aragon*, I'm again dealing with powerful people. They're people who have power without having done anything to deserve it, but they're convinced they have a monopoly on the truth. The main theme of these two plays, if you look at them closely, is the injustice of the powerful towards people who have no resources. A good example is the story of Zénon, who they call "Zénon le souillon" ("Zenon the slovenly") in the last part of *C'est ici que le monde a commencé*. Here it's the small society he lives in that takes the place of the people with power.

D.S. — In *Le roi d'Aragon*, an English-Canadian capitalist is kidnapped by some monks. You seem fascinated by men of the Church, and you like to make characters of them. In *Les fous d'amour* (Jumonville, 1973), all the characters are monks. You appear to admire the imagination, the mystery, the bearing and especially the energy of certain Church figures. The preachers, with their pure, excessive emotions in the best Manichean tradition, were to some degree literary characters.

A.T. — Every human being you meet in your life can be a literary character. All it takes is for them to inspire us at the proper irrational moment. Then you can let them be born again in the full light of fiction, and with a bit of luck, you can infuse them with a new life more real than the first. On the other hand, I've always been intrigued by people who renounce the joys of life for the joys of an afterlife. It seems to me that they must make it so hard for themselves to go on living! They're deeply repressed. To some degree it's because I want to be present when they finally let themselves go that I try to put myself into their skins from time to time. I don't think I could ever be a monk without going a bit crazy now and again.

D.S. — As one of your titles puts it, your monks are *Les fous d'amour* (literally "mad for love"). But they strike me more as followers of the Marquis de Sade than as children of Mary.

A.T. — No, no! Not at all! My monks are all good monks who would never dream of calling their vocation into question. However, they are passionate beings like other people, and at certain moments, because of certain circumstances, their passion has no choice but to come out into the open. Why do you suppose that monks shouldn't be plagued by their passions? If they weren't, there wouldn't be any merit in their doing what they do. You can certainly repress some desires for a certain period of time, but it may happen that these desires are so strong that they come to the surface and cause a crisis. You don't stop being a human being just because you become a monk. There were all sorts of problems in the monasteries in the Middle Ages, and I'm sure that there are still some today.

D.S. — Thank you, Adrien Thério, for talking to us about your life and your work. I wish you more stimulating books. The people from the Chemin Taché, your pleasure-loving monks and all your characters are awaiting you. Your readers too.

Gilbert La Rocque, or the Novelist as Interpreter of the Subconscious

Gilbert La Rocque died of a cerebral haemorrhage on November 26, 1984, at the age of forty-two. Referred to by several critics as the "Faulkner of Quebec," he has left behind him a remarkable body of work. Monsieur La Rocque lived beside Mount Saint-Hilaire with his wife Murielle, his daughter Catherine and his son Sébastien.

Gilbert La Rocque died barely a month after the publication of his final novel, *Le passager*, in which the central theme is an obsession with mortality. The novel thus offers an astonishing premonition of his own imminent death.

I was fortunate enough to interview Gilbert La Rocque a few weeks before his premature passing. My 1983 interview is thus supplemented by what tragically turned out to be the final interview granted by one of Quebec's most remarkable publishers and writers.

* * *

Gilbert La Rocque was born in Rosemont in 1943. Here is what he told me about the circumstances in which he grew up.

G.L.R. — I lived in Rosemont until I was eleven; by definition, then, this is the milieu that has left the clearest impressions in my mind. By the time I was eight I had a job in the Brébeuf School library — in fact I was the only librarian. I read a lot. One of the books I remember was entitled *Les secrets de la maison blanche. The Secrets of the White House*, written anonymously, was a rather sadistic and violent book set in the Middle Ages. At that time I was already fascinated by subterranean passages and diabolical stories. Even today I still like subterranean passages. I hardly dare think what a psychoanalyst would make of this: no doubt something quite absurd...

When I was eleven we moved to Montréal-Nord. By that time my most important influences had already been absorbed. My father was a tinsmith. His dream when we were living in Rosemont was typical of all the other workers living with their families in confined quarters: he wanted to buy a bungalow. This was a widespread phenomenon at the time, you know; it was the beginning of a kind of exodus of the Rosemont working class out into the suburbs. For them the Garden of Eden was finally within reach: a little house in Montréal-Nord. This dispersal of families away from the Angus Shops, which had provided their bread and butter for years, was due to new possibilities of transportation. Once you had to live very close to the factory where you were employed, but the arrival of the family car suddenly allowed people to move out of those ghettoes into places where there was a bit of fresh air.

I did five years of classical college, up to "belles-lettres," and then quit. I worked for a while as a tinsmith and after that in heavy construction and then in a bank. Finally I ended up spending eight years at City Hall where I played around at being a clerk. The work was so routine and so deadly dull it made me sick. Luckily, being a civil servant wasn't all that demanding, so while I was at City Hall I was

able to write my first two novels — or at least the better part
of them. Then in 1972 I managed to get myself hired as
senior editor at the Editions de l'Homme, after which I
became literary director of the Editions de l'Aurore. Then I
got a grant from the Quebec Government which allowed me
to write *Les masques*, and at present I'm literary director of
Québec/Amérique.

In 1977 I wrote four drama programmes for the "Scé-
nario" series on television. I reintroduced my character
Jérôme, who was the hero in my first novel, but I changed
him completely. The suicide's gone. Suicide is replaced by
madness and the rifle is replaced by a garden in the living
room, but it's all the same thing. However, the garden acts as
a symbol of Jérôme's insanity, and that's the main reason my
television script was called "Le refuge."

D.S. — When did you begin to write?

G.L.R. — I was writing poems when I was fifteen...like everyone else! What I was writing was really bad, too, and Jacques
Hébert was right in rejecting the first manuscript I sent to
the Editions du Jour.

Two or three years later I'd completely given up poetry:
I'd seen the light. So then I started writing stories that in
some ways resembled what I'm doing now. Only the subjects
were different, but subjects aren't all that important anyway.

D.S. — In your second novel, *Corridors* (1971), there is an
hallucinatory presentation of the F.L.Q. phenomenon. Did
the inspiration come to you spontaneously, or did you have
political and social goals in mind?

G.L.R. — I wrote *Corridors* before the October Crisis in 1970.
Even if the theme of the F.L.Q. was in the air at the time, I
had no intention of writing a political or social whatever. Of
course you can't prevent a novel like that from having some
social overtones — that's obvious! But basically the social and
political sea in which my characters are swimming is simply
a material necessity for the construction of the novel. It all

comes of its own accord: you imagine that you're going to talk about yourself and only about yourself by projecting yourself here and there among your characters...and before you know it you find you're pouring out some sort of social- ist tirade and the ink on your paper suddenly takes on politi- cal colours. Well, so much the better, or so much the worse! In any case there comes a time when it's too late to change anything at all — the work no longer belongs to you. And then everyone's free to see whatever they want in it; whatev- er a person discovers by rooting around in the depths of a novel is right, and whatever it is, it was put there by the author — only, he didn't necessarily know it! It's a question of intuition, I imagine, or that famous subconscious! There are elements of knowledge we absorb without being aware of it — a bit like breathing air. That may explain how we can have premonitions of things that are about to happen: the October Crisis or other crises are already contained in the mental and physical environment which will give rise to them. In any event, October came along and confirmed the things I'd been feeling.

D.S. — In *Corridors* the young character Lili keeps a diary in which she provides a lucid description of life in her family: her father is a blue-collar worker, glued to the TV; her mother produces babies and drifts away in impossible dreams; her sister is a prisoner in the convent; and her brother Raoul is a champion at cursing and motorcycle racing. Is this a sort of autobiography? Did you keep a diary like that?

G.L.R. — No. I never kept a personal diary. Obviously it's not easy to get away from the autobiographical context, and to some extent even the texture of a writer's characters is imposed upon him. I did have a sister in fact, but she died when I was a year old so I don't think you can say I really knew her, especially since she was born dead! As for the brother, I only have one and he's never had a motorcycle; actually he's not at all like Clément's brother in *Corridors*. In any case, where the characters come from is perhaps not as interesting as people sometimes seem to think: they're always signs that point to something else and their only value lies in the impulses from which they were conceived.

I was familiar with the background described in *Corridors* from living in Rosemont. As I said before, I knew that whole scene: people trapped like ants in an ant-hill, no money, no car or anything, forced to live not too far away from the all-consuming factory in the Angus Shops. To a large extent my characters are a sort of projection of my memories of a particular past that memory has made almost mythical. They are also parts of myself. There's no getting around it. Every human being is a universe, a microcosm: the raw material is there; it simply has to be extracted.

My novels are not rigidly structured, at the outset. It's like life: anything can happen. In the beginning I make a fairly loose plan; I write a lot before I start doing the final verson of a novel. It's as if the act frightened me a bit every time, as if I had to skulk around it as long as I can, inevitably — and guiltily — postponing its arrival. After all, once you've got your fingers stuck in the cogs of a novel, all the rest of you gets caught up too, and sometimes it hurts. Luckily writing holds some surprises. The rest of it, the organizational work that's so necessary at the end, is every bit as hard as manual labour. After one of my books has been published, it's up to the readers and critics (the ones who actually read it before talking about it; there are still a few around, but they're a dying race) to tell me exactly what I've written…and it's often highly instructive — or entertaining.

D.S. — Even before *Après la boue* (literally *After the Mud*) was published in 1972, I'd noticed how important mud was as a leitmotif in the world of your novels. In *Corridors* mud is presented in an atmosphere of nightmare, as a sign of betrayal and apathy in various characters. In *Serge d'entre les morts* (1976), mud represents the lethargy of a guardian grandmother, the "slow, obstinate, grinding contemplation of something already no more than a bit of mud, no more than the irregular pulsations that now constituted the rhythm of her life, the seasons of her sluggishness" (p.18). Could you talk about this obsession with mud and muck — all these things that slop and splatter?

G.L.R. — Everyone has mud in their head and their heart, you know. Some of them spurt out quite a lot, but people don't realize it! They're blind, deaf and dumb, drowning in their own ocean of mud without even being aware of it. Mud is an environment, an unconscious state of mind. It's also a symbol or a brutal symptom of the lower depths of my being. There comes a moment when the novelist must of necessity become the interpreter of his subconscious and initiate a process of self-accusation. It results in whatever it results in — one gets the characters and situations one deserves.

D.S. — Corridors and mythology in general form another leitmotif in your work. The Minotaur in *Serge d'entre les morts* goes running through the alleys in "horrible Montreal, dog turds, the vomit of alcoholic bums, their hiccups overcome, collapsing, staggering at the foot of a staircase" (p.13); the funeral parlour resembles the muddy half-light of a corridor. Where does your obsession with corridors come from?

G.L.R. — A corridor can be the uterus, a sort of rebirth. When the little boy in *Corridors* goes running through his grandmother's hallway, he reenters the womb of his past. It may be a regression into a kind of security that real life will never offer him. It's a bit like an absolute escape, a kind of walk backwards through the corridor leading to insanity. It reminds me of a kind of collective schizophrenia that's not exactly unheard of around here. Just like a single being, a whole people throws itself headlong down the corridor of its clear conscience, so that it can then reassume its state of immobility — as if tomorrow were as stagnant as yesterday, and as if time were like a sick dog chewing on its tail. There are also corridors that lead to the depths of oneself, and often those corridors leave you floundering around in pure nightmare. Besides, when I was young — let's say between six and ten — I would have whole series of nightmares, horror added to horror as one night succeeded another. I didn't want to go to sleep at night, knowing only too well what awaited me. I could feel myself taking off into the tunnel of terrors leading from one night to the next. In these nightmares — or rather in the episodes of this one nightmare — I would see a big red woman who chased me all over the place. She didn't hurt me: she was simply there, wounding me just by the ugliness of her ghastly face and her huge, deformed, blood-red mouth.

D.S. — In *Serge d'entre les morts* I was very much taken with the introduction of a theme that seems to me fairly new in your work: the theme of "Nothingness." Your characters drift away into the void, "sink upright into the black putrefaction of a swamp" (p.108). The people in your novels are plagued by what you call the "motionless Nothingness" and the "horror of eternal night." What does this "Nothingness" with a capital "n" mean?

G.L.R. — In *Serge* there's a guy who's tottering on the edge of the void in terms of his parents, his friends and his country. For Serge this Nothingness is a reality he experiences every day. It's certainly not an abstraction but rather a positive phenomenon that he can comprehend. His life is filled with absences, failures, emptiness…In retrospect I'm reminded of Mallarmé's famous tomb "by lack only of bursting bouquets pervaded."

D.S. — The other word you write with a capital letter is "Madness." The "sumptuous wings of Madness," so apparent in *Serge*, also made an earlier appearance in *Après la boue* with the character of Eva, the unfortunate aunt who is always sleeping off the effects of cognac and parading naked in her yard. Tell us about Serge's grandmother, that old lady with madness in her eyes; always clutching her rosary, she's a form of degradation rocking away in her squeaky wooden chair, a prophetic ghost who never seems to die.

G.L.R. — The grandmother is not entirely what you would call a living being: she's an awareness. Her mind is elsewhere but she has the gift of intuition, which is the most important faculty for any novelist worthy of the name. She *knows*, even beyond the signs. She's more than a character; in a certain way she's the pivot on which the whole novel turns, since like the narrator she's been blessed with a certain gift of omniscience, sitting there in the centre of her spider web. As someone who is insane, the old lady also symbolizes Madness, all alone with the wind in her window and her memories of the girl she once was, the young woman down near Cap-à-l'aigle in the Charlevoix area who would watch as the sun rose along the river and stayed suspended right in the middle of the sky. But now it's dusk. In the upstairs bedroom, Madness and Time are rocking away in the form of this old lady — who also represents the novelist and creative people in a general sense. As for the image of the rocking chair, it no doubt comes from one of my aunts who had an enormous goitre and a mouth full of solid gold; she used to rock in her chair from morning till night. Serge's grandmother is also the progenitor who has perpetuated the race and now sits rocking in her corner without saying a word. She doesn't even budge, since her back-and-forth motion isn't a real movement, unless you interpret it as the movement of a clock, like the swinging pendulum in a grandfather clock. In any case they're not the movements of life. Serge and Colette are the ones who are alive, who move around. As the title indicates, Serge will be emerging from among the dead. His greatest virtue is to have realized that the others are only corpses, either in fact or in terms of their power. They're dead people who whisper in the walls, or dead people who are still on their feet. I'm tempted, by the way, to take up this character again, looking at him from a different angle and at a later time in his life. That whole business isn't finished yet. What I'm writing is all one piece of work — not books but one book, seen through the different facets that make up the whole thing. I want to build a complete *oeuvre*.

D.S. — Memory, "the big bag of memories that bursts open in the middle of the night" (*Serge*, p.53), is a fascinating theme in your work. Has memory had an influence on the way you write? I'm thinking here of *Serge d'entre les morts*, a novel which is all written in a single stream-of-consciousness sentence.

G.L.R. — Yes, in fact the actual technique of the novel is based on memory. The writing closely follows the analogical links that automatically come into operation when we let our memory flow freely. It's also a technique that only worked for that one novel; I couldn't use it again in any extensive way without getting too bogged down in it. For the specific needs of *Serge d'entre les morts*, I found certain stylistic techniques that enabled me to translate thoughts spontaneously and take shortcuts so that several images could be telescoped into one single dynamic thrust. Look here on page 84, for example (Gilbert La Rocque reads me the following passage from *Serge d'entre les morts*):

> I've got my big flowered dress on they bought it for my birthday daddy said yes it's nice I look good enough to eat he says just like a flower when he comes home it's great I guess I do love him he thinks she's pretty I know because I curl my hair in the morning I have ringlets down to my neck pride I'm not supposed to look at myself in mirrors the devil might come cloven hooves crooked horns Father d'Ars saw him the head or foot of his bed burned by hellfire will burn the unclean have committed sins of the flesh.

Serge owes his name to its resemblance to the Latin verb *surgere*, which means "to get up." In a way I'm telling my hero, "Get up from among the dead!" It's his family who are the dead. And he does break free of them, thanks to corrective memory.

D.S. In issue eight of the literary magazine *Lettres québécoises* André Vanasse wrote an article dealing with sexuality in your novels. The grandmother in *Serge* is literally "pregnant" with a slow death imposed by society. Let me refer to a marvellous passage in *Serge d'entre les morts*:

> I knew the heart of the house had stopped beating and that the great silence of inner deaths had taken up residence forever as in a land fate has sacrificed and condemned to sterility, I knew it and understood how through all time it was a monstrous rotten vulva that was swallowing us back up again (p.11).

You often express yourself through sexual images, don't you?

G.L.R. — For Serge the "sexual" is a symbol of liberation. Like the majority of Québécois, Serge was caged up in his taboos. He can't accept his sexuality; it always remains restricted to the level of desire and unassumed transgression. It's sexuality that devours itself, up to the moment Serge manages to connect with an object capable of crystallizing his desire. But when I was writing that, I saw something else too. All through the entire community there was a sort of constant self-abortion, a negation of the self, a perpetual recognition of impotence. Whether it was before or after the Parti Québécois' victory on November 15 doesn't make much difference: when your hands have been tied together for too long, they stay stiff. It was that liberation I was thinking of when I wrote *Serge*. But it's only a secondary theme, of course.

There's a good reason why Serge makes love with an anonymous person and is thus able to break free of his family ties and his personal compulsions. Sex is always present but in a muted form. Sexuality is crystallized around Colette, who becomes an all-encompassing symbol. Serge is impotent when faced with the real object of his desire, but later it works with a surrogate who is a caricature of what he needs to become free. Actually, Colette is a false sister: Serge can desire her but not possess her. The taboos fall and yet they don't fall. It's very perverse and very contradictory.

D.S. — The theme of death is scattered throughout your work. You take pleasure in "the remnants of this family in which people seem far more involved in dying than in doing anything else" (*Serge*, p.59). Is it a question of death in itself or rather a manifestation of something much larger?

G.L.R. — Like many people, my characters die from their extravagant dreams and from the weight of an alienating society. They never stop dying, day after day and hour after hour. Getting up at six in the morning, taking care of seven kids or taking off with a lunch pail under your arm to go earn a miserly wage: this is a way of dying bit by bit, from morning to evening all day long. There's no lack of movement, but the people pretending to laugh, going through their funny little lives not knowing anything, are corpses; they're dying from their futile attempts, their murdered dreams, their aborted plans and from the great emptiness of the deep identity they'll never be able to assume. That's why you can say that in *Serge*, real death is not represented by the father's accident but rather by the people who spend their lives dying. The grandfather is killing himself with every day he spends working in C.P.'s Angus Shops, but behind him I could see a whole people being asphyxiated.

D.S. — There's a strange "coincidence" in your third novel. On the night of his father's death, Serge discovers love — at least a dream of love — by going to sleep in the room of Colette, a cousin who has become his untouchable "sister." Why do you bring love and death together in this way?

G.L.R. — I won't start in on the grand themes that several writers, like Georges Bataille for example, have brilliantly set out and developed in their work. In any case I wasn't conscious of putting love and death together in that way. It's another one of those tricks the deep self plays on us. It's always triggered by something in the subliminal circuits of consciousness. After you've been asked a number of questions like that one, you start wondering to what extent you can even claim responsibility for the work you thought you'd created. Or at least to what extent you deserve to think of yourself as the craftsman behind it. The game of writing is probably only an artificial process that allows unconscious forces to be released. Words are the crystal ball, the tarot cards or the magic spell that let you go into a trance and say something other than what you thought you'd said. And in my opinion, that's where the phenomenon of creation attains its full importance. When you manage to gain access to the great reservoir of your unconscious, you reach through to what is universal. You can't explain it; you just do it and feel it.

D.S. — You create unforgettable metaphors using insects: the grandmother is a squashed fly or a listless spider; the house is being gnawed away by termites; a slow, collective death is described as silence crawling on insect legs. In *Après la boue* the memory decomposes like a fruit riddled with worms. And above all there's that butterfly, with Serge wanting to protect its fragile wings. Why are you so fond of insects?

G.L.R. — Sometimes it's very difficult to know why you like or dislike something. I think the insect world is fascinating, perhaps because it's not like anything else and is therefore completely foreign to us. The insect world is almost like a world of extra-terrestrials. They're foreign to us, and usually we find them repulsive. Sometimes they're absolute symbols of decomposition and they make us uneasy in almost a metaphysical sense. But at that point you've stopped perceiving them objectively. You know, you can overcome your feelings of repugnance. For example, all summer long in my garden I live on intimate terms, as it were, with some enormous spiders that I occasionally feed; for their part, they take responsibility for getting rid of a great number of insects that would like nothing better than to chew away at my vegetables. In any case such is life: on a symbolic level, insects will always be part of what humans find deeply frightening, they'll still be there in the delirium tremens, and they'll also win out in the long run.

D.S. — I'm going to ask you what some writers think is a rather stupid question, just to please the journalist in *Les masques*. Who are your favourite authors? Who had the greatest influence on the central theme of your work — exploring images of the subconscious — and who most influenced your narrative technique, the juxtaposition of fantasies, flashbacks and external reality?

G.L.R. — My reading is quite varied. Actually, there are a great many authors I like. It depends on the day and how I'm feeling. Still, I could mention in fairly random order Balzac, Mallarmé, Villiers de l'Isle-Adam, Proust, Céline, Faulkner, Joyce. Enough! There'd be no end to it. In any case I think it's better to avoid letting yourself become hypnotized by influences that are overly exclusive. We gain something from tons of writers. I think that even reading manuscripts in my job as a publisher — even the looniest ones — leaves me with something that, once it's been distilled and transformed, will influence my writing in some way. Basically, when you look at it from that angle, one's whole life is a book. It's at the level of experience, memory, the way you relate to yourself and so on, that the real sources of influence and the raw materials for my books are to be found. In any case there will always be too many "cerebral" or "intellectual" novels that present a strictly literary world — after all, a novel is written from the sum total of what we are, not only from our heads.

D.S. — In 1979 you published your first play, *Le refuge*, which was written for television. In *Le refuge* you use the camera to convey the internal sequences, the inevitable oscillation between the conscious and the unconscious. Also in that play you bring back the characters from *Le nombril*.

G.L.R. — *Le nombril* was written years ago, and I wanted to see what the hero of my novel would become when I looked at him now that I was older and had a different view of things and of myself. The main character in *Le refuge* is thirty-some years old, and rather than committing suicide or wanting to commit suicide at the end, he quite simply goes mad. It's six of one and half a dozen of the other! If you made a close comparison of *Le nombril* and *Le refuge*, I don't think you'd find any difference in orientation. There's still the same escape syndrome, the same dizzying flight from reality, whether through death or insanity.

D.S. — After reading *Les masques*, a novel in which a woman journalist pesters a writer with a lot of stupid questions, I was rather uneasy at the idea of asking you for an interview. However, your doubtful journalist is not a sensitive reader, which I hope isn't true in my case. She wants to talk about things that are clear, like the characters' childhood, not about the obscure things like the river, for instance.

G.L.R. — In the novel I made the journalist pregnant — in the story, that is — because I had an urge to describe the breed of journalists who only want precise facts. Basically this is what happens in the novel. That sort of thing is of no importance, whereas there's so much to be said about the hidden side of the writing, what the words manage to suggest about the obscure depths of the novel. It may also be that I'm difficult to interview. Really, the prospect of being interviewed doesn't excite me all that much. Also, it's obvious that there are bad readers all over the place. I'd even go so far as to say that people who *really* know how to read are almost the exceptions. And of course that's also true of journalists and critics. After all, there is more to a novel than the plot (well, not always, but that's a different story); there are hidden, or at least discrete, meanings to be discovered — all those concealed things that you must be able to locate and interpret in the density of the text.

D.S. — How do you react to someone like Madeleine Ouellette-Michalska, the feminist critic at *Le Devoir*, who concedes that she was very much taken with *Les masques* but who accuses you of "archaic misogyny." Here's a quote: "Every meeting with a woman in the flesh — the journalist, the girlfriend Louise — leads to another of those frenzied races through the subterranean world. As with Miller, they can't do without it yet they indulge in it with disgust and misgivings."

G.L.R. — As you know, feminist criteria are relatively new to our structures of thought, whereas the deep impulses — at the instinctual level, let's say, and with regard to sexual matters, among others — are very much archaic impulses; they are in the process of changing, of course, but not to the point where this new way of feeling has really become implanted in the mental reflexes of men. Ouellette-Michalska talks of misogyny, for example, when the woman is perceived as a sexual object. Oof! But if it's a woman who gets excited about a man who arouses her sexually or sensually, no problem. I think the problem is elsewhere. Very often men are reluctant to tell a woman she's beautiful out of fear of being taken for a sexist, an admirer of women as objects. As for indulging in it "with disgust and misgivings," what can I say? Madame Ouellette-Michalska has every right to interpret my novel. After all, isn't that why it was written?

D.S. — The writer in *Les masques* speaks of his novel being written within himself; he talks of "the character on paper he himself became each time he wrote 'I' in the sort of parallel life he maintained through the great lie of his writings." Is writing a "parallel life" in this sense?

G.L.R. — Writing a novel is not an exact transposition of reality. Kerouac, for example, wanted to relate the precise facts about what he had experienced. However, through the combined play of memory and imagination, he too ends up deforming and magnifying the ups and downs of his life. I'm using him as an extreme example, of course. After all, Brecht's distancing effect happens to varying degrees with different writers. When a novel is being written, two forms of memory come together: the real past — but here again memory distorts — and the novelist's own memory or "false memory," which is a sort of amalgam of memory and imagination. That's what I'm talking about in *Les masques.*

D.S. — I really like the title of your novel. You use the concept of the mask to explain your perception of literature: "There always comes a point where it's very difficult to unravel identities — the true one and the fabricated one, identity as written and identity as experienced, mask and face, costume and skin."

G.L.R. — Obviously all that is also connected to the problem of "false memory." With regard to the title, as always I discovered it a long time after I'd finished the novel. The title imposed itself. The true purpose of a great work of art consists in *unmasking* reality, that is, seeing beyond appearances. Life is but a mask. Matter is a mask and people all wear masks. The work of art itself is a mask behind which one gets a glimpse of the creator attempting to reorganize the elements of what he calls his "inspiration"; we glimpse him in the very act of struggling to unmask a reality which keeps slipping away in the ubiquity of signs.

D.S. — The "Rivière des Prairies" just to the north of Montreal is the river which kills Eric, but more importantly it's also an environment that allows you to descend into the "watery depths" of the subconscious.

G.L.R. — If I were a psychoanalytic critic, I would of course make a connection between that and the brown sewage pipes of the outhouse, that famous ancestral outhouse described at the beginning of the book. The novel is structured around liquid images: fluids, discharges, liquefaction, etc. It's a novel that flows like a river, as it were — flows, not gushes! The Rivière des Prairies is a nice metaphor (not to mention a very old one — it's not something I invented) for the flow of the life of the main character, with its troubled waters and whirlpools, with all the shit it carries along with it and all the safes and other junk that pollute it. The river also has a completely secondary function: to drown Eric, my protagonist's son. Mind you, I could just as well have had him killed by a locomotive but it wouldn't have had the same symbolic dimensions. And in any case you mustn't forget that from the very start the whole novel was conceived of as being structured around that river. To some extent the river is the novel's backbone; it regulates its internal rhythms and can legitimately be considered as one of its main characters. Obviously it's a lot of other things as well — but to talk about this would mean rewriting the same novel!

D.S. — In *Les masques* death is presented as a sort of

> rite through which one must pass, the trial of the great Passage, an initiation in the secret chambers of the pyramid, where in any case something would represent the perfect opposite of the primal or primordial cry: the terminal cry in which everything is exhaled when all is used up or consumed and when life has ultimately crucified us and expelled us. It is the rattling gasp at the end of the road.

G.L.R. — In the context of *Les masques*, and no doubt in actual fact, death is the door through which we can enter into something else. For the father character in a more particular sense, however, the death of his child is a sort of initiation through which he is able to reach another level of understanding of his own personality; the pain has triggered a process of self-appraisal. In the end, it's much more complicated than that. You have to have read the novel.

D.S. — You take us on a strange trip in your last novel, *Le passager* (literally *The Passenger*).

G.L.R. — A novel is always more or less a trip, at least in the mind of the reader — after having been a trip in the mind of the novelist. To justify the title I must say that the theme of the car is rather important: all that driving back and forth between Montreal and Saint-Hilaire.

D.S. — I have the impression that it's often while travelling that we dream the most and create the most.

G.L.R. — Yes, but it's quite possible to travel in an armchair as well, without necessarily having taken any special substance that makes you "trip."

D.S. — *Le passager* is about a trip that is much more internal than external.

G.L.R. — Yes, but external too; there is a change from one place to another. The main character has to be seen as a passenger on board himself. That's very important. He'll be forced to get off before the end of the trip...but I'll stop there, since I don't want to give away what happens. It's up to the readers to plunge into it.

D.S. — You're a publisher, and in *Le passager* you have a good time making fun of the publishing world, and especially the world of literary criticism.

G.L.R. — That's true, but I also make fun of the world in general. It's difficult, I think, to maintain a lucid view of the contemporary world and not end up caricaturizing it, because people are quite simply caricatures.

D.S. — Montreal is everywhere in your novel. Its famous "single bars" or "cruising bars" provide another source of humour.

G.L.R. — Yes, just as the literary circles act as a sort of catalyst that sets off another level of action. The bars you're referring to act as yet another catalyst which triggers another aspect of the phenomenon of writing.

D.S. — I was quite taken aback by the violence in *Le passager.* Your novel contains a lot of violence: real, repressed and perhaps above all imaginary. It's one of the most violent Quebec novels I've read, although there's a gentle streak in it as well. I wonder whether to some degree violence isn't an essential part of the creative process?

G.L.R. — Violence is everywhere, a little like the caricatures we were talking about a minute ago. Violence is present all around us, especially in our society, but in a novel there's a way to make something out of it, just as you can with fantasies, or anything else for that matter. Subjects are not very important; it all depends on the way you deal with them.

D.S. — *Le passager* isn't only a novel of caricatures. It's also perhaps your most poetic novel. Mount Saint-Hilaire is literally enchanting — it gives a meaning to life. You live very close to Mount Saint-Hilaire. Without it, I wonder whether *Le passager* could have been written.

G.L.R. — In any case, it would have been different. I live in Saint-Hilaire and I've noticed it's a microcosm that is, as you so aptly put it, enchanting — even without any form of artistic involvement at all. There are a lot of creative people who live in that area. I live close to Mount Saint-Hilaire and it did influence part of the novel. That becomes apparent as soon as you start reading it.

D.S. — In a way there are two geographical extremities, Mount Saint-Hilaire and Montreal: two opposites.

G.L.R. — Yes, and the way they complement one another shapes the way the main character behaves.

D.S. — *Le passager* is also a sequel to other novels you've written. You return to situations and characters that have appeared elsewhere.

G.L.R. — Without necessarily being a sequel, I hope that it does show a greater maturity. As we get older, I hope that what we call talent matures at the same time.

D.S. — Speaking of maturity, what interests me here is precisely the mastery of your writing. Your sentences are musical; you put a lot of emphasis on the rhythm and the way the words sound.

G.L.R. — Writing is based on what is often erroneously called style. If the writing is successful, you can call it anything you want. Nathalie Sarraute was able to keep going on for almost a hundred pages about a door-knob; it's not necessarily interesting, but it's quite a feat. It was Céline who said that grand subjects in novels are all well and good, but they're accessories. When you write a novel, you're producing writing. That's what's important: being able to mobilize the reader, starting out with the subject you have but using it with the instruments you have at your disposal — this is what writing's all about.

Jean Barbeau and Popular Fantasies

When I interviewed Jean Barbeau for the first time in 1977, he was living in Amos. As Secretary of the food cooperative, cultural organizer for the Secondary School and President of the Regional Executive of the Parti Québécois, Monsieur Barbeau had no desire whatsoever to live in a big city. "Being a writer in Montreal is often just navel gazing," he said. "You can't get away from literary people. Here, I can get on with writing and living."

Jean Barbeau considers himself primarily a writer. Writing is his work, and he had no hesitation in stating this to the people of Amos, even if it has sometimes meant explaining what is involved or defending his profession as a useful and necessary activity. Amos, a city with barely 10,000 inhabitants, has two arenas but not a single live theatre. When *Le chant du sink* was staged at the high school, however, it was a great success. And Jean Barbeau was stubbornly trying to convince O'Keefe that theatre was just as worthy of support as broom-ball!

The Abitibi region means a lot to the Barbeau family: peace and tranquility; magnificent landscapes; the flowers skillfully photographed by Madame Barbeau, a native of Amos; the moose that Monsieur Barbeau used to hunt every autumn; the log cottage at Lake La Motte, and the saw-mill they bought to build the extensions to their cottage. During my first meeting with the Barbeaus, we spent a long time talking about nature: the swamplands, the endless kilometres of deer paths, or how to cut up the carcass of a magnificent moose. And I too began to develop a feeling for the land, a sense of harmony with the natural world around me.

Three years after my trip to the Abitibi, the Barbeaus decided to move to Montreal. I asked Mr. Barbeau what had brought about this unexpected change.

I've been living in Montreal since 1980 and actually I feel pretty good about it. I find Montreal tremendously stimulating, and as far as work is concerned, the results have been very positive. For example, I've written some songs and monologues for my good friend, the actress Dorothée Berryman. Together with a composer and musician named Daniel Deshaime, we turned these into a show called "Dix-huit ans et plus..." which we performed last fall in Quebec City and Montreal. That wouldn't have been possible if I hadn't been living in Montreal, since the three of us worked in close cooperation. Very often we had to get together, discuss things etc.

Right now I'm in the process of doing an adaptation of a famous Quebec novel, *Le Survenant* by Germaine Guèvremont, which is going to be made into a film for television. I met the producer of the project here in Montreal. We developed certain connections which convinced him not only that I could do the work but also that we'd be able to work together.

For three years now I've been writing plays for summer theatre, in conjunction with Claude Michaud. Working with him continues to be a very productive experience. Again, because I'm in Montreal, I can meet with Claude quite frequently; we go to hockey games together, discuss things, get to know one another better.

I also spend a lot of time with my friend Claude Maher, an actor and director who's often the first one to read the initial version of my work. The fact that he remains objective makes him

an invaluable critic who helps me to think things through in my writing.

I have a list of projects that I hope to accomplish, so I can see lots of work ahead and fresh challenges in the years to come. What I really like about what's happening is that I'll have the opportunity to try my hand at different kinds of drama writing, and at the same time try to maintain my own position in the theatre world.

Jean Barbeau was born in 1945 in Saint-Romuald, a suburb of Quebec City. I asked him if the milieu he grew up in had influenced his decision to become a writer.

My father was a bus driver for a sort of fly-by-night company. He was never sure of having work from one week to the next. We weren't poor, but the family lived in modest circumstances. What I remember most of all is how resigned my father was, how docile he was in terms of religion and the political establishment. He was the kind of guy who'd been absolutely neutralized by moral values, a misfit like Goglu, a character in one of my plays. However, the desire to get out of it all, which I instilled in Goglu, comes from me. My parents didn't have any influence on the general environment. They were good French Canadians who had stopped evolving when they were about thirty; in social terms, they were basically losers. Nevertheless, my parents did give me an education which set me apart from the others.

Jean Barbeau wrote his first plays when he was at college in Lévis, but he feels that his first "real" play was *Et Caetera*, written in 1968 while he was at Laval University. He spent two years at Laval, but he found the university atmosphere stifling. He was bored by the courses and discouraged by the lack of any real links with the outside world. Most of his time was spent with the theatre troupe "Les treize de Laval," which was founded in 1969.

Et Caetera shows the influence of Pirandello; I had just read his *Six Characters in Search of an Author*. My play looked like a collective creation that was written by a single person. For me it was mostly a technical experiment, trying to learn the ropes. It dealt with the nature of drama, and it used a style of language borrowed from the French theatre, from writers of the absurd like Ionesco. Still, there were a few dialogues which used local Quebec French. I was experimenting with theatre techniques. It was an apprenticeship for which I owe a lot to Jean Guy, a director from Quebec City who was also one of the characters in *La brosse*. In those days "Les treize" were mainly performing French repertory, such as Ionesco and Boris Vian, and we saw ourselves as quite avant-garde. It was the time when university theatre was making a comeback. The question of Quebec theatre never arose. But when I got there, some people were already talking about it, like the actor Raymond Bouchard, for instance. There was no course on Quebec drama at Laval University. I remember plays like Ionesco's *The Bald Soprano*. I got involved in theatre because I liked it. It was theatre itself that first interested me, not Quebec theatre.

After his experience at university, Jean Barbeau, in cooperation with a number of actors, founded the "Théâtre quotidien de Québec" in 1970, and from that time on he has been living on his theatre work. The group's first play was *Le chemin de Lacroix*, staged at the Chantauteuil. The author also undertook to be the director, and the main thing he learned was that he was "not ready to direct plays. It ended up being a group effort." In 1971 the Trident Theatre in Quebec City inaugurated its "Salle Octave Crémazie" by presenting *0-71*. This play, still unpublished, describes the former "national sport" of Quebeckers: "Three different bingos," adds Barbeau, "in 1947,58, and 70...a mosaic, almost a fresco, three tableaux to show how Quebec society had evolved, from the forbidden bingo of the Duplessis era to the commercial circus of the 1960's." In the same year, 1971, the Théâtre populaire du Québec presented *Ben-Ur*. The author worked in collaboration with the director Albert Millaire: "I was a consultant for Albert, and that wouldn't have been possible if I hadn't had the experience at the Chantauteuil."

In each of his plays, Jean Barbeau provides useful, precise instructions for staging. In that regard, his contact with directors and his technical knowledge have certainly been helpful for him. In 1973 the "Sans l'sou" Troupe from Amos staged *La coupe Stainless*. "It wasn't a real theatre troupe, in terms of staffing. Compared to 'Les Treize,' it was a return to amateur theatre. I wanted to work again with people who liked theatre, and I did the directing myself."

Before discussing his best-known plays, I had a few more general questions to ask Jean Barbeau. Naturally I began with the most pertinent one: "Did the P.Q. victory on November 15, 1976 bring any changes to you as a writer?"

It changed me tremendously! I can't write the way I used to. There's no longer even a crumb of pessimism. You feel like exploding, being an optimist. The 15th had as much impact as the October Crisis in 1970, or Bills 22 and 63. It was a creative stimulant, but this time it went in the direction of white instead of black. Before, I was often fed up with the political situation.

At this point I broke in to remind him that even if the political situation in Quebec had been bleak, he had never written any real tragedies; his plays were more comical than anything else.

Yes, that's true. The greatest tragedy was played out a long time ago, on the Plains of Abraham. How could I write anything blacker than that? In my plays, I am speaking for myself, obviously; I'm just not able to write a real tragedy, like Tremblay's *Marie-Lou*, even though I saw it four times.

And so it was Monsieur Barbeau himself who brought up the name of Michel Tremblay. Since I had been hesitant about making the inevitable comparison myself, this gave me a chance to ask him if he'd been influenced by the author of *Les belles-soeurs*.

I'm sorry that certain people make superficial comparisons between us. I'm not in competition with him. The "Osstidcho," an extravaganza put on by Charlebois, Deschamps and Forestier, had a lot bigger influence on me than Tremblay. That show, which took place in Quebec City in 1969, really juiced me; I told myself that if they could be that direct, that close to the colloquial language of Quebec, then I could be too. Why look any further for a language to use? I came out of it absolutely amazed.

I went a step further in suggesting that Yvon Deschamps asserts the language he uses in his monologues is based on caricature.

I stick to the spoken language and use it to create humour. It's a language rich in imagination and images, and I exploit it to make people laugh!

I then added that he must have done a lot of work writing it down, since he is one of the most successful authors in codifying popular Quebec French and transcribing its rhythms. Jean Barbeau has so far refused to apply for a grant from the Quebec Government because "the former minister Cloutier had a pretty closed mind on the subject of *joual.*" "But all that," he went on, "is a question of cultural colonialism. I've tried to follow standard French practice: I write *quétaine*, not *kétaine* ("kitsch," "corny"). I developed a way of writing down words like *à c't'heure* ("right now") or *c't'affaire* ("no kidding"). I reproduce the spoken language; I'm not trying to create a style."

The names of Pierre Beaudry and Louis-Paul Béguin came up, both of whom used to write supposedly "linguistic" columns in *La Presse* and *Le Devoir* respectively. Barbeau made fun of them, calling them extremists in the same sense as people who would like to turn *joual* into a national language: "*Joual* exists. It's *one* way of talking, and Béguin makes us look ridiculous with his campaign against the Larousse dictionary, which has started adding some *joual* expressions. You don't have to learn *joual* in school; you learn it in the street. But people shouldn't dump on it. All national groups, the South Americans for instance, have their own levels of language."

Why does Jean Barbeau "frenchify" certain anglicisms in his plays?

I play with levels of language. I don't react to anglicisms with any feeling of disdain. When it's a question of atmosphere or context, it's often easier to say *slaquer* for "to lay off" rather than *mettre à pied temporairement*, as the French from France say. I don't panic when I hear an anglicism but I don't like it when they're used too freely. I just want people to realize they can use anglicisms as long as they are aware of it, because often it's more practical.

We continued talking on the subject of language and concluded that, at a certain level, an anglicism is not necessarily a sign of ignorance but rather an aspect of Quebec reality. In Jean Barbeau's plays, there are several French characters who "correct" their "cousins" from Quebec. The author explained as follows:

I really was taking an ironic look at the pretentiousness of a lot of French people I knew in university circles. However, not all Frenchmen are like that. We have to get beyond the reactions of French people who laugh at our accent. It's time they accepted us as we are! It's time we started having real exchanges between France and Quebec!

Let's now move on to your first major play, *Le chemin de Lacroix* (1971). The play introduces Rod Lacroix, an unemployed labourer who is clubbed down on St. Jean Street in Quebec City by two cops. Lacroix is the kind of guy who "works like an idiot all day long for a crust of bread"; his mother is a miserable creature, "a twenty-five cent whore." He does his Stations of the Cross, not with religions pictures, but with tough cops who accuse him of being a "communist," "separatist," "terrorist," "extremist," "anarchist," "artist", "sovereigntist," "dope addict" and "P.Q. supporter." The cops piss in his face. At the last station, however, Rod decides to "self determine," to shout out to the world all the misery of the "losers" in Quebec. What does the name Lacroix (literally "The Cross") signify?

I thought of the title on Easter weekend, with the memory of the still-recent Bill 63 in my head and the police with their billy clubs. That may be the only play I ever wrote completely in *joual*. The "Osstidcho" was still fresh in my memory and *joual* had shown how effective it can be, how direct and colourful a language it actually is. When I put the Frenchman from France and the Québécois on stage at the same time, talking about a fight in the street, the spectators could easily understand how ridiculous Thierry (the Frenchman) came across and how genuine Lacroix was. Putting the two ways of speaking side by side was both hilarious and revealing.

Jean Barbeau claims he is not exaggerating when he writes of police violence: "I've had friends who had their fingernails torn out because they refused to let themselves be fingerprinted."

In 1971, the Théâtre du Nouveau-Monde staged *Goglu*, a play that was televised by Radio-Canada in 1974. Godbout, a taxi driver, and Goglu, a disillusioned worker, are chatting on a "senior citizens'" bench in Quebec City. Both are waiting impatiently for their old age. They watch the American boats gathering up pulp-wood on the river; their only solace is an occasional shot of rubbing alcohol, the odd hockey game at the Forum — "Ice-cream, crème à glace, revel...Chocolat, gomme, peanut!" — softball and French fries. For them, happiness is as illusory as it is for Michel Tremblay's character, Germaine Lauzon: "I could see myself on an island...with lovely grey sand, palm trees, sparkling clean water and a sort of smell of sweet rushes all around." They are completely and utterly fed up. Goglu gives vent to his anger in a gesture of rage and despair: he "whacks off" behind a tree, "shooting" another baby into the river of loneliness. While the play is simply a product of Jean Barbeau's imagination, Goglu has become almost real. The author sympathizes with him and often talks about his character; he remembers another Goglu ("a nice nickname," and in French the name of the migrating bobolink), one of his college friends in St-Romuald, "not the least bit like Goglu in the play."

In *Manon Lastcall* (1970), Jean Barbeau attacks an elitist conception of culture. Maurice, a museum curator with an affected manner of speaking, meets Manon, who is very much a working-class girl. She goes to work as a guide in the museum, and suddenly the museum starts to fill up like a "bar and grill" or a cheap drinking spot. She explains the paintings in the museum by using simple language that is completely devoid of jargon, and there are always people left when the "last call" is sounded at the end of the day. The Minister of Cultural Affairs is scandalized by Manon's tendency to talk in *joual*. Maurice, however, sleeps with her in a rapturous love affair *à la québécoise* and pays no attention to the honourable Minister, "a pedantic knick-knack" who is left hanging on a coat-hook. What is the meaning of Maurice's conversion?

At the beginning of the play, Maurice is a highly affected character who has no roots. He lives in an artificial world of paintings and ministers. At the end, however, he assumes his place in the real world, taking off with a working-class girl. It's a sort of *Pygmalion* in reverse, a send-up of the former minister Jean-Noël Tremblay and all his preciousness. I made him into a fresher and more natural character. Manon reminds me of Madame Bellay, who was a very well-known eccentric in Quebec City. She was an exhibitionist who turned up at almost every show in town dressed in the most extravagant outfits. Her costumes were even shown at the Quebec City Museum and it was the most popular exhibition of the year. She brought the Museum to life by being outrageous. Culture has to have colour and spontaneity.

Joualez-moi d'amour (1972) again deals with the theme of making culture more accessible to the common people. Jules, an austere man who talks in a "very polished manner," turns out to be impotent with a French prostitute and remains so until he starts speaking his "real" language.

It's a play that I wrote as a reaction to various things. I was fed up with being told that the way I spoke was "colourful." The call-girl in the play speaks her own version of *joual*, which is French-from-France slang. That didn't occur to any of the critics! She had accepted her language, her past and the life she was leading. Nobody was bothered by the fact that she didn't speak "correct" French. She uses slang words like *piaule* ("pad," "place") and *mec* ("guy"). But when Jules spoke *joual* to her, as one equal to another, people were scandalized.

Before writing the play I'd gone to see Tremblay's *La Duchesse de Langeais*. The Duchess made herself more "butch" by speaking *joual*. You have the same thing in *Joualez-moi d'amour*, where Jules becomes more virile by speaking the language of his mother. It's a sort of portrait of different registers of language, and the message is "If you deny your mother, you won't get very far. Accept your own language! After that, anything can happen."

Along with *Ben-Ur*, *Le chant du sink* (1973) is one of Barbeau's most complete plays in the theatrical sense. The dialogue always goes beyond mere verbiage, conveying the themes of the play through a combination of puns, verbal inventiveness, images and refrains. There is a panegyric to the drainpipe, a poem in honour of slums, an allegory about the Machine changing the people of Quebec into rats, a mime about "Pape-Herman" ("Pope Peppermint" and other virtually untranslatable puns), and a whole series of word-plays involving Bell Canada, Hydro Québec, Imperial Oil, steam pipes, prayers and so on.

Although Jean Barbeau claims not to have been thinking of Greek drama, its influence can be felt in the four *inspiratrices* (both "intake valves" and "muses") who act as a "chorus" for Pierre, a drunken young playwright who is strapped into a straitjacket, incapable of self-determination, and headed for the asylum. The play contains a bewildering cast of characters created from various aspects of Quebec's history and popular culture: Verchères La Bataille (a transformation of Madeleine de Verchères), who believes in a free Quebec despite Pierre's mistrust of her Marxist jargon; Esther Larousse, who represents Her Majesty the French Language of the Academy; Bernadette La Thamaturge ("Miracle Worker"); Barbi la Débauche, "the goddess of sex, who gives a celestial piece of ass" and exudes a sort of Baby Doll sensuality; and the mother, Gisèle, a waitress who, disgusted by the "song of the sink" and her crook of a boss, decides at the end of the play to become an active Parti Québécois supporter.

My first question to Jean Barbeau was a natural one: "Pierre wants to be a playwright, since 'The Theatre is the only place where you can still say what you want.' He is not ashamed of the way he speaks; he wants to portray the lives of common people; he wants to prevent the Québécois from assimilating into the 250 million 'blokes'; he comes from an underprivileged background; and he's considered a madman because he talks in images about the people of Quebec being turned into rats by the Machine. Is this fictional Pierre actually a self-portrait?"

The problems are the ones I was facing: being caught up in language and caught up in a political situation. Those were the constraints imposed on writers in Quebec at that time, and dealing

with them through Pierre did me an enormous amount of good. I was able to identify what was bugging me.

Jean Barbeau went on to explain that Verchères La Bataille was not really related to the historical character, but was rather a personification of nationalism and a kind of political dilemma.

The idea of independence is often difficult to accept. It's not the historical dimension that troubles you, it's the hassle involved. You had to be a separatist. This is one facet of the problems faced by anybody who's a writer in Quebec. Jacques Godbout put it very well when he talked of the necessity of producing a certain amount of maple syrup every year.

The title of *La coupe Stainless* (1973) is a take-off on the Stanley Cup, and the play is described as the "little broom-ball epic" of the French-Canadian people. Ti-Bum Samson represents the young hockey or broom-ball players who, when they start imitating Number 9 of the Montreal Canadiens, forget about the "congenital" defeatism of the Québécois. Here Barbeau has created a parody of the Québécois who are winners in the hockey rink but losers in their own country. At the end of the play, Ti-Bum Samson gives up playing Samson on the ice; putting broom-ball behind him, from now on he will work to defend the "unknown heroes of the struggles against conscription, anti-labour governments, and the paid peddlars of our national unity." Monsieur Barbeau's wife breaks into the conversation to explain to me that broom-ball is one of the most popular forms of entertainment in the Abitibi region; the people of Amos are still talking about a legendary match between the Laurentide team and the O'Keefe team! The author of *La coupe Stainless* continues:

Broom-ball is truly a national sport in the Abitibi. I chose it instead of hockey so that I could set the action in a small village. It's a fable, a parable. For too long the heroes in Quebec have been hockey players, who win only when they're on the ice. In *La coupe Stainless* the character leaves the rink behind, knowing that he can be a winner on other fronts. Maybe I had a prophetic vision when I wrote that play!

The short monologue *Solange* (1973), written expressly for the actress Dorothée Berryman, paints a portrait of "a little hick from the country," a former nun specializing in Gregorian chants who was expelled from the convent because she was a little too fond of caressing the pretty little girls. She sees evil everywhere: "They stuffed so many things into your head...It's like having tar on your clothes, you don't know how you'll ever get rid of it." Solange is chosen by society to be a creature of God, but instead she falls madly in love with a bearded socialist who is arrested as a terrorist.

I wrote *Solange* in '71, just after the October Crisis. I've always liked those typical religious stories, like the one about the nun who thinks she's going to meet Christ one day in the street. Solange meets a bearded member of the F.L.Q., takes him for Christ, and has a son with him. She still believes in God, and there's nothing crazy about her. She loves her husband in prison, she believes in revolution, and she'll bring up her son to believe in it too. It's both violent and non-violent at the same time, a kind of collective delirium.

Of all Barbeau's plays, *Citrouille* (1975) is the one that caused the greatest controversy. The critic Martial Dassylvia in *La Presse* accused the author of being too moralistic. Evelyn Dumas, in the now-defunct *Le Jour*, raged that "*Citrouille* plays on a variation of pornographic male fantasies by simply inverting the secular theme of men who humiliate, batter, mutilate and rape women." *Citrouille*, however, had a greater success than any of the other plays. At present the author is working on a screenplay involving a completely revised version of *Citrouille*, which is to be made into a film by Justine Héroux, the wife of film-maker Denis Héroux ("I'm counting on Justine not to make a film that in any way resembles *Valérie*," cracks Barbeau). A brief synopsis of the play goes as follows: three women, rather like witches celebrating a black sabbath, lock a man up in a cottage, intending to cure him of all his male prejudices in 48 hours. Mado, a naive lesbian from the country, Rachel, who is reminiscent of Lenin, and Citrouille, a determined, down-to-earth feminist, set out to take their revenge on men: they dress up Michel Lemoyne like a "bunny," they slash the tires of his "phallic" car, they burn him with his male chauvinist cigar, and they make him watch them act out commercials for beauty products. It all becomes a fantasy in which the myth of the male seducer is turned on its head. As for the ideological criticism levelled at the play, Jean Barbeau has this to say:

> *Citrouille* is the most difficult play I've ever written. I wrote it in a burst of enthusiasm for women's liberation. It was my feminist side coming out, along the lines of Germaine Greer or Angela Davis. I have no regrets about the play. Obviously I created sterotypes and caricatures using all the most superficial images: a lesbian, a doctrinaire intellectual, a kind of a tom boy character with a very sharp tongue. It shouldn't be forgotten that *Citrouille* was written by a man. It's much more the description of a man than of three feminists. I don't pretend to be speaking on behalf of women. And the reversal in the play, with the woman raping the man, is primarily a theatrical trick used for comic purposes. Confinement and mutilation fantasies are as much aberrations for men as they are for women. Some of the spectators were able to grasp the simplifications involved.

We moved on from *Citrouille* to a discussion of *Ben-Ur*, which I consider to be a particularly effective play because of the variety of its theatrical devices: alternating dialogues, temporal and physical distancing effects, fade-outs, a rotating stage, songs, word-plays, and "anthropological data" that serve to stereotype the characters. Performed in 1971 by the Théâtre populaire du Québec, the play shows the evolution of Joseph Benoît-Urbain Théberge, known as Ben-Ur, who is described as a "tacky little French Canadian who's getting fed up to the balls." He doesn't like his "cheap, silly, stupid" name, either as the Ben Hur of the American film, or as the Ben Hur who carried Christ's cross for Him. Ben decides to quit school. He works at the corner grocery store, in the bowling alley, on a trailer selling French fries which ends up in bankruptcy, and even for Brinks, which sent several (empty) armoured trucks to Toronto in an attempt to convince people that an independent Quebec would scare away big business. Eventually he gains entry into the underworld typified by Jacques Ferron's Papa Boss. His father takes refuge in drink and his mother, ensconced in her rocking chair, endlessly recites her rosary. His only heroes are characters like Zorro, Elliot Ness, the Lone Ranger, Tonto and Tarzan, all of whom are exploiters in their own way. There's no way he can adulate any of Quebec's heroes, such as the Indian killer from New France, Dollard des Ormeaux, or the hockey players found on bubble-gum cards. Where did the play's title come from?

It comes from Raymond Cloutier of the "Grand Cirque Ordinaire" theatre troupe. We were talking about Quebec heroes, Joan-of-Arcs and Ben Hurs, who become anti-heroes in the play. Ben-Ur is a synthesis of the other characters I've created. I'd always talked about small-time guys. With Ben, it's the biography of a guy who's oppressed; he sets the pattern for the typical Quebecker, marked from birth by being named Joseph and constantly dreaming of something better. He's just stuck there, frustrated, a victim of his heredity. His heroes only serve to oppress him further.

I really got off on comic strips, the White Man who's King of the Blacks in Africa. The bad guys in the comic strips were actually the good guys. Ben-Ur, with his dreams of being Tarzan, is participating in these imperialistic attitudes. We had to cut the character of Zorro in the performances because we were short of time, but he's another symbol of the false dispenser of justice, with all his talk about California becoming part of the United States, as if it couldn't have remained independent.

In 1976 Jean Barbeau wrote a play in collaboration with Marcel Dubé. *Dites-le avec des fleurs* is described as "light entertainment," and according to Barbeau, the two authors "complemented and reinforced one another." However, I was interested in talking about *Une brosse*, performed by Le Trident in 1975 and known in France under the title *Ivres pour vivre*. In this play, two laid-off workers are waiting in vain for a telephone call about a new job. They go on a binge and become "pollutioners" by littering the sidewalk with their empty beer cans. Just as Goglu dreamed of his island, these two have a fantasy about going fishing for bass. They despair of ever being able to move out of their stinking "foetus apartments," and they're part of the class that "licks the asshole of America." Suffering from "an indigestion of multinationals," they're nevertheless greatly enamoured of Cadillacs. One time when they're completely smashed, they kill a prostitute and a policeman in a violent, clown-like episode. Jean Barbeau told me that some spectators had been scandalized by the violence, whereas others had better understood its essentially theatrical nature.

The murder of the policeman means that order is being destroyed. What's important is that the two unemployed labourers get themselves stoned on gunpowder and alcohol, and they finally react to the reality of the city. They act against the laws. They live in violent surroundings and anarchy is the only way for them to get out of their bind. Alcohol is the dramatic pretext for bringing the violence to a resolution. The subject is universal in this case; it's not even a Quebec play. The two men are symbolically married using the ring from a beer can. The ceremony for the battle against violence is initiated.

Une brosse is a synthesis of my plays, much like *Ben-Ur*. The other plays are individual works. *Une brosse* is a continuation of Rodolphe Lacroix and Goglu, who are also acquiescent. Here the acquiescent characters decide to put their frustration into action.

I got the idea for writing the play when my wife Monique's nephew saw somebody taking a bath in Lake La Motte and shouted "pollutioner!" Later, someone on the "Carnet Arts et Lettres" programme on Radio-Canada told a long history about the etymological origins of that particular word. We were at the cottage and we laughed ourselves silly about it!

In 1979 four plays by Jean Barbeau were published by Leméac. *Le Théâtre de la Maintenance*, which was performed in 1974 by the Nouvelle Compagnie Théâtrale, is a sort of play-within-a-play where the maintenance workers, whose job is to clean up the stage, decide to put on their own play. It's an appeal on behalf of collective theatre and everyone's right to have theatre in their life.

The Nouvelle Compagnie Théâtrale commissioned me to write the play so they could present it in their "Operation-

Théâtre" series, which was designed to initiate young students into the world of theatre. If you want more precise information, all you have to do is look at the preamble in the Leméac edition of the play.

Contrary to what you say, it's not "an appeal on behalf of collective theatre and everyone's right to have theatre in their life." Theatre *is* a collective experience, like life. And there is some theatre in every person's life. You just have to analyze how people behave when they're in love, for example. In that play I simply tried to imagine some typical characters and situations that young spectators would be able to recognize and identify with. I placed these characters and situations in a theatre environment and I set them into action. By rounding off a few corners and simplifying things a little, I established an amusing, unpretentious parallel between theatre and life.

For Jean Barbeau, theatre is a way of living, and writing thus becomes a way of transforming the world.

"Writing is the power to transform the world — an illusory power to a large extent, but also real to some degree. More precisely it's the power to reorganize the world according to my own preferences, so that it can transmit my "message." This can involve presenting certain realities (cultural, social, linguistic or political) and having them evolve artificially in a world that works according to rules I have chosen myself or according to a specific mode (comic or tragic). Writing is an illustration of life which provokes the audience into thinking in a way that can take it on a completely opposite path from the one I've described.

There's also another power that is specific to theatre: through the magic of images and words, hundreds of people assembled in the same place can all be moved to laughter or tears at the same time.

Le jardin de la maison blanche (1979) presents four characters who symbolically meet one another in a coma: an insane "macho," an exploited black man, a tatooed woman and a girl who is sick. What point were you trying to get across with this bizarre meeting?

I wanted to express what I perceive as the loneliness and disarray of the minorities in America. First of all, this meant to some extent broadening the concept of a minority beyond its exclusively ethnic, linguistic or cultural connotations. The American minorities that I'm dealing with in this play are women, couples, immigrant workers, Blacks, of course, and the Québécois, which goes without saying; however, there are also the "social" minorities, such as people who are addicted to violence or drugs. The dream of America is to put all the disparities into a melting pot so that here, on this fabulous continent, it will be possible to achieve the dream that everybody is equal, that everybody starts out with the same opportunities.

The results, however, are quite another matter. The fact that each of these minorities is unable to express its own dynamism sets off conflicts that lead to a sort of artificial existence, an "existential" lethargy that is an expression of both spiritual confusion (Babel) and an inability to live fully. This is the coma in which the characters in the play are floundering. The coma is America itself, which is why I called the play *Le jardin de la maison blanche (The Garden of the White House)*.

In *Une Marquise de Sade et un lézard nommé King Kong* (1979), a dull little civil servant and his wife, who spends her time reading dime-store novels, reach beyond the boredom of their lives by indulging in their fantasies. Whatever the obsession, be it the Marquise de Sade or the giant gorilla, it's still a way for them to find a bit of happiness.

Well, actually, no! To put things into perspective, let's say right off that I wrote this play on a whim. I wanted to write about couples, knowing full well that I'd inevitably have to get involved in dreams and fantasies as an alternative to the agonizing banality of everyday life. So I simply tried reversing the data dealing with the problem of writing, going full steam ahead with dreams and fantasies. However, for this couple I wanted to create a banal everyday existence that was preposterous and bewildering, along with utterly conventional flights of the imagination: for the woman, the jungle and warfare you find in dime-store novels; for the man, the mythology of Spanish-Italian-Moroccan coproductions featuring the strongman Hercules. As a bonus for the masculine character, I added a personal fantasy, Cyrano, who also appears in *Le Théâtre de la Maintenance*.

Thus there are two sorts of imaginations at work, one cinematographic and the other literary (popular literature, granted, but literature all the same). There are two modes, two cultures, almost two sexes. The two kinds of imaginary scenarios can no more connect with one another than can this man and woman in their everyday lives. At first glance, then, it's an amusing trifle. At second glance, it provides a certain view of what it means to live as a couple.

Emile et une nuit (1979) presents what seems to be the predominant message in Jean Barbeau's most recent plays: language, words and self-expression are seen as the best means of improving our lives. *Emile* is perhaps Barbeau's most poetic piece of writing so far. Thanks to the beauty of language, to which the rubby-dub in the Métro is deeply attached, a suicidal boy named Etienne is brought to an acceptance of life.

It was a disappointment for me — the show, I mean — in spite of Jean Marchand's marvellous performance as the bum, Emile. The script, which was already fairly difficult, was weighted down and obscured by pretentious staging. I wanted it to be along the lines of Woody Allen and they made it into something Bergmanesque, in spite of my objections.

However, I remain very attached to that script in spite of its weaknesses, or perhaps precisely because of them. But most of all it deals with the power of words capable of suggesting an "elsewhere," a "great beyond," an "other life." I use a lot of quotations of poetry in that play because for Emile, the rubby-dub, as for me, poets are the ones who have been most successful in evoking the "other world," which in this case resembles the world of Ideas (a platonic concept which is also illustrated by the poets I quote from). It's the world of Ideas from which we emerged and to which we aspire to return. "Real life is elsewhere," to quote Rimbaud. That's what Emile tells the young man who wants to commit suicide. But at the same time he tells him that to commit suicide is to give up the essential quest for the "elsewhere," which is not the same thing as the void the young man wants to throw himself into. In this quest, words (especially connected with poems) are the keys that may open the gates to this "great beyond," the *azur* that Mallarmé spoke of.

I keep coming back to Plato and the myth of the cave, which can be seen as a sort of recurring theme throughout the play. We are all prisoners, chained to the floor of a cave. What we see as life (reality) is only the shadows, projected into the cave, of people standing around a fire at the entrance to the cave. Words, poetry (and any creative activity in the large sense) allow us to break the links that keep us chained and prevent us from reaching the outside.

La Vénus d'Emilio (1980) is a play dealing with the familiar themes of hockey, marriage, and sex. The author has stated that this play is his first real comedy.

That's a bit of an exaggeration. After all, there was *Manon Lastcall* and *La coupe Stainless*. In any case, *La Vénus d'Emilio* is a remake of a radio script entitled *K.O. technique à la troisième période* (1970), which was adapted as a one-act play in 1975 under the title *K.O. technique* (performed in the Lunchtime Theatre programme at the Théâtre du Nouveau-Monde). It was also rewritten as a comedy in two acts for the Théâtre La Relève à Michaud. Thus the origins of the play go back to 1970, and in this sense, looking back, it's the first real comedy that I ever committed.

I should add that what I mean by comedy is a play that doesn't deal with any of the social subjects that might have a bearing on the conflicts we are experiencing. In this sense, *Citrouille* is not altogether a comedy. On the other hand, what makes *La Vénus d'Emilio* interesting is that I have two plots going on at the same time; in themselves, the two plots shouldn't lead to conflict but they end up doing so because of our craze for hockey, which borders on fanaticism. To give a brief résumé of what happens, it's the story of an old maid who wants to force her fiancé to pop the big question on the evening of the "historic" first match between the Montreal Canadiens and the Quebec Nordiques; meanwhile, the fiancé, the father and the old maid are all hockey fanatics, and the poor old thing is trying to monopolize the living room where the television set is located.

In 1981, the Théâtre La Relève à Michaud, in St-Mathieu-de-Beloeil, staged *Coeur de papa*. How does Jean Barbeau see this play in relation to the rest of his writings?

The simplest way of putting it would be to say that it's part of a series of lighter plays that I've started to write these past few years, specifically for summer theatre. I live from my writing and I use summer theatre to buy my independence. I've always thought of myself as lazy. Actually, "irregular" would be a more accurate term. Being compelled, every year for the past three years now, to write for a specific audience, in a particular context, and having to respect quite specific schedules and deadlines — all that has forced a certain discipline on me. It's also made me aware of a whole other side to the business of writing drama that I hadn't known about before. For a certain while, a lot of Quebec dramatists (and lots of other creative artists and entertainers in Quebec) saw it as their mission to carry Quebec on their shoulders. In these conditions, it was necessary for every word and every gesture to serve the cause. It's an obligation that is noble, worthy and demanding, and for a long time I felt it couldn't be reconciled with writing that is more relaxed and free of commitment.

Now I don't think that way anymore. I consider that it would be absurd to suppress things I have inside me that are expressions of my sense of humour, my *joie de vivre* and my basic good health. You can't spend your life running after a "masterpiece" or a definitive work. So this new attitude I've adopted over the past few years has led to plays like *La Vénus d'Emilio, Coeur de papa, Minuit, Chrétiens* (a sort of Christmas story in which a couple of old thieves dressed up as Santa Claus decide to break with the criminal past they have in common), and *Les gars*, which was performed in English as *The Guys* in Vancouver. I make no bones about it. A good comedy is every bit as difficult to write as a serious drama.

Pierre Morency: Enchantment and the Symbols of Existence

Originally from Lauzon, the poet and playwright Pierre Morency has lived for many years in Quebec City, where he has established himself as one of the capital's most influential poets. With six collections of poetry and four plays to his credit, Pierre Morency is clearly a professional writer: in both a spiritual and financial sense, he lives from writing. During the interview he was kind enough to grant me, I was deeply moved by his spontaneity and by the enthusiasm with which he discussed his vocation as a poet. In a world where poetry seems to be less and less popular, Pierre Morency is determined to defend his craft, and he does so with vigour and sincerity.

Pierre Morency's first collection, *Poèmes de la froide merveille de vivre*, was published in 1967. At that time, the majority of Quebec poets were what might be termed "repressed" or *empêchés* (literally "prevented," as the poet Gaston Miron put it), since the colonial situation prevailing in Quebec prevented them from feeling free and writing liberated love poems. For these poets, women were subjugated to the land, occasionally even to the point of being depicted as the *femme-pays* ("land-woman") who sums up all the painful uncertainties of the nation itself. In *Poèmes de la froide merveille de vivre*, however, the reader discovers genuine love poems. No longer is it a question of moving *towards* love, as in Miron's "Marche à l'amour." Here, love is something you *make*:

> My love my love this day is a greenhouse
> Notice how closely I resemble that tender maple
> My feet in clay my head in leaves
> You are there close to me and still I seek you out
> I have planted you within me like a geranium

Morency deals with a variety of subjects in this early work. Sometimes the theme of the land is dominant. Quebec oscillates between birth, conveyed through images of birds, trees and light, and imminent death, described in terms of silence and cold. Like so many other poets in this period, Pierre Morency wants to put an end to "frozen words." The collection contains some very beautiful patriotic poems inspired by the shores and waters of the St.Lawrence. The best are at once surrealistic and lyrical, structured by a captivating rhythm. Traces of Villon and Apollinaire can be heard in "Ballade du temps qui va":

> Like streams my friends move
> Time flows away like a river
> We all go by backwards
> But we roll on in our own way
> As do clouds or clear water
> But we see our fathers die
> And men go by like water.

The *Poèmes de la vie déliée* (1968) clearly shows that Pierre Morency is one of the few poets who speaks of love simply for the sake of love. Suzanne Paradis has stated that, because of Morency, Quebec poetry was able to come to terms with men and women finally touching one another. At certain moments the poet resembles Anne Hébert, suffering from a confined love that produces strange feelings of excruciating joy: "In our little iron rooms/ We are sitting in one another/

Cut and pierced by blades of flesh." At other times the poet lets himself take off into the realms of erotic experience, "all tongue and thigh," in which man "melts" on the woman's breast "like the beak of a crazed bird." His language remains surrealistic, yet it is in no way gratuitous or obscure. In *Poèmes de la vie déliée* we also find ironic attacks against those who are condemned to live in the City, "celebrating the wedding" of their stomachs to "a big steel desk."

Au nord constamment de l'amour (1970) combines the two basic themes in Pierre Morency's poetry: on the one hand, there are hymns to love; on the other, the cries of a poet "fed up with rotting among the bones" of indifference, uncomfortable with life in the consumer society, unsure of his balance, walking, as in the title, "constantly to the north" of his own actions. Morency wants to "fly in every birdsong" and "flow in the streams." In his view, nature is primordial, yet unfortunately modern man tends to be distant from it. The poems read smoothly, the experiences behind them having been carefully translated into a metaphorical register that never sounds artificial.

Pierre Morency is a poet who believes in the power of the imagination and who exploits our creative faculties. His writing is very close to the fantasies of childhood, which explains why three of his plays were written for children. Even the one play he wrote for an adult audience, *Les passeuses* (1976), stresses how necessary it is to have magic in our lives. The three widowers in *Les passeuses* have all graduated from "the university of living." They manage to escape the despair of old age through words and stories. They teach us to marvel at small things; for example, one of the old widowers finds delight in a simple butterfly, "a monarch, one of the most beautiful butterflies in all creation, a miracle." From one book to another, Pierre Morency presents us with his impressions of love, capitalism, fantasy, and nationalist commitment. In his most recent poetic voyage, *Torrents*, he returns to the anonymity of our collective origins; making peace with the Indians — "in the Indian's quiver I must have been struggling I was full of old blood" — he is at last able to come to terms with his body and his life.

* * *

D.S. – You have a graduate degree in literature and you've taught at Laval University. Was it this background in literature that made you take up writing? Has it had an influence on you?

P.M. – It probably did have an influence, except that, as naive as it may sound, I actually went to university to learn how to write. I'll tell you a bit about how it happened.

After I finished classical college, I directed a theatre troupe and was already starting to get fairly interested in poetry. I was writing quite a lot, but I found myself isolated in Lévis. I didn't know a soul and I really had very little idea how to improve my writing. So, I had an idea. I said to myself: people who want to be doctors study medicine, and people who want to be engineers study engineering. Therefore I went off to study literature so I could learn to write. I arrived at the Faculty of Arts in 1963. In those days the professor and critic Clément Lockquell used to greet the new students with the questions, "What do you intend to do? Why are you here?" I told him I'd come to learn how to be a writer! At that point he just about fell out of his chair with laughter. "Well, my good fellow," he said, "you've chosen the wrong place to come to. You'd be better to pack up your things and take off around the world." I replied that I couldn't do that, since I had commitments that meant I had to keep working. So, finally, they rigged me up a programme based mostly on French and grammar. I did it in three years and all the while I was teaching full-time to earn my living. I did actually take a few courses in poetry, which may have taught me something, but the ones I liked most were courses in linguistics, the evolution of words, and philology. I think that all writers, whether they're poets or novelists, are word maniacs. I can't conceive of a writer who didn't have a passion for words: where they come from, how they take form. The deep truth about a country or a period can be seen through its favourite words.

I didn't write much while I was at univerity. I was sort of held back by criticism in the sense that the literature courses weren't designed to make you like books but rather to teach you about the various critical approaches. But my friends and I spent a lot of time discussing creative writing, which is what counts in the long run. There was the singer Sylvain Lelièvre, the writer Jacques Garneau and a lot of others. We would talk about poetry — floundering around in the unknown.

The summer after I finished my degree, everything just started flowing for me. I wrote about that in detail in issue 3 of the magazine *Nord*. I'd get up very early in the morning, read a few poems to warm up, and then I'd sit down at my writing table.

I should also point out that the period when I was studying coincided with the resurgence of Quebec poetry. Books by Roland Giguère, Paul Chamberland, Paul-Marie Lapointe, Fernand Ouellette and Gilles Hénault were beginning to make a breakthrough in Quebec. Gilles Vigneault had a lot of influence, too. One of the greatest shocks I had at that time was discovering Gaston Miron through his poem "La marche à l'amour," which Guy Robert had published in *Littérature du Québec* in 1964.

D.S. — What does being a writer mean to you?

P.M. — Oh, that's a very big question! First of all I must say I've always felt somewhat embarrassed to hear myself referred to as a poet. Why? No doubt out of a totally inappropriate sense of false modesty. Seriously, though, the word "poet" does carry with it a load of very serious connotations and it's a word that should be used carefully. In one sense, there's a whole side to poetry that I detest: as much the verbal affectation as the pretentious, condescending intellectualism. In that sense, I don't think of myself very much as a man of letters. But if you accept the fact that the poet is a person who bases his life on inner realities, who believes that real life is elsewhere, that the enthusiastic transformation of language can change people, that poetry is never completely poetry, and especially that the poet is a man or woman who writes poems — in that case, then, I am a poet.

Still, I'd like to reply to your question more clearly, perhaps by reading you something I wrote in my notebook recently. I'm not sure it will be of any use to you, but let's give it a try anyway. "The need for poetry in a poet who is busily working to earn a living for himself and his blind

children resembles a little gust of wind that happens to find
its way inside a flute lying forgotten on a table. As for the
hand that stops up the holes and makes the music play, this
the poet will find in the leisure hours he wrests from his
essential occupations; he will gain it from the time allocated
for rest, will invent it from his ever-present energy, to the
extent that the propensity to weight and silence clearly
emerges from the field of unconscious shapes that prey upon
us, preventing us from living more largely.

"To be a poet is to invent, in spite of social orders and
the general law of silence, the man one is in the depths of
one's being, man moulding himself through new songs and a
pure perception of what is real. Always to reinvent, always to
reach beyond the present state of abstract knowledge by fran-
tically working on what is concrete, on what is a constantly
new relationship between mineral, vegetable, animal and
social reality and the ordinary man propulsed into the necessity of living. The poet does not recoil from any avenue:
he will caress crowds, survey microscopes, change beds, clean
his glasses, buy paper, be crazy about ink and drawing, spend
time with the weak and the strong, plunge a knife into morals,
give only to the downtrodden, remove the decorations from
the privileged, sing in the courtyards, piss in the temples,
bleach banners in Javel water, love animals to the point of
tears, plant within himself the song of the mockingbird and
the flight of the buzzard, go into ecstasies over a wild plant,
build himself a tumultuous lair in the middle of the city,
sound the rhythm of the true celebration, open himself to
women and men, take his place on the same ray as a healthy
child, deliver his wife of a child, win out over sleep, take
frequent walks in nameless streets, name each emotion the
very moment it is felt since emotions are born and fade away
in the full obscurity that quashes us, lend his ear, listen to
the song of things given to silence, be silent most often when
crying can be heard, be revolted by the loss of human time,
bend down towards the entrance to the tunnel, remember his
mother and the belly of his father. In this pre-war period,
the poet will avoid speaking of peace, preferring to work
with the words knowledge, nature, tribe, power, blindness,
light, crowd, shelter, fog. He will keep away from schools,

preferring to hang around shopkeepers and women. He will be revolted by any image of the poet that is overly favourable and will occasionally serve himself in the office of absent civil servants. With people in power he will be like a cat, forgetting their caresses and dreaming only of horror.

"And then he will write poems using words that have been sleeping a long time in his own private coffers. At the moment they spurt forth, he will be simple enough to be enthusiastic, firmly enough anchored to be fraternal, alone enough to be free. He will read other poets patiently and crazily. Everything that is said to him he will turn inside out like a glove to grasp what is true. His truth will be his beauty, his verses will move faster than television. Any slogan will make him vomit on the table to which he's been invited. He will not try to change modes, choosing instead to plunge into the sea in search of more breathable air. Every way of thinking has been learned. Everything learned has been taught. Everything taught has been taught by someone who owns it and is trying to protect his possessions. The poet, if he can manage it, will be rich enough to be poor and vice versa. The poet is to the writer what the wolf is to the dog." Whew! The passage is a bit long, but it has the advantage of explaining what I think in a poetic way.

D.S. — Do you set out with the same attitude when you're writing a play as when you're writing a collection of poems? Do the two sorts of writing stem from the same vision?

P.M. — Yes, probably they do come from the same vision of things. I believe that poetry is first of all a way of existing, of living one's life, of eating up time, of chewing away at the heart of time which is heading towards death. It's a choice that you make in your adolescence. Some people discover it, censure it, repress it and forget it. They end up basing their lives on the realities of promotions, career, power and illusion, whereas others direct themselves towards things based not on having but on being. Little by little they become impassioned with being, with human enrichment, knowledge, listening and unity. In my own case, for example, I'm mad about the natural sciences: it's one aspect of my way of living that eventually leads to writing, to poetry and drama. Even when I'm writing a play, I'm writing poetry. In our day and age, the genres are no longer completely distinct from one another. Luckily our century killed off the literary genres.

D.S. — Yes, but the reality you describe in your plays is nevertheless quite different from the reality in your poetry.

P.M. — Obviously, when I write a poem it's me who's talking — and through me, of course, all the people who have made me, everything that shapes me every day of my life: words, animals, climates , silent cries of pain, the secret rhythm of the city. However, at some point in time I find myself being invaded. What I'm saying here is real. Characters start unfolding within me; they start talking and living and taking their place in an imaginary situation that is actually more real than factual events. That's when I feel the need to write a play. The realities I describe in my plays are perhaps located at a different level from the ones that show up in a poem, but they're realities I have to deal with in my life as a man who is part of a community.

D.S. — As you so aptly say in one of your plays, children understand and appreciate these realities.

P.M. — I am aware that children are very important in my work. I've written for children, and children are also present in my poems. But you have to be careful: children's literature should be looked at very closely. Think of the writings of Tolkien; there you have a veritable modern mythology presented in the form of a children's story. Nevertheless, I feel very close to children and I marvel at their openness, their curiosity and their passion for discovering things. It's also true of myself, for example; when I walk in the natural world I hear the plants growing, I hear the roots living, I hear the seething life of all creatures. That's why I'm so interested in birds. They have a mystery about them — the mystery of life, basically, or the mystery of a memory that precedes even the existence of people on this earth. I'm quite close to believing that man's deepest dream is to be a bird.

The passion I feel for nature has led me to think, like René Char and Édouard Glissant, that nature expresses herself through the poet. She expresses her present disarray and tells of what is threatening and destroying her. She also expresses her enormous strength, her rhythm and cadence, her great cycle oscillating between life and death. It was Goethe who said, "Nature has no language but she creates tongues and hearts through which she feels and speaks." What I mean here is not some evanescent and vaguely bucolic piece of poetry: it's a reality in which I'm evolving more and more.

D.S. — I now have a practical question for you. How do you earn your living these days?

P.M. — Actually I live from my writing, if you accept the fact that my radio work partly involves writing. I receive royalties from my plays which have been performed almost constantly in one place or another over the past ten years. Also, I've been given a few government grants. And then there's radio. For some time now, I've been working for the French F.M. network of the CBC. I write programmes in which nature plays a central role. For instance, I did a series of 13 one-hour programmes dealing with vegetable and animal realities that everyone comes in contact with two or three times a day: food. Among other things I looked at bread, corn, onions and honey, and through them I made some incredible discoveries. I tell you, by using the ordinary old potato I went on a fantastic trip through time and space!

D.S. — It was a literary programme, though. You weren't really talking about potatoes.

P.M. — When I do radio programmes, they're both poetic and scientific at the same time. No, it's not really that. They go beyond both those kinds of knowledge. I try to convey flavours, pleasures, emotions, the secret connections between things; I try to develop a sense of complicity between the radio audience and the natural world. In actual fact I deal with history, anthropology, mythology, zoology and botany. And poetry serves to hold all those things together. It's the same thing with my programmes about birds and my record called *Une journée chez les oiseaux (A Day with the Birds)*.

D.S. — You might say it's "science-poetry," as compared to science-fiction.

P.M. — Well, I'm not sure... That was Novalis' great project... In my own case, when I'm sitting in front of a microphone, all I'm trying to create is good radio. I've always refused to think of the audience as imbeciles and I give them the best of myself. It's the same thing when I write a poem. The American poet Thoreau used to say, "You don't write any better than you're worth." A variation on this is that, with radio, you can't give anything but the best of yourself; otherwise the audience gets bored. Also, radio provides the poet with a whole new field to explore. Could that be one way of resolving the dilemma between oral and written poetry?

To come back to your question, there is one thing I find surprising these days. On the one hand there are several poets who use language that resembles a scientific equation, and on the other hand various scientists move around very comfortably in the realms of pure imagination. So, who are the real poets? One thing is certain: modern poets are facing a great challenge from science and technology. They shouldn't fool themselves about this. Science has become a child of poetry. Was it Rabelais who wrote "Science without conscience is sure to trouble the soul"?

D.S. — Would you care to talk about the magazine you worked with, *Estuaire*? Was it you who founded it?

P.M. — There were four of us in the beginning. But, you know, I don't really feel like talking about that. *Estuaire* was one of the great dramas in my life. Quebec needed a genuine poetry magazine, a central laboratory, as Max Jacob put it. After a year and a half of teamwork, I preferred to withdraw from it. Unfortunately I'm a bit too much of a solitary worker.

D.S. — When you write about the city, your poetry seems to me to be less pessimistic than the Montreal poets. You condemn the cruelties of urban life, but you're nevertheless able to breathe in the city. Is that because you're from Quebec City, not Montreal?

P.M. — Actually, to begin with I'm not a Quebec City poet. I wasn't born here; I was born in Lauzon, on the other side of the St.Lawrence. That's an interesting question you asked because the first thing that came into my head, while you were still formulating your question, is that when I saw the city for the first time, from Lauzon or Lévis, when I was very young, I thought it was so beautiful. Quebec City, seen from the other side of the river, is really captivating. At least it was beautiful at that time, before certain tall buildings came and altered the skyline. The first time I actually walked through the streets of Quebec City, when I was eleven years old, was an unforgettable discovery, a tremendous pleasure, almost a shock. Imagine a child from the outskirts discovering a city with those harmonious houses, those parks, those lively streets and then that enormous river opening up into the estuary. The city was marvellous. But I balk a bit when people say "Quebec City poet" because I don't consider myself as such in the restrictive, chauvinistic sense. Also, I happen to have very little contact with the people who call themselves Quebec City poets. I find that ridiculous. If there absolutely must be labels, let's say that my work table is located somewhere in Quebec between Fort Chimo and Montreal.

D.S. — Yet it seems to me that Quebec City has given you a vision of the world quite different from that of Quebec poets in general.

P.M. — It's true; I hadn't thought much about that. I've always been a bit torn about Quebec City, a bit contradictory in what I've had to say about it. On occasion I've said some very harsh things about Quebec City. I've described it as a city that's asleep, a city that's too calm, too frugal, too closed and too sensitive. But deep down you know that behind all that slightly aggressive impudence there's really a great deal of love and affection. It's like Baudelaire's "I hate you as much as I love you." In actual fact I realize that I really am very much attached to Quebec City. It's become my birthplace.

My family was very poor when I was a teenager. At various times I would get a bit of money together and take off on the boat for Quebec City. In the evenings I would go to the little cafés and I'd listen. I was in a hurry to be older so I could check out the yards and the houses and everything. Because a city is something important. In human terms it's more important than the country. For me, nature is also part of the city. Nature isn't only trees and fields; it's not only the country.

D.S. — You really do see nature as part of the city. This is something one notices continually in your poetry.

P.M. — In Quebec City you're so close to nature. It's one of the few cities that's full of possibilities. Also, poets are more interested in what is *natural* than what is *cultural*.

D.S. — In *Poèmes de la froide merveille de vivre* you make an association between love and nature, between passion and plants and animals and all the different elements of nature. Does this metaphor seem to you to be a human truth, something almost instinctive?

P.M. — For me it does have a lot to do with instinct, I'm sure of that. Your questions are making me aware of a lot of things. It's got a tremendous amount to do with instinct; it's a celebration, it's life laid out before me, arousing my impulses, my need for love and giving and tenderness. For me, you know, that comes from a long way back. I've gone through a long, terrible tunnel these past few years, a very arduous descent into the depths. I discovered a lot of things that have certain connections with creativity and poetry. I realized that my chilhood, however tragic or dramatic I remembered it being, was not actually as dramatic as I had thought. Of course it involved the discovery all around me of human brutality and the relentless violence that exists in all beings. But this was compensated for by the tremendous pleasure I got from the natural world. I was always out in the woods or exploring a stream. That's where I made my first wonderful observations; that's where I felt comfortable. It was also out in the natural world that my sexual awakening took place. It's very strange. It was in the natural world that I dreamed the most; nature sustained me, yet I obviously didn't know the names of all the living creatures that surrounded me.

It's true that, for me, women and all the feelings that come from women, all the feelings I have for women and children and other men — all this was coloured and nurtured by the natural world. But then again, nature is cosmic and more connected with things we don't see, like underground streams. My father's work was drilling artesian wells, and in the house I grew up in there was always talk of things that were underground. There are a lot of wells in my poems. My father would come home happy because he'd finally managed to find water after drilling for several days. He would talk to us about the water spurting out of the well — nourishing water, the purest and best in the world.

D.S. — Speaking of water, you and Gatien Lapointe have written what I consider to be Quebec's most beautiful verses about the St.Lawrence. The St.Lawrence has had a lot of influence on you.

P.M. — Yes, once I even compared it to my spine. For me the St.Lawrence is something physical. I see it with my eyes, as an object I'm looking at, as a reality that is external to me. Still, it's bizarre: it's as though I didn't really see it, it's as though it were running through me. There's something in this that connects with the philosophical ideas of Heraclitus. For instance, Heraclitus says that people who go into the same rivers always bathe in new waters; you can never dive into the same river twice. I think that's a basic philosophical reality. Imagine a boy of six or seven who just has to go out of his house, down the hill, and there he is on the banks of the St.Lawrence. All he has to do is plunge into it. The St.Lawrence gave me a tremendous number of things, including all my imaginative faculties. One of my basic perceptions is how quickly time passes, how it flows by like water, and I've also developed a sense of haste, a sort of feverishness, a thirst for obscure kinds of knowledge.

D.S. — *Au nord constamment de l'amour* shows the greatest social involvement of any of your collections of poetry. You also make a connection in it between yourself and Henry

Miller, who described himself as being dazzled by the grandeur of the world falling to pieces. Were you influenced by
Miller?

P.M. — Yes, he's an author I discovered somewhere around
1968-69. He had an influence on my life but not on my poetry.
There was something about him I found seductive: his explo-
siveness, his liberty, that marvellous freedom in the city. I
sensed quite clearly that the values that were important to
him were important to me also: human values as opposed to
the white-bread values of America, contact with people,
friendship. I was quite taken with his tremendous sensual
and sexual liberation. At that time I was in a kind of cage,
and even now, you know, I'm still a long way from writing
that kind of work. I even discovered some of Miller's sources
that he never talks about. He does talk a lot about his sources,
but not about the real ones. One of Henry Miller's most
important sources was the American philosopher and poet
Henry David Thoreau, author of *Walden*.

D.S. — I've noticed that fire is often used as a metaphor in
your poetry. You say that man is summoned to a new beginning through fire, that he must constantly seek a passion for
living which comes as much from trees as from the woman
he loves. In fact the symbols of water, fire and birds all
express the rebirth of the passionate man who fights against
boredom and mediocrity. Why are you so fond of these
symbols?

P.M. — I'm very touched by what you've just said, because
those realities are certainly very important in my life. However, they're so deep within me, at a level so far removed
from reflection or reason, that I'm not really conscious of
them. They live within me and they surface in my poems,
but in my everyday life I never talk about them. Not about
fire, anyway, although I talk about birds, of course.

D.S. — No, that's obvious, but fire, water and birds are creative obsessions for you.

P.M. − That's become increasingly clear in my poetry. The basic world in each poem, which emerges through various symbols, is still relatively limited. I think that every work of poetry only deals with a few basic realities, which at a certain point in time are constantly reinforced by changes in the realities around you, by new discoveries and new life experiences. But the same basic cluster of important symbols are always present in the work, and in my case they come from my first discoveries of the world.

D.S. − The title *Lieu de naissance* (*Birthplace*) underscores one of the obsessions in your poetry: the image or images of birth.

P.M. − Okay, but you must have seen in my poems that the reality of death is also always there; it's a sort of reverse side to birth.

D.S. − But in your poems and plays the old people are in the process of being reborn, discovering the word and the world of nature.

P.M. − The three old men in my play *Les passeuses* are three sides of myself that die so that a new man can be reborn; they die separately because they don't get along very well. At the end they become very closely tied up with one another; I would have liked it if at the end of my play these three old men could have become one, could all three have been welded together into one man. In a deep sense, this play expresses how necessary I feel it is for a new man to be born. You know, a lot of individuals often go through a terrible crisis when they're in their thirties: you either come out of it or you don't. A lot of people put on their tie and slippers, sit down in their armchair, and die. Others opt for a deeper reality, probably because of the terrible fire burning inside them and also because of the water that is always deep down; when it spurts forth, it's probably because of happiness, and one thing I'd really like to stress is the extreme pleasure, the enormous pleasure that comes from self-expression, from

poetry and from writing in general. I see myself a bit like a
tree trunk through which various forces are moving, or like
a well with very deep water in it. And when you give expression to that, you get a great deal of pleasure — it's like the
pleasure of ejaculating. For me writing involves work that is
nerve-wracking, hard on the stomach and full of anguish; at
the same time it's work that brings so much pleasure that it
becomes a kind of drug: you can no longer stop yourself
from writing. The life forces are so strong for a poet that he
refuses to die "with his slippers on."

D.S. — So old age is a state of mind.

P.M. — Something happened in my life recently that really
shook me up and affected me. It was when my wife gave
birth to our daughter Catherine a year and a half ago. My
wife wanted me to be present for the delivery. I was a bit
anxious but I wanted to be there with her. I was practically
part of her body when she was in labour. At the moment the
baby was born, I felt a sort of dazzling flash of beauty in my
head and my body. And I suddenly had the impression that
I was completing my own birth, a birth that had begun happening 36 years earlier. A man who takes 35 years to be born
is a hell of a slow mover. I have the feeling my poetry won't
be the same any more.

You know, I think I'm basically a lyric writer, a vitalist.
Yes, deep down I'm more lyric than didactic. Let's say a lyric
realist. I feel like the reed that René Char talks about,
perhaps, or like the flute we were talking about earlier. I feel
something passing through me and I'm a maniac for music
and songs, although not the usual sorts of songs. It's not a
nice little melody that tickles your ear-drums. No, for me
songs are one of the basic realities of life and human expression; songs exist first of all in nature. I can't conceive of
poetry that doesn't sing. When I speak of songs, I'm talking
about rhythm, breath, beat and nakedness as much as about
profusion.

D.S. — That means poetry that expresses what?

P.M. — It means poetry that expresses the living forces of life, an enormous need to affirm life against everything in us that dies.

D.S. — Let's talk a bit about theatre now. Why did you change literary genres after having previously written three or four collections of poetry? Was it something deliberate, thought out?

P.M. — Well, it happened almost naturally. It was originally the theatre that got me into writing. My first experiences with poetry involved reciting poems from the stage. Later I started acting in plays when I was at college. I even founded a theatre troupe when I was 20 years old. At that point I hadn't written many poems, just one or two off the top of my head, poetic little love-letters to my first girlfriends. In theatre there's a great deal of poetry: when you read Racine you're reading a poet. So theatre has always been a part of my life. It's a side of my character. Like all timid, awkward creatures, I discovered that to finally shake myself loose a bit in the city and the community, I had to get involved in theatre.

D.S. — In *Les passeuses* you make the most of the richness of popular language. Your poetry, on the other hand, contains very little colloquial Quebec French. Does this mean you think that poetry should not be written using so-called "vulgar" language?

P.M. — I don't agree all that much with what you're saying because in my poetry there are actually quite a few words that are part of the language spoken in Quebec. For example, I write "Je varnousse dans le rêve des insectes." The verb *varnousser* is an old French word, *vernoucher*, which means slowly to become active. My poetry is deeply influenced by the spoken language. I keep my ears open when I'm roaming around. Almost all idiomatic expressions come from the people. Quebec French is a vivid language. I have notebooks filled with observations. Eventually, at some point an observation gets transformed into a poetic image. For example, I was talking recently with a guy who said, "I was as happy as a king in the froth." Expressions like this are very, very important. Some of them can be found in dictionaries, but there are a lot of others that are still out there in the rough and that have never been used by a writer. So in that sense I think that the spoken language is the richest one for the poet, or for writers in general. However, there's also the written language; actually, I do a lot of reading and I get a lot out of what I read. The spoken and written forms of language seep into the sort of secret laboratory you have inside you. Everything gets transformed.

D.S. — Why did you write plays for children?

P.M. — It's strictly a question of circumstance; I was asked to write them. I must admit it amuses me. I feel perhaps a bit freer to invent stories that are completely crazy. But I have noticed one thing, that there's a lot of myself in them, a lot of things from my life, a lot of the deep conflicts I've experienced.

D.S. — Would you like to write children's plays intended for an adult audience?

P.M. — Yes, but it's something I only dream of doing. I don't know when I'll be able to — perhaps when I'm really old and really simple. My dream is to write a play from which both children and adults would learn something. The children wouldn't get bored and the adults wouldn't either.

D.S. — Something like a Quebec version of *The Little Prince?*

P.M. — Yes, where there would be animals on the stage, a whole lot of magical things that would be strange and new and unreal. Because what we call unreal is actually only another side of reality.

D.S. — You still remain a poet when you're writing for the theatre. You have a poet's way of seeing the world.

P.M. — Precisely.

D.S. — This could cause a few difficulties when you're staging a play.

P.M. — Yes! I'm quite aware of that. Any director who is interested in my work has to respect that side of me.

D.S. — Are you going to become more and more a playwright or more and more a poet?

P.M. — No, they go together. I don't see that there's any antagonism at all between the two things. Also, theatre without poetry would bore me. The plays that last are always the work of poets. Quebec audiences are becoming more and more demanding in that respect.

D.S. — Do you write every day?

P.M. — No, there are mornings-after, trips, outings, unforeseen events, sicknesses and so on. I scribble a bit almost every day but I don't write every day.

D.S. — Do you intend to publish your radio scripts?

P.M. — Well, with my programmes about food, for instance, I don't really know. They're written in a certain way and they're meant to be read aloud. I don't know what sort of effect they'd have in printed form. With my programmes about birds, it's a different question. For years I've been gathering an incredible amount of documentation and research. I wrote them all for radio, but I'd like to redo them in book form. As a matter of fact, I have a project in the works with Gilles Vigneault, my first publisher.

D.S. — You want to publish your research on birds, but don't forget that birds are an important symbol in your literary work.

P.M. — Precisely. Oh, wait a minute! What was it Paul Éluard said in one of his earliest poems?

> I need fish to hold my crown around my brow
> I need birds to speak to the crowd

That should be a good ending for the interview!

Donald Smith: Author and Interviewer

Born in Toronto, Donald Smith studied at York University, Université Laval, the Sorbonne, and the University of Ottawa. He is the author of several books on French-Canadian literature and culture, and has co-authored, with Sinclair Robinson, the *Practical Handbook of Quebec and Acadian French* (House of Anansi, 1984).

Professor Smith teaches Quebec and Acadian literature at Carleton University and works as an editor for the Editions Québec/Amérique in Montreal.

Other books by Donald Smith

L'Ecrivain devant son oeuvre. Montréal: Québec/Amérique, 1983.

Practical Handbook of Quebec and Acadian French/Manuel pratique du français québécois et acadien, with Sinclair Robinson. Toronto: House of Anansi Press, 1984.

Gilles Vigneault, conteur et poète. Montréal, Québec/Amérique, 1984.

Gilbert La Rocque, l'écriture du rêve, with G. Dorion, R. Robidoux and A. Vanasse. Montréal: Québec/Amérique, 1985.

Éditions

Pleure pas, Germaine, by Claude Jasmin, with Sinclair Robinson. Montréal: Centre éducatif et culturel, 1974.

Index